LOVE BY DESIGN
CLUB RAPTURE: RISK AWARE BOOK ONE

KATE HAWTHORNE

Love by Design

CLUB RAPTURE: RISK AWARE BOOK ONE

KATE HAWTHORNE

CONTENT NOTE

Love by Design includes a scene of under-negotiated power exchange that leads to an attempted on-page assault (between one main character and a third party) and later conversations about said assault.

If this content is triggering to you, please proceed with care. If you have specific questions, please reach out to the author.

CHAPTER 1
SILAS

Marshall Covington had gray hair around his temples. It wasn't something I'd noticed until he sat down across from me and my father under the glaring fluorescent lights of the conference room, but the salt was definitely salting. Reclining back in my chair, I turned my attention away from him to stare out the window. The sunlight and the blue sky were preferable to the too-bright artificial light, but it was only four in the afternoon, and I had at least three hours of work left to do after we wrapped up this meeting that most assuredly should have been an email.

Marshall Covington owned an architectural design firm.

And so did my father.

One was better than the other, but Marshall was yet to realize he was outmatched. If not by my father's talent and reach, then by mine. I was more than twenty years their junior, with fresh ideas and a solid understanding of concepts that hadn't even existed when the two of them had gone into business.

My dad had been one of Marshall's professors in design school, or that was the story I'd been told. Marshall was capable, but he was arrogant and rude. He'd left critical feedback on the graduate survey about my dad's teaching, and the grudge had never died down. Things had only gotten worse once my dad left teaching and opened his design firm. Marshall was getting himself established, and the two of them had run neck and neck against each other, rising up through the ranks in the city, putting newer firms out of business before they even got started.

Both men were sickeningly competent and capable. But they were both getting old.

I would turn twenty-five in three days, which would mark twenty-five days and nine months that my father had been preparing for me to follow in his footsteps. My mom, before she passed, had been the only thing that gave Stanley Ayres a work/life balance. She'd been gone for just shy of seven years. After she died, he walked away from teaching—something he'd been doing part-time for years—and threw himself headfirst into the firm. It was only after my mom's passing that the competition between my father and Marshall really started to take off.

It had always been there, but it quickly became so much worse. A grumbled name around the dinner table, a contract lost here and there, but after we put my mom into the ground, my father's focus shifted from her to Marshall. I was even an afterthought in most cases, which was a relief…sometimes. He'd put so much pressure on me for all of my life to be smarter, to be better, to be more innovative…sometimes I just wanted a break.

Three months back, a new bid request was circulated for a massive commercial and residential project tucked against the hillside just off the Cahuenga Pass. It was worth millions of dollars, and my father threw us both into the bid process without even taking a breath first. The prep had been tedious, the estimation some of the hardest I'd ever tried to manage, and we were down to the wire.

Two firms in the running.

Ayres and Covington.

"I'm not walking away from this," Marshall said to my father with a definitive pronunciation in his words that made it clear to me he was done with the conversation. There was no further argument to be had. I swallowed hard and turned my attention away from the sidewalk and back to my father's rival.

He was dressed for a Friday, navy slacks and a crisp white button-up, no tie. The top button of the shirt was undone, revealing a tan throat that fanned out into a muscular chest. I imagined Marshall had a work/life balance, with muscles like the ones he kept so neatly hidden beneath the starched seams of his shirt. As he spoke, he popped his cuffs undone and rolled his sleeves up toward his elbows, revealing more tan skin, more muscles, these dusted with dark brown hair untouched by the gray that had already begun to wisp over his ears.

My father, on the other hand, had gone gray long ago. Gray hair to match his gray suit, and a complete lack of interest in anything that would have broken up the familiar monotony of his life.

My father had called Marshall down in an attempt to smooth-talk him out of the running entirely, which had been a flawed plan from the start. I'd told him the offense would make him look weak. It would let Marshall know we weren't as sure-footed with the bid as we should have been, but since my mother passed, he listened to reason less and less.

And to me—even *less*.

My father was going to run Ayres Design into the ground before he even handed me the keys. Winning this project was probably the only thing that would ensure I had a business to inherit, but neither of the two men in the room with me was going to budge on their morals—or their ideas.

"You're going to lose it then," my father warned.

Marshall made a lilting noise in the back of his throat, and

I sat up straight, folding my hands together on the cool mahogany table, hoping to look like the attentive and talented son everyone knew I was.

Marshall glanced at me, his blue eyes flashing with amusement.

"You can come work for me, you know," he said, and to my left, my father made an indignant sound. "I read the article you published in *LA Design Digest* about using solar panels to power water purification in tandem with greywater and rainwater collection systems."

Marshall's tongue darted out, worrying a spot in the corner of his lower lip.

"And?" I prompted.

"It was brilliant," he said simply.

"It's a cost most won't be willing to pay," my father interjected. "It's not practical or necessary."

Marshall bit the inside of his cheek. I saw how it hollowed, how he swallowed back whatever he wanted to say next, and I found myself learning forward, desperate to hear another word of praise—or argument—from the man my father had spent three decades making an enemy of.

"Like I said." He stood up and cracked both his thumbs before sliding his left hand into his pocket. I stood up immediately after him, another ingrained trigger. The meeting was over, time to smile and shake hands, time to say goodbye, time to get back to work.

Marshall threw a quick glance at me—fleeting, dismissive —and I fought the urge to sink back down into the chair beside my father. Instead, I stuck my hand out to initiate the shake.

"I know my father and I will both hate to see you lose the bid, Mr. Covington," I said.

He slid his palm against mine, curling his fingers around the underside of my hand. Squeezing hard, I countered back with as much pressure as I could manage, but his fingers were as muscular as the rest of him, his grip punishing.

"As you say."

He let go of my hand, threw a disdainful glance down at my father and turned for the door. It was halfway open when he stopped, one foot in the main part of the office, the other nearly there. Marshall turned back to my father, who was still seated at the table, and he frowned.

"You're going to ruin his career before it even gets started if you don't listen to him, Stanley."

That had my father out of his seat, hands flat on the table, entire body angled toward the door. "I don't need business advice from you."

I wiped the sweat off my palm and onto the front of my slacks.

"Wasn't business advice," he said, throwing one last glance in my direction before letting himself out of the conference room and closing the door behind him with a loud click of the latch.

My knees shook, so I returned to my seat, pushing the chair back at least to stretch my legs out and dry my palms again.

"I told you not to publish that article," my father said without looking at me.

"I didn't publish it. I submitted it."

"You know what I meant."

I did.

"You've had a good run with this, Dad, but it's literally a new century. Can we at least try some of these ideas?"

"This industry is filled with men like me, Silas. Men *my* age. They'll see things my way, not yours."

I sighed, looking up at the ceiling until I was properly blinded by the lights that had already betrayed Marshall Covington's age. "Don't you think any of them have sons or daughters? Come on, Dad. I'm not the only person out here thinking this way. Buildings are being designed with these very same concepts in other parts of the world—"

He cut me off, "But not here."

"Not yet."

My father shook his head and held up his hand in a signal I knew meant the conversation was over.

"I won't hear it, Silas."

"Covington isn't going to lose this bid," I warned.

I hadn't seen his offering, but I knew it would be better than ours. My father had shot down nearly every idea I'd come up with, opting for tradition instead of innovation. It was a wonder we'd made it to the final round, but he was probably right. The decision was most likely being made around a table like ours, with men like him…not men like me.

My father stepped away from the table, wiped his hands together like he was wiping them clean of me.

"If you think you're so smart, Silas, redraft the proposal."

Breath caught in my throat. "What?"

"Redraft it the way you think it should be done."

"And you'll go with it?" I asked.

"I'll look at it," he said.

I scoffed, rolling my eyes at the notion. "I'm not going to put time and thought into you simply indulging me. I know you don't take me or my ideas seriously."

"If I didn't take you seriously, you wouldn't work here."

"You'll really consider it?"

"I'll look at it," he repeated, which was more of a concession than he'd ever given me before. Even when I was in school, fighting my way through finals and design projects, he'd never cared unless it lined up with his philosophy of architecture. An unexpected and unfamiliar feeling sparked somewhere in the middle of my chest.

"You'll look at it."

"I'll look," he said, pushing himself up to his full height and heading for the door.

"Okay. Thank you."

He shook his head, like the idea I would put more time into trying to impress him was ridiculous, and in a way, I supposed, it was. My mom had always been the cheerleader for us both, even when our ideas were at odds. I missed her often, but I missed her most when I had accomplishments I wanted to share. I hadn't told my dad about the article being published because I knew he wouldn't care. It could have gotten us new clients, but he refused to implement my ideas, and he refused to let me take on clients without his heavy-handed oversight.

If we didn't win this proposal, it was going to be the end of the firm, and I'd have to leave. I refused to let my career be ruined, but there were only so many minutes I could stay on a sinking ship. The problem was if I left the firm, I'd have to leave my dad too. He wouldn't accept me branching out onto my own or going to work with anyone else. My leaving—to him—would be the ultimate betrayal. And then I wouldn't have my mom or him.

I'd be alone.

"This is your chance," I said to myself, a pep talk that would never be enough to make me ready to face my father in the way he was asking.

I closed the lid on my laptop and stacked the remaining project files and their folders on top of it, then grabbed everything and headed toward my office.

It was almost five now, and it was a Friday, but there were designs for other projects that needed to be finalized and sent for approval before the end of the day, and those had somehow landed on me. I listened to my father bang around in his office, shutting everything down for the weekend. He didn't even stop to make sure I had my list of items to complete before the end of the night. He didn't confirm I'd be sending off the final bids on three smaller projects in El Segundo or that I'd be responding to the Q&A from a potential residential build in the Palisades. He didn't have to because he knew I would. He had raised me to be reliable and, for the most part, I was.

He flipped the lights off in his office and left without saying goodbye.

I spent two more hours behind my desk before checking the last item off my to-do list, then I closed my computer and grabbed my phone. Flipping off the rest of the lights as I went, I made sure everything was shut down and locked up. The trashcan in the lobby hadn't been emptied, I realized, and I made a mental note to talk to our receptionist Kelly about it on Monday, but I stopped, the idea half-formed in my brain when I realized the trash had been emptied.

There was only one thing inside the fresh bag.

The most recent issue of *LA Design Digest*. The one with my article inside.

CHAPTER 2
MARSHALL

The only thing worse than having four younger brothers, I imagined, was having four younger *half-*brothers.

After finishing up the joke of a meeting with Stanley and his son, I was early for my weekly family dinner, which wasn't so much a whole family, just me and the four younger men I shared fifty percent of my genetic makeup with. As the oldest of the herd, I clocked in at thirty-nine. The second oldest brother, Finn, was thirty-five. Then came Hunter, who was also thirty-five. Because while all of them were half-brothers to me, they were also half to each other, and our father, Willem Covington, had never met a woman he didn't want to bed.

Which is how we ended up with Smith, the youngest by far at twenty-five.

Same age as Stanley Ayres' kid, who wasn't really a kid at all, but an overworked and overlooked shining star of his generation and our field. It was too bad for him—and the world as a whole—that he was going to burn out before he even had a chance to get going. Stanley had been pigheaded since I met him at school, and old age clearly hadn't made him any wiser. He was going to ruin his business and his only son's life if he didn't get his head out of his ass.

My brothers and I had taken bets on more than one occasion about how many other Covington brothers were floating around, but it had been years since any had come out of the woodwork. My father had gotten rich at the right time, thanks to some well-played stocks back in the eighties, so anyone foolish enough to get pregnant by him never kept it a secret for long. The women would be paid off accordingly and given the choice to keep the child or…for lack of a better term, sell him.

My father—*our* father—wasn't cruel. He was simply pragmatic.

It was crass to explain to people outside of our circle, but all four of our mothers had taken the latter deal, relinquishing parental rights in exchange for a sum of money that none of us would ever know about. In return, we were raised together for the most part, tutored and trained and boarded, wrapped up with expensive college educations and hand-selected internships, then sent into the world.

Smith was not only the youngest, he was also running headlong toward his teens by the time he'd come around. I had already graduated from college, and Hunter and Finn were well on their way. The house we'd all grown up in was practically empty when Smith landed on the doorstep, and the end years of his childhood were far different from ours. More isolated and more lonely, but for the most part, he'd turned out all right. The twins, as I called them, even though they weren't, had tried to be present for Smith, and I even tried to come around more, but our youngest brother hadn't wanted any of it.

Not until he'd graduated himself, and then it was like meeting a completely different person. Smith Covington accepted his diploma and tossed his cap into the air like he'd tossed away a death sentence. It wasn't until after he had finally settled in his first post-graduate job that I realized how hard he'd been fighting behind the scenes to keep himself together emotionally.

He refused to talk about it, and the three of us gave up trying to press the matter. As far as we could tell, Smith was as well-adjusted as anyone could be in his situation, but it was shortly after his graduation that we'd started our weekly little get-togethers. If he saw through our motives and knew it for the check-in we meant it to be, he never said anything, which was for the better.

To be honest, the touchpoints weren't just for him anymore. All of us had our struggles. My current one being Stanley Ayres and his attempts to trip me up from securing the Walterson Homes project off Cahuenga. He'd steal it right out from under me if he stopped talking long enough to listen to his son, Silas, but there wasn't much Stanley loved more than the sound of his own voice so I didn't think it was likely.

I'd gone straight to the restaurant after leaving the meeting with Ayres, where I'd tucked into our usual booth and ordered a glass of red wine, which I was halfway through when Finn showed up.

"Are you ever not working?" he asked, collapsing into the seat across from me with a dramatic huff. He stretched his arm across the table, clasping my laptop and turning it to face him.

"I'm just reviewing the numbers on this bid," I told him, leaning back and rubbing hard at the bridge of my nose. "You know I hate math."

"And yet it's your whole job."

"In the fun way, not the boring way."

Finn snorted and adjusted the angle of the laptop, setting it down on the white tablecloth so he could get to work. He scratched mindlessly at the side of his nose and scrolled back to the top of the page I'd been stuck on. "Leave this to your capable baby brother."

With some complicated math degree from CalTech, Finn was more than capable, but if I told him that, his head might explode. Either way, I was happy to let him triple-check the bid for me and sit back to finish my drink.

Smith was the next to show up, sliding in to flank me with a tired sounding groan when his ass hit the booth. His wavy hair flopped down over his face, and he puffed out his lower lip to try and use his breath to blow it back…to no avail.

"Long day?" I asked.

He flagged down a waitress with a curl of his fingers and ordered a fresh round for the three of us, plus a drink for Hunter, who'd never been on time for anything a day in his life. Not even his birth, Finn liked to remind him, or else he would have been the older one.

"I'm thinking about changing my name," he announced.

"Coming from you, I'm not surprised. What would you change it to?"

"My mom's name is Hartford," he said.

Finn glanced up from my laptop, one brow raised. "Smith Hartford? That sounds like a brand of breakfast sausage."

Smith gave him the finger, and Finn returned his attention to my bid.

"That full of disdain?" I asked.

He frowned and shrugged. "I don't feel ownership of it the way the three of you do?"

"What do we own?" Hunter asked, breathless and late. He dropped his brown leather messenger bag against the side of the booth before sliding in and obnoxiously knocking into Finn's shoulder.

"The Covington name," Finn said, not looking up but still reminding us of how unfairly well his brain worked.

"I was thinking of changing my name," Smith muttered. "I don't want to talk about it."

"You don't even eat sausage," Finn said, snapping my

laptop closed and looking up at me. "You had some errors with some of the line items, but I cross-referenced them with the source files in your project folder, and you have better margins now. So that's a win. I also programmed it to extract the data automatically, so if you drop a new quote in, it'll populate."

"How did you do that?" I asked, taking my computer back from him and setting it in a slim laptop case between me and Smith.

"It would take me longer to explain to you than it took me to do. Just trust that it's done, and it's done properly."

"I do," I assured him.

The waitress returned with all of our drinks—fresh wine for me, a matching glass for Smith, a Manhattan for Finn, and a vodka soda for Hunter. We cheers-ed, clinking our glasses together before lapsing into our normal kind of Friday night conversation. I told my brothers about the project I'd been working on for months and the disastrous meeting with Stanley and Silas. Finn talked about the internal debate he'd been having with himself about pursuing grad school or not. Hunter complained about a recent case filing, and Smith just gestured in the air and took another drink of his wine.

"Who did you say you met with earlier?" he asked me instead of talking more about himself.

"Stanley Ayres and his son."

"Silas?" Smith asked, scrunching his nose.

"Silas," I confirmed. "Do you know him?"

Smith and Silas were the same age, but I knew from Silas's biography in the article I'd read that he and Smith hadn't gone to the same college, and I knew for sure they'd not attended the same high school.

"Friend of a friend," he muttered, cheeks flushing.

"Indeed," Finn said, huffing out a laugh.

I studied my younger brother for a tell, but he kept his eyes trained on his lap until the color in his face returned to normal, only looking up again after he'd taken a substantial swallow of his wine.

"Silas has the potential to be a brilliant architect," I said. "If only his father would stop suffocating him."

"The opposite of our father then?" Smith countered.

"You'll appreciate it when you're older," Hunter promised, and I knew he understood our father in the same way I did. He was far from the best, but he was the best we had. It was his name and his money that had given all of us our lives, and he'd asked for nothing in return. It seemed he prided himself on knowing the name would carry on after him and that it would carry on well. Maybe that would happen in spite of him, but I'd long ago made peace with the kind of man my father was compared to the kind of men who fathered my friends.

I was nowhere near as practical as him. Finn had once gotten drunk and suggested Willem Covington was a sociopath, but I had always found him to be a product of his own environment. Hunter and I didn't hold his detached parenting style against him anymore, at least not in the way Smith seemed to. My whole life, Dad had his girlfriends and he had his hookups, and before my brothers had joined the family, I'd idolized that way of life. I thought my father was the pinnacle of all things, and when I eventually learned otherwise, it was too late.

Reaching up, I subconsciously tucked my hair behind my ears. Not that it was long enough for that, but it was going gray, and I was the oldest of all my brothers. While I held no ill will against my father, I didn't want to be like him anymore. I'd modeled myself after him because I had no other role models to look up to, and by the time I'd reached Hunter's and Finn's age, there were dozens of notches on my bedpost and not a single serious relationship under my belt.

I rubbed my fingers and thumb around the stem of my wine glass, glancing across the table to see the twins deep in conversation about something that would only ever involve them, so I angled my head toward Smith.

"You don't have to change your name to not be like him," I said softly enough for him to hear, but not the other two.

"I don't want to be like him."

"You're not."

Smith reached for his wine, sliding his thumb and fingers around the stem the same way I'd done, then he lifted it to his mouth and took a drink. "You don't want to be like him either, do you?"

"It's not a goal I'm actively pursuing, Smith."

He rubbed his lips together, and it was so easy to see him as the angry, abandoned ten-year-old he'd been when I met him for the first time. Sometimes I wished I could have done better by him, but I was fresh out of college, fighting so hard to make the Covington name my own.

"You're *not* like him," he said to me, like the question had only meant to confirm his suspicions that Dad and I weren't the same man.

"I know," I said, doing my best to commit the observation from Smith to my memory for later in case I forgot it.

Which I sometimes did.

CHAPTER 3
SILAS

By the time I got home, I was somehow in a worse mood than when I'd left. I'd spent the whole drive stewing about my father, my brain helpfully playing back Marshall Covington's smooth voice as he complimented my work over the top of my father's constant dismissals. Slamming the front door behind me, I dropped everything just inside the door, then I toed off my oxfords and shuffled into the living room, hoping my roommate Lincoln was there. He wasn't, but the steady thump of EDM coming from down the hallway led me straight to him.

I found my roommate—and friend—standing in front of his full-length mirror, wearing nothing more than a pair of tight leather pants. I flung myself down face-first onto his bed, muffling a frustrated cry into his pillow. Lincoln turned down the music and sat beside me on the bed, his talented fingers plucking my shirt to untuck it from my pants.

I rolled onto my back and let him finish the job, tugging out the tails before undoing my belt and pulling down my fly. Without a word, he stripped me of my slacks, then he finished unbuttoning my dress shirt, fingertips drawing a swirl around the base of my throat as I shrugged out of the confining material. Collapsing back onto his sheets in only my boxer briefs, relief trickled up my body, accelerated by the careful slide of Lincoln's hand.

"Rough day?" he asked.

I hummed in response.

"Come out with me tonight," he said, pressing on my hip until I rolled to my side and then back onto my belly.

"I'm not in the mood," I grumbled.

Lincoln chuckled, kneading the globes of my ass until I groaned and arched up against his grip.

"You're always in the mood."

"I'm not."

He released one side of my ass, only to spank it. Not hard enough to count, but enough to remind me he was right. I was always in the mood.

"Come out with me," he said again, getting rougher with his handling of my ass. I fought the urge to hump his comforter, even though it wouldn't have been the first time.

"Linc."

He lay down beside me, body half on top of mine, the cool press of his leather pants sending a shiver up my spine. He hooked one leg over mine and pushed my thighs apart, grinding against my hip.

"Let me share you tonight," he whispered, the proposition licking hot as fire against my ear.

The reality was, I wasn't his to share. Lincoln and I were friends, and we were roommates, and sometimes we kissed and sometimes we played, and even if he used words like *let me share you tonight*, we both understood he only facilitated something for me that I was too scared to search out for myself. There were nights that I asked Lincoln to dominate me, and there were nights he asked me to submit to him, just like there were nights we tangled our bodies together on the couch and fell asleep. More often than not, though, we did none of those things.

Lincoln was my friend, first and foremost.

Above all things.

And it was the closeness of our friendship that helped him understand there were times I needed more than what he could—or would—give to me. Even if I didn't always have the words to ask, he still knew. And it had been so long since I'd had a boyfriend, even longer since I'd had a boyfriend who was dominant and liked to see me submit.

I'd met a guy on an app right after my last birthday, Joe, and we'd lasted a few months, but our relationship was quick to run its course. I worked too much for his tastes, but I wasn't in a position to step back from my responsibilities at the firm. And now I had to work even harder because I needed to make sure my father didn't run his legacy into the ground before passing it on to me.

I wished he would fucking retire.

But before Joe, there was a slew of men whose names I'd be pressed to remember. Men who didn't last more than a date or two for all kinds of reasons. Some of them weren't kinky, some of them were too kinky, some were the wrong kind of kinky, some of them weren't smart, and some of them were jealous of Lincoln. He'd told me once I was being too picky, but I never agreed.

I knew what I wanted, and I wasn't going to settle for less.

For as horrible as my father was to me about work, I knew it was only because he'd used every ounce of his love and kindness with my mother. They'd been together since college, and he doted on her like I'd never seen anyone else do before or since. It was only after she died that he turned sour to the core, but I still remembered the capacity for kindness that used to live in him, the devotion.

I wanted that.

But until I found it, I'd fuck.

"Share me with who?" I asked.

The leather of Lincoln's pants was warming up from being exposed to my bare skin, and he rubbed himself against me like a cat.

"Whoever I want," he whispered. "Let me find a man to take you over his knee and spank all the stress of the week right out of you."

The idea sounded like heaven, and I lifted my hips off the bed. "Can't you do it?"

"Not as hard as you need it, and we both know it."

I sank back down into the sheets. "I don't want to get dressed," I complained.

Lincoln snorted and untangled our legs, then he shoved me onto my back.

"What if I get you dressed?"

My cock surged to attention in an embarrassing way that had my hands snaking between my legs to cover the bulge. He didn't miss it, because he never did. That was another problem, I'd realized months before. Lincoln was so in tune with my moods and my needs, so attentive…everyone else paled in comparison to him. And the worst part was, it had all come naturally. If he'd tried to learn me, he never made it obvious. He just showed up in the ways that would always count the most, and I loved him for it. Lincoln—platonically and physically—was everything I wanted, but I'd never felt romantic attachment for him.

I'd told him that once, early in our friendship over a shared box of cheap wine. I'd cried about it even, wanting to love Lincoln in all the ways *I* wanted to be loved. He was just as drunk as me, and he'd brushed my hair out of my face, kissed the corner of my downturned mouth, and told me love was shit anyway.

"Hmn?" he prompted, and I covered my face with his pillow, muttering a muffled curse into the case. "You liked that, and you know it."

"No, I didn't."

"You like being told what to do, and you like being used. There's no shame in it." He kissed the shell of my ear, and my lashes fluttered. "Let me dress you up and take you out, find a nice man with big hands to get you off, then I'll bring you home safe and tuck you into bed."

All in all, it sounded like a perfect night…but I was so raw from the exchange with my father and with Marshall that I wanted to go back to the office, dig the magazine out of the trash, and papercut myself to death with it. I wanted to bleed all over my father's desk, all over the proposal bid—which was so fucking lacking—until he understood how much of myself I put into the job and how little of himself he put into *everything*.

"I don't want to wear leather," I conceded.

"I know you don't." Lincoln ruffled the hair on the back of my head and climbed off the bed, leaving me to stew in my own thoughts for almost too long. I was seconds away from calling out for him when the bed dipped again with his weight.

I didn't look up, but helped him maneuver my legs into a pair of tight jeans. He grunted, trying to hike them the rest of the way up my thighs, then collapsed beside me with a laugh.

"You'll have to get those the rest of the way on," he announced.

"Yes, Sir," I teased, forcing myself into a seated position beside him.

"Arms up, lazybones."

I obliged and he slid a plain black t-shirt down over my arms. I wriggled into it, then stood with a jump to get the pants fully on.

"Those were probably not the best choice if you wanted a spanking tonight," he said, lips pursed.

"You picked them," I reminded him. "And besides, if they want me, they'll have to work for it."

"And we know how you love that." Lincoln rolled his eyes

at me, and I waited for him to finish getting dressed. He fingered a leather harness that sat on his dresser, glancing in the mirror to see my thoughts in the reflection. I shook my head, and he left it be, opting instead for a snug black t-shirt that he tucked into the tight pants.

"Are you ready?" I asked.

"Almost." He sat down on the foot of the bed and stretched his legs out, wiggling his bare toes.

"Linc," I groaned, heading for his dresser and then his closet.

"I didn't do it on purpose," he promised. "I didn't even know when you were going to be home."

I grabbed a pair of black socks and his leather boots, then sank down onto my knees at his feet.

"I don't believe you," I fake-grumbled, getting each of his feet into the socks before situating the tops underneath the cuffs of his leather pants. His boots were next, one foot and then the other, and there'd been a time I'd accused him of liking me on my knees better than my back. He'd protested and scoffed, then pressed the toe of his boot against the bulge between my legs, and we both knew who liked what.

Lacing him up, I patted his calves, then pushed up until I was standing.

"You can kiss them," he suggested, giving his booted feet a wiggle, kicking one against my bare ankle.

"You'd like that."

"*You* would like that," he countered.

"We'll never know." But the heat surging between my legs and the shared memory between us confirmed we both knew. It was just…a boundary between us.

A limit.

"My turn," he said quickly, taking my hand and leading me down the short hall that separated our bedrooms. Lincoln gave me a gentle shove onto the bed, and I went willingly, fighting back a tangle of complicated feelings as Lincoln went to his knees in front of me and busied himself with returning the favor. Instead of boots, he laced me into my sneakers, then helped me to my feet.

"Thank you," I whispered.

"For the shoes?"

I shook my head. "For always knowing what I need."

He chuckled and slung an arm over my shoulders. "Maybe it's not as selfless as you think, Silas. Maybe I want to watch."

Heat burned my cheeks, and I turned away, even though I was certain Lincoln didn't need to see it to know how much I liked the idea. Our friendship was an easy thing, a perfect thing, but it was murky sometimes. I dreaded the day that would become a problem, so instead I tried to pretend like it wasn't a possibility.

"What is your goal for the night?" I asked him once we reached the door, doubling back to his bedroom to dig my wallet and keys out of the pockets of my discarded slacks. I stopped in the bathroom to mess up my carefully-styled hair, and Lincoln leaned against the door frame, arms crossed in front of his chest, green eyes sparkling.

"My goal is to hand you off to someone with stronger hands than me, and while you're getting beaten into the oblivion you're so desperate for, I'll be getting a blow job somewhere."

"I thought you wanted to watch," I teased, arching a brow.

"Only if a better opportunity doesn't present itself."

Flicking off the light switch and plunging us both into shadows, I asked, "Should I be hurt?"

Lincoln smiled and inclined his head toward the front door.

"That's the plan, Silas. That's the plan."

CHAPTER 4
MARSHALL

After too many drinks and an otherwise uneventful dinner, I said goodbye to my brothers, then locked myself in my car to catch my breath. It was a few minutes shy of ten when my cell phone vibrated against my thigh. Without opening my eyes, I fished the device out of my pocket and swiped the screen on, making a mental guess with myself about who the message was from.

"It's an email from Stanley," I said to no one. "He's withdrawing his bid."

It was not an email from Stanley, but instead a text message from my friend Justin.

JUSTIN

Are you done with your brothers?

I chuckled.

Forever or for now?

Either.

Yes.

> Good. Come have a drink.

I closed my eyes again, brows raising, and I rubbed the bridge of my nose until it hurt.

> I had wine with Smith at dinner

> Come have wine with Micah at Rapture then.

> He says please.

> I'm sure he does. He says it quite nicely.

> He's mad at me for a punishment from earlier. Maybe if he gets to see his favorite person who doesn't share a bed with him, he'll be in a better mood and stop making my life so hard.

> A menace, then?

> He's giving me and Keith a run for it.

Justin and Micah had been married more years than I could count, but about five years ago they'd opened their marriage for a third, a man named Keith. I hadn't known them then, but I heard after the fact it had been quite the start of things, with Keith shaking up more than just their sheets. I didn't envy Justin, a dominant partnered up with a submissive and a switch, but it seemed to work well for them.

> What time?

> We're leaving now, so before 11.

> I'm too old to be out that late.

> Liar. See you soon.

Dropping my cell phone into the cup holder, I didn't bother keying out a reply. Of course I would go meet Justin,

Keith, and Micah at Rapture because they were my friends, it was a Friday night, and I had a lot of steam to burn off after my meeting earlier in the day. Heading to Rapture, having another drink or two, seeing my friends, and seeing where the night could take me sounded like just the thing I needed.

Rapture was an abandoned church-turned-BDSM club tucked against the foothills of the Pasadena mountains. It was secluded and blasphemous, and I'd spent more time there than I'd ever admit, even under oath. I enjoyed going there to dance and I enjoyed going there to fuck. Justin and his husbands were extremely close friends with the owners, Landon Miller and Verity Jones, two people I'd also become rather fond of over the past couple years. Landon's partner, Gregory, wasn't around much, but Verity's partner, Aaron, followed them around like a Doberman on a short leash. Not that I could blame him. Even though I'd never had a chance to shoot my shot, it was undeniable that Verity was unequivocally kind and universally appealing.

Aaron was a lucky man.

Landon and Verity had bought the church and converted it into a veritable den of iniquity, and it had grown and turned into the most exclusive club in Los Angeles. On the weekend, the private lofts upstairs were packed with millionaires in five-hundred dollar suits drinking thousand dollar bottles of bourbon, half-naked men over their lap or against the wall. There were always varying stages of undress and debauchery, and one of the things I loved the most was the calculated unpredictability of Rapture.

I never knew what I'd get, but it would always be a good time.

So, I drove to Pasadena, and I parked in the dirt parking lot, staring up at the huge stained glass rose window over the wooden front doors of the club. The interior lights reflected through the massive stained glass panels and cast colorful shadows into the parking lot and the alley. The beat of the music vibrated through the space, encouraging my heart to pick up the pace and my legs to get out of the car. It was close enough to eleven that I could go inside and get a glass of wine while I waited for Justin, Micah, and Keith to show up.

Back when it first opened, Rapture used to be a typical kind of nightclub where you could show your ID and get through the door. But as the years went on and their popularity grew, they shifted to a members-only model. Names matched to background checks, guest lists, the whole nine yards. It created a different sort of experience that spoke to the new kind of clientele, and I thought it only changed things for the better. It was nice to go into a space designed for pleasure knowing that there was no one in there who would try to blackmail someone or do anything underhanded. Even the guest passes were closely monitored to create a safe space for not just the employees, but also the members.

After the slender man at the front cross-checked my ID, I tucked it back into my wallet and headed into the club. Rapture was two floors, the first being the former sanctuary which Landon and Verity had turned into an enormous dance floor and sprawling bar. The upper was the old choir loft, which had been converted into a small public play space with private rooms down a short, dark hallway. There was a patio on the main floor, bathrooms, and not much else.

I hadn't been to the club in a few weeks on account of how much time the bid was taking, but when I walked in, I found an entirely new first floor spread out around me. The dance floor and bar were much the same, but a wall had been put up that sectioned off a piece of the dance floor. It didn't take more than a quick look to realize they'd built another private area, similar to the vibes of the quiet, upstairs loft.

The walls were painted a dark shade that looked black to me, and a stained glass window cut into one of the walls that let the reflections of the strobe lights over the dance floor shine through was the only real source of light in the space. Much like upstairs, there was a St. Andrew's Cross tucked into a corner, a leather spanking bench, and an array of mismatched but comfortable-looking seating.

It was on a plush leather couch that I found Justin, reclined back with an ankle resting on his knee and a weary look on his face. He had a half-empty glass of scotch in his hand, and he smiled when he saw me.

"Of course this place is your first stop," he said.

I sank down onto the couch beside him, leather creaking beneath my weight. There wasn't a bar in the room, and there was only one other couple, standing in the far corner with their heads together while they shared a conversation.

"How long has this room been here?" I asked, looking around again to make sure I hadn't missed anything on my first perusal.

"Two weeks maybe?"

"How long did it take to build?"

"Less than that." He sipped his bourbon, visibly relaxing. "You haven't come around in a while."

"Work has been a lot."

"It always is," he agreed, glancing toward the door.

"Where are your better halves?" I asked.

"Keith ran off with Verity, and I sent Micah to fetch you a drink."

"I just got here."

"I knew you were coming," he said with a smile. "And if Micah is going to be a brat to me, the least he can do is take care of you."

I followed his stare toward the doorway, still vacant of either of his partners.

"What's been going on?"

"Nothing, he's just been argumentative this entire week. At

first I thought he just wanted some attention, but then I thought maybe the answer was no attention—"

"Which made things worse," I guessed.

Justin groaned, but he swallowed it down, adjusting his posture when Micah stepped through the doorway, three drinks balanced between his hands. He set down another bourbon for Justin, something for Keith, then he handed me a glass of red wine.

"Nothing for you?" I asked in lieu of a greeting.

With a frown, Micah reached into his back pocket and pulled out a bottle of water.

"We love a hydrated husband," I teased, beckoning him down for a hug, which he gave without protest. Micah grumbled in my ear, and Justin reached between us, hooking his finger around the thin leather of Micah's collar and hauling him down onto his knees. Micah huffed, unscrewing the cap of his water and taking a guzzle.

Watching the two of them together was always adorable, but when Keith was in the mix, it was like a whole new layer to their dynamic. Keith was submissive to Justin all the time, but dominant to Micah some of the time, and much like an outing to Rapture, there was no way of telling what I'd get when I went out with the three of them.

"Thank you for my wine, Micah," I said, angling my glass toward him before taking a drink.

"You're welcome, Marshall," he muttered.

I could tell there was more that he wanted to say, but instead he rubbed his thumb over the tattooed wedding band on his left ring finger.

"Are you having a rough go of things?" I asked.

He worked his jaw back and forth.

The couple in the corner moved away from the wall and toward the spanking bench. They kissed loudly, hands roaming over bodies.

"Do you feel like a dash of voyeurism tonight?" Justin asked, glancing toward the corner with the furniture.

"Not quite yet," I said.

He nodded his agreement and helped Micah to his feet. Micah took Keith's drink, and the three of us made our way out of the new private suite and onto the dance floor. Justin led the way and Micah hung back, but whatever the tension was between them, avoidance wasn't going to sort it out. I gently bumped the back of Micah's shoulder and propelled him forward.

"Dance with your husband," I whispered into his ear, reaching out and catching Justin to drag him back. Their bodies crashed together, and it wasn't anything more than muscle memory for Justin to lift his hands and grab Micah before either of them stumbled.

"Did you trip? Are you okay?" Justin asked.

Micah narrowed his eyes at me but turned his stare toward his husband. "I'm fine."

"I'm going to go find your third," I shouted over the music, making sure the two of them stayed aligned before leaving them in the middle of the dance floor and heading for the bar.

If Keith was with Verity, he'd be easy to find. Verity was always a beacon in the crowd, whether they were dressed masculine or feminine or, in extremely rare occasions, in nothing more than their underwear. But this time, I found Keith first, leaning against the bar, nodding along while Verity talked to him, gesturing with long and elegant hands and an animated face.

I approached from behind Keith, dropping my chin on his shoulder and smiling at Verity until they blushed.

"Stop using me as a tool to seduce unwitting strangers," Keith said, dropping his hand and smacking my thigh.

"Verity is hardly unwilling, and they're far from a stranger."

Verity waved me off, rolling their eyes at me.

"You look good enough to eat, Verity," I said with a sly smile.

"Aaron already has," they countered, "repeatedly. But thank you for the observation."

"Mind if I cut in and steal this handsome third from you?" I knocked my head into Keith's curly mop of dark hair.

"Please, take him." Verity leaned in and kissed us both on the cheek, then spun on their heel and headed off toward the back.

With my chin still on Keith's shoulder, I walked around until we were facing each other, immediately seeing the worry lines around the corners of his dark eyes.

"What's going on?" I asked.

"Micah is just…I have no idea. I was asking Verity for some advice."

"Get anything helpful?"

"Maybe."

"The three of you are my favorite throuple and I hate to see you like this," I said, grabbing Keith by the shoulders and steering him toward the dance floor.

Micah and Justin were easy to find. They'd gotten close, and Justin had a possessive hand around Micah's throat while Micah gyrated suggestively against his hip. I fit Keith in at Micah's back, pushing the three of them together like a sandwich.

"Don't come back until you've fixed whatever is wrong," I said, smacking Justin on the ass for good measure.

He gave me the finger, but the smile on his face and the way he looked at Micah, then at Keith, was the only confirmation I needed to know everything was going to be okay. I nodded, and Keith nodded back, then I took another drink of my wine and headed back for the first floor suite. Maybe a little voyeurism was in order after all.

CHAPTER 5
SILAS

Lincoln was right. Getting out and going to Rapture had been a good call. He and I danced together in the middle of the dance floor, the sweat from his chest dripping against my back. His hand on my hip, steering my body in whatever way he determined would be most appealing. It was nice to shut down and forget sometimes. He'd already found someone for himself, a wisp of a man who smelled like gardenias, pressed against us both from the side, his fingers skating delicately across Lincoln's waist.

"There's a man watching you," Lincoln murmured in my ear, and I slowly blinked my eyes open.

"Which one?"

"Over by the new addition," he said. "He's just kind of swaying there."

I hummed, finding the man Lincoln had spotted. He was definitely watching, his stare raking over me heavy enough to feel it even with the dozens of people between us. He looked from me to Lincoln to…

I angled my head to the side. "What's your name?"

"Riot."

I snorted an amused sound in the back of my throat. "Riot?"

"What's wrong with Riot?" he snapped.

"You just don't look it," I said.

"What do I look like?"

"You—" Lincoln interrupted, turning Riot's face toward him with a gentle press against the underside of his chin. "Look like a man about to suck my cock as soon as I find someone to spank my best friend here."

Riot sputtered out a gasp, and I rolled my eyes, stare shifting back to the man on the outskirts of the dance floor. He was older than me, but that didn't mean much. Dressed in all black, like he wanted to fit in but he wasn't sure how.

"You want to suck my cock, don't you?" Lincoln asked.

"I do," Riot purred.

Heat burned low and hot in my belly from the thought of Lincoln and Riot, and also from the promise of a rough spanking in my very near future.

"I'll go talk to him," Lincoln said, separating from me and Riot.

"I can do it." I turned and dusted a quick kiss across Lincoln's mouth. He tasted like cherries, which meant he'd been stealing kisses behind my back. The fire inside of me stoked to something very close to raging.

I swerved my way across the dance floor until I reached the man in question. He leaned against the wall, a drink in hand, and when I got close enough to make out his features in more detail, he rewarded me with an almost shy smile.

"Hey," he said.

"I saw you watching me," I murmured, my nerves spiking from the adrenaline that always came with finding a new hookup.

"Are you with those two?"

I glanced over my shoulder to find Lincoln and Riot wrapped up in each other, arms and tongues tangled.

"One of them," I said. "In some ways."

"Not all?"

"Not the ones that matter."

"Are you submissive?" he asked, and I laughed, dipping my chin toward my chest before locking my eyes on his.

"Do I look like it?"

He opened his mouth to speak, then closed it again. "You look like you need to be taken down a couple of pegs," he said.

It should have been a red flag.

Honestly, it should have been.

It was.

But from the corner of my eye, I saw Lincoln and Riot stumble into the private room, and I suddenly found myself overwhelmed with the need to know what Riot looked like with a dick in his mouth. And the conversation from earlier still held true. I needed a good spanking, and Lincoln had found someone to facilitate that. The club was safe. Everything would be fine.

"I'd like to see you try," I taunted him deliberately, then headed after Lincoln. Around the corner into the newly constructed play space, and I found it barely occupied. There was a couple sitting on the couch, lost in a conversation that looked a lot like aftercare, and Lincoln in the corner with Riot already on his knees. We made eye contact, and he lifted a brow, his concern morphing into excitement when the man he'd scouted followed me into the room.

"On the bench," he said, palm connecting with my back. He guided me toward the spanking bench, and I let him. "Pants around your knees."

"I don't even know what to call you," I said, undoing my fly and shoving my pants down to my thighs.

"You can call me Sir."

I laughed. "Pass."

He pushed me onto the bench.

It should have been another red flag.

Lincoln had his hands in Riot's hair and his hips moved in slow, measured thrusts. I bet his cock would taste like cherry lip gloss at the end of the night. It was my own distraction that caused me to miss the man clipping cuffs around my ankles, attaching me to the bench. I caught him when he came around to do the same to my wrists, and I rocked back into a seated position to stop him.

"Slow down there, buddy," I warned, holding up a hand to stop him. "That's not how this works."

"How it works is you do as you're told."

In the corner, Lincoln was coming, lost to an orgasm that he shot straight into the back of Riot's throat, and the man in front of me grabbed my wrist and tried to haul me forward so he could cuff me to the front of the bench.

"Stop," I told him.

He ignored me.

Riot made a gagging noise.

The couple on the couch…. I had no idea about them. I couldn't hear anything, and when I tried to turn to look behind me for help, the man tugged me—hard. My chest came forward, I landed against the bench with a thud, and then I only had one hand free.

"Lincoln," I tried to call out for my friend, but the music in the room was almost as loud as it was on the dance floor and the restraint had it so my voice traveled straight into the floor. Panic reared its head, slamming against my rib cage alongside my frantic heart.

"Stop fighting me," the man complained, trying to grab my other wrist. He succeeded, and I was bound to the bench with my bare ass up in the air. "You're supposed to do what you're told."

"Let me go," I said again, fighting the cuffs.

He reached into his pocket and pulled out a balled up bandana, then he shoved it so far into my mouth that when I sucked in a breath, the corners of it tickled the back of my throat, threatening to choke me. Sweat prickled my temple, and my fingers tingled with anxiety. Another set of feet came into view, not Lincoln, and my stomach sank. I had no idea who this other man was or what I'd gotten myself into. All I could do was hope Lincoln realized something was wrong before it got too far out of hand.

"Is this consensual?" a new voice asked. It was almost familiar, but I couldn't make out anything over the quickly rising panic.

I shook my head frantically, trying to use my tongue to spit out the gag.

New fingers attached to new hands made quick work of unclasping the cuffs around my wrists, and I was back upright as soon as he finished my second cuff. I yanked the bandana out of my mouth and flung it in his face, furiously tearing open the cuffs while the stranger who'd saved me went around back for my ankles.

"Silas?" It was Lincoln's voice from the corner, coming out of his post-orgasm haze, and I didn't want to know what the scene in front of him looked like.

"I'm fine," I promised him, wishing more than anything I could climb off the bench and pull my fucking pants up.

As soon as the last cuff was undone, I did just that, yanking my pants up and taking a step away from the bench.

"I told you to stop," I said to the man.

"Silas?"

My name again, but this time from behind me. From the man who'd saved me.

My brain connected the memories before I'd finished turning toward him, before I even saw him.

"Marshall," I muttered his name, wanting to dig a hole under the club and bury myself there.

A thousand thoughts raced across his face, half of them clear as day, but he finally settled on asking, "Are you all right?"

All things considered, it was the best thing he could have asked, but the one with the most complicated answer.

"I'm fine," I said, which tasted like a lie, but it was real.

I was free. I was unharmed. And I was protected.

Marshall's expression morphed from concern to fury, all of the latter directed at the man who'd just had his hands on me.

"What part of stop wasn't clear to you?" he asked, voice barely louder than whatever dance beat the DJ was spinning.

"I didn't think he meant it," he tried to say dismissively, and my body bowed forward, overcome with the need to vomit all over my feet.

"Do you know him?" Marshall asked, the question traveling over my head, so I assumed it was directed at Lincoln.

"Yeah."

"Then help him," Marshall ordered. I heard the sound of his shoes clicking against the concrete—he was still dressed for work, still dressed from our meeting—and then the other guy gasped, and something slammed into the wall.

Lincoln helped me right myself in time to see Marshall fist the other guy's shirt and shove him so hard into the drywall I worried they'd have to patch the wall. Marshall whispered something into his ear that turned the other man a sickly shade of green, and then they were both on their way out of the room.

"Sit, Silas," Marshall called out to me over his shoulder, and there was no argument to be had about it. Maybe another day or another time, but not now. "I'll be right back."

And then the room was quiet.

The other couple was gone. Riot was gone. It was just me and Lincoln, and Lincoln helping me around the room until the backs of my legs connected with the couch and I sank down into the cushions.

"I'm so sorry," he said, grabbing my face and tilting my head all around to inspect me.

"It's not your fault."

He angled my chin up to check my throat, but what he couldn't see was my tongue stuck to the roof of my mouth, the tang of someone else's dried sweat seeping into my tastebuds.

"I picked him."

"You're not my Dom." I grabbed Lincoln's desperate hands to bring him to a stop. "You didn't do this. And it could have been worse. I'm really fine."

"He was going to assault you." Lincoln pressed the issue. "Right in front of me, and I—"

I covered his mouth with one of my hands before the words could get out of his mouth.

"I'm begging you to not make this about you."

He swallowed hard and nodded, and I dropped my hand into my lap.

I could still feel the cuffs around my wrists.

"Can you go get me some water?" I asked, voice cracking.

"I don't want to leave you alone."

"He's not alone," Marshall said from the doorway, a bottle of water in hand. He untwisted the cap and extended it to me. I took it and guzzled the whole thing in less than three gulps.

"And who are you?" Lincoln snapped.

I smiled down at my lap, appreciating the way he was ready to defend me at a moment's notice.

"I know him," I promised my best friend.

"From where?"

"Work." I flicked a glance up at Marshall, who didn't look concerned in the least that I was who I was and he was who he was, and that we'd just gone through this shared experience together. He did look concerned, though. Just…about me.

"Work," he confirmed.

I gave Lincoln as much of an honest smile as I could manage, but his coddling was the absolute last thing I wanted.

"I'm fine, Lincoln," I said again, willing it to be true. "What happened to Riot?"

My best friend looked at me like I'd asked him if pigs could fly.

"He went to the bathroom."

The flush on Lincoln's cheeks confirmed just *why* Riot had scampered off for a quick dose of privacy.

"Go find him then." I nudged him until he reluctantly stood up from the cushion beside me. "I promise I'm okay. Go have fun, and I'll come find you in a few minutes. I need to…"

I trailed off, because if I told him I needed to be alone with Marshall, he wouldn't go. The guilt was eating him up, but I didn't have it in me to convince him this wasn't his fault, and it wasn't his problem.

"I'll stay with him," Marshall said, which seemed to give Lincoln some ease.

He took a tentative step toward the door, and then another.

"I won't leave this spot until you come back."

"I'll make sure of it," Marshall confirmed.

Lincoln either believed us or knew arguing would get him nowhere. With one last look, he left me and Marshall alone in the private playroom, and he took all of the air with him. I sucked in a breath, dropping my elbows against my knees. It hurt to breathe, it hurt to come apart.

Marshall took the seat Lincoln had vacated, and he settled one strong hand on my knee, the other on my spine.

"You're here, Silas," he said, drawing a circle on my back with his palm. "All you have to do is breathe. Can you breathe?"

"It doesn't feel like it."

"Just one. In through the nose, okay? We'll do it together."

I tilted my head to look up at Marshall, who had his shoulders up near his ears like he was ready to take a breath. I managed a nod, blinked back tears, then breathed in through my nose. We exhaled together, and without being asked, repeated and repeated and repeated. His presence was a stronger salve than anything I'd ever experienced before, and I wondered how I'd never picked up on him before. In all of our meetings, all our business engagements…I'd never even thought of Marshall in a place like this, but if asked, he'd probably say the same about me.

I pushed back until I hit the couch, the stretch of his forearm across my shoulders like a shock blanket. Scrubbing a hand down my face, I swallowed back the last lingering threads of panic, then blinked back the tears I'd refused to shed.

I was fine.

I was *fine*.

"What do you need, Silas?" Marshall asked me softly, after it no longer hurt to fill my lungs. His voice was so quiet, he had to be so close to my ear to hear him over the drumbeat, and he was so strong, so warm…so very safe.

The answer tasted like sand, but sand was better than sweat.

"Just this," I told him. "I just need this a little while longer."

CHAPTER 6
MARSHALL

Walking in on an assault was something I never wanted to experience again. Walking in on an assault against Stanley Ayres' kid? Another. Though, Silas was hardly a kid, was he? The same age as Smith and probably twice as accomplished—if he could get out from beneath his father's heel. It took all my strength to not put the pretend Dom through a wall when I saw the way he ignored Silas, but as soon as we were out of the playroom, his posturing turned into a slew of apologies. He was new. He didn't understand. He hadn't been taught. Any of them could have been legitimate reasons, but none of them were a valid excuse.

"Find a mentor," I'd told him before throwing him off to security and heading back in search of Silas.

The only thing that tamped down my anger was the warm press of Silas's body against mine. The way he made himself so small to tuck in against my side, empty water bottle clutched tightly in his fists. Slowly, I pried his fingers off the plastic, hoping he could relax further.

"I'll stay as long as you need," I said, and I meant it.

Of their own volition, my fingers stroked short, calm lines

up and down the length of Silas's arm. I lost track of time, the two of us there quiet in each other's arms until, at some point, he said, "You're not going to tell my dad, are you?"

The idea was preposterous. "Why would I tell your dad?"

He shrugged, shifting against me.

"You're a grown man, Silas. Whatever you do in bed isn't your father's concern." I paused, tracing my tongue across the front of my teeth, debating if the next part warranted saying. In the end, it did. "I am concerned, though."

"Why?"

Silas moved his head against my shoulder, messy curls dragging across my jaw and bottom lip. I flattened his hair and rested my chin against the top of his head.

"It shouldn't fall on you, but from what I saw, you weren't going to fight him. You were just going to—"

"I would have fought harder. If it got to…if I ended up needing to. I just…panicked," he interrupted, pushing up and out of my arms, and I immediately knew I'd said the wrong thing.

"I know, I'm sorry. That's not how I meant it…" I snapped my mouth closed because how could I tell him that I would be forever worried about him now. That I was the oldest of four and I was a caretaker by nature, and now I knew this about him, that I would always wonder if he was safe. If he was making good decisions.

"I know," he said gruffly, sinking down into the couch beside me instead of against me.

"If I hadn't walked in, Silas."

"I *know*," he said again, far more petulant than the first. "But don't you dare come at me with some misguided sense of judgment that I shouldn't be out here doing what I'm doing or doing it with strangers. Everyone starts as a stranger."

I raised my hands in surrender, brows up in my hairline. "I'd never judge," I assured him. "I wasn't judging."

Silas blinked at me, swallowed hard, shoulders sinking, and it looked like he was trying to bury himself in the couch again. I held my hand out for him, and he stared at it a beat before slowly settling his palm against mine. With a gentle tug, I pulled him up from the depths of the leather cushions and back against me.

"Is this okay?" I asked.

"Yes," he muttered, like he hated the truth of it.

"This is what you wanted, right? Just a little more of this?"

He nodded into my armpit.

"I'll shut up then."

Another quiet minute, maybe two, maybe five.

Silas's friend hadn't come looking for him and Justin, Keith, and Micah were nowhere to be seen. That probably meant they were all fucking in the bathroom—not each other —and that was the best possible outcome for all parties involved.

"Did you really read my article?" Silas sounded meeker than he had since I'd walked into the room in the first place.

"Twice."

"And you meant what you said?"

"Every word." I buried my nose in his curls and breathed him in. His hair smelled like lavender and sage, wild and delicate at the same time.

Silas exhaled loudly. "We're going to lose the bid, aren't we?"

I didn't have it in me to lie to him, not after what he'd been though. "Probably."

Another heavy sigh.

"I don't want to talk about work," he said.

"Okay."

Another silence, longer than the last. The music on the dance floor kept shifting and changing; the only constant was the steady bass that vibrated up from the floor and right into the bottoms of my feet.

"Why are you here?" he asked me next.

I huffed out half of a laugh. "I imagine the same reason you are."

"Jesus, no. I…I didn't mean…"

I wanted to kiss him.

"Not the exact same reason," I amended. "But the same result."

"Fuck."

I'd never heard him curse before. It made me feel the same way as cinnamon sugar did on my tongue, surprised and pleased all at once. I ignored the feeling, tamped down the heat it stirred between my legs.

"I meant why are you here right now. In this room. With me," he said.

"Because you said this is what you needed."

"And why does that matter?"

I knew it was grossly inappropriate to tell the son of my longtime business rival the answer to his question, but the situation was too sensitive to support a lie. That, and it wasn't in my nature to be dishonest, especially about matters of power exchange and sexual activities.

"I'm not your Dom, Silas. But that doesn't mean I'm not—"

"Someone else's," he tacked on before I could finish the thought.

"No." I bit the tip of my tongue until the pain grounded me back into the moment. "This is just how I am, Silas."

He hummed, and I couldn't make sense of the sound of it. Didn't know if he agreed with me or found my answer lacking.

Finally, he said, "This is so embarrassing."

"For whom?"

Silas snorted and pushed away from me again. "Me, obviously."

"Why?"

"Are you serious?" He moved farther away, stood up, and it was my first real chance to *see* him. Tight black jeans that left *nothing* to the imagination, a tight black t-shirt, and battered sneakers that had definitely seen better days. It was wrong to lust after Stanley's son, I definitely knew that, but there was no stopping my mind from racing through a dozen imaginary and very sexual scenarios anyway. None of which I would ever act on.

Especially not after what had happened to him.

Especially because of who he was to me.

"Very serious."

"How is this not embarrassing?"

"It was a scene, Silas. A scene gone wrong, but a scene just the same. Is it embarrassing when you come so hard you cry? When you get spanked until it's difficult to breathe and you choke on air? When you have to ask for permission to crawl to the bathroom to relieve yourself after—"

I stopped myself, covering my mouth with my hand to actually contain the rest of the words in my mouth. Silas's lips parted, jaw hanging slack, and his fingers flexed against the outside of his thighs. He swayed forward, and I was more than ready to catch him if he fell.

"After what?" he rasped.

I shook my head. "It doesn't matter."

"It very much matters," he said quietly. "Marshall."

I stood up, took a step toward him. He took a step back, not cowering, but so he had enough room to tilt his head to gaze up at me.

"Don't play with fire, sweetheart," I warned.

His tongue darted out to moisten the corner of his lips, and I zeroed in on the motion, the deliberate and teasing swipe, covering just the corner, then half, then the entirety of his bottom lip.

"I want to know," he said.

I took another step toward him, and we were so dangerously close. I could easily slide my hands around his waist, pull our bodies flush, let him feel the way my cock throbbed for him.

"There you are!"

Lincoln, Silas's distracted and horny friend called out from the doorway. His voice was like a glass of cold water, thrown on us both. Silas stumbled away from me, the backs of his legs colliding with another chair. His arms flailed out like propellers as his body swung back, ready to fall. I lunged forward, hooking my arm around the small of his back and sinking down into my own center of gravity to haul him to his feet. It brought us together like I'd wanted earlier, but with far more violence. He weighed more than I expected, and we both tumbled backward onto the couch.

I landed hard against the seat, legs splayed with Silas neatly tucked against me, protected from the fall. He wasn't protected from my arousal, though. His thigh sank between my legs and the heat and rigidity of my erection were unavoidable. He sucked in a surprised breath, eyes going wide as his brain connected the dots of what was happening. I tightened my arm around him, a primal instinct I had no control over. His body felt so fucking good against me.

"Oh, shit." Lincoln laughed from the door, another rush of ice over the top of us.

Silas scrambled out of my arms, and I cursed his friend under my breath as we both righted ourselves.

"I said I would come find you," Silas said.

"It's been over an hour."

It felt like ten minutes.

It felt like the whole night.

"Are you okay now?" Lincoln asked. "Are you ready to head home?"

I bit my lips between my teeth to stop from snapping at him. There was no way Silas was okay, no matter what answer he gave. I knew that, and Silas knew that, but whether he would admit it or not was another thing entirely.

"I'm fine," Silas lied, and I frowned at him.

He wasn't looking at me, but anyone could see the tension in the fake smile he offered up with the answer.

"I feel horrible, Silas," Lincoln said.

Another apology.

"It's not your fault."

I cleared my throat, and Silas did finally look at me.

"Are you okay?" I asked him softly.

He worked his jaw, clenched the muscles, then gave me the same bullshit smile he'd given his friend. "I'm fine, Marshall. Thank you."

I leaned in close, my next words meant only for him. "I don't believe you."

"You don't have a choice."

"I don't like this."

"Why do you care?" He gave me another saccharine smile, then turned his attention over my shoulder to his friend. "I'm ready."

I wasn't in a position to argue with him. Silas wasn't my submissive, and he wasn't my concern. He'd used me for comfort, which I'd given willingly. I would have done it a thousand times over, but being discarded after his friend's return had me feeling more used than I could ever remember. So much of my private life was transactional. Sometimes there was money exchanged; sometimes it was just an agreement between two willing parties. I was used to things that didn't last, and yet…

"Thank you," Silas said again, and I looked at him, maybe seeing him for the first time.

He was a man trying so hard to stand on his own in all of the ways that counted most to him, and unfortunately that meant standing away from me. I wasn't ready, though. I *wanted*. And I lifted my hand slowly between us so he could see what I was asking for. He didn't move away, didn't shake his head, didn't falter. Brushing my fingertips across his warm, pink cheekbone, I committed to memory the way his pupils dilated, the way his lashes fluttered.

Shoving my hand into the pocket of my slacks, I cleared my throat and took a step away. Cool air rushed between us, and we were both awake. The tender moments between us broken. Gone.

"It was my honor, Silas," I told him quietly, more words meant just for his ears.

He bit his lower lip, dragged his stare away from mine, then he walked out.

CHAPTER 7
SILAS

did not go to bed with Lincoln when we got home from Rapture. He barely said another word to me, save to check if I was okay, before walking me straight to my own bed and tucking me in. I tossed and turned for an hour before kicking off the blankets and stalking down the hallway to his room. He was also awake, and he lifted the covers for me without argument. Sleep came quickly after that for the both of us, Lincoln's arm wrapped protectively around my chest.

I woke hours later, still in his bed, but alone.

Closing my eyes, I covered my face with both of my hands, annoyed at how prevalent Marshall Covington's face was on the backs of my eyelids.

Last night when he'd asked me if I was okay and I said yes, it was a lie. But in the morning light, it felt a little more true. Partially thanks to the way he'd sat with me and comforted me after doing whatever he'd done with—

Shit.

I'd never even gotten that other man's name, and I was about to let him strap me to a bench with my pants around my ankles.

God, I was a fucking idiot.

A fucking idiot who needed a whole pot of coffee to recover from the embarrassment of the night before. It was one thing to make a bad call with a prospective sexual partner in the privacy of your own home. It was another entirely to do it in public…in front of my father's business rival.

"I hear you rustling!" Lincoln shouted from the kitchen, which meant there was coffee ready for me and maybe even breakfast.

I climbed out of bed and shuffled down the hallway, rubbing sleep out of my eyes as I stumbled into the kitchen. Lincoln shoved a mug of coffee across the counter and into my waiting hands.

"I'm glad you're speaking to me again," I said, raising the mug to my mouth.

He gave me an unamused look. "I don't even know why you're speaking to *me*."

"Because you didn't do anything wrong."

"I found him," Lincoln protested.

"I don't want to do this with you again." I sighed, taking my coffee to the couch. "I smell the bacon, so bring some with you."

Lincoln grumbled under his breath but joined me on the couch with his own coffee and a plate of bacon that he dropped unceremoniously onto my thigh. I picked a strip up and chomped down on a fatty end piece.

"Is this apology bacon?" I asked with my mouthful.

"Is it working?"

"No, because I don't want an apology. I'm an adult. I can make bad decisions too, and this time I did. That's all. Okay?" I grabbed Lincoln's face, pinching his cheeks in so he looked like a cranky wall-mounted fish.

"Who was that other guy last night?" he asked.

I picked up another slice of bacon and folded it into his mouth. He chewed it, one eyebrow arched.

"Someone from work," I said.

Lincoln swallowed. "Tell me more."

Lincoln was no stranger to the pain points of my job or the long hours I worked with my father. He knew almost as much about architectural design as I did, learned purely through osmosis, so as soon as I told him it was Marshall, realization dawned across his face like a sunrise.

"Please don't," I begged.

"Marshall Covington like *the* Marshall Covington, like the man your father would send into space with nothing more than his birthday suit Marshall Covington?"

"That's him." I reached for my coffee and another piece of bacon so I would have something to do with my hands.

"You didn't tell me he was kinky."

"I didn't *know!* Jesus. How was I supposed to know that? That's not really the kind of thing that comes up over our usual business meetings, you know."

There wasn't enough coffee in the world.

"He's hot," Lincoln said.

"He's…"

My cheeks burned, remembering the way his arms had felt around me, the way his fingers felt against my cheek, the way he breathed with me until I wasn't scared of dying any longer.

"Hot," Lincoln said again.

As if my guardian angel sensed I needed a reprieve, my cell phone started to ring from somewhere in my bedroom.

"I've got to get that," I said, clambering to my feet.

"Literally saved by the bell," Lincoln grumbled, grabbing for the plate of bacon before it fell onto the couch. I ran down the hallway, chasing after the ringtone and finding my phone properly plugged in on the nightstand where it belonged. At least I'd managed that much before going to bed.

My finger swiped to accept the call—a force of habit from work—before my brain had time to register the name. By the time I put two and two together, it was too late, the phone was pressed against my ear and my mouth was moving.

"Hello?"

"Silas," Marshall rumbled, and I screwed my eyes closed, sinking down onto the floor. "Good morning."

"Is it?"

A pause. "Isn't it?"

"I slept like shit," I admitted.

He made a sound so displeased I felt it down to my marrow, and again I found myself wanting to burrow into the ground and die. But now for entirely different reasons.

"Have you had coffee?" he asked.

"Yes."

"And breakfast?"

"Two slices of bacon."

Another sound, this one more of a pained grunt. "That's hardly breakfast."

"Did you call to criticize my eating habits, Marshall?"

"No," he said quietly. "I didn't. You're right. I'm sorry."

"Why *did* you call?" I asked, finally letting the floor take me. I splayed out in the middle of my room like a sad little starfish, phone clutched against my ear like a thingamabobber.

"I wanted to check on you. See how you were doing."

"Why?"

"Because I was worried about you after last night."

"Why?" I pressed.

"Because you were nearly assaulted," he said.

"Nearly."

"Silas."

Marshall said my name like my correction had disappointed him, and I didn't know what was worse. That he sounded like that or the way his disappointment made me feel.

"I'm fine," I told him. "Same as last night."

"You said you didn't sleep well."

"Maybe I never sleep well," I countered.

Marshall sighed heavily into my ear and then, "Silas."

But it sounded different that time, tired and unsure. Weary. Hopeful.

"I promise I'm okay," I said.

He was silent for long enough that I picked up on the cadence of his breathing, accidentally matching mine to his because it felt good to be in sync with him again. Because it reminded me of being in his arms the night before.

"You don't believe me," I whispered.

"No."

"Why not?"

"Because if I was you, I wouldn't be okay," he said.

"Well, you're not." I swallowed hard. "How can I convince you so we can go back to pretending this never happened?"

Marshall made a dismissive noise in the back of his throat. "I can't go back, Silas."

"Good thing we're going to lose the bid then. We'll be out of business and not your—"

He interrupted with a rushed, "Meet me for lunch."

"—problem. I'm sorry. What did you say?"

"I said meet me for lunch," he repeated, not a question.

"Marshall." I sighed.

"Prove to me that you're good, and I'll leave you alone."

"I'm not sure you will," I grumbled.

He laughed like we both knew I was right.

"I'll text you an address. Do you want me to call you a car?"

"I'm shocked you're asking."

He was quiet for two seconds too long, and I worried I'd said the wrong thing. My palm sweated against the case of my phone, and I was so close to opening my mouth and telling him I'd been teasing when he spoke first and cut me off at the pass.

"All things with consent, Silas," he said quietly.

"You *told* me to have lunch with you," I reminded him.

"Tell me you don't want to."

This time, the silence was mine because we both knew I did.

"I don't need a car," I said instead.

"Do you want one?"

"Marshall, please," I begged, slamming my eyes closed and stabbing my fingertips into my eye sockets until my vision sparked around the edges.

"I'll text you an address, Silas," he said, then he hung up.

We hadn't agreed on a time, but in my gut I knew we didn't need to. The expectation was heavy and silent between us that I would get off the phone, make myself presentable, and then plug the results of his next text message into my GPS and hit the road.

The text came through before I'd even managed to lower the phone away from my face, but I didn't bother checking in. I slid my phone across the room and rolled onto my hands and knees, dragging my cheek back and forth the carpet until the skin was tender. I needed to shave, but the short hairs were another abrasion that kept my feet and my brain firmly rooted in the present moment

"You're fine," I told myself. "It's just lunch. It's just Marshall."

Knowing it was Marshall somehow made it worse, but I swallowed down as much trepidation as I could manage and pushed myself up to standing. Lincoln was still in the living room, but I knew him well enough to know he was on the couch with his neck craned backward, ears straining to eavesdrop on my conversation.

"It was Marshall," I called out from the hallway. "Meeting him for lunch."

I didn't wait for Lincoln to say anything else. The bathroom was close, and I made sure to lock the door behind me to make sure I maintained privacy. Shoving my pajamas down to my ankles, I ignored the way my cock caught on the waistband, already thick and half-hard from…from what, I wasn't sure. It couldn't have been the phone conversation with Marshall because…

It just couldn't.

Under the spray of the shower, I continued to pay my cock no attention, but it only got harder, and it got harder aggressively, if that was even a thing. By the time I'd washed my face and my hair, precum had pooled on the tip of my dick, and it was on account of the way my brain wouldn't stop thinking about Marshall and the way his arms had felt around me the night before.

I'd been so safe there on the couch with him.

"Fine," I conceded to myself, making a tight fist around my shaft with one hand and bracing myself against the wall of the shower with the other. Dropping my forehead against my forearm, I made quick work of the orgasm my body was so insistent about receiving. It came hard and rough, the release violently shooting against the tiled wall before being rinsed straight down the drain.

My knees knocked together as I stroked myself to empty, and I shivered from the peace of it. If there was a way to be fulfilled from an orgasm, I found it there in the shower, Marshall's hands at the forefront of my brain. The only thing that would have made the release more perfect was if I could have shuffled naked across the hallway and climbed back into bed for another two hours.

I debated texting Marshall and telling him never mind, but I was dry and I was dressed, and my fingers were already keying the address he'd provided into my phone. Lincoln eyed me warily from his perch on the couch, the last slice of bacon hanging out of his mouth like a cigarette.

"You good, Si?" he asked, watching me like a hawk as I sat down beside him to put on socks and lace up my sneakers.

I nodded.

I wasn't okay five minutes later when I got into my car and stuck my phone up onto the magnet mount, though. Because the address Marshall had texted me was very definitely residential, not commercial.

Letting out a nervous breath, I swiped open to my text messaging and typed one out to him, my car still in park.

Is this your house?

MARSHALL

Yes

Simple and straightforward, just like him, just like everything between us had been for the entirety of our relationship. Marshall was the same at work as he'd been at Rapture—astute, aware, and alert. He carried himself with the air of a man who never argued because he never had to defend himself. He always knew the right things to say, the simple collections of syllables that could so readily disarm a man. He did it in the boardroom, and he undoubtedly carried that energy into the bedroom. Things between us hadn't gone that far, but with the hint of cum still fresh on the tips of my fingers, I realized I might not care if they did, and that was really, *really* fucked up.

CHAPTER 8
MARSHALL

Silas knocked on my door with every ounce of over-confidence I'd expect a recently traumatized but currently posturing man to have. In another time, I would have made him wait, would have wanted him nervous, but admittedly that was the last thing I wanted with Silas. I was waiting by the door when he arrived, and I opened it quickly, his arm still raised to knock another time.

When he saw me there, he gave me a quick onceover, his face not giving much away about his reaction to my appearance—worn jeans, a threadbare undershirt, and bare feet—before he returned his stare to my face.

"I'm here," he said, throwing his arms out a little dramatically, "and I'm fine."

Sighing, I stepped to the side to make room for him to come in.

Silas stepped onto the white tile of my entryway, looked back at my bare feet, then kicked his shoes off without asking if it was necessary. With socked toes, he nudged his black sneakers—the same ones from last night—into a neat line against the baseboard, then he followed me into the living room without complaining.

I'd made him lunch because he needed to eat, but I ignored the way his stomach growled once he saw the pasta salad and sandwiches I'd set out on the coffee table. Gesturing for Silas to take a seat in one of my chairs, I took the one opposite him and waited for him to say something. Again, in other circumstances, it would have been different, but Silas was skittish as a mouse even if he tried to pretend otherwise.

"You really read it," he finally said, leaning forward and tapping the cover of the most recent issue of *LA Design Digest*. It was the one with his article that I had read, more than once.

"I told you as much."

His stomach growled again.

"Eat, Silas." I pushed one of the sandwiches closer to him, and he picked the plate up without being told a second time.

He worked his way through half the sandwich before setting the plate back onto the table and pushing it away. Half was better than nothing.

"See?" he prompted, brushing his hands down the front of his chest. "I'm fine. Can I go?"

"I want to talk about what happened last night."

"I don't."

"Why not?" I asked.

"Because nothing happened."

"So you weren't tied to a bench by a man you didn't know who would have raped you as a worst-case scenario and injured you at best?" My tone was snappish, but Silas's complete lack of awareness about what had almost transpired at Rapture was too cavalier of an attitude for me to bear.

He stared at me, swallowing hard, like the words were a truth he didn't have the stomach for.

"I'm fine, Marshall," he said again, the syllables far more measured. Pressing his palms against the top of his thighs, he leveraged himself to stand. "Thank you for lunch."

"Sit down, Silas."

And he did, cheeks burning bright as hot coals.

Silas worked his jaw, looked from me to the food to his lap, back to the table again before asking, "What did you think about my suggestion in the article to use solar power tied in with the water purification?"

"You know I think it was amazing," I murmured, leaning forward to bring our bodies closer together. "What were you after last night?"

"A good time."

"Wrong answer."

"I'm not sure the technology is there yet to purify graywater in the way we need it for future development and use," he croaked.

"What do you need, Silas?"

"But there's some guys in Europe who are making a lot of progress with the tech."

"Silas."

"We're probably a few years away from that kind of advancement here," he whispered.

I could hear the way his exhales trembled in the space between us.

"Did you get what you wanted last night?"

His body swayed forward, and he blinked long and hard. "I…"

He licked his lips, and I watched. I *watched*.

"My research was really inspired by integration with nature that you see in buildings like the Pabellon de la Reserva."

"Silas."

It was obvious my thought pattern around Silas Ayres had shifted irrevocably when I walked in and found him with his pants down and his ass up, but that had no bearing on the opinion I'd had of him before last night. He was smart, capable, extremely forward-thinking, if not burdened by the narrowmindedness of his father. He had the makings of being a groundbreaking architect, but he needed the freedom to design his own ideas, not someone else's. He'd always been Stanley's son, and obviously that hadn't changed, but I had. He was the son of my former friend, my business rival.

He had no place in my home with his shoes off, with his pulse hammering against his throat so hard I could see it. Holding him in my arms at Rapture had awoken something in me that had been long dormant. Having him in my house now, with my food in his belly and his hands only inches away from mine only served to stoke a fire that I'd never meant to start.

"No," he whispered, so soft I barely heard it over the beating of my own heart.

"If this is a no, you can leave." I tried to make myself lean away from him, but it was impossible.

"No, I meant…no, I didn't get what I wanted last night."

Heat raced between my legs, blood thickening my cock to a girth it had no right being, all things considered. Silas was here because I'd asked him over, demanded it maybe, but only because he'd suffered a trauma and I wanted to make sure he was processing it and not avoiding it. My brain and my body were on different wavelengths, though, and I needed to control myself so the wrong one didn't win out.

I forced myself to lean away from him just long enough to breathe and ask, "What did you want?"

"A spanking," he murmured.

I exhaled through my mouth, cheeks puffing out like a squirrel, and I reached forward, gently pressing my fingers against Silas's chest. His eyes went wide, and I gave him a gentle push backward. He'd leaned in so close during the exchange he was barely on the seat, and I knew he needed the fresh air as much as I did. His back hit the cushions, and he blinked rapidly, then covered his cheeks with his hands and turned away from me.

"Sorry," he muttered.

"What for?"

He shrugged awkwardly and let his hands fall into his lap, fingers tangled.

"Next time you want a spanking, I'll give you a spanking."

As soon as the words left my mouth, I stood. Gathering the plates from the table, I carried everything into the kitchen and dropped it on the counter with enough force I was shocked when the porcelain didn't shatter on impact. Bracing myself against the edge of the counter, I bowed forward and let my chin hang against my chest while I caught my breath. It was easier to breathe when Silas wasn't in the room, but then he was.

I felt him behind me before I heard him, the nervous but sure energy rolling off of him like waves crashing against the shore. Squaring my shoulders, I stood up straight but didn't turn toward him because I couldn't be responsible for what happened next if I did.

"I want a spanking," he said.

I clenched my jaw so hard I worried my molars were about to shatter. "I didn't mean right now."

"Why not?"

"Because you're still processing everything that happened last night." Bracketing my hands on my hips so I didn't reach for him, I spun around to face him, finding him red-faced and ready.

"You keep saying that, but you're wrong."

"You're being bold, Silas," I warned.

"I want a spanking," he said again, taking a step toward me, encroaching on the precious untainted air I'd been desperate for.

He wanted a spanking, and I wanted to give it to him— there was no doubt about that. Silas was one of those men who was so naturally submissive, the fact he was also a masochist wasn't anything less than a cherry on top. He was the kind of man I'd spent most of my early adult life searching for before giving up and settling on nothing more than casual hookups.

I wanted to spank him more than I wanted my next breath, but I wanted to spank him more than once so I knew I couldn't.

"Then let me tie you up," I said.

He winced, a visible recoil and the look of defeat that flashed across his gorgeous face confirmed he finally understood that I was right. He wasn't ready, even if he wanted to be.

"Is that a requirement?"

"No," I told him honestly. "But until the idea doesn't terrify you, I'm not going to touch you at all."

Silas cursed under his breath and stalked out of my kitchen. His exit brought breathable air back into the space, and I took a desperate lungful of it before following after him back into the living room. I was relieved to find him in a chair again and not in the entryway lacing up his sneakers. I slowly sat down back beside him, propping my elbows on my knees and bringing our bodies close again. His resignation tempered some of my arousal, and I tentatively hovered one hand over top of his leg.

"Can I touch you?"

"Yes," he rasped, and I slowly set my hand on his thigh.

He was slimmer than he looked, my fingers curling around to the inside of his leg when I spread them out. His muscles tightened, then relaxed, like he was unfurling beneath my touch, a reaction that did nothing to ease the ache that had developed between my legs.

"I want you to be fine, Silas," I said, fingers flexing against his jeans. "I want you to be fine because I want to spank you. I want to tie you up. Tie you down."

He inhaled sharply, swaying toward me.

"I want all of those things and more."

"More?"

"More," I repeated. "But only if they're freely given, and you are… not free to give right now."

"Why?" he asked, glancing up at me from beneath the fan of his dark and curled lashes. "Why me? Why now?"

He was closer to okay than I thought with a question like that, an intuitive understanding that something between us had shifted out of the shadows and into the light, and that neither of us were able to shove it back into the darkness. At least, not entirely.

"I like the way you felt in my arms last night," I admitted.

It was simple.

It was honest.

"Is that all?"

"Isn't that enough?"

Silas made a thoughtful noise, and I squeezed his thigh tighter, drawing his attention to my face.

"I've always thought you to be intelligent, Silas, if not stifled by your employer." I paused, and his nostrils flared at the mention of his father, but he didn't argue the point so I continued. "You're young, talented, attractive, and now that I know…"

The corner of his mouth angled up into a smile.

"Now that you know I like it rough."

I swallowed hard. "That's not…I…some people like those things softly, Silas."

"I don't," he said, stare flickering down to my hand around his thigh. My fingers had splayed wider, incher higher.

"And now that I know," I repeated, dragging my teeth across my bottom lip while I tried to get my thoughts back into line. "I want."

We'd leaned in at some point, unknowing. The hot bursts of his exhales landed against my damp lip, my cheek. His breath didn't shake any longer, and neither did mine. My hands, though, another story entirely. I raised one to his face anyway, cradling his jaw against my palm and groaning when he pressed his cheek into my hand, lashes fluttering. The touch emboldened him, empowered, and he stared at me with those brilliant eyes of his, so full of understanding and of want.

"I think you're safe, Marshall," he whispered.

"I'm…*fuck*."

He grabbed my wrist and dragged my hand to the front of his face, kissed my palm. "You're what?"

"I'm your father's…. I'm old enough to…"

He kissed me again, this time with teeth.

"You're safe for me," he said again, one more kiss. "And I'll call you, I promise. As soon as I'm safe for you."

CHAPTER 9
SILAS

On Friday afternoon, my phone rang. I was sitting across the conference table from my father, both our laptops flipped open. He cursed under his breath when my phone vibration startled him, so I snatched it up and again—without looking at the screen—answered the call.

"Hello?"

My father glared at me from his seat, so I pushed my chair back and walked out of the room, pulling the door closed behind me.

"Is this Silas Ayres?"

I checked the screen, but the number wasn't saved in my phone.

"Yes. Who is calling?"

"Silas, hi. This is Landon Miller, I'm one of the owners of Rapture in Pasadena."

"Oh." My breath caught in my throat. "Hi."

"Is now a good time?"

"Uhm. Hold on," I mumbled.

I glanced toward the closed conference room door, then headed to my small office in the far corner of the workspace. I locked the door behind me and leaned against it for good measure.

"Now is fine," I said.

"I hope I'm not being forward here, and you can tell me the topic is off the table, but I was made aware of an issue that happened on Friday night at my club, and I want to address it with you. I mean, I want to make sure you're okay and I want to let you know what we're doing to make sure it doesn't happen again."

My knees gave out, and I slid down the wall until my ass hit the shitty office carpet. Propping my elbows on my knees, I closed my eyes.

"What do you think happened?" I asked.

"Without mincing words, Silas, it sounds like it was very close to assault."

I made an unhappy sound. If Marshall had anything to do with this phone call, I was going to be so beyond angry. The words Landon fed me could have come straight out of Marshall's mouth.

"Did Marshall put you up to this?"

"What?" Landon laughed. "No, quite the opposite. He told me to leave it be."

"So why didn't you?"

"Because Marshall Covington doesn't own my club, and it's not up to him how I choose to run my business."

I would have loved to see the conversation between the two of them play out because I knew when it came to talking with Marshall it was very much either his way or the highway. Though, I supposed that wasn't entirely true. He'd not rebuffed me when I expressed interest in him on Saturday…something I'd been embarrassed about ever since. I'd held him and I'd kissed his hand, and I'd practically begged him to dominate me. None of it had turned him off, and the promise I'd made him to revisit everything later…

It hung heavy around my shoulders.

I meant what I told him, that I wanted to be safe for him. I understood power exchange was a two-way street, and I somehow knew I wasn't in a place to offer him the same things he offered me, but making good on the bargain meant I'd have to have this conversation with Landon. That I'd have to admit what happened to me.

"It wasn't assault," I told Landon, something I would stand firm on.

"How would you classify it? The way I understand it, you were cuffed to a bench, expressed a desire to stop, and that desire was ignored."

"In some cases, that's a great start to a weekend," I said.

"In your case?"

I sighed, banging my head against the door.

"I told him to stop and he didn't, that's true. But he's— what's his name by the way?"

Landon made a noncommittal sound. "His name is Barrett, which he's told me I can tell you. If you asked."

"You talked to him?" My knees trembled again, and I straightened my legs out in front of me.

"Of course."

"And what did he say happened?"

"I want to know what you say happened," Landon countered.

"He…Barrett…he did cuff me to the bench, and I did tell him to stop, and he didn't. If Marshall hadn't…" I cleared my throat. "It wasn't assault. It was…under-negotiated, at best."

"And at worst?"

"Thankfully we'll never know," I said.

Landon exhaled, and the slow cadence of it matched my own breath. I chewed at the inside of my cheek while I waited for whatever he had to say next, moderately annoyed that my mind kept drifting back to Marshall and the way it felt to be in his arms…in his *space*.

"The point I'm trying to make is he wasn't entirely at fault."

"No," Landon agreed, "but the dominant does carry more of a burden when it comes to these things."

"Debatable."

"I'm not saying you're without fault. I hear you taking accountability and that makes me confident that you won't find yourself in that sort of situation again. I want to let you know as well that Barrett's membership has been suspended."

"Oh."

"It won't be reinstated unless he agrees to a mentorship," Landon said.

"A what? How?"

"I'm not going to air out his personal life, but if Barrett wants to return to Rapture in any capacity, he needs to understand the expectations that come with engaging in that sort of play."

"I thought you had a pretty thorough screening process," I said, biting my lips between my teeth.

"Financially and socially. There's not much we can do about the rest." Landon cleared his throat, tone turning more business-like. "Either way, Barrett knows what he has to do if he wants to come back. We're also installing monitors in the loft and the downstairs playroom to act as a second set of eyes for our guests."

"That's good." I swallowed hard. My right foot was asleep, and I would have rather chopped it off than let the next question come out of my mouth, but I didn't have a saw in my office. "And what about me?"

"Hmn?"

"What do I have to do to come back? Is my membership also suspended?"

"You're not suspended, and it seems to me you already know what you need to do," he said.

"Negotiate more clearly on the front end."

"A partner can only hold a safe space for you if you're an active participant in creating it," he said. "I'm confident that you know that better now."

The light bulb went on over my head, and I groaned.

"I do. Thank you."

"Feel free to save this number, Silas," Landon told me. "If anything else comes up or you have other concerns about the safety measures in place at the club, please let me know."

"I will," I croaked. "Thank you."

I hung up the phone without saying goodbye, not intentionally, but because my hands were shaking so badly I fumbled the whole thing and disconnected the call on accident.

"Fuck." I crawled onto my hands and knees, letting my head hang low, the weight heavy between my shoulders. I bowed my back and arched it, repeating a pose I used to do in yoga but hadn't thought about in years.

I hadn't heard from Marshall since I'd left his house on Saturday afternoon, but I'd thought about him every day since. At the time, I hadn't understood what to do to make myself safe for him. I hadn't even understood why I said it, why I wanted to. Marshall, on paper, was not a good road for me to walk down. He was closer to my dad's age than he was to mine, and he was our biggest competition. My dad would disown me if he ever found out, but…was it worth it?

I stretched my arms and legs until I starfished myself on the floor, then I rolled onto my back and stared up at the ceiling. It was shitty pressboard panels and annoying overhead fluorescents that I never bothered to turn on. Everything in the office was dated and old, and I didn't want to drown in the past the way my father was. Marshall wasn't a way out, but he was a breath of fresh air, and I didn't realize how much I needed to breathe until I'd been with him…breathing.

Picking up my phone, I opened the notes app and started typing out a message I wanted to send to Marshall. I knew better than to do it in the messages app because my fingers weren't steady enough to trust. Some of the things I wrote him felt silly, childish even, but they needed to be said so I wrote them anyway, and instead of sending the message, I slid my phone across the room.

The words would keep, and it was barely three in the afternoon. I had at least two and a half more hours of work to finish before I could head home for the day. Forcing myself onto my feet, I headed back into the conference room, finding my dad still poring over whatever he'd been tangled up in on his computer. I'd been multitasking, splitting my attention between the bid and another article the editor of *LA Design Digest* had asked me to write.

"I can't look at these numbers for one more second," my dad said, closing his laptop and pushing it toward the center of the table.

I glanced up at him, brow raised.

"Maybe a change of scenery," I suggested. "Go work at a Panera or something."

He snorted. "What do you think I am, Silas? A millennial?"

I rolled my eyes and tabbed my own screen around until the outline of my next article took up the prime real estate of my screen.

"Go take a walk then," I suggested. "Get some fresh air and come back to it with better eyes."

"Why don't we just call it a day?" he proposed.

"Excuse me?"

"I own the place," he reminded me, as if I could ever forget. "The work will be here next week. I know the deadline is pretty close, but I think we're giving Marshall a real run for it."

I was too beaten down from my call with Landon to argue. I took one last look at my outline then closed my laptop. "Calling it a day sounds good."

My dad stood up from the table and picked up his computer, tucking it under his arm. "Bright and early Monday?"

"Bright and early," I agreed. "I'll lock up."

I didn't move an inch while I listened to my father busy himself around the office, packing his computer away and getting his coat from the rack. His routine was predictable, his early departure was not. Once he was safely out of the building, I dropped my forehead against the table and groaned.

Eventually, I peeled myself out of the chair. I knew when I got back to my office the note would still be on my phone, waiting to be sent. It was admittedly more than he asked for, but it was the only way to answer my end of our weekend agreement. And all complications aside, I was interested in Marshall. He was handsome, he was competent, he was clearly dominant, but beyond that.... I liked the way I felt around him.

Marshall's arms were like a weighted blanket, a warm and welcome kind of restraint. When he'd touched me, it was with nothing less than tenderness, consent…want. And fuck, how he wanted. The things he'd said had my brain hazy from the promise of it all.

I'd only ever known him as my father's biggest competition, the threat to our livelihoods, but all of that had shifted now. He was so much more than the box I'd helped my father push him into, and little pieces of him unfurled with every conversation or exchange we shared.

Lincoln and I had played for so many years, wondering about the ideal kind of man for each of us. We both knew I needed a dominant man who wasn't scared of a challenge, but I'd spent years settling on boys playing pretend. I realized, much to my horror, that if I could have crafted a partner for myself from scratch, he would have looked a lot like Marshall Covington. Maybe he would have been a little closer to my age, but the gap in our years did the opposite of turn me off. At the end of the day, Marshall had been there when I needed him, and he was ready to be there now that I wanted him.

In my office, I slid my laptop into my bag and grabbed my things. The office felt safe without my dad haunting the halls, but I needed fresh air. Getting out of work early meant there wasn't any traffic, so I made it home in record time. Once I was inside, I dropped my bags and went straight into a shower. Marshall showed no signs of leaving my brain, so after I dried off and got dressed, I dug my phone out of my back pocket and carried it to the couch. Swiping open to the notes app, I reread the paragraphs I'd put into it earlier, then I copied it, pasted it into a text message, and hit send. For the first time in my life, the direction of my future was in my own hands. There was no going back, and even if there was, I didn't want to.

CHAPTER 10
MARSHALL

It was a curious thing, how I'd gone thirty-nine years without speaking to Silas daily, but after plucking him off that bench on a Friday and very nearly kissing him on a Saturday, six days of silence was akin to absolute torture.

"You," Finn said, sliding into his usual seat across from me, "look distracted."

"You just got here," I drolled, taking a lazy drink of my wine.

It was Friday night again, time for our usual dinner, and I was first, as always, with Finn not far behind. I gestured to the drink I'd already ordered for him and leaned against the back of the booth with a weary sigh.

"You're exhaling dramatically," he said, narrowing his eyes. "Are you seeing someone?"

"Why would my breathing indicate my dating status?"

"That's not a no." He grinned at me and scrunched his nose.

"What's not a no?" Smith was next to arrive, taking the seat beside me. I'd also ordered him a drink, and one for Hunter as well.

I glanced at Smith from the corner of my eye, trying to not

catalog the similarities and differences between him and Silas. Just because they were the same age didn't mean anything. It meant nothing. My brother was as much his own man as I was, and same with Silas. The age was nothing. My relationship with his father…also nothing.

"Marshall is seeing someone," Finn said helpfully.

"I am not."

"You are?" Smith asked, shoving my shoulder like he was angry I'd been keeping a secret from him. In reality, if I did confess about Silas to any of my brothers, Smith would probably be the first to hear about it, with Finn being the last. Though Hunter was a vault and would probably take the secret to the grave if I didn't willingly tell the other two.

As if to prove my point, he arrived last, taking his place next to Finn and not asking any of us to bring him up to speed on the conversation.

"I'm not," I said again.

"Not yet."

I glared at Finn, ready to snap. My nerves had been frayed all week, and I wasn't sure if it had to do with work or with the way my brain never wanted to stop thinking about Silas. The way we'd left things on Saturday after lunch was painfully open-ended, but there'd been so much promise in his words.

Tucking my hands under the table, I rubbed my thumb mindlessly over the spot he'd kissed and bitten. I wanted to taste him for real, more than the aftertaste that came with pressing my own mouth against the heel of my hand after he left, chasing after anything I could get of him. I wanted his teeth on me again, I wanted him hurting and desperate and snapping at the bit.

There was something wrong with me.

"Let me up," I said to Smith, knocking my shoulder into his.

"Calling your boyfriend?" Finn teased.

"I have to piss, you degenerate."

He laughed, and Smith slid out of the booth so I could go to the bathroom. I'd never been more thankful for the private restrooms at Cunningham's than I was after slamming the door closed and twisting the deadbolt. I didn't need to relieve myself, at least not by using the restroom. I turned the water on cold and splashed some on my face, desperate to drop the temperature of my cheeks. If I couldn't get my mind off Silas, dinner was going to be excruciating, not just because of the distraction but because my brothers would see right through my lies. I wasn't dating anyone, but I was very interested in remedying that as soon as possible.

In the pocket of my slacks, my phone let out a quick buzz, the alert of an incoming text message. If it was Finn teasing me about this imaginary boyfriend of mine, I would sneak out the back and abandon our Friday meals for the rest of time. It wasn't Finn, though. It was Silas, which was somehow worse. That cloying energy burned at my cheeks again, and I turned to rest my ass on the counter and read what he had to say.

Tapping open my message app, a long, colored bubble filled my screen and then some. Silas apparently had a lot he needed to say.

SILAS

Spoke with Landon today and he told me about Barrett's membership being suspended. He says you didn't have anything to do with that, but I don't know if I believe him. It seems like something you would do. I also accepted responsibility for my part of the whole thing. For under-negotiating, for ignoring what I knew were red flags. I'm very lucky you walked in, Marshall. I don't know if I ever thanked you for helping me, but if I didn't...thank you.

Anyway, Landon said something that really resonated with me. He said a partner can only hold a safe space for me if I help create it, and I didn't do that with Barrett, but I'm going to do it with you. I'm going to be safe by being clear. I'm terrified to send this, so I hope this doesn't blow up in my face, but I do want the things we talked about on Saturday. I want you to restrain me and spank me. I don't think, no…I know I'm not ready for gags right now, but I am a submissive, Marshall. And I want to submit to you. I'm not asking for anything more than that right now. A little bondage and a good spanking, maybe hopefully some rough sex too. I don't care that you're older than me. I don't care if you know my dad. This isn't about him. It's about us.

I read the message no less than five times, my throat growing drier and my cock harder with every pass. Silas's forwardness in asking for what he wanted was one of the sexiest things about him. I'd seen it last weekend in my living room and again just now with the text message. He wasn't offering me a blank check with his body. He offered me a very specific list of wants to make up a carefully controlled and well thought out scene. I could do all the things he asked for. I wanted to do all of those things. And I'd told him no before because I didn't think he was ready for it, but maybe neither of us had been.

There were a few things I wanted to talk to him about, but none of them were suited for text message so my reply to Silas was short and simple

Publicly or privately?

I set my phone on the counter and splashed my face again.

The pink was a permanent fixture, it seemed, only getting darker when Silas's reply came through.

> Private.

> I'll give Lincoln your address so he knows where I am and a time limit to hold out without hearing from me before calling the cops.

I huffed out an amused laugh, wondering what that breath would have given away if anyone had heard it.

> You have been putting thought into this, haven't you?

> Yes.

> Tonight?

> What time?

> I'm at dinner with my brothers right now. How does nine sound?

> Nine is good. I'll tell Lincoln if he hasn't heard from me by eleven to send help.

> Let's make it eight, Silas. And give me until twelve.

> I want to take my time with you.

> eight and twelve then. At your house?

> Yes. Unless you would feel safer at a hotel.

There was enough of a delay in response I knew he was actually weighing the pros and cons of my house versus a hotel.

Which would you prefer?

Silas, there will hopefully come a time between us where my preferences guide decision-making, but tonight isn't that time.

I pushed the heel of my hand down hard between my legs, willing my unruly erection to settle back into line so I could go rejoin my brothers.

Your house is good.

Then I'll see you at eight.

I glanced at my watch, it was just after six.

Enjoy your dinner, Marshall.

Cursing, I slid my phone back into my pocket and then tucked my cock up into the waistband of my briefs. The erection was clearly not going anywhere, but I was not going to give my brothers fodder to tease me through the whole rest of the meal.

By the time I got back to the table, the food was there, obviously ordered in my absence. I kicked the side of the booth so Smith would get out of my way, and I felt all three sets of their eyes on me as I returned to my seat.

"Is the boyfriend in the restaurant?" Finn asked, poking at his salad.

"There is no boyfriend."

"You look like you just fucked," he said, angling his head to the side and giving me a very slow onceover. "You're flushed."

"Do you ever get tired of hearing yourself speak?"

"Very rarely," he said with a grin.

I turned my attention down to the salmon I ate every week. It was always properly seasoned and well-cooked. It was predictable. Silas was not predictable. I dropped my right hand onto the edge of the table, letting my fingers hold the weight while my palm curled around the side to steady myself. The restaurant wasn't tilting on its axis; that was just me.

My three brothers lapsed into a casual and teasing conversation with each other, and I managed to fight my way through half the salmon before giving up. I turned down a third glass of wine, which earned me a raised eyebrow from Hunter, but no admonishment or question from the rest of them. Time ticked by achingly slow, and at seven-fifteen, I bumped into Smith with my shoulder.

"Just because I only had two doesn't mean you have to stop at two," I said, remarking on the fact he'd quit drinking when I had.

"I didn't have lunch," he said back.

"Two is enough then," I said, and Smith smiled at me. "Let me up again. I need to get home."

He moved out of the way without argument, and Finn opened his mouth to call me out, but Hunter smacked him hard in the center of his chest.

"Everything is fine," I assured them. "I've just been working long hours this week, and I'm feeling a little sluggish."

"You work long hours every week," Finn countered.

"And yet I still slog through to tolerate your company every Friday."

He gave me the finger, and I gave Smith a hug.

I loved my brothers, all of them, even if they each had their own idiosyncrasies that drove me up the wall. I was sure my emotional detachment bothered them sometimes too, especially Smith, who looked up to me more than any of us ever had to our father.

"Let's get together soon," I said to Smith, out of earshot of the twins. "Just the two of us."

He nodded, not giving anything away.

I left cash for my drinks and dinner, then jogged back to my car. The drive home took a lifetime, thanks to traffic on the 405, but I made it home with ten minutes to spare. There wasn't time to do much besides take my shoes off and turn on the lights, pour myself a glass of wine, which was more out of habit than anything else, and then Silas was on my doorstep, finger pressed against the doorbell.

"This is fine," I said to myself, padding my way from the kitchen to the front door. The wine remained untouched on the counter. I wasn't going to drink it; I just hadn't been thinking. It was routine, but Silas…Silas was not routine.

I steadied myself with another telling breath, then twisted the doorknob open and let him inside.

CHAPTER 11
SILAS

I had been nervous, to the point that I almost turned the car around at least four times, but as soon as Marshall opened the door and I saw him standing there in his slacks and his button-up, bare feet and exposed forearms, everything—once again—settled into place.

"Silas."

My name was a low rumble somewhere in the back of his throat that sent gooseflesh racing up my arms.

I stepped into his foyer and toed off my sneakers, sliding them together against the wall so as to not take up too much room without being invited to do so.

"Marshall."

"It's good to see you," he said.

I glanced up at him. "The niceties are awkward."

"Am I not normally nice?" He inclined his head toward the living room, and I followed after him. There was a glass of wine on the table, but everything else looked exactly as it had the week before. The *LA Design Digest* still took center stage on his coffee table, the cover folded back to an open article. It was the one after mine; I knew it on sight.

"You're nice enough," I said.

He gestured for me to sit, and I sank down into the over-stuffed cushions of the chair I'd been in for lunch.

"I appreciate the text you sent me." He dragged his tongue across the front of his teeth, his stare solely focused on me. "I can tell you put a lot of thought into it."

I didn't know what to say to him about it, so I just nodded my agreement. The message itself had been rushed, but not in thought, just composition. I worried if I hadn't gotten it out on the first go, I never would. Not that I was careless with the whole thing, just…I knew myself well enough.

"Before we get started, I want to be clear about some things," he said. "I've set an alarm on my phone for five minutes before twelve. I won't have you missing your text to Lincoln."

I nodded, almost dumbstruck at the forethought. "Thank you."

"And next, I want to know if penetrative sex is on the table for you tonight?"

It was almost too formal of a question, too abrupt of a segue, but the thought of it still had my eyes aching to roll up and back into their sockets.

"Very much so," I answered, sounding embarrassingly breathy even to my own ears.

"With protection."

"Of course."

Marshall nodded, propping one ankle up onto the opposite knee. He curled his fingers around his calf, and it was impossible to not imagine him curling his hand around my body in much the same way. I was horny and amped up on adrenaline, an addictive combination.

"Are you okay with edging?"

"Yes," I rasped.

"What about orgasm control?"

"Isn't that the same thing?"

The corner of his mouth twitched into a dangerous-looking smile. "Not quite."

"I don't know then," I whispered.

"Do you want to find out?"

"Not against the idea."

Across from me, Marshall conversated like we were in the middle of a business deal, and I could barely string three coherent words together to answer his prompts. It was going to be a very long night.

"What about oral sex? Hand jobs?"

"All of it."

"Giving or receiving?" he asked.

"Yes."

That answer earned me a very proud-looking smile, and I was suddenly concerned about melting into nothing more than a puddle of precum in the middle of Marshall Covington's living room.

"Beyond that, just bondage and spanking tonight, right?"

"It doesn't have to be *just* that," I said, already feeling greedy for the older man.

"For our first time, Silas, I want the boundaries to be exceedingly clear."

I swallowed hard. "Alright."

"Can I mark you?" he asked next. "Your ass and the backs of your thighs."

I nodded. "Yes."

"Do you have a safe word?" His fingers flexed around his leg, and I was helpless to look away from him.

"Red is fine," I managed. "Do you?"

Marshall arched a brow, looking pleased, and I tried very hard to ignore the way my chest swelled in response. "Red is fine."

A short silence drifted between us, and I was reminded of how much I hated that awkward phase between negotiation and action, reminded why I skipped it more often than I should. But after the previous weekend, it wasn't something I would do again. Landon's words sat like boulders in the back of my mind, and even though talking about the things I wanted to have done to me made me want to crawl out of my skin, it was necessary. The conversation was Marshall and me both building the space I expected him to hold for me through the rest of the night.

"Okay," he said next, standing and tapping his palms against the tops of his thighs. "Ready?"

I nodded and stood, following him down a hallway and up a flight of stairs. There were three doors on the landing, one closed and two open. He led me to the farthest door, and I'd never seen a space more *Marshall* in my whole life. The floors matched the ones downstairs, a sleek and pale, thick-planked wood. I walked ahead of him, surveying his space. His bed was exceedingly simple, a narrow platform with no discernible headboard or footboard, and I wondered what exactly he was going to tie me to when I noticed the extremely low-profile bolts on the corners.

His sheets were white.

The comforter smooth.

"Should I call you sir?" I asked, looking back at him over my shoulder. He was less than a foot away, and I could smell the rich cedar of his soap or his cologne, or whatever made him smell like a forest I was more than ready to get lost in.

He closed the gap between us, carefully sliding one hand around my waist and bringing our bodies flush. "Not until I've earned it."

"Marshall then."

His lips were against my ear, the pleased hum he loosed in reply deep enough to send a shiver down the entire length of my spine.

"Marshall then," he repeated, letting his lips trail from my ear to the back of my neck. "Take off your clothes, Silas. Show me what's mine for the night."

He didn't move away from me, so I had to fumble out of my pants and my shirt with his chest pressed against my back. Even when I had to bend down to get out of my socks and my underwear, he didn't relent. My ass knocked into his groin, and he made a low sound at the contact. His cock was hard as steel already against me, and when I stood straight again, he notched our bodies together in perfect alignment.

"I would love to take you over my knee, Silas," he whispered against my ear, hands roaming over my hips in a slow and curious exploration. "Tuck your cock between my thighs and let you fuck my legs while I spank you until you're black and blue."

My eyes lost the battle, rolling back entirely with so much force my head hit the front of his shoulder.

"But that's not bondage, is it?"

"Kind of," I murmured.

He chuckled. "Not what we agreed on, though. And not what either of us meant. Now come over here and get on your knees."

He walked me toward the foot of his bed and knocked his knee into the back of mine. I went down, first onto my right knee, then my left, and Marshall's steady hand on my shoulders tipped me forward, just enough to make my back arch.

"Good boy," he said. "Don't move."

There was no way I would dare to move from the spot, but that didn't stop the way my arms and legs vibrated like leaves ready to fall. My palms were sweaty as fuck, and I was desperate to wipe them onto my thighs before he came back to me, but I was even more needy to follow instructions and have him call me a good boy again. Instead I swallowed hard, tried to breathe, and watched Marshall's broad backside disappear into a walk-in closet. I would have paid good money to see what he had in there besides slacks and button-ups, but maybe that would be another night, another time.

I'd counted thirty of my own breaths by the time he returned with four matching leather cuffs in hand, a black spreader bar, and something shoved into his pocket that definitely hadn't been there before. Marshall came around behind me, dropped everything on the floor, and went to his knees. He was still dressed, the cool glide of his clothes against my bare skin one of the sexiest things I'd ever felt. He took my right arm into his hand, dragging his fingers from my elbow down to my wrist.

I had to close my eyes.

Marshall lifted my arm and kissed the delicate skin against my wrist bone before wrapping the leather cuff around it like a seal meant to keep the feel of his mouth against my skin. His fingers slowly danced back up my arm and across my back, down the other side where he repeated the same gentle kiss, the same leather restraint. The only sounds in the room were the labored pant of my breaths and the slow, steady cadence of his.

How was he not absolutely unraveled?

"You're a vision," he murmured, dragging his fingers down the sides of my back and over my hips. His weight shifted behind me, then he touched my ass, the backs of my thighs, behind my knees, and lower still. "Better than anything I could ever design on my own. I wish you could see yourself."

I was less than a second away from suggesting he turn me toward a mirror so I could, but the words stopped dead in my throat when his lips grazed over my ankle bone. My head jerked to the side, ready to look over my shoulder to see what I knew had to be true. The only way he could get his mouth that low was if he'd prostrated himself on the ground behind me. But his words rang loud in my ears, a present reminder of what he expected of me in those moments.

Don't. Move.

A kiss and a cuff, the same journey from one leg to another, then another brush of his lips against my opposite ankle bone and the cool wrap of leather sealing it in. He was back after that, body pressed against mine, hands constantly moving and exploring my skin the way I wished I could explore his.

"Your obedience makes my cock ache, Silas," he whispered against my ear, bucking his hips against me so I could feel the cock in question. It was—somehow—harder than before, and even hidden by the layers of fabric between us I could tell he was endowed. He snaked his hand around to the front of me, the tips of his fingers barely touching the base of my shaft. "Does your cock ache too?"

"Yes," I whimpered.

"You're trembling." He slid his hand down my shaft, rubbing me with his palm. The tip of my dick was embarrassingly wet with precum, and he smeared it around, making a very pleased sound.

"I know."

"Do you want to stop?"

"No." It was a breath, a puff of desperation out of my mouth.

Marshall dragged his cheek against mine, though with our size difference, he was more against my temple, the fringes of my hair. He pressed against me, using his body to push against mine until I moaned and melted against him. Somehow still on my knees but also resting most of my body weight against his chest.

This was what I'd been after. Every time Lincoln wanted to find me a man with strong hands, all I'd really needed was a man like Marshall. Not only did he have strong hands, he knew how to use them. He knew how to use *me*. Marshall had asked for more time, an early arrival and a later departure, but at the rate things were going, I was going to come and call it a night in thirty seconds.

The slow drag of his palm across my shaft had turned into a heavy pressure and my hips surged forward, chasing after more of his touch. He made a very quiet tutting noise in my ear, tongue clicking against the roof of his mouth.

"I said don't move, Silas," he warned. "That includes those unruly hips of yours."

"S-sorry," I stammered, squeezing my eyes closed and clenching my jaw. Trying to bring my body back under my control when all I wanted to do was surrender to it was a massive feat, but I knew when I'd managed it because Marshall kissed the shell of my ear.

He gave me another good boy, then finally wrapped his fingers around my shaft. His grip was wet and tight, and two slow strokes later, I cried out, "I'm going to come."

Marshall's hand was gone before I finished the sentence, my cock spasming wildly in the air. I sucked in a breath and swayed forward, but Marshall banded his other arm around my chest to stop me from falling face-first onto the floor. He pulled our bodies back together, sank down onto his heels and took me with him. The pose wasn't uncomfortable, but it wasn't quite natural, and then his hand was back around my cock, stroking lazily from root to tip.

I shook violently in his arms, pressing my chest forward to test the strength of his hold, which was more than sufficient. He huffed an exhaled kind of laugh against my ear and stroked me faster until I was right back there ready to shoot my load all over his hand.

"Marshall," I whined. "I'm so close. I'm right there."

"I know," he said, sounding almost apologetic as he took his hand away again. "You're right on the edge, Silas. Right where I want you."

I sank down into his lap with a defeated whine, and then he took my cock again into his hand and walked me right back to the cliff but refused to let me jump.

CHAPTER 12
MARSHALL

By the time I was ready to spank him, Silas was a trembling, sweaty mess of a man. His cock had grown long and thick in my hand, the skin stretched in a way that looked almost painful. The tip of his cock was nearly purple, precum leaking from the slit like a faucet. I swiped up some of the wetness with the pad of my thumb and raised it to his mouth as an offering. He moaned, nipping at me before sucking me in past his teeth.

"Slowly, slowly," I warned, shifting the angle of my thumb so I could add two fingers into his mouth. Pressing against his tongue, Silas sucked desperately at my fingers, and I cradled the back of his head with my free hand to keep him steady. "Good boy, do you want one more?"

He moaned so low that it vibrated up the length of my arm, so I obliged him with a third finger. My reach spread his jaw wide, and as I stretched toward the back of his throat, his body seized with a gag. I pushed the back of his head forward, curling my fingers into his skull.

He choked, taking my fingers up to the last knuckle. Spit slid down his chin and his lips were spread so far apart to accommodate my fingers, and I really did wish we'd negotiated some kind of recording rights because I was already going to jerk off about this encounter for the rest of my days. Being able to call it up and rewatch it was a reward I probably hadn't done anything to deserve.

"This is how deep I expect you to take my cock, Silas. Do you understand?"

He mumbled a yes, and I withdrew my hand from his mouth, using his cheeks to dry my fingers. I pushed him down, hand splayed out in the middle of his back.

"Spread your arms out," I said, and he did.

I put enough space between us to get his wrist cuffs attached to the bolts on either side of my footboard, then I fastened his ankles to the spreader bar. The position looked uncomfortable, but not enough to cause him more discomfort than I wanted him to feel.

"How's that, Silas?" I asked.

"Good. It's good."

"What's two times two?"

He made a noise that sounded like it would have been a laugh if he wasn't already fraught with arousal. "Four. Why?"

I reached into my pocket and pulled out my gloves. The kidskin leather was cool to the touch, but it warmed as soon as I slipped my fingers inside, flexing them to help the leather mold and form to the shape of my hands.

"Just making sure you're still here."

"Mmmn. I am," he purred.

I had lube in my pocket alongside a gold-foiled condom, waiting for the right time, which was—unfortunately for me— still rather far off.

"What's your safe word?"

"Red."

"Good."

I gave one last look at the sight of Silas on his knees, legs spread wide and arms spread wider. His cock hung parallel to the floor, smearing wetness across his stomach with every beat of his heart. Turning my back, I stood over the top of him, one leg on either side of his hips, then I sank down into a squat. Sliding one hand beneath his stomach to hold him up, I rubbed slow and smooth circles across the pale swell of his ass. The spreader bar helped keep him open, his asshole accessible if I wanted it to be, which…

I did and I didn't.

I needed to keep up my end of our negotiated scene before fucking him, because I could tell from nothing more than the way he moved and moaned against me that once I got inside of him, I'd be completely undone. Needing to put me out of my own misery, I lifted my hand and brought it back down, a hard and sharp slap of leather against skin. Silas sucked in a breath, and I repeated the motion in the same place but harder.

Another gasp.

So I went harder.

Still…

Silas moaned like a whore, his body moving like he was trying to fuck the air, so I spanked him again but lower, the leather covering my palm landing hard and true against the delicate fold of skin between his thigh and his ass cheek.

That was the impact that finally earned me something louder than a whimper.

I got him quick and strong, five more times in the same spot, then five more, and Silas was gasping for air between the moans. Kneading the skin I'd just been spanking, I moved to the other side, starting low and hard without the warmup. Silas was greedy when it came to keeping noises to himself, forcing out breathy pants and gasps and the quietest moans. All of it enough to make my own dick throb against my thigh, but not enough to make me feel like I was giving him the kind of spanking he was truly after.

Thinking quickly, I undid his wrists and hauled him up onto the bed. I reattached his wrist cuffs at the headboard, sank my weight down onto the small of his back and resumed spanking him with better leverage and more power.

"Oh, fuck." Silas's voice was muffled in the sheets, but he was far more audible than he'd been before. I went hard on him after that, against the globes of his ass, down the backs of his thighs and up again. On more than one occasion, he tried to squirm and twist away from me, but the spreader bar between his ankles kept him open how I wanted him.

As surprised as Silas had been to learn I was a dominant, I was more surprised to find out he was a submissive, even more so a masochist. It spoke to the fact there were so many things neither of us knew about each other, and one other thing Silas didn't know about me was that I had the stamina of a man half my age, and I wasn't even close to getting tired of striking him.

Twenty minutes in, the thrust of his hips into the sheets lost its consistent cadence, and I was quick to lift his midsection off the bed, taking away the friction he'd been chasing after.

"No," I warned, putting my body over his, fisting his hair and yanking his head up to give my mouth access to his ear. "You will not come on my sheets, and you will not come without permission."

"Marshall," he begged, he whined, he *pleaded*.

"Do you understand me?"

"I can't just—"

I twisted the hand in his hair and bared my teeth against the shell of his ear. Rutting against him, I ground my cock between the cleft of his ass, my slacks against his tender thighs.

"Do you understand?" I repeated.

He swallowed hard. "Yes, Marshall."

I shoved his face back down into the sheets, taking the pillows away in favor of sliding them into place beneath his hips. It gave him something to fuck, but it gave me a better angle to spank him, and I'd been very clear with him about my expectation that he not come.

I laid into him forcefully after that. Enough strength behind each movement to make my forearm ache from exertion. After twenty minutes, I tore off my gloves and gave him my skin, which earned me more of the sounds that made my dick leak. The lube and the condom burned a hole in my pocket, but it was barely after nine and I didn't know if I would get a chance to have Silas ever again.

Finally taking a break to catch my breath, I rocked back onto my heels, drawing stars and swirls across the patchwork bruising that had already begun to form on the back of Silas's legs. He let out a shaky whimper, arching after my touch in search of more. I drew my way over his hip and down between his stomach and the pillows. His cock was rigid and hot to the touch.

"You're so wet for me," I told him, dragging my thumb through his slick slit. "Do you ever like to top?"

He shook his head, whispered, "No."

"That's good." I made a tight fist around his straining dick and stroked. "Some men look best on the bottom, I think."

"Marshall."

"Hmn?"

"I need to come."

I laughed, a low rumble in the center of my chest. "The only thing you need to do is what you're told, Silas. And I definitely haven't told you to come."

"Marshall," he whined, hips thrusting against my hand.

"I'm nowhere near ready to fuck you."

That was a lie. Maybe the biggest one I'd ever told.

"Let's get those muscles moving, sweetheart. Don't want

you to get sore." The endearment slipped out without much forethought, but I liked the taste of it just the same.

Moving around the bed, I unclipped one of his wrists and then sat down with my ass where the pillows should have been, my back flat against the wall. I attached Silas's wrist to the bed again and tugged him closer so his face was buried in my lap. I pulled the pillows out from beneath his hips and told him to hold himself up on his knees. His hair was soft and damp against my fingers, and I threaded my fingers into his hair to maneuver his face against my bulge.

Silas mouthed my cock through my pants, and I was grateful he couldn't see the absolute pleasure wash over my face from the heat of his mouth. I was as affected by him as he was by me, if not more, but I needed to maintain the appearance of control. At least for the night.

After enjoying the feel of his face, I fought open my pants with my free hand, revealing my cock to him for the first time, up close and personal. My shaft slapped against his cheek, and Silas's lashes fluttered. He was so fucking sweaty, already so wrecked.

"You're huge," he groaned.

"Sssh." I brushed the tip across his lips, and he opened wide for me. "Do you remember where I told you I wanted my cock to go?"

He nodded eagerly, swallowing my length until his nose was pressed against my stomach. He gagged once he had me fully in his mouth, the convulsion of his throat muscles against my crown not doing anything to hold me back from my own end.

"Lift your legs up if you want to stop, Silas. Do you understand?" I asked.

He made an affirmative sound that sent a shiver straight into my balls.

"Show me."

He lifted his legs, the spreader bar still holding him open, then he collapsed them back down to the bed.

"Good boy," I told him again. "You don't have to do anything but suck, alright?"

In response to that, he sucked *hard*.

I folded myself over the top of him so I could reach his ass and then I started up another fresh round of spanking. By the time my arm got tired again, I was a mess, sitting in a pool of Silas's spit, my mattress probably soaked to the core from how much his dick was leaking into the sheets. His ass was a gorgeous shade of purple, the same vibrant hue his dick had been earlier in the night, and I couldn't hold off any longer.

Grabbing Silas's hair, I pulled him up off my lap.

He choked on all the air, spit strings smearing across his chin and his cheeks, tears racing from the corners of his eyes. His arms were still spread wide on either side of me, cuffs bound to the bed. He was like a butterfly, spread and pinned, awaiting dissection.

Instead of undoing his restraints, I stood in place and walked around to the bottom of my bed. Sinking onto my knees behind him, I finally pulled the condom and lube out of my pocket. At the sound of the foil tearing open, Silas sobbed, entire body swaying like a wave had crashed over the top of him.

I poured a fair amount of lube onto both of my hands, ready to walk him so close to the edge he'd finally be scared to step off. I speared two slick fingers into his asshole and grabbed his cock with the other hand. Silas cried, gasping for God, calling out for me. His balls were so tight, tucked against his body, and with every stroke up his shaft, my knuckles brushed him and he let out another curse.

Another prayer.

"Marsh—" He couldn't even get my entire name out.

I let go of his cock and put a third finger into his ass.

It was then that he started to weep openly, but he didn't lift his legs around me, didn't mutter the word that would make it all stop. My patience was thin as it had ever been, and I finally needed to give in before both of us lost our minds. I withdrew my fingers and made quick work of replacing them with my cock.

It only took one smooth pump of my hips to seat myself fully inside of him, and Silas's back arched as I sank all the way home. I grabbed his hair again and pulled his head back toward me, more than happy to increase the curve of his spine so I could get even deeper into his body. I took his waist into my other hand, and then I started to move.

There was no warm-up, no warning, no more questions.

I fucked Silas so hard, I knew I'd give myself bruises on the fronts of my thighs. Over and over and over, and he was crying and screaming and begging to come, and I wanted to get deeper, deeper, deeper before I let him finish.

"We're so close now," I promised. I wanted to dig him down into my bed, but I was still dressed and couldn't get my leg up over his body to do it.

"I—"

"I know, sweetheart," I promised, pulling him until his arms were straight, the angle assuredly enough to cause him the kind of hurt we both knew he liked during sex. I let go of his hip with my other hand, shifted deeper and to the side as much as I could manage, then I spanked the side of his ass, the outside of his thigh.

Again.

Again.

Again.

My vision went dark and frayed around the edges and I relented on Silas's hair, throwing him face-first down into the sheets.

"Come, Silas," I demanded, and he let out a sharp, painful wail and went tense beneath me then, entirely boneless.

His body trembled and spasmed, and I leveraged myself on top of him to drive down into him. It only took two more thrusts for me to give into my own pleasure, and then I fell over the edge, Silas's name a whispered promise in the space between us.

CHAPTER 13
SILAS

Marshall's tongue licked a hot line up the side of my neck.

My cheek pressed into the sheets. My hips still arched from the pillows he'd shoved between me and the bed. My body had never been so thoroughly used.

Every touch was electric, half an inch too far over the line of pain to be pleasurable anymore, my skin reduced to nothing more than nerves and need. His strong hand kneaded my ass cheek, and I whimpered for him.

"I could so easily become obsessed with you," he whispered, easing out of me, but even for all his gentleness, it felt like being split in two.

I bit as much of the bedding as I could get into my mouth, hoping it would stifle the sound of my unhappiness.

"I know. I know." Marshall petted his hands down the small of my back. "Rest now."

So, I did.

I closed my eyes and let him take the pillows away, let him uncuff me from the bed, from the spreader bar. His fingers were skilled as he undid the clasps on the cuffs themselves, his mouth soft as he pressed kisses over the ones he'd sealed in at the start of the night.

"No more multiplication tables?" I mumbled, rocking my head side to side before landing back on my cheek.

Marshall—who was still fully dressed—helped move me onto my side, wrapping his arms and one leg around me like an entirely different and more affectionate sort of bondage from earlier.

"You're more present now than you were then."

I hummed, tilting my head up and back to try and get a look at his face, but his hold made it nearly impossible to wriggle away. I tested my shoulder against the spread of his arm, and he lifted enough that I was able to untangle myself to turn and face him.

"Am I?"

Marshall hummed, stroking my embarrassingly sweaty hair away from my face. "A bit," he murmured. "Do you have a shower in you?"

I reached out tentatively, pressing my hand against the middle of his chest. His heart beat hard and steady, pushing up against my palm with every pump.

"Alone or—"

"Not alone," he said.

"Then yes."

He smiled, a fleeting thing I wanted to chase after.

Marshall helped me into a seated position, then slowly slid my legs over the edge of the bed until my feet hit the floor. We stood up together, and he didn't even give me an option besides leaning my body weight into his. Marshall supported me and my shaky legs out of the bedroom and into the en suite bathroom which was just as modern as the rest of his house.

"Is that a steam shower?"

"Yes," he said. "There's a bench in there too. Go sit, and I'll be right behind you."

"I don't get to watch you get undressed?"

"Did you want to?"

I angled my head to the side. "Why wouldn't I want to?"

He made a thoughtful sound, then gestured toward the shower with his chin. "Go sit down. I'll be right there."

If I had more energy—or more stamina—I would have pouted. Instead, I did what I'd been told…which was kind of the whole point. After shuffling into the shower, I sat on the bench, wincing and readjusting my weight to lay off the ache in my ass and my thighs. There were definitely going to be bruises, and I wanted to see them, but I'd have to wait. Marshall followed after me, reaching in to turn on the water and the steam feature before pulling the door closed and sealing me in.

Resigned to wait, I dropped my head against the tiled wall and closed my eyes, wondering if I'd somehow slipped and woken up in some kind of alternate reality. There weren't enough words for the things Marshall had done or the way those things had made me feel. The negotiation had been so clear, the expectations of the scene planned but not predictable. Just thinking about the ways he'd bound me and touched me had blood thickening my cock again, which should have been near impossible considering the way he'd drawn out my pleasure in his bed.

I dropped my hand into my lap, my fingers making a loose fist around my cock, and as if he had a sixth sense, Marshall opened the shower door and caught me, making a noise in the back of his throat that sounded far more pleased than it did disappointed. I slid my hand off my cock, opening my eyes and blinking him into focus.

The shower had already started to fill with steam, but the gust of air from Marshall's entry cleared enough of it for me to make out the thick swell of his thighs, the v-cut of his hips, and the smooth planes of his stomach. His cock hung long and hard between his legs. He handed me a bottle of water, the plastic crinkling loudly in my grip. I took a trembling drink, then closed the bottle and set it beside me on the bench.

"Still horny?" he asked, eyeing me curiously after closing the shower behind him.

Suddenly, the space felt so much hotter than before.

Smaller.

I didn't know what to say, so in reply I lifted my hips from the bench so he could see my quickly growing erection.

"Obsessed," he said under his breath, and then he sank down to his knees with the grace of a man who knew how good he'd look once he was there. Steam whirled around him, and water rained down over both of us, and Marshall spread his hands apart against the insides of my thighs and pushed my legs wider to make room for his shoulders.

"You don't—"

"Put your hands behind your head, Silas. Thread your fingers together and don't fucking move."

Marshall took my whole cock into his mouth and his throat like he'd never even heard the words gag reflex before, let alone have one. I cried out, bucking up from the bench even though he'd told me not to move. Tightening the hold I had on my hands, I willed myself back down, my desperation turning into not much more than breathy moans and whimpers as Marshall tried to suck my sanity out of my dick. I was tired and sore and pleased and *wanting*, and in the thick air of the shower, it was easy to get lost in the heat of Marshall's mouth, the all-consuming feel of him.

My next orgasm knotted itself together, a ferocious and violent thing at the base of my spine, and seconds before my body fell into the release Marshall's throat promised me, he rocked back onto his heels, breathing heavily and wiping his mouth with the back of his hand. I banged my head backward, grateful for the padding of my own knuckles and the equally angry erection I could make out between Marshall's flexed thighs.

"Drink some more water," he said, which was the actual last thing I'd expected to come out of his mouth.

My hands went for the bottle, opened the cap, raised it to my lips, all on their own. My brain was tangled up with the need to protest, lost in the shock of an orgasm denied. I set the bottle back down on the bench and returned my hands to their place at the back of my head.

"It's barely after ten," he told me next, standing and bringing his cock to eye level.

Sucking him earlier, when I'd choked around the length of him while he spanked me, had been one of the hottest blow jobs I'd ever given, and I was eager for a repeat, but Marshall didn't give me that instruction. "We've got another hour at least before I need to bring you all the way back down."

"I don't have to go home at midnight," I protested. "I just need to check in."

"What are you proposing?"

I hated how often I found myself at a loss for words with this man, how many times he forced me out of my comfort zone to give voice to my needs and my wants. It was an embarrassing thing to speak up, sometimes.

"Nothing," I said.

Marshall frowned, reaching for a scrub puff and a white bottle of something I assumed must be soap. "Don't lie."

I bit the inside of my cheek. "I don't know. I wasn't."

"What do you want?" Marshall lathered the soap and cleaned his chest, his stomach, and lower still. The steam made it hard to see, harder to breathe, or maybe that was just…

"I wanted to stay, but it's not my pl—"

"Then stay."

"Not my place," I finished.

He added more soap to the puff and pulled me to my feet.

Instead of washing me, he brought our chests flush and rubbed against me a little bit like a cat. His erection dug into my stomach, and only after he'd transferred almost all of the suds from his body to mine did he turn me around and use the puff on my back. When he reached my ass and my legs, he switched to his hands, using his fingers to press and prod at the tender muscles.

His mouth grazed across my ear, and he whispered, "Whenever you're with me, sweetheart, it is very much your place to ask for whatever you want."

"I want to stay," I said. "And I want to come."

He smiled and brought his soapy hands between my legs, leisurely and loosely stroking my dick.

"You can stay," he said, "and you can come, but not yet."

"Marshall."

"I like you a little desperate." He walked us one step over and the water rinsed both of our bodies clean. "I like the way you look on the edge."

"Are you going to spank me again?"

"Do you want me to?"

"Yes, but…" I trailed off, swallowing past my doubt. "But like the way you said before."

He dragged his hands lower, hefting me off balance by the insides of my thighs until one foot was propped on the bench. If we hadn't agreed to use condoms he could bend me over and thrust right inside.

"You want me to take you over my lap and let you slide your cock between my thighs until you come?"

"Yes," I rasped, sounding so terribly breathy.

"You have no idea how much I want that." With one arm still around me, Marshall turned off the water, leaving us in the steam. "But not tonight."

"You said to just ask." The words came out sounding so

whiny I wished I could catch them in my hands and shove them back into my mouth.

"Your ass is a kaleidoscope of all my favorite colors, Silas. I don't want to overdo it."

"I can take it."

"I know *you* can, but there's two of us here, right?"

He wrapped me in his arms again, rested his cheek against the side of my head, and I melted into him with a content little purr.

"Right," I agreed.

"So let me wrap you up in the softest, warmest towel I can find, let me take you back to bed so I can kiss every single one of the bruises you let me give you."

He was already walking me backward out of the shower, only breaking away from me long enough to source a towel to wrap around my shoulders. "And we can talk about what we want to do together next time, and the time after that, and—"

"Can I still stay?" I asked, cutting him off.

"You can stay."

"In bed with you?"

Marshall huffed out an amused breath. "Where else would you stay if not with me?"

"I don't know, like a guest room or something."

"If you're with me, you're with me." He walked me back into the bedroom and sat me down on the edge of the bed. The cuffs were strewn across the floor, the spreader bar discarded near the condom wrapper. The sheets were sweaty and twisted into knots.

Marshall surveyed the mess we'd made, the corner of his mouth tipped up into a curious look that might have been a satisfied smile, but I was too tired to be sure. He'd been right with the decision in the bathroom. Even though I wanted him to spank me again, even though I wanted to come. I was beyond exhausted, already crashing from the high of our scene.

"I'm going to go get your cell phone so you can check in with Lincoln, then I'm going to get fresh bedding so you can tuck in under the covers. Is that all right, or do you want me to stay?"

I squinted, shocked at the choice, even more floored at my answer.

"Maybe stay for another minute," I said quietly, and then Marshall was beside me on the bed, and I was curled safely again in his arms.

CHAPTER 14
MARSHALL

Silas spent the night in my arms. He slept like a log, unmoving beyond the swell of his chest on every inhale. When he woke up the next morning, the sleepy way he smiled at me before dropping a kiss against the center of my chest was enough to ruin me for other men entirely. As if the night before hadn't already done the job. He hadn't argued when I brought him coffee and a bagel, and then he was gone before ten. My house sat achingly empty like it had forgotten that until the night before, I'd been more than enough of a presence to fill it.

It was Saturday and was meant to be a slow day for me. No work at all. I wasn't even supposed to open my laptop up to check my email. At least that was what Finn had said when he'd told me to come over in the afternoon to help him paint his office. My brother could afford to hire it out, but I was relatively certain he was trying to send me to an early grave, and his refusal and subsequent ask for help was just another tool in his plot.

Either way, he was my brother, so after I drank my own coffee and had my own toast, I put on an old pair of basketball shorts and a weathered college t-shirt and drove across town to

Finn's place. He was in the driveway when I got there, on his hands and knees with his ass sticking out of the open car door. I parked next to him then came around to the driver's side of his car and smacked him hard enough across the top of his ass for it to hurt. He yelped, and fell backward onto the concrete, his cell phone clutched in his hand.

"Is this a new way to cruise that I'm too old to understand?" I asked.

"I dropped my phone between the seat and the console," he said, dusting off the screen and standing up.

Finn was tall, but still a few inches shy of my six-foot-two frame. We were similar in the way cousins were similar, features that looked reminiscent of each other without being carbon copies. Our father's DNA was clearly too weak to make a stand across all four of our mothers.

"If you say so." I gave him a shove toward his front door. "What color are we painting your office, and why aren't you paying someone to do it?"

"I don't remember the name, but it's some pink they use at MoMA," he said. "Pouting room or something."

"Do you often have tantrums in your office?"

"It's supposed to be a calm neutral," he said, stepping over the threshold and into his house. It was an old ranch house that he'd done enough work on for the insides to look brand new and the outside to look like it was fresh in the fifties. I personally hated Finn's maximalist style, but after he'd closed on the property, he managed to forget I was a designer until it was too late for me to walk back the monstrosity that had already become his living room.

"There's nothing calm about your house," I said, ignoring the cacophony of color to my right. I followed Finn down the hallway to the bedroom he'd converted into an office, finding his massive desk in the middle of the room, covered with a plastic tarp. He'd taken down all of his ornately gold-framed paintings and stacked them against the front of the desk, each getting their own covering to keep them safe from the catastrophe that was about to be the paint job he'd solicited me for.

"And I'm not hiring it out because you're free, and I did the analysis on the cost of my time versus my skill set, and—"

I interrupted him, lifting a hand in surrender, "Alright, Finn. Just say you want some one-on-one time with me next time, though."

He rolled his eyes at me, and I laughed, dropping into a squat beside him to look down at the already open can of mauve paint.

"Calming, you say?"

"That's what the article said."

He handed me a roller brush, and I groaned. "I read the article."

"Of course you did."

I killed time by painting my palm and my forearm with the dry roller, waiting for Finn to dump the paint into the tray and tell me where he wanted me to start. When he pulled out an extension rod, I raised a curious brow.

"I want to color wash it," he said, moving quickly to dip his roller into paint and smear a garish streak across the ceiling before I could protest. We both blinked up at the streak of pink on his ceiling, and I chuckled under my breath.

"This is going to feel like being back inside the womb," I teased, picking a wall to start. There was no way my arms had the strength to handle the ceiling, not after the spanking I'd given Silas the night before.

Painting turned out to be a welcome distraction because it was mindless and my mind was otherwise occupied with Silas. Finn blathered on about something I wasn't quite listening to, which explained how he caught me off-guard asking, "So how was your date last night?"

"Good," I said, before realizing what I'd admitted to.

We both froze, and I turned slowly, finding Finn standing on top of his desk, paint roller raised and a triumphant smile on his face.

"Good?"

"It wasn't a date," I corrected.

"What was it?"

There were a dozen answers, and none of them were right. I settled with, "It was a hookup."

"Did he stay the night?"

"Yes."

Finn lowered the paint roller. "That's…"

"Don't," I warned.

"You don't ever let people stay over, Marshall," he said, like I didn't know.

"It was an extenuating circumstance," I said, but my cheeks burned, and they had to be a darker pink than the wall I'd just been painting.

"Fucked him until he forgot how to drive?"

"It wasn't a date," was all I could say.

"What's the not-date's name?"

"Does it matter?" I re-wet the roller and turned back to the task at hand, which was decidedly *not* playing the game of conversational chess with my brother.

"Very much." He started painting again, the wet roller squelching against the ceiling behind me.

"Silas," I finally said.

The roller stopped, and I knew he'd put two and two together. On account of his job, my brother was extremely detail-oriented. And on top of that, he was a brilliant listener, even when you thought he wasn't.

"Ayres," he said.

"Yes."

Finn let out a low whistle, and I dropped the roller into the paint tray, deciding it was time for a break. Finn repeated the motions, collapsing onto the floor beside me with his legs crossed and his fingers drumming steadily against the tops of his knees.

"The son."

"Yes," I said again.

"Smith's age?"

I sighed and nodded.

"You never struck me as the type to like them young," he said. It was almost a tease, but the truth in it was too sharp for either of us to pretend.

"He's not *young*. He's just younger than me."

"Smith is young."

"He was young when he came to us," I corrected. "He's his own man now, and you know it. Just because you still see him as a baby—"

"Don't you?"

"Of course I do," I said, shrugging helplessly. "But Smith and Silas are not the same person."

"No, I imagine they're not." Finn tipped his head to the side, puckering his lips in thought. "Do you want to tell me how you ended up on a not-date with the son of your biggest business rival?"

"I'd hardly call Stanley a rival. He's not competition for me."

Finn chortled. "He's giving you a run for it with the Cahuenga Pass project."

"That's only because Silas is getting bits and pieces of his own ideas into the design," I said. "Stanley on his own is as dated as your house."

"I should be offended, but I know you don't mean it."

"Don't I?"

My brother laughed at me, then pushed to his feet, surveying the painting we'd gotten done already. "Let's take a break. Have a drink and we'll get through the rest after."

"This is going to need two coats."

"Hunter is on deck tomorrow, don't worry." Finn held out his hand to help me up, and I took it. He was surprisingly strong, hauling me to my feet with ease and giving me a quick slap on the back for good measure. We went into the kitchen where he pulled two beers out of the fridge, cracking them both open and pushing one across the counter toward my waiting hand.

"Now that we're free of the fumes, you can tell me how you ended up in bed with this Silas kid."

"He's not a kid."

"You know what I mean," Finn volleyed.

"You know what *I* mean."

He let out a very tired-sounding breath. "How did you end up in bed with this Silas *man?*"

I wanted to tell him it was an accident, but that would have been a gross misstatement. Everything with Silas had been well thought out and calculated, down to the way I fucked him and for how long. I'd orchestrated this, and there was no way around it. The problem was my brother and I talked about a lot of things, and I was sure he had his suspicions about me—and I about him—but we'd managed to never actually discuss our preferences in the bedroom.

"I met him at a bar," I said. "He was about to get taken advantage of, and I stepped in."

"What a hero."

I glared at Finn and took a swig of my beer.

"I called him the next day to make sure he was okay, and we sort of hit it off and made plans."

"Plans for your not-date." Finn was so fucking amused at the conversation, leaning against his fridge with his head bouncing around like a bobblehead.

"Exactly," I said.

"And he spent the night."

"Yes."

"This is a dumb question, but are you going to do it again?" Finn scratched the side of his mouth. "I can't imagine it's advisable."

"It's probably not the best idea, but…" I trailed off because we both knew if I let him spend the night, that there was definitely going to be a repeat.

Finn let me stew in that for a bit, and we both drank the rest of our beers in mostly silence. He polished off the last swallow, smacked his lips, and said, "Remind me of the issues with the ki—with Silas's dad? Why does Stanley have it out for you?"

Scrubbing a hand down my face, I frowned at the memories from college.

Stanley Ayres was older than me, but not by much. I'd had him as an adjunct professor for one of my first-year design classes, and he had all of the bitterness required for the role. Even back then, his design talents were stilted and stifled, and I hadn't been scared to tell him as much. I'd pushed back against the syllabus from the start, which had rubbed Stanley wrong through both semesters of course work, and I made sure to let the administration know about it.

It was the only class I'd ever gotten less than an A in.

"We've never seen eye to eye on a single thing," I said. "And he gave me a C once."

Finn snorted and I finished off my beer, tossing both of our empty bottles into the recycle bin.

"Let's finish this first coat." I took one step back toward the hallway, and Finn reached out, grabbing my arm to draw me back toward him.

I looked at my brother, studied the way he studied me. Maybe we were more similar than I'd thought because it was easy to see my own expressions in the tight knit of his brow and the worry in the dark shadows of his eyes.

"Just tell me you're not doing this to get back at an old man over a twenty-year grudge."

"Whenever I'm with Silas, his father is the last thing on my mind."

"Tell me this isn't a midlife crisis."

I shook my arm out of his grasp. "I'm not even forty yet."

"So close," he murmured, the tension relaxing out of his mouth.

"This isn't anything like that," I promised my brother, taking another step back toward his office so I could finish painting it crybaby pink. Then I admitted the truth of the whole thing to him, "Finn, I'm sincerely interested in Silas."

"Oh," he said, giving me an apologetic look. "Well…shit."

CHAPTER 15
SILAS

On Sunday night, Marshall called.

I was on the couch with my head resting on Lincoln's shoulder, his feet propped up on the coffee table. He'd tried to pump me for information about my night with Marshall, but I'd kept as much of it as close to my chest as I could. It wasn't that I was keeping Marshall a secret or anything; it was more that I hadn't found the words to explain the way I felt about our night together.

Lincoln had seen my bruises first thing when I got home, his brow knitting together into a tight and worried line.

"It was consensual," I assured my best friend, who looked doubtful. "He set an alarm so I wouldn't be late calling you. It was probably the most well-negotiated scene I've ever done."

He still didn't look convinced, but he was quick to draw himself back when I ignored his pressure for more details. Instead, I shifted the conversation to Riot, who it was clear Lincoln wanted to see again, but for some reason hadn't. Whatever his reasons for self-deprivation, I wasn't terribly interested in breaking through them. The only thing I wanted to do was dwell in the lingering afterglow of one of the most intense scenes and best orgasms I'd ever had.

Lincoln and I had skirted around each other most of the day, but the evening brought us together, and he was scrolling through his phone looking for a place to order takeout from when mine started to ring. He glanced at my screen and raised a brow, opening the menu for our favorite Chinese restaurant.

"Are you going to get that?" he asked, pointing at Marshall's name on my screen.

"Are you going to get *that*?" I countered, tapping a picture on the menu of barbeque pork chow mein.

"Obviously." He added it to the order.

"Obviously," I said, swiping to answer the call and untangling myself from the couch. "Hello?"

"Silas."

I hated that I loved the way he said my name, a bit like a prayer, a bit like a reckoning.

"Marshall."

"How are you feeling today?"

"Tired," I said, giving Lincoln the finger when he made a circle with one hand and aggressively speared his other hand into it over and over again. "Sore."

"You gave me quite a workout too."

I chuckled, feeling proud. "I'm sorry?"

"I don't think you are."

"Not really," I murmured, heading down the hall toward my bedroom for some privacy. Closing the door behind me, I pressed my back against it and shut my eyes. "Is that wrong of me?"

"Not in the slightest. I like you honest."

I didn't know what to say to that, so I kept my mouth shut and the call lapsed into a silence millimeters on the tolerable side of awkward. Scrubbing a hand down my face, I pushed away from the door and crossed the room so I could sit down on my bed. It was smaller than Marshall's, the sheets dirtier, the thread count lower. It wasn't that I was poor, it was just that…he had better taste. I wasn't sure, but in the quiet on that call, I was painfully aware of every difference that existed between us.

Clearing my throat, I asked him, "What can I do for you, Marshall? I mean…why are you calling?"

"I'm calling to check on you after our scene," he said, "but I'm also calling you because I wanted to."

"You don't seem to be in the habit of depriving yourself of the things you want."

"Neither do you," he said quickly.

"No. I'm not." My breath hitched. "So…"

"I haven't been able to stop thinking about you since you left on Saturday morning," he admitted, the words coming quietly, almost rushed. "I told my brother about you earlier today."

Something about the revelation took me by surprise, either the fact he had a brother or that he'd already told his brother about me.

"I didn't know you had a brother."

"I have three."

"Older?"

"All of them younger," he said.

"Oh."

"I told him I was interested in you."

"What did he say to that?" I asked.

"He wished me luck," Marshall said. "Told me not to fuck it up."

"What is *it*? What shouldn't you fuck up?" Something that felt a lot like hope sparked to life in the middle of my chest.

The sound that left Marshall next was primal, low and rumbling like a thunderstorm that had me falling onto my back and covering my eyes with my forearm. It was unfair almost, the way he could take me apart without even trying, without even being in the same room as me. We'd been together once.

Once. Was I already so fucking ruined for other men? Suddenly, none of it even seemed worth it. The peacocking and the game playing, the flirting and the teasing. Without a shadow of a doubt, I knew no person would be able to handle my body as steadily and correctly as Marshall Covington did. There was no point in pretending another man would ever compare. No point in pretending I wanted anyone except for him.

But then Marshall said the last thing I'd expected from him, "I don't…it's been a long time since I've dated someone, Silas."

"What then?"

"I want to see you again, the way I saw you Friday night."

"You want to fuck," I said.

He hummed. "Is that what we did?"

Yes.

Maybe.

"Not entirely," I admitted. "You want to scene again?"

"Is *that* all we did?" he asked again, and then a sigh. "I haven't dated anyone since college, Silas."

"What are you saying?"

"I'm saying I want to earn the right to hear what it sounds like when you call me Sir. I'm saying I want you to trust me enough to let me take you bare. And I want to see you again," he went on. "I want to see you soon. I *only* want to see you."

"In what way?"

"All of them."

"But you don't date," I whispered.

"I corrected myself. I said I *haven't* dated."

"And you would date me?"

Marshall paused. "I'd do everything with you. For you."

"You don't even know me," I said, even though I was already absolutely as gone for him as he apparently was for me. I would have knelt at his feet and kissed the tops of his shoes and then thanked him for the privilege if that was what he wanted. If that was what he allowed.

"I know what you look like when you come apart for me, Silas. Everything else is unimportant."

"What about my dad?"

He let out a disgusted noise. "What about him? This has nothing to do with him."

"You know what I mean."

"You mean that you're the son of my biggest competitor? That you're almost fifteen years younger than me?"

I wanted to dig a hole in the ground and bury myself in it. "Well, when you say it like that."

"I'm not going to tell him anything," Marshall said simply. "It's not his business."

"If we're together, he will find out."

"It's not his business," he said again. "But I'm also not interested in keeping secrets. If you belong to me, I want everyone to know it. Including my brothers, including your best friend, including your father."

I blinked hard, grunting at how the conversation had already gotten away from me. From fucking to dating to *belonging*. And I didn't know what to do besides laugh. It started as a breathy exhale, then turned into something that had my stomach quivering and my eyes watering. The whole thing was so preposterous. How had I gone from what my life had been two weeks ago to what it was now?

"Come over tonight," Marshall pressed. "Let me see you again. Silas, I haven't even kissed you yet—"

"I can't," I said quietly, pressing my fingertips against my bottom lip. "Lincoln was ordering us takeout when you called."

"Tomorrow then. Come over after work."

"And what?" I rasped.

"We'll get dinner. We'll negotiate. We'll set some rules."

"Rules about what?"

"What happens next," he said.

I put my phone on speaker and set it beside my head, then I rolled onto my side, halfway into a fetal position. All of the nerves in my body had disconnected themselves and then put their structure back together wrong. Everything inside of me was misfiring, sparking, smoldering.

"Alright," I agreed, sounding breathier than I ever had before.

There was a small pause and then Marshall asked, "What did Lincoln get you for dinner?"

"Chinese."

"Rice or noodles?"

"Rice for me," I said.

"White?"

"Fried."

The inquisition over my preferences in Chinese takeout had no right sounding as sexy as it did, but every word out of Marshall's mouth was enough to light me up. It was a relief in some ways to have heard his earlier confessions. To know he didn't date but wanted to date me. That he'd told one of his brothers about me. I wasn't the only one here out of my depth.

"What do you want for dinner tomorrow?" he asked.

The answer came quickly. "I want you to choose."

On the other end of the call, Marshall sucked in a sharp breath. "I'll choose," he agreed.

My dick was hard over a conversation about dinner, and it was nearly impossible to breathe.

"Do you need to go now?" he asked.

I glanced at the door, knowing that even though he hadn't knocked, there was no way Lincoln wasn't close. I'd been cagey with him about how the night with Marshall had gone because I didn't want to sound like an overeager child, but knowing things were balanced between us...I wasn't so scared to tell my best friend anymore.

"Lincoln is probably waiting for me."

"I'll let you go then. Come over after work tomorrow. Whenever you're ready."

"Okay."

"Okay," he whispered back to me, the smile loud through the speaker. "Have a good night, Silas."

"Goodnight, Marshall."

The call had no sooner disconnected than Lincoln was knocking on—and opening—my door. I rolled to the side to make room for him, but the way he launched himself at me it was hard to avoid the impact of his body on top of mine. The breath left both our lungs with a whoosh, and I choked, shoving him off so I could get into a more upright position.

"You have to spill now," he said. "I heard too much to let you keep it all in."

"You shouldn't have been eavesdropping."

"Probably not, but I did. So, tell me about Friday."

Lincoln used his shoulder and hip to move me around the bed until we were both flat on our backs, stares turned toward the ceiling.

"Friday was…I don't even have words for it," I said.

"And you're seeing him tomorrow?"

"Yes."

"Is he your boyfriend?"

"No," I said quickly, but the denial lodged in my throat and almost tasted like a lie. "I mean, that sounds silly."

"Why? Because he's your dad's age?"

"God, Linc. No. He's not as old as my dad." I groaned, but Lincoln just laughed at me.

"He is kind of hot in that middle-aged man kind of way. Do you think he wants you to call him Daddy?"

Reaching behind me, I grabbed my pillow and yanked it around, bringing it down hard on Lincoln's face and smothering the tail end of his obnoxious laugh.

"He's not my Daddy," I argued, even though heat burned low in my belly at the thought of it.

"Boyfriend then," he said again.

"We're going to talk about it tomorrow," I said.

Lincoln steamrolled over me in the way he always did when he was excited about something. "Boyfriend and Dom."

I wanted to protest it, but all I could manage was another whack against his face with the pillow. I didn't hate the idea of Marshall being my boyfriend, and I definitely liked the idea of him being my Dom. He'd said on the phone he wanted me to belong to him…

What else could he have meant, if not that?

CHAPTER 16
MARSHALL

I spent the whole of Monday looking forward to seeing Silas after work, and not even an annoying onslaught of text messages from Finn could sour my mood. He'd taken my confession about my interest in Silas and run with it, refusing to let me know a moment's peace about the whole thing. He'd told Hunter as well, because my usually stoic and reserved middle brother even sent a message about it as I was getting ready for bed Sunday night. The only saving grace was that Smith seemed to still be in the dark. I was nowhere near ready to tell my youngest brother that I was involved with someone his age. Someone he knew from school.

It was just before seven when Silas showed up at my house, still dressed for work and looking like he'd been through the wringer. When I opened the door to him, his shoulders sagged, and he shuffled inside, toeing off his shoes again without being told.

I liked that about him.

"You look like you've been through it," I said as a greeting.

He gave me an exasperated look.

"Bad day at work?" I asked.

"The day you came for that meeting, my dad told me I could redraft the bid for him."

Something a lot like dread pooled in my belly, and I hated it was my first reaction. Bidding against Stanley meant I would get it for sure, bidding against Silas? That wasn't such a sure thing. He was too bright and too forward-thinking for that sort of assumption.

"You didn't tell me that," I said.

He glanced up at me, tired. "It didn't really come up, Marshall. I didn't think we had that kind of relationship."

"No." I shook my head, gesturing for him to follow me toward the kitchen. "You're right. I just—"

He snorted. "Are you worried now?"

"Yes," I said simply.

I wanted Silas to see how good he was at his job, how smart he was. Even if I wasn't sleeping with him, going against him for a competitive bid would have been a lot more work than going head-to-head with his father.

He bumped his shoulder against mine before climbing onto one of my barstools and letting the counter support his weight. "You're safe. I haven't been taking it seriously."

"Why not?"

"He said if I redrafted it, he would look at it, not that we would use it. And he thinks my ideas are too revolutionary. I don't see there being any world where he actually takes my work seriously."

"You should come work for me," I blurted, which earned me a wide-eyed look of shock from an otherwise weary-looking man. "Or not."

"That feels like a gross misuse of power at this point."

"How so?"

"You'd be my boss?" He said it like a question. "But you'd also be my Dom and my…boyfriend?" The last word caught in his throat. "All three seem overwhelming when you put them together."

"But you can take the last two on their own?"

Silas's cheeks burned a very pretty shade of pink, and he looked far less tired than he had when he'd arrived, but he didn't give me a verbal reply.

"You're wound tight as a bowstring, Silas. Do you want me to help you relax before we eat? Before we talk?" I tapped my thumb against my forefinger, hovering near him and hating how much the anticipation had me feeling like a snake ready to strike.

"I don't even know," he grumbled, scrubbing both hands down his face.

"What do you want?" I asked. "What do you *need*?"

Silas clenched his jaw down hard, and he banged his elbow onto the counter, catching his chin in his hands like he needed the help to stay upright. He threw a look up at me from beneath the fan of his dark lashes.

"You tell me," he muttered. "You choose."

The decision was right there on the tip of my tongue. It was so very close, and I knew it would solve his problem. It would bring the relief he needed, but if I'd learned anything… if he had learned anything, it was that negotiations had to happen with a clear head.

"I wish I could, but we're not there yet, sweetheart. I can't make those decisions for you until we've already set the ground rules."

He made the unhappiest noise, and I kicked the stool around so we faced each other, then I wrapped my arms around him and let him rest his head against my chest. I could give him this, for now. Gingerly, I stroked my hands down Silas's back, breathing heavily as he exhaled against me.

"I know," he reluctantly agreed, nodding his forehead against my sternum.

I bent down to kiss the top of his head, inhaling the scent of tangerines.

"Let's eat, and then we'll talk, and then we'll see where the night takes us."

At the promise of the last part, Silas groaned, and I had to put space between us because the rumble of his need rattled me down to my bones.

"What's for dinner?"

Instead of telling him, I went to the fridge and decided to show him. Earlier I'd made a chicken salad and a caprese plate, which felt like a nice enough meal without trying too hard. I didn't know where we'd end the evening and didn't want either of us to eat anything too heavy. Silas leaned forward and peered down into the salad bowl.

"Did you make this?"

"Why? Is something wrong with it?" I looked down at the salad, the shredded cheese on top, the croutons, the crisp lettuce.

"Nothing's wrong," he said.

"Yes." I pulled the plastic wrap off the salad and the caprese, then got us plates and forks. "I made it."

"It's interesting to picture you standing here at the counter slicing chicken up and picking leaves of basil off the stem."

I had a bottle of white wine chilling in the fridge, and I poured us each a reasonably small glass.

"I don't normally cook," I admitted, "but I was trying to impress you."

Silas laughed at me a little, then took the wine and raised his glass for a toast. "To me being impressed," he offered.

I clinked the rim of my glass against his and took a drink of the wine.

"May I serve you?" I asked, setting the glass down on the counter.

He hummed thoughtfully. "I would have expected the other way around."

"All things have a time and a place, Silas."

He stared at me, licking his lips in a way that spoke of deep thought, not seduction, and then he swallowed hard and gave me a quick nod. I scooped some of the salad onto a plate for him, then a neat stack of mozzarella, tomato, and basil. I repeated it for my own plate and took the empty stool beside him.

"That's as good a segue as any, I suppose," I said, waiting for him to take a bite before continuing. "About what I would expect from you…in a relationship."

Silas chewed thoughtfully, swallowed, then used the side of his fork to cut off a piece of mozzarella. "I'm surprised you expect anything since you said you didn't date."

"My father was—and probably still is—a womanizer. My brothers and I all have different mothers, none of whom are still in our lives. I didn't grow up with a healthy role model when it came to relationships, but just because I don't date doesn't mean I don't know what I would want if I did."

He took another bite, washing it down with a sip of wine.

"And what do you want, Marshall?"

Fuck, I loved the way he said my name. I liked hearing it more than I could ever imagine enjoying the sound of the word *Sir* rolling off his tongue. He managed to infuse far too much promise and threat into the two simple syllables.

"I want you to tell me what you need," I said. "I want to know what kind of ache brings you out to Rapture looking for a man to take you over his knee and spank you until you can't breathe."

"It's not just that," he whispered.

"Tell me."

"God." Silas dropped his fork and covered his eyes with his fingertips. "This is embarrassing."

"It shouldn't be," I reminded him.

"It's nice to not disappoint someone for once," he said, edgy, chasing the confession with the rest of his wine.

My finger twitched, and I rubbed it against the seam of my slacks to stop myself from reaching for him. The urge to touch Silas was so very tangible, but if I touched him, I would never want to stop, and I needed him to continue being honest, telling me what he wanted from me.

"You like being dominated because the expectations are clear," I said, and he nodded. "But it's more than that, isn't it? You like the pain."

He tapped his temple. "It quiets everything down a bit."

"But more than that?"

"It makes me hard," Silas said.

"You know that would be enough, right?" I ate some salad, had some wine, and dropped my voice low. "Even if the other things didn't come into play, wanting it because it made you hard would be enough."

"I know," he whispered.

"Does it also make you hard to give up the decision-making? To submit that fully?"

"I've never thought too hard about that part," he said.

"Maybe you should."

Silas picked up his fork and finished off the caprese I'd served him. I climbed off my stool and went to get him water, since the small serving of wine was more than enough for us both, all things considered at that moment.

"It makes me feel good in other parts of my body," he finally answered.

"But does it make you hard?"

Silas licked his lips slowly, staring hard at the salad left on his plate. "Yes."

"It makes me hard too," I told him. "I like being in charge."

"Why?" he asked.

"I need the control, I think. It probably has to do with how my brothers and I were raised."

I thought about how we'd all been given up by our mothers, abandoned to a man who cared more about making more sons than caring for the ones he already had. It created a tension in the house from the four of us toward him, but an irreversible sense of comradery between us. There was no one who would support me more than my brothers would, and no one I would support more in return.

At least…there hadn't been before.

"Does it get exhausting?" Silas asked.

I huffed a laugh out of my nose. "I've never done it long term."

"Not even in college?"

"Not in the ways I wanted," I said.

Silas chewed the inside of his cheek hard enough for me to see the outline of his teeth. I reached up and tapped his cheek and he immediately released the skin. I smoothed my touch over his cheek and down to his jawline before letting my hand fall back into my lap.

"So back to it then," Silas said quietly, his body swaying toward me like he was chasing after the feel of my fingers again. "What do you want, Marshall?"

I'd done nothing but think about the answer to that question since the very first time I saw Silas with his bare ass in the air at Rapture, and the answer remained unchanged.

"I want to know how much you'll give me," I admitted, "and then I want to know how much you'll let me take."

Silas swallowed audibly. "Have I eaten enough dinner?"

I looked at his nearly untouched plate. "No."

The unspoken question hung in the air between us, and I knew he was waiting for me to be brave enough to reach out and grab it. There was no question we both wanted it to very certainly the same degree, but I didn't want to be the one making the final call and neither did he. Neither of us wanted to be the one who pushed the other too far.

But it had to be, in the end, didn't it? That was partially my role, my job here.

"Eat some more salad, Silas," I commanded, and he picked up his fork with trembling fingers, spearing some lettuce onto the tines and lifting it to his mouth. He wasn't trying to eat in a sexy way, but the fact it was an order he'd been given and an order he'd followed was hot in and of itself. I studied him in silence while he finished all of the chicken salad I'd served onto his plate, and after the last bite, he set the fork down to his right and folded his hands into his lap—the perfect picture of submission.

CHAPTER 17
SILAS

"Did you like that?" Marshall asked me, voice barely louder than my heartbeat. "Being told to do something mundane like eat your dinner?"

The immediate answer was a loud and resounding yes, but the explanation of it was a little more complicated. This level of submission was uncharted territory for me, and it sounded like it was maybe the same for him. Or at least a road very untraveled. I'd spent most of my adult life focusing on the sexual side of submission, of bending over and being spanked, of getting fucked or denied. I liked all of those things… most of them, at least. I didn't think anyone truly liked denial, but the payoff was always worth it, so it felt like a reasonable trade in the end. But it had always been about sex before. Sitting beside Marshall and eating a salad because he told me to wasn't about sex at all, although my body failed to get the memo that what was happening wasn't foreplay.

"I did," I answered, because complicated or not, it was the truth.

"If we dated—" Marshall paused, dragging his tongue across the front of his teeth. "I would want to do this more."

"Have dinner?" It was an attempt at a joke that fell painfully flat. My nerves were fucking flayed.

"I would want to choose our meals," he said thoughtfully, ignoring the failed tease. "It would be my responsibility to make sure you ate enough, that you got enough sleep."

"I'm twenty-five," I reminded him. "Not five."

He nodded. "And yet."

"And yet," I repeated.

I looked down at my hands, fingers tangled together in my lap, and the absurdity of not knowing what to do with my hands was laughable. I'd been on dates before. I'd scened before. Marshall had already been inside of me, so why did this conversation feel so glaringly intimate and exposing?

"I don't want to strip you of your free will," he said next. "I quite enjoy seeing what you do on your own, but I do want that responsibility, Silas."

"It's ownership," I rasped.

"Yes."

"Is it both or nothing?" I asked.

Marshall's tongue still worked across the front of his teeth, and he made a small sucking sound before he pinched his lips together to quiet the noise.

"What if I said yes?"

"I don't know."

"What about it bothers you?" he asked next. "Why is it okay in the bedroom but not out of it?"

"I have a life, Marshall." I brought my hands up to the edge of the counter and pressed my palms flat against the cool marble. The temperature change worked quickly to reduce my anxiety over the conversation, and my shoulders sagged in relief.

"Of course you do. I don't want to change that."

"How, then?"

"If you have a bad day at work with your dad, Silas, I want

to know about it so I can make sure you take care of yourself afterward. So I can tell you to take a shower, or go to dinner with Lincoln, or come to my house and let me take care of you. I don't want you to hole yourself up. I don't want you to be alone," he said, and it all sounded so nice.

It sounded so fucking nice.

"Are you worried I'm going to take you away from your life?" he asked.

"I don't know," I admitted. "I've never done this before."

"This might be odd for me to say, all things considered, but I believe you're overthinking this one a little." Marshall let out a small chuckle, then climbed off the stool, smoothing his hands down the front of his slacks to ease away any wrinkles. "Put the dishes in the sink, Silas, then join me in the bedroom. We can talk more there."

My legs moved on their own, getting me upright while I watched Marshall disappear from my sight. I stacked the empty plates and silverware, carried it all to the sink and rinsed them off. I ran some water through the empty wine glasses wishing I'd had more than a few sips while also understanding the reason for it. I dried my hands on a navy blue dish towel, then headed for the bedroom.

Marshall sat at the foot of the bed, his forearms resting on his knees. When I walked in, he looked up at me, one brow arched in an unspoken question. I gave the room a quick onceover, finding the bolts in his bed frame still in place, the sheets just as clean and white as they had been the first time I stepped into the room. Nothing was out of place, everything was in order, and in that moment, everything made sense.

"I don't want you to think I don't want to do it," I blurted, flipping my hands upside down and sliding them around the back of my neck until my fingers joined together in my hairline. "I just haven't done it before."

"Would it be easier for you if we start without it? If we integrate it slowly."

"I'm not sure." My cheeks burned, but I was focused on not hiding from this man.

"You did so well already tonight. You came over, you ate, you cleaned. It's not so bad, is it?" He straightened up, squared his shoulders.

I shook my head. "It wasn't bad at all."

"Your bad day at work is nearly forgotten, isn't it?"

At first, I didn't know what he was talking about. The scrunch of my nose had Marshall looking as smug as he deserved. Then I remembered the rest of my day. The argument with my dad about my own version of the proposal, the knowing that it was busy work that wouldn't go anywhere. I'd come over, annoyed and stressed, and without a single rough touch, Marshall had found a way to clear all of that out of my head.

"Yes," I whispered, blinking hard.

Why did I want to cry?

What a relief to finally be known this way.

"That's all I want." Marshall crooked a finger, beckoning me closer. "I just want you to feel good. I want both of us to feel good."

I shuffled toward him, closing the space between us. When I reached the gap between his spread legs, he pointed at the floor, and I sank down to my knees. I dropped my weight back onto my heels and settled my palms on the tops of my thighs. He studied me, fingers twitching like he wanted to reach out and touch me, but he never stretched far enough to make the connection. I found myself leaning forward, chasing after the heat of him, the feel of him.

"We can talk about the rest later, but I want to be clear in what I want right now," he said. "Are you clearheaded?"

"Yes. You can ask me a multiplication up to twelve and I could answer it."

The corner of his mouth quirked up. "Duly noted, Silas. Thank you, but I don't think I'll have to do that yet."

"Okay," I whispered.

My fingers tingled, and the muscles in my thighs quivered. I was so desperate for whatever was going to happen next, for whatever kind of release Marshall had in store for me.

"Tonight I'd like to bind your wrists behind your back. I want you to suck my cock until I come. I want you to choke on it, Silas. I want your tears to mix with your spit, to mix with my cum. All of it on your tongue."

"Shit."

He flashed a smile, tilting his head to the side. "Then I want you to come without your hands, without penetration."

I had no doubt Marshall could get me off hands-free, but there was a more pressing question.

"How?"

"I want you to rut into the sheets while my cock softens in your mouth. I want you to come all over my bedding, and then I want to taste you. I want your tears and your spit and my cum returned to me after you finish."

"Jesus fuck," I choked, letting out another curse or five under my breath.

How was this man real?

"Because your tears are mine, aren't they? Your spit? Everything about you belongs to me, doesn't it?"

I wanted to die because I'd never heard anything more right in my life. My jaw went slack, words trying to form into sentences but falling short.

As if he knew, Marshall smirked and asked, "Does that sound—"

I cut him off, finding the only word I needed, "Perfect."

"Go to the nightstand. Get the cuffs and bring them here."

I scampered around the bed, yanking open the drawer and finding the same cuffs as last time. There were no condoms, no lube, and I wondered if Marshall had been planning this chain of events all along. If he somehow knew we'd end up here when I hadn't even been certain of it.

Back at the foot of the bed, I handed the cuffs to him, and he gestured in a circle with his finger.

"Strip naked with your back to me. I want to see how I left you."

The bruises from Friday night had only gotten darker with each passing day, and I made sure to show off my ass when I hinged at the hips to shove my pants and my underwear down. I slipped out of the rest of my clothes, then waited for his next instruction.

"Do they hurt?" he asked.

"Sometimes."

"Walk backward," he said, and I stepped back toward him until he told me to stop. His large hands bracketed my waist then slid down over my hips, around the top of my ass and down to the backs of my thighs. He pressed at the ones that hurt and ignored the ones that didn't, and it was another mystery to add to the list of questions I had about how Marshall Covington knew me so fucking well.

Fortunately—or not—the attention on my marks made my cock painfully erect, and when he attached the cuffs around my wrists, precum leaked from my slit. He kissed my wrists again, the same way as before, the same gentle reverence before tightening down the straps, and then he spun me to face him, bringing my erection to eye level.

"It's a wonder how much your body loves this."

I didn't know what to say. I wasn't even sure I had words left, anyway.

"Let's add some bruises to your knees, shall we?" he asked next, even though it was hardly a question at that point.

I went back to my knees between his legs, ignoring the way saliva pooled in my mouth while he undid his fly and pulled out his cock. He rubbed it against my face, dragging his slick crown across my chin and my cheek before taking it away. My instinct was to chase after him when he scooted up the bed toward the headboard, spreading himself out against the wall like the king I imagined him to be.

"Crawl up here," he demanded, and I was grateful the bed was low to the floor, but I would have figured it out even if it was ten feet tall.

With my wrists bound behind my back, I hobbled onto the bed and knee-walked toward him at the top. He looped his thumb and first finger around the base of his dick and pointed it toward me.

"Come suck it, sweetheart," he said.

I dove between his legs, taking as much of him into my mouth as I could on the first swallow. Marshall groaned, cursing quietly, then followed his exhale up with a hushed murmur of my name. He threaded the fingers of his free hand into my hair, guiding me down to take more of his clean and hard length into my mouth.

He wanted me to cry, and he wanted me to make a mess, so I used his erection to choke myself. The muscles of my throat flexed around the tip of his dick and his hips lifted off the bed, pushing him deeper. I gagged and sputtered around him, sinking farther around his length because I didn't have the support of my arms to hold me up.

My dick was already leaking smears of precum across his sheets. I bobbed up and down his length, squinting hard when he fucked up against the roof of my mouth. Tears spilled out from the corners of my eyes, sliding down my cheeks and into my mouth, and Marshall made a very pleased sound as he pushed deeper into my throat.

The trim hairs around the base of his shaft tickled my nose

as I took the whole of him into my mouth, and I choked around him, needing more air but not finding it. His hand was still steady against the back of my head, applying only enough pressure to make sure I didn't stop sucking him.

"Two out of three," he murmured, hips chasing a frenetic pattern against my face. "Don't swallow, Silas. I want to taste it all together. Do you understand?"

I managed a nod, and then he was done.

Cum shot against the roof of my mouth, the back of my tongue. It was impossible to not swallow, with spit and cum spilling out of the corners of my mouth as he continued to fill me with his spend.

"Good boy. Good boy." He stroked my hair back from my face, his entire body trembling beneath me. "Just like that. Now show me how you make yourself come."

I should have been embarrassed.

Restrained with my arms behind me, my face covered with spit and tears, cum leaking out of my mouth. My own cock was so hard it could have hammered nails, and sealing my lips around the base of Marshall's shaft to keep his cum and his dick in my mouth only made me harder.

Getting myself off was going to be easy.

I spread my legs, grinding down into the previously pristine bedding. The plush comforter wrapped around my cock like a soft hand, and my brain immediately wanted to know what it would be like for Marshall to stroke my cock with his leather gloves he'd worn on Friday. I pumped my hips harder, groaning at the weight of his cock in my mouth, still hard against my tongue.

My orgasm came on slowly, a dangerous and steady climb from the tips of my toes to the base of my spine. At some point, my pleasure twisted and knotted, and I couldn't breathe, couldn't think. My hips moved faster, rougher, and then it was over. I spilled my load onto the sheets with a pathetic gurgle.

Cum still sprayed out of my cock when Marshall grabbed me by the throat and hauled me up onto his lap. My still spurting dick rubbed against the wool of his slacks, and he used his hold around my neck to bring our mouths within kissing distance.

Then he stopped.

"I just realized I haven't kissed you yet," he murmured, brushing his lips against mine.

Hadn't he?

I was certain Marshall had taken every part of my body inside and out already.

Certain of it.

"I don't want it to be like this, though…" he trailed off, pressing his thumb against the underside of my chin. I was a quivering mess from the orgasm, cum still leaking from my cock, hands still bound behind my back, naked against all of Marshall's clothes. He regarded me up close, breath mingled and lips so close to the connection he'd already promised me. "Open, Silas."

I dropped my mouth open, sticking my tongue out enough for him to see his cum pooled on top. He closed the space, but instead of *kissing* me, he took my tongue into his mouth, sucked it like it was a dick until I couldn't taste him anymore. He reached deeper, licking up the inside of my cheek, the backs of my teeth. He was, if nothing else, a man of his word. This was a tasting, not a kiss. And I found myself left wanting when he pulled away.

Hungry when he licked his lips and let out a satisfied growl.

I was somehow horny and sated all at the same time, enjoying how it felt to be on his lap, supported by his hands. Even if the thought of the kind of submission Marshall wanted had scared me at dinner, in this moment, it was the only thing that made sense. Of course I would offer him that part of myself. I would offer him anything because, somehow, he knew me.

As though he'd been in a trance, Marshall shook his head and pressed his body against the headboard and the wall.

"Back to the floor," he said. "On your knees again."

I was loath to be away from him, but I managed to swing my body to the foot of the bed and then off. My knees hit the floor, and I hoped there would be bruises like he'd suggested. I wanted his marks all over me because I never wanted to forget how good it felt to kneel for him.

He followed me off the bed and stood in front of me, his cock still out, now limp against his thigh. I was at the perfect height to suck him again, and part of me hoped he would ask. Part of me wanted to come to his house after work and put his dick into my mouth and not take it out until it was time to leave again. I could ask for that. I wondered if he would like it or if he would think it was weird.

I tilted my head back, blinking up at him. My lashes were still wet, tears still welling out of the corners of my eyes. Marshall hummed, swiping my tears away, then brushing his thumb dry across my lower lip. My mouth was already salty from his cum, more so now the memory of it. My chin quivered at his touch, and it should have been embarrassing.

It should have been a lot of things.

He bent down and brought our mouths so close together again, another brush of his lips like the last time. Not quite nothing, but not quite a kiss.

"We didn't negotiate a kiss," he murmured, tugging my chin down.

"Please, Marshall," I whined. "If you don't kiss me, I think I'll die."

"You'll do no such thing."

"I'll beg."

"Don't threaten me with a good time, sweetheart."

"You said you didn't want it to be like this," I said, blinking hard. I was ready to scream, ready to cry again. "What did you want it to be like?"

He made a thoughtful noise, then came down onto his knees. He was still taller than me, but it was closer to eye level than before. Reaching around behind me, he unlatched the connector on the cuffs, then undid them entirely. He rubbed my wrists, paying extra attention to the kisses he'd left first beneath the leather, then he lifted my arms one at a time and kissed them again.

"Tell me *I* can kiss *you*," I whispered, stretching my fingers toward the side of his face. He pressed his lips against my wrist and looked at me earnestly, then he gave me the briefest nod.

It was all the consent I needed.

I took Marshall's face into my hands and crashed our mouths together. He slid one arm around my waist to steady me, and beneath my mouth, he parted his lips and made room for my tongue. I moaned, throwing the whole of my body weight against him, and it was no surprise he managed to hold us both. I licked into his mouth the way he'd done to mine, but instead of to taste, it was to explore.

Deepening the kiss, I climbed halfway into his lap, wrapping my legs around his waist and sinking down to sit on top of his dick, which was now half-hard again. I wanted him to fuck me like this one time too. Where we were so close together the only air we could breathe was what the other provided.

God, I wanted, and I wanted, and I wanted.

And for the first time in my life, I was scared the wanting would unravel me entirely, but then Marshall dug his fingers into the bruises on my ass and there wasn't anything else in the world that mattered besides him.

Again.

CHAPTER 18
MARSHALL

Tuesday was hell.

I couldn't get a single thing done, my brain far too wrapped up in Silas and the way every nerve in my body came alive when he kissed me.

When *he* kissed *me*.

He was so submissive and yet so sure, nothing like the man he'd been the night I walked in on him in the private playroom at Rapture. The fact that had only been days ago was just as astounding as the rest of him. The speed at which my feelings had manifested and developed was for textbooks. Put a picture of my face right beside the words *infatuation, obsessed, consumed*.

Watching Silas go home at the end of the night had wrecked me, but he'd smirked and reminded me we hadn't negotiated a sleepover. My own rules coming back to bite me in the ass when all I wanted was to take him into my bed and keep him there until I'd never be able to wash the smell of him out of my sheets.

Might as well add my picture next to *possessed* too.

I had struggled through the morning, wanting to text him but not wanting to add *desperate* to the word list as well, so when Hunter reached out about getting lunch, I jumped at the chance. He was closest with Finn, and even then he was reserved, so it was a rare treat when he wanted to get together one on one.

As soon as it was close enough to lunch, I shut my laptop, slid my cell phone into my pocket, and locked up my office. The weather was nice, so I decided to walk the half-mile instead of driving. Hunter had picked some ramen restaurant in a strip mall, and he was already sitting at the counter when I arrived. The seat beside him was open, a glass of water already waiting for me. Sliding up into the seat, I bumped my shoulder into his.

"Hey, baby brother," I greeted.

He made an unimpressed noise. "I'm four years younger than you and a decade older than Smith."

"Practically an infant," I teased.

"Then Smith is a fetus?"

I chuckled and took a swallow of water. "Isn't he?"

"Sometimes it seems like it." Hunter sighed heavily, and I was suddenly worried he'd called me up for lunch because something was wrong with our youngest brother.

"What's up, Hunter?" I asked, only to be interrupted by the waiter coming to take our order. I shrugged, and Hunter ordered for us both, waiting a beat after the waiter had left to answer me.

"It's about Dad," he said.

Dread filled the pit of my stomach, worse than when I'd thought something was going on with Smith. "What about him?"

It had been years since Finn and I had spoken to our dad. He'd done his part, we'd agreed, getting us through high school and college, keeping us alive, though not nurtured. We didn't see the point in trying to build any lasting familial relations with him, so we hadn't tried. Smith had tried and failed to lay the foundation for a father/son relationship. After giving up, he'd turned his sights on me, and I was more than happy to fill those shoes for him. Hunter, on the other hand, had kept track of things without staying close. They spoke twice a year, Dad giving Hunter updates about his financials—for the inheritances—and Hunter letting him know the four of us were still alive.

"He's not dead," Hunter said. "But…"

The way he trailed off had me unsure of what was going to come next. Not dead, but dying? Did he have cancer? I was getting older than the rest of them; was it something I should get checked for? Was it hereditary? Oh, maybe he had a heart attack…a stroke.

"Spill it."

He exhaled, cheeks puffing out and deflating slower than molasses. Hunter was quiet, but he was rarely at a loss for words.

"There's another brother," he finally said, chewing on his lower lip and avoiding my stare.

"What now?"

The waiter was back, sliding two bowls of steaming hot ramen and the most perfect-looking soft-boiled eggs in front of us. It smelled delicious, but I found myself worried I was about to throw up all over the noodles. I reached for the glass and took a drink of water, swallowing down the bile and my nerves. I was the oldest of us, and it was my responsibility to stay level-headed about things.

To be reasonable.

"He's been made aware of another son," Hunter said.

"Son," I repeated. "At least he's consistent."

My brother huffed out a laugh and cracked apart his chopsticks. He'd clearly been sitting on this news for a while if he was able to dive into his meal like he'd just told me he bought a new car or rented a new apartment. I opened my chopsticks up because it felt like the thing to do, even though I wasn't sure I had it in me to eat anymore.

Finn would be amused to all hell by the news.

Smith would be devastated.

"Ask me the rest." Hunter slurped up a mouthful of noodles and pork, finally glancing up at me.

"How old is he?"

"Twenty-eight."

"Where does he live?" I poked the tip of my chopstick into the almost runny yolk of the egg. My stomach growled, and I gave in, picking up the whole thing and shoving it into my mouth.

"San Diego."

Of course. Dear old dad never went far from home.

"Why now?" I asked.

"His mom passed. It was all in the will."

"How long have you known?"

"Since yesterday." My brother dove in for another hunk of ramen, and I twirled a few strands of noodles up around my chopsticks and managed a bite.

"Have you talked to him?" I asked. "What's his name?"

"Drew. Andrew."

"Not Covington?"

He shook his head. "Andrew Neil Calavert."

"What a name," I drolled. "What did Dad say about it?"

"He's known awhile, but he respects the contact schedule so he was saving it for the next time we talked. He said Drew is an only child—"

"Was," I corrected.

Hunter rolled his eyes. "Was an only child. Would be open to meeting us."

"What does he want from Dad? Or what does he get from Dad, rather?"

Hunter had managed to eat almost all of his ramen while I

processed the news of another sibling, and he shoved the bowl away from him with a grunt. He folded his hands together on top of his otherwise flat stomach and heaved a breath.

"He doesn't want anything as far as I can tell. He gets added to the inheritance, but other than that…" he trailed off.

I finished eating.

"He wants to meet us?" I asked.

"He would be open to it."

"What do you think?"

Hunter shrugged, and suddenly he was a teenager again, so young and unruly, so angry about the hand we'd all been dealt with mothers and a father like ours.

"I think whatever we do, we do together. We need to talk to Finn and Smith, but I wanted to talk to you first. I think Smith…"

"He's not going to take it well," I said.

Hunter shook his head.

I pushed the half-eaten ramen away and scrubbed a hand down my face. This was not the lunch I'd been expecting to have when Hunter had reached out earlier in the day. But I also shouldn't have been surprised. Dad's lack of affection for prophylactics was the most predictable thing about him.

"You want me to talk to him before Friday."

"I think it would help," he said. "I don't want him to be caught off-guard."

"If I talk to Smith separately, Finn will be pouty that he's the last to know."

"Shit, you're right."

I needed something stronger than water to get through the rest of this meal, the rest of my day.

"We tell them both on Friday," I suggested. "I'll just be available for Smith after. And you can talk to Finn if he needs anything."

"Less than ideal, but it works."

"There is no ideal here, Hunt." I shifted my weight to get my wallet, and Hunter was protesting before I'd managed to even get fingers around my cash. I wasn't like our dad in a lot of ways, but only some of them. "No arguing," I told him, throwing two twenties down onto the counter between our bowls.

"Sorry to drop this on you." He stood up, rolling his head around his neck until he got the crack he was after. "But thank you for lunch."

"Thank you for being the point of contact."

I slid my wallet back into my pocket and walked with my brother to the door. Back outside, the sun was bright, the sky was clear, and everything was as it had been before I'd walked inside and had my world turned upside down.

Another brother.

Fuck.

"Before you go, though," Hunter said, mouth pulling into a smirk. "Do you want to tell me about your boyfriend?"

"I don't have a—" The protest died in my mouth, and his smirk turned into a very knowing smile.

"Finn told me all about it."

"It's new," I muttered.

"He's young."

I exhaled, threading my fingers together at the back of my head. I arched my back, inches away from staring up into the sun and blinding myself completely. Maybe things would be easier that way.

"Does Smith know?" Hunter asked.

"It's too new for any of you to know, but Finn is Finn."

Hunter pulled his car keys out of his pocket, pressing the fob and unlocking his black BMW. "You can't tell him both things at the same time, you know."

"I know."

I didn't like the idea of lying to Smith, but Hunter was

right. Smith could maybe handle the addition of a new brother, if it was a good day, or he could handle finding out that I was finally in a relationship with someone—closer to his age than mine. There didn't seem to be a way where both could be delivered at the same time without feelings getting hurt or wires getting crossed.

"Drew first."

I nodded my agreement.

"See you Friday." He gave me a two-finger salute, and I stayed on the sidewalk, watching the taillights on his car until he turned a corner and was out of sight.

With a reluctant groan, I started the short walk back to the office, cursing my father and cursing myself. I'd spent the whole morning practically begging for a distraction from Silas, and the universe had delivered in the most dramatic fashion possible.

Back at the office, I flipped open my laptop and stared at the calendar. I didn't have much time left to finalize and return the proposal for the Cahuenga Pass project. There was no question I'd win it, especially if Silas wasn't going to redo the work his father had insisted on butchering out of the gate. There wasn't anything else for me to do with the numbers or the design.

It could wait until tomorrow. I'd give it one final review and then send it off.

I'd celebrate with my brothers on Friday about it, a counter to the news Hunter was going to drop on the rest of them. That would be a fair enough balance, I hoped. And then if all went well, I would see Silas on Saturday. I would get to kiss him again, get to tie him to something uncomfortable, and fuck him again.

But it was so much more than that now. For both of us. I would be able to feed him again, serve him dessert again, wash the folds of his thighs with soapy fingers, and maybe make him come in the shower. The list of things I wanted to explore with him was never-ending, and daydreaming about them was the only thing that would get me through the monotony of my workdays.

Dropping my cell phone onto my desk, I opened up my messages app and fired one off to Silas, not sure if he would have time to reply immediately or if it would have to wait. I didn't imagine Stanley was a fun boss to have, and I was relatively sure he made Silas work through lunch most days.

> You distracted me last night with that tight, wet throat of yours. We need to talk more about the non-sexual things. I can't stop thinking about you. About all of it.

I hit send before I could think better of it.

Maybe add my picture next to *pathetic* or *whipped*.

He replied almost immediately, which I hadn't expected.

SILAS

> I want all of it. I know we have to negotiate it a little, but I do want to do it with you.

> Can you talk?

He answered by calling me.

"Silas."

"Hi." He sounded winded, quiet.

"Are you sure you can talk right now?"

"I'm in the conference room alone. I have time," he said.

"I'll never ask anything of you that will put you in harm's way, Silas. I'll never make a demand of you that will jeopardize any of your relationships, including ours."

"I know," he whispered. "I want that to be enough. I want to start, and I want…"

"What do you want, sweetheart?" My fingers flexed into a fist, relaxed, flexed again.

"I want you," he said, clearing his throat. "I want *you*."

"Send me a text with your sexual limits before the end of the day. Is that clear?"

A soft moan. "Yes, Marshall."

"Do you have plans after work?"

"If we don't have plans, I have plans with Lincoln, but—"

"Do you need to spend time with him tonight?" I asked. "Since you were with me last night?"

"I can do both," Silas said. "I can have dinner with him and then come over afterward."

"I want the list before you get to my house."

"I understand."

Heat burned between my legs for how much I wanted this man. For how out of my mind the mere *thought* of him made me.

"Good boy, Silas."

He whimpered.

He fucking whimpered.

"I've got to go," he said quickly, sounding more hushed than he had before. "I'll see you later."

The call disconnected loudly in my ear, and I dropped the phone onto my desk with a groan.

I was going to put Silas's father out of work for good, which would in turn put Silas out of a job. We both knew it, but neither of us had ever discussed it. I had a new brother, and that news was going to be received about as well as a grenade. I was in a relationship with someone almost half my age, and I didn't feel bad about it in the slightest.

It was too much.

Too much.

And I was so fucking fucked.

CHAPTER 19
SILAS

Much to my father's disapproval, I left work early. He kept hounding me about an updated version of the bid, and I kept pushing him off. The fact he thought I could whip it together in a handful of days spoke volumes to how unimportant he thought my ideas really were. There was deliberation and care and understanding that had to go into designing plans that would incorporate the kind of innovation required to stay at the forefront of our industry. It wasn't as simple as drawing up new schematics and adding greenery.

Resigned to ignore him, I texted Lincoln so he could order ahead for dinner, then I headed home. Our apartment smelled like olives and hummus when I arrived, and Lincoln was bent over the dining room table, spreading containers out so we could both reach them from our usual seats.

"Honey, I'm home," I called out from the door, adding a Ricky Ricardo kind of inflection to my voice. Kicking the door closed, I dropped my laptop bag by the door and toed off my shoes, and then I let my nose carry me to the table. Lincoln sat down and grinned up at me when I got there. I kissed the top of his head and collapsed into my own chair with a groan.

"Long day?" he asked.

"Long week."

"It's Tuesday."

I snorted and stared up at the ceiling. "My dad is being the worst again."

"I don't know how you work with him." Lincoln leaned toward the center of the table and picked up a clear container of hummus. He set it between us, and I passed him a pita chip.

"At the time, I didn't have much of a choice," I grumbled, and it was true.

When I was in school, I didn't get any internships after graduation, so taking a job with my dad had felt like the only option. In hindsight, it had just been the easiest, and now it wasn't anything more than a trap filled with quicksand.

"Do you now?"

"I could look for other work, but I don't have a lot of experience on my resume."

"Just because dad is dated doesn't mean you don't have experience," he countered, pointing at me with a half-eaten pita chip. "You got that article published, and you're working on another one, so they'll see you're not stuck in the past just because your boss is."

"Yeah," I agreed, even though my heart wasn't in it.

"I'm sure you don't want to talk about work. Shawarma or gyro?"

"Shawarma," I said.

Lincoln passed me a white Styrofoam container overflowing with rice and shawarma. I opened it up and breathed in the smell of all the herbs, then shoved a forkful of meat into my mouth.

"Let's talk about your boyfriend," Lincoln said right as I swallowed.

The shreds of chicken roped together in my throat, and I

choked. Pounding my chest to get the bite down, I narrowed my eyes and glared at my best friend.

"What do you mean?"

Lincoln arched a brow. "Isn't he?"

"Who?"

"Marshall."

"He's not—" I stopped, catching myself in the lie.

Marshall was my boyfriend, technically, I guess. He was also my Dom, even though we were still figuring out the logistics of how those two things would work together.

"Exactly." Lincoln grinned at me. "You sounded like you'd been to heaven and back the first night you went over there and emergency-called me to check in, but you haven't said anything to me about him since, beyond assuring me all those pretty bruises on your ass were consensual."

He wasn't wrong.

It wasn't that I'd been avoiding Lincoln, I just didn't have the words to explain how I felt about Marshall or what our relationship was. It was fresh to me and very fresh to him, and there was no way to articulate that to a third party.

"It's new," I settled on.

"Obviously." He reached over and scooped up some of my shawarma with a plastic fork and then said the next part with his mouth full of food. "Is he a good Dom?"

The flush on my cheeks should have been the only answer Lincoln needed, but I nodded. "Yes."

"A good boyfriend?"

"We're still figuring it all out."

"Is it a 24/7 thing?" he asked.

"Figuring it out," I repeated, pushing the container of gyro toward him so he would stop talking and start eating, but Lincoln was nothing if not dedicated, and he was solely focused on me and Marshall.

"Does your dad know?"

"Definitely not."

"Are you going to tell him?" he asked.

"I'd love to not."

Lincoln made an unimpressed sound. "You can't hide forever."

"Can't we?" I asked.

He shook his head, the hint of a knowing frown on his face. "No."

"Hey." I poked him in the arm, and he made a dramatic show of rocking his whole body from the touch. "What's that about?"

"Nothing," he lied.

I poked him harder, and he rolled his eyes. "It's Riot."

Snorting, I grinned at my best friend. "That can't be his real name. I don't care what he says."

"It is." Lincoln frowned harder, smearing hummus onto his fork and using the dip to pick up some shavings of gyro. He filled his mouth and chewed, ignoring my stare.

"Alright."

I worked on assembling something for myself to eat. It was probably more food than would be advisable, considering my plans for the rest of the night, so I took one more bite of shawarma then searched out the container full of salad. Lincoln gave me a slow and sarcastic blink but didn't say anything. We were on the verge of him either calling out the change in my eating habits and what that meant for the rest of my night or him being honest with me about whatever was going on with him and Riot. I hoped for the latter, but there was no telling how things would go.

He ate a couple more bites of his meal in silence, then sighed. "He's not out."

I squinted, laughing out loud before swallowing it all back down when I saw the serious expression on Lincoln's face. "Wait. Are you serious?"

He nodded.

That night at Rapture was mostly a blur…by design. Not that I'd tried to black out any of the things that happened to me, but because Marshall saving the day overshadowed all of it. Sitting on the couch with him after it was all done, breathing with him, and feeling how steady his heart beat…nothing else mattered.

"He seemed pretty out to me, Linc," I finally said when it was clear my best friend was not going to pick up the conversation again.

"On Friday nights at a sex club, maybe. But not in real life."

"And that's a dealbreaker?"

He cocked his head to the side and pursed his lips. "Isn't it?"

"I don't know." I shrugged. "Like, I'm out and I think Marshall is too, but our relationship isn't out."

"I don't want to talk about Riot," he muttered.

"You really like him," I said.

"I really don't want to talk about him." Lincoln cleared his throat and turned his attention on me, eyes laser focused. "I want to know if our relationship has to change now that you have a boyfriend and a Dom."

"What do you mean?"

He rolled his eyes and dropped his fork.

It seemed neither of us had much of an appetite anymore.

"The way we've always been, Si. We're not…normal friends."

"We're very normal," I protested. "There's nothing wrong with us."

"I love you," he said, and I answered him without missing a beat.

"I love you."

"I've never wanted to have sex with you."

I snorted. "Should my feelings be hurt?"

"No, dumbass. I'm saying that everything between us is platonic. It always has been, and it always will be. But we share a bed sometimes, and we kiss sometimes. We cuddle *a lot*, and we used to scene—"

I cut him off, grimacing. "We can't scene anymore."

"What about the rest?"

It was almost an absurd question, because why should anything in my relationship with Lincoln have to change just because I was now involved with Marshall? Lincoln was my best friend, and that was the only thing he would ever be. But would Marshall see it that way? Would he be okay with the knowledge that sometimes on the nights I wasn't with him, I'd be in bed with Lincoln? Our physicality was such an important part of our friendship, something both of us needed…I didn't want to lose that.

"I'll have to talk to Marshall," I said.

It was all I had in the moment.

"What if he hates it?" Lincoln worried his canine tooth with the tip of his tongue. It was a nervous habit he'd had for as long as I'd known him, and even with his mouth closed tight, I recognized the movement of it. "What if he says no?"

The prospect of losing my relationship with Lincoln made me sick, but the thought of giving up Marshall didn't make me feel much different.

"He won't say no."

"He doesn't seem like the type to share."

"It's not sharing," I said. "My relationship with you isn't the same as my relationship with him."

"You kiss us both."

"I've kissed him once," I said, smirking before covering my face with my hands.

Lincoln reached over and smacked my hands out the way. His eyes were wide, and his mouth parted in shock. "Once?"

The bomb about that piece of our intimacy had landed just as I'd hoped. Not that I was deliberately trying to distract him, but I didn't have the answers either of us needed. I'd have to talk to Marshall about it after dinner when I went over to his house.

There was apparently a lot for us to talk about after dinner.

"Once," I confirmed. "And it was just last night."

"Please tell me how that happened."

"We just…he's really big on negotiating what happens in a scene and not changing it up. We never talked about a kiss until last night."

He scrunched his nose and leaned away from me, crossing his arms in front of his chest. "Is that weird of him? To be so strict?"

I shook my head. "It's not…it's not bad. It's actually really fucking hot. The way we talk through things before we do them, but I think now that we've agreed we're *together*, he'll be more willing to change within a scene."

"Is every time you have sex a scene?"

I opened my mouth to answer but fell short. I wanted to say no, but the answer—so far—was yes. And if Marshall was meant to be my boyfriend *and* my Dom, then I imagined yes… every time it would be a scene. Or maybe none of the times would be a scene, it would just be us.

"So far," I answered. "But I don't think that will be forever. I have plans to see him later tonight, and we were supposed to talk about all of that."

"What do you want from him?"

"Everything."

Lincoln worked his jaw back and forth, stare hazy, like he was looking through me instead of at me.

"That's serious, Silas."

"I know."

"So serious you only had two bites of your favorite dinner."

He pulled the shawarma away from me and closer to him, repeating his same hummus as glue trick with the chicken before shoving a forkful of meat into his mouth.

"Trying to be courteous," I said. "All things considered."

He made a thoughtful sound as he swallowed, and I was just glad his appetite had returned.

The course of our conversation had given me whiplash. From work to Riot to Marshall to us. I hadn't realized until this conversation just how much of my life was currently in flux. It was like standing on a cliff and being ready to jump, even though I had no idea what I'd find at the bottom.

It was easy to feel safe when I was with Marshall. His dominant nature and easy kind of caretaking style were enough to make sure I never doubted my security with him. It was the days without him where everything was called into question.

"He's good to you, then?" Lincoln asked, tone completely different from before.

"He's amazing."

"I'm happy for you. You deserve that."

"Hey."

He glanced up at me, and I scooted my chair closer, knocking our shoulders together before resting my head on his. The closeness to Lincoln felt as right as it ever had. So much so, I wasn't sure how I would react if Marshall took issue with it. Lincoln's and my physical affection was as important to our friendship as our conversation.

"Hey."

"You deserve it too."

Lincoln snorted, sighing heavily and dropping his head against mine.

"Let's worry about you for now. We can deal with me later."

I pretended to dry heave, the attention too much. "Thanks, I hate it."

"Too bad."

We sat in silence for a minute, the spread in front of us quickly getting cold. I tapped my fingers against Lincoln's thigh, and he offered me his hand. Threading our fingers together, I lifted his hand to my mouth and kissed his knuckles.

"I love you," I whispered, dropping our joined hands down to the small gap between our thighs.

"I know," he said. "I love you too, Si."

"Should I be worried about you?"

He squeezed my hand. "Not yet."

"You'll tell me?"

On top of my head, I felt him nod.

"Promise?" I asked.

"I promise." Lincoln cleared his throat and untangled himself from me fully. "Now help me pack this all into the fridge. Sounds like you have a hot date."

CHAPTER 20
MARSHALL

Silas arrived later than I'd expected. I wasn't more than ten minutes away from texting to check on him when he showed up on my porch in a pair of low-slung gray sweats and a threadbare USC t-shirt, messenger bag looped around his neck like usual.

"Sorry I'm late," he said with half of a shrug.

"We never settled on a time."

I stepped out of the way to let him in, knowing his first stop would be getting his shoes off and kicking them into a neat pile by the door. Next, he slipped off his messenger bag, ready to set it on the floor, but I took it from him before the leather could hit the tile.

"I'll go put this in my room."

His cheeks pinked and he nodded.

"Why don't you head into the dining room? I poured us some wine."

"Thank you," he said quietly, padding off in the opposite direction of my bedroom.

I carried Silas's bag into my room and set it in the closet, then I found him perched on a stool with the wine in hand. He spun the glass around in a circle, aerating the bubbles, but not taking a drink.

"Is this all I get for the night?" he asked.

"That depends."

"On if we fuck?"

I sucked in a silent breath and sat down beside him, not sure where his defensiveness was coming from but more than ready to find out.

"On if we fuck the way we both like."

Silas cocked his head to the side and asked, "Do you think you wouldn't like fucking me normally?"

"I'm sure I'll like fucking you every way I can."

He finally raised the glass to his lips, taking the smallest sip imaginable. "If you're my boyfriend and my Dom, doesn't that make everything a scene?"

The question made me wish I'd poured us both a whole bottle and not two ounces.

Instead of answering his question, I made an observation. "You seem uneasy, Silas. Did something happen at dinner?"

He frowned, taking another swallow of wine. He set the glass down and started to spin it again, making me wonder if the movement was a nervous habit, giving me the idea of tying him down and forcing him to be still and face whatever was eating at him.

"I want to talk to you about my relationship with Lincoln." Silas turned his stool so our knees knocked together, and I made room for him to notch himself between my thighs.

"Talk."

He was a bundle of nerves trapped in the body of a man, twitchy and unsure in a way I'd never seen from him before. Not that my experience with Silas's moods was vast. The time we'd spent together was minimal in comparison to the time I'd spent with my brothers or the time he'd spent with Lincoln. I settled my hands on the tops of his thighs, hoping the weight would in some way calm him.

"He's my best friend." Silas looked at me, looked away, looked at me again.

"I know."

"We...our friendship..." He grimaced, turning his face downward. He traced his thumbs across the tops of my knuckles, and I was very worried he was about to tell me something that was going to break whatever this deal between us was. I didn't know what the confession would be, but Silas's body language had me prepared for the worst.

"You can tell me," I said, even though part of the answer felt like a lie. "Whatever it is, I want to know. Do the two of you fuck? Is that it?"

Silas exhaled with a laugh, his shoulders caving inward, and he curled his fingers around the sides of my hands, tucking them up against my palm. Apparently I'd said the right thing—which I didn't quite understand—because the earlier tension that had locked his spine straight had vanished.

"God, no." He made an almost disgusted noise. "We've never slept together. We scene sometimes, rarely. But, no... we're...we do sleep together, but not for sex. Just for sleep. We're...God, this is so weird to say. We're physical with each other, but not sexual."

I worried the inside of my cheek, giving myself a minute to think before I reacted. Silas pressed his fingertips against my palms, one at a time, almost like he was tapping out a beat.

"Do you hold hands?"

"Sometimes."

"And you share a bed?"

Another grimace. "Sometimes. Not always."

"You hold each other while you sleep?" I asked.

"Yeah," he said. "Sometimes."

"What else?" I prompted, seeing something lingering in the backs of his eyes that wasn't yet in the space between us.

"We kiss," he blurted, "and I understand that you—"

I groaned, taking one of my hands out of his grasp and covering his mouth before he could manage another word.

"Stop," I warned him. "Don't assume a single thing about whatever you think my response to this is going to be."

He pursed his lips, the slightest pucker against my palm. Eyes wide over the side of my hand, he nodded, and I let my hand fall away.

"You and Lincoln have a platonic relationship, yes?"

"Yes. Yeah. We're not…we're not interested in each other. I don't want him the way I want you."

"And that's mutual?"

Silas nodded, brows knit together in worry.

"Are you certain?" I asked.

"It's been this way for years," he said. "We talked about it a long time ago, and we're definitely on the same page."

"If the two of you are only friends, why do you kiss each other?"

"Because it feels good?" He phrased it like a question, adding a shrug. "Not good like it turns either of us on, good in like…I don't know how to explain it. It's more than a hug. It's just…I don't know, Marshall. I can stop. We can stop. That's what I wanted to talk to you—"

I covered his mouth again, giving him a weary look to remind him of what I'd just said.

"And you're here now, asking me if you have to lose those things with him to have me?"

He nodded.

In another life, the answer would have been a quick and resounding yes. With any other partner, it would have been a yes. But there was something so inherently different about Silas, different about my feelings for him, that made the prospect of telling him it had to stop feel like a cruel and unusual punishment.

"I want you to feel loved at all times, sweetheart." I pulled my hand away from his mouth and slid it around his cheek, my fingers stretching around the side of his neck and into his hair. Silas leaned into me like our bodies were made to fit together, mold together this way and all ways.

"I don't want you to scene with anyone besides me, but the rest…" I paused. Thought. "I have more questions about the kissing."

"Ask me," he rasped.

"Does it make you hard to kiss him?"

"No." He shook his head. "It's more of… like a warmth in my chest. Like a hug."

"A mouth hug," I murmured, chuckling under my breath.

"We don't do it a lot. Just…sometimes it happens or, no. It doesn't *just* happen."

Anyone else would have been a no. Anyone else wasn't Silas.

"I understand what you mean," I said. And, somehow, I did. "No more scenes. Lincoln is not to be dominant to you in any way."

"Yes," he agreed, breathy, still pressing his cheek into my palm. He reached out, grabbing both of my thighs with his hands for balance as he swayed closer to me.

"No one is dominant to you except me."

"Yes, Marshall."

He used my name again like an honorific, and it was embarrassing to admit how badly it made me want to melt into the floor.

"The rest is…fine."

His entire face changed, morphing from worry to shock to a relief that had his eyes filling with tears. Silas blinked hard, forcing them down, and he practically crawled across the space between us until he was balanced in my lap on a barstool that was definitely not rated for both of our weights.

"Do you mean it?" he asked, our noses brushing together, lips inches apart.

I'd only kissed him once.

I wrapped one arm around his waist to hold his balance, pressed my fingers into the back of his head with the other.

"I'm always your Dom, Silas, but I won't always tell you what to do," I said. "Does that make sense? I don't want to dictate every facet of your life, but when I give an order—"

"I'll follow it," he said.

"In or out of the bedroom."

"Yes."

"I meant what I said before, that I won't ever do anything to jeopardize any of your relationships. I won't ever ask you to do anything that will hurt you—or anyone else, for that matter. I won't put you in danger, even though sometimes it might feel like it."

Silas moaned, hips rocking against mine.

"Give me some limits," I said. "Tell me how far I can go."

We were almost too close together for the conversation to be as balanced as I needed it to be, but it was impossible to keep my hands off of him. I'd already shown so much restraint, and Silas tested my resolve at every turn. With his bravery, with his honesty, his talent, his unbridled passion for his work…for me.

"No marks that will show at work," he bit the words out like every one of them was a fight. "Don't ignore me as a punishment."

"I would never."

"I'm not a huge fan of canes, but I would like to be."

My dick surged to full-mast. "I love canes."

"Good." Silas chewed his lip between his teeth. "What about you?"

"I won't abide a brat, Silas."

"Understood," he said, nodding quickly. "Anything else?"

"I'll use red if anything needs to stop, same as I expect from you. Also, aftercare is a non-negotiable. I'll always make sure we have time for it. That I have time for you."

Precum leaked against my underwear.

I'd always enjoyed the discussion and the negotiation of a scene, the way talking about what I was about to do was like foreplay in and of itself. The hint of arousal with it all, the tease and the promise. But this, like all things with Silas, was so much more than that. The man in my lap was dangerously close to consuming me, and he didn't even know. Could he tell how affected I was by the sight of him? The proximity of him?

"Yes," he said, and I shuddered, realizing he was agreeing to my limits, not commenting on a thought he'd never heard. "Does this mean you want me to call you Sir now?"

Very back in the present moment, I trailed my hand down his cheek, over his arm, down his side to his waist. I held him hard, held him steady, encouraging him to grind down into my lap to chase the friction he was after.

"Have I earned it?"

Silas exhaled against my mouth, breath quivering as it ghosted across my lips.

"I think so," he whispered.

Something burned and expanded in the middle of my chest, pressing against my sternum and my ribs. I swallowed hard to keep whatever it was inside of me, unsure about the repercussions of letting it out.

"Then, yes."

"When?" he asked.

"Whenever you want, Silas. Or whenever I tell you. But it doesn't have to be all the time." I dug my thumbs into his hips. "I do very much love the way you say my name too."

He let loose a sound that was half-groan, half-sigh.

"What do you want from me, Marshall?"

Anything.

Everything.

"I want to kiss you," I admitted.

"What are you wa—"

I didn't bother letting him finish the sentence. I no longer needed permission. Our mutual consent was a band wrapped around the both of us that we'd always wear. I'd check the tension on it often, make sure it was still comfortable and right, safe in the ways that mattered, but we had our understanding now.

I slanted my mouth against his and gave him exactly what we both wanted.

CHAPTER 21
SILAS

Kissing Marshall felt a lot like coming home.

With a groan that I felt all the way down to my bones, Marshall stood up. I wrapped my legs around his waist to balance myself, relishing in his strength as he carried me out of the kitchen and into the bedroom. He sank down onto the bed with one knee, then ever so gently laid me onto my back.

He never broke the kiss.

I unwound my legs from his waist so I could make more room for him between my thighs, but he tapped me on the knee and grunted into my mouth. I put my legs back around him and my arms too, for good measure, shivering when he reached between our bodies and shoved down the waistband of my sweatpants. There was more fussing, and then Marshall's strong hand circled around both of our cocks.

He tore his mouth away from mine, kissing his way up my jaw and to my ear, down the side of my neck where he grazed his teeth across the thin and sensitive skin behind my ear.

"Come with me," he whispered, rutting against me while we both fucked through his tight fist. "I'm going to keep you up all night, Silas. Come now so you can last for it."

It was a promise and a threat, and Marshall kissed me again, spearing his tongue so deep into my mouth. I had no option but to yield for him in every possible way. His hand was rough and tight, and he came first, the entire weight of his body bearing down on mine as hot bursts of cum coated the length of my dick. He adjusted his grip enough to smear his cum all over my shaft, and when he wrapped his fist back around my cock and sank his teeth into my lower lip, it was over for me. I came hard, unexpectedly so, shouting and arching off the bed. The only thing holding me down was his weight on top of me, my limbs still twined around his. Marshall slowed everything, his body, his hand, his kiss, then he rocked back onto his heels and stared down at the mess we'd both made of ourselves.

"You unman me," he murmured.

His stare was heavy as he looked me over from the top of my head down to my thighs, nostrils flaring when he grabbed my sweatpants and tugged them down. I lifted a leg, and he stripped me of my pants and underwear, tossing it all over his shoulder without so much as a second glance. My shirt was sticky with cum, and he grabbed the hem next, tugging it up and over my head before adding it to the pile of clothes on the floor. He was still fully dressed, his cock soft and plump against his thigh.

"Forced orgasms?" he asked softly, curling his fingers around my shaft. His hands were so much bigger than mine, fingertips meeting in the middle where mine barely reached around the thickest part of me.

"Right now or another time?"

"Yes."

The breath left my lungs, and I sank down into the sheets.

"Yes," I answered.

"Denial?"

I squeezed my eyes shut and nodded.

"Nipples?"

"Yes."

"Is there any part of you that's off-limits?" he asked, stroking with almost no pressure in his grip at all.

"No."

His hand reached the tip of my dick, and he slid his thumb through my slit, pressing the corner of his nail against my piss hole. "Not even here?"

"I...I've never."

"Is it off-limits?" he asked again, lifting his thumb away and returning his attention to my shaft. It was a simple move, but then nothing with Marshall was simple. He didn't have the consent he was always chasing, so he would refrain until he did.

"No," I told him. "I would try it."

"I would start small, Silas." He applied pressure to the head of my dick, pulling down to spread my slit open, expose me. "I would only stretch you until you forgot how to speak."

Shivering, I fisted the sheets and groaned when my hips lifted off the bed, clearly entranced at the promise of his threat.

"Blindfolds?" he asked next.

I nodded.

"What else?"

My cheeks burned, and I told him, "I like being told what to do."

I didn't have strong feelings one way or another about humiliation, but I did find in most instances it made me hard.

"Praise?" he asked next. "Humiliation?"

"Sometimes yes."

"I think you like praise all the time." He tested the correction, tightening his hand around my erection to gauge my arousal. "Humiliation sometimes, maybe. In context."

In reply, I whimpered.

Marshall hummed, moving through his mental checklist. "Clearly you like bondage and spanking."

"Very much." My shaft pulsed against Marshall's palm.

The conversation was killing me. He touched me with such tenderness, and all I wanted was for him to rough handle me right into another orgasm.

"And you like it rough."

"Yeah. Yes." My nodding turned more aggressive. "Dangerously so."

He pursed his lips, turning his head at a slight angle to continue his appraisal of me. "Elaborate."

"I like when it hurts. I like if I'm a little scared I've gone too far," I admitted.

"And you've pursued this with strangers?" he asked, letting go of my cock and grabbing my thighs. Marshall hauled me a couple of feet down the bed until the backs of my thighs were on top of his, my lower half higher in the air than my upper half.

"Sometimes."

He walked his fingers over the tops of my legs until they were nestled against the insides of my thighs, and then he pinched me.

Hard.

The sharp stings were blinding, and my body instinctively fought against his, thrashing to chase escape but only twisting myself deeper into the shocking pinch.

"That's careless," he said, releasing my skin.

"I know."

"I encourage your friendship with Lincoln in whatever form the two of you need that to take, but you will treat my body with more care than you have been. Isn't that right, Silas?" He delivered a sharp slap against the quickly blooming pinprick bruise. "This body is mine now, right?"

"Yes," I whimpered. "Yes. Yes. I'm sorry."

And I was.

"Good." His fingers turned gentle, soothing the places he'd just hit. "How do you feel about exhibitionism?"

"Depends."

"On?"

"Context," I said.

He made a thoughtful sound. "Duly noted. What about free use?"

"I…" My tongue stuck to the roof of my mouth.

"It wouldn't be entirely free. It would be people I selected. Vetted. There would be rules, of course."

"You take care of your things," I murmured, and Marshall smiled down at me like I was a prize worth winning. "Also context, I think."

"Thank you for being honest with me." He petted his hands down my thighs toward my knees, and the only thing I wanted to do was bare myself entirely for him. With the current line of questioning, we were well on the way. "Breath play?"

I managed another nod.

He narrowed his eyes. "You like to be forced, don't you? You like to fight."

My entire body burned with embarrassment. No one had ever put two and two together so quickly—ever—before. Not even Lincoln. It was one thing to like rough sex; it was another to like being on the wrong edge of that kind of thing. One was okay to ask for and the other…not so much.

"Sometimes," I confirmed, covering my face with both of my hands.

Marshall, of course, wasn't having it. He grabbed both of my wrists with one hand, using his body weight to lever over me. Pinning my wrists against the bed and bending my legs so my knees shot up toward my ears, he rutted himself against me. The prong of his belt dug sharply into the sensitive area right beside my balls, but it only made my cock harder.

"What else do you like?" he asked, nipping at my earlobe. "What do you want?"

"I want to submit," I answered.

"It's that simple, is it?"

"It feels the opposite of that for most people." God, it was hard to fucking think with his mouth moving so slow down the side of my neck.

"I'm not most people."

"No," I agreed.

"And neither are you."

I shook my head, and he sealed his lips around my collarbone, kissing me messily there, but gently. No marks.

"You want to just submit sometimes, don't you?" he asked, licking the place he'd just kissed.

I closed my eyes, trying to imagine how it would feel if he sucked a bruise into the bone.

"Want to give it all up, pain or not…sex or not."

Fuck, it was painful to be known. "Yes."

The Sir was right there on the tip of my tongue. It felt so perfect in the moment, laced with all the knowledge and understanding, and he'd told me not to use it until he'd earned it, and hadn't he earned it? Wasn't all of this him earning it? The consent, the negotiation, the understanding…the care.

"Sir," I blurted it out, and he went still, face still buried into the crook of my neck. "Yes, Sir. I want to submit."

His dick pulsed against my groin, but other than that, he was entirely unmoving and quiet. Seconds passed, minutes, an hour, a day—I didn't know—until finally Marshall smiled against my skin, his teeth slick and cool. He shifted his weight and reached between our bodies, pressing his fingertips against my hole. Not hard enough to breach the ring of muscle, but just enough to test the resistance.

"You want to submit," he repeated.

"Yes."

"To me."

"Yes," I said again.

"If I ever go too far, you'll tell me to stop?" he asked.

"I'll use my safe word."

Marshall groaned, moving his fingers away from my hole. He curled his hands around the backs of my thighs and hiked my legs higher…until my hamstrings burned, then he lifted his body up enough to see my face. He didn't look anything like the man I knew. Marshall was undone, hair a little loose, pupils bigger and darker than I'd ever seen.

"Is stop not a safe word here, Silas?" he asked.

"No." My mouth moved more than words came out. I shook my head to double up on the answer.

"Okay," he agreed, matching my head shake with a nod of understanding. "Thank you for telling me. What about no?"

I shook my head quicker.

"Don't?"

"No," I rasped.

"The only safe word is red?" he asked.

"Or whatever you tell me to do if I can't speak," I whispered.

"So gags are a yes."

"Yes," I croaked.

Marshall inhaled deeply, dragging his hands over my legs, up my stomach, and toward my chest. "I can't decide if you're a dream come true or an absolute nightmare."

A nervous laugh bubbled out of my throat. "Probably both."

He smiled, laughing in a much less obnoxious way. "You're probably right about that."

He kept his hands moving all over my body, drawing lines and circles up my ribs and down my stomach when he wasn't busy cradling my cock and balls in his hand. The attention was simple and too much all at the same time. It all felt like a precursor to something more, but nothing more ever came. It was mindless soft touches, careless swirls that felt like they had no real direction. I closed my eyes and imagined him a cartographer, committing the lines and peaks of my body to memory for future exploration.

After a while, the anticipation died down, my nerves with it. I was no longer waiting for him to do something more severe, something more sexual. His exploration and attention had turned me into a pool of Jello on his bed, content and malleable under his touch. The shapes and lines were foreplay on their own, and though I was sure none of his touches were drawn with the intent to arouse, they still did.

By the time his hands made it back between my legs, my cock was achingly hard, thick and leaking against my stomach. With the flat underside of his middle finger, he drew a line from my balls to my crown, then retracted it back down. Over and over again, until the muscles on my legs quaked.

"You're trembling, sweetheart," he said softly, turning his hand so my dick slid across the heel of it. It was the most contact he'd given me since he'd stopped talking, and I was only seconds away from crying about it. The weight of his hand was slight, but the relief was more than welcome.

I hadn't even realized he'd been walking me toward another orgasm until it was there, hot and heavy in my balls. I didn't even have to warn him about it. My breathing hitched, and Marshall finally made a fist around the base of my cock, squeezing, squeezing, *squeezing*, until he'd guided me back from the cliff. Sucking in a sharp breath, I blinked hard, tears fighting to break free against the backs of my eyelids. The sheets were wet in my fists, and I'd gone from trembling to vibrating. His touch was no longer gentle, my body was on fire, and everything was torture, and when the realization inside of me shifted, Marshall saw it.

Of course he did.

He stroked my cock from root to tip, bending down over me. I opened my eyes in time to see him spit on his fingers, to feel the heat of his saliva slick my shaft.

"There you are," he murmured, and there was no way he could have been talking about me because I'd never felt more lost.

"Hmn?" I blinked hard, tears sliding free from the corners of my eyes. If he saw them, at first he paid them no mind, so neither did I.

"Now that you're properly mine, now that you're properly ready." His fingers were thorns around my dick, even with the spit, especially with the spit. "Now, Silas…we can begin."

CHAPTER 22
MARSHALL

Cleary, I had died and gone to heaven.

A thousand things I wanted to do to Silas and now that I had the opportunity, choosing where to start was beyond comprehension. He looked like a dream on my bed, naked and flushed and so very horny for me.

So very submissive.

His pupils were so dilated I could barely make out the golden amber of his irises, and the way he stared up at me like I hung the moon was intoxicating. He licked his lips, pulling them between his teeth to stifle a moan, and I knew exactly what I wanted to do with him. I rocked backward and climbed off the bed, holding up a finger and gesturing for him to stay still. Silas wiggled down deeper into the sheets, his hooded gaze tracking me from the bed to the closet and back again.

I produced a leather blindfold and beckoned him closer with the crook of my finger. For someone who was as strung out on lust as he was, he moved quickly, flipping onto all fours and crawling toward the foot of the bed before easing off and making his way toward me. His ass swung in the air like he knew exactly what he was doing, the purples and greens of the bruises I'd left for him still the most brilliant kaleidoscope I'd ever seen.

Instead of bringing him to his feet, I bent down to his level and fastened the blindfold around his eyes. It wasn't one of those flimsy strips of fabric meant for casual playtime. No, it was a sturdy cutout of leather with raised pads around the outer rim effectively sealing the wearer's vision off entirely. After checking the Velcro at the back of his head, I stroked my fingers through his hair and down the front of his face.

"How many fingers am I holding up?"

Silas exhaled loudly. "If you weren't touching me, I wouldn't even know where you were."

I grabbed his face, hard, fingers digging into his cheeks and yanking his face upward toward mine even though he couldn't see me. "How many fingers?" I repeated.

"I don't know, Sir," he answered, appropriately chastened.

"That's better." I let him go and gave myself the opportunity to study the top of his messy hair, the slope of his back as it curved into his ass. He looked so fucking good on his knees, but something was missing. I left him in the middle of my room and went back to the closet, returning with the cuffs I'd used on him the first night. I fastened his wrists together behind his back, then stepped to the side to admire my handiwork.

It was nowhere near the state I wanted to see him in, but the conversation about limits and our own agreement was still so fresh. I didn't want to push either of us too far and ruin things before they even had a chance to get started. Silas wanted to submit, and he looked so gorgeous on his knees, I decided I wanted to keep him there as often as possible.

"You were so close to coming earlier, weren't you?" I worked my fingers through his hair, down the sides of his face toward his cheeks.

"Yes, Sir."

Fuck, I loved the sound of that.

"I ruined it for you, didn't I?"

"Yes." The answer was scratchier, like it was harder for him to say and still be honest. "Yes, Sir."

I hummed, kicking my foot into the space between his legs. I lifted up, pressing against the underside of his balls and drawing a low groan out of him. With the hand that wasn't in his hair, I stroked my cock, pointing it down for a couple of pulls before tapping it against the corner of his mouth.

"You can come again after you make me come," I told him, smearing precum around his parted lips. He opened them wider, and I slid onto his tongue. His mouth was just as hot and wet as I remembered, and I thrust slowly toward the back of his throat.

Silas had a bit of a gag reflex, which I loved. I pushed past it until his body convulsed, then I pulled all the way out.

"Can you snap, Silas?" I asked, pinching myself off at the base so I didn't spray my load all over his face.

"Yes."

"Show me."

He gave me two decent snaps from behind his back, and I put my dick in his mouth again.

"That's how you tell me if you want me to stop," I said. He managed a nod and then choked around the head of my dick a second time.

I went slowly with him, one inch after another after another. Every time he gagged, his throat convulsed and held me tighter. I wasn't going to last long at all, but I needed to do better.

"After I come, you can use my leg to get yourself off. Do you understand?"

Another jerky nod. He tilted his chin back like he wanted to look up at me, but all I could see of his face was the thick black blindfold keeping me out of his vision. I traced my thumb across the places his eyelids would be, wanting to know how much he liked his predicament.

"Ride my leg while you suck me," I said, letting my hand fall away from his face. "I want to feel how much you like choking on dick. How much you like being blind to what's coming next."

Silas groaned and situated himself over the top of my foot, inching closer until his erection pressed against my ankle and my calf. His pleasure vibrated through me, and I grabbed the back of his head, holding his mouth still. His hips never stopped moving, chasing after pleasure that he was already dangerously close to, considering I was yet to get off.

A tight tug on his hair was enough warning for him to slow his pace and focus on his mouth, hollowing his cheeks and using so much spit it leaked down his chin and my balls.

"You sound like a slut, sweetheart," I murmured, taking his face into both of my hands so I could properly fuck his throat. "You sound perfect. Now open wide and let me finish myself off."

Silas whimpered, and I tightened my hold on his head. I fucked into his mouth hard enough that it was impossible for him to keep his teeth off of me, but the streaks of pain only spurred me on harder. He humped himself against my leg again, making breathy and wet noises of pleasure that were drowned out by the roaring in my ears.

He sucked me like his throat had been created to be painted with my cum, so I made sure to give it to him. My second orgasm rolled down my spine like a tidal wave, and I moaned out Silas's name as I shot my load against the back of his throat. He barely even sputtered, working the muscles of his throat to swallow my cum into his stomach instead of letting the copious amounts of spit in his mouth rinse it down his chin. I bucked against his face, the aftershocks of my orgasm almost enough to knock me off my feet.

After I finished, my grip on his head turned softer, and he made a needy little whine. He flattened his tongue against the underside of my shaft and sucked at my dick like he was trying to get me hard again. The connector chain on the cuffs rattled, and Silas began to move against my leg like I'd put a time limit on his release.

Three pumps of his lips later and he cried out around my cock, taking me all the way down to the root. His body fell forward against me, and hot cum burned against my calf through my slacks. It was hot and sticky, and it glued him to me. I slipped my hand around the back of his head, holding up his weight while his body trembled through the rest of his orgasm. My cock was still in his mouth, getting harder every second, so I eased back and tucked my erection into the waistband of my underwear. I'd deal with it later, after checking on him.

"Hey." I tipped his head back, traced the outline of his mouth with my thumbs. His lips were shiny and swollen. "Stick out your tongue."

He did, and it was pink and perfect like his cock. Not a drop of cum to be seen.

"You swallowed all of it, didn't you?" I asked, even though we both knew it was rhetorical. I tugged his lower lip before letting it go.

"Yes, Sir."

"Did you even taste it, or did I come too deep for that?"

"Too deep," he whispered.

"I'll make sure to be more generous next time."

Silas hummed. He moaned. "Thank you, Sir."

Slowly, and only after making sure he could support his own weight, I extricated myself from him. He made a sad noise but held himself steady. I took a step back to study him, the pale flush on his chest, the smears of cum down his cock and his stomach, the way his mouth hung open like he was desperate for it to always be filled. He was truly a vision, like nothing I'd seen before or would ever see again.

Absentmindedly, I picked at the beginnings of a hangnail on my cuticle, catching my own breath while leaving him suspended in that post-orgasm haze of uncertainty.

"I want you to know you've made me a very happy man tonight," I said, and I meant every word.

His slutty gaping mouth tipped upward into a smile. "Thank you, Sir."

"I also want you to know I love the way that honorific sounds coming out of your mouth."

A bigger smile.

"You look so beautiful on your knees, I want to keep you there."

"Yes, please."

"How's the blindfold?" I asked.

"So good," he murmured.

Fuck, he *really* liked it. Silas was a submissive down to the core of his being, and it was suddenly imperative to me that I figure out how to be enough for him. I'd never doubted my skill as a Dom before, but I'd also never played with a submissive like Silas.

There was no room to miss, no chances to make mistakes.

"I'm going to go wash up," I said. "Don't move."

"Yes, Sir."

He was so breathy, so obedient.

I watched him for another minute, then went into the bathroom. I stripped out of my clothes and turned on the shower, then quietly lingered in the doorway, leaning against the doorjamb to watch Silas. True to his word—and my command—he didn't move. He barely even shifted, hardly breathed. The cuffs rattled once, but other than that, I watched in awe as Silas sank deeper and deeper into his submission.

When my own knees began to hurt, I went back to the

shower and finally stepped under the spray. I rinsed myself quickly, only washing where necessary, then I turned off the water. I toweled off on my way back into the bedroom and still no movement. If the hitch in his breathing hadn't given him away, I would have wondered if he'd fallen asleep like that. I came to a stop in front of him and dropped down into a squat so we were eye level, even if he didn't know it.

"I want you to stay the night," I said.

I want you to stay every night.

"I would like that."

"I also want to talk to you about rules. Expectations."

Silas swallowed, chin tilting up a little. His face chased after the sound of my voice like a sunflower followed the sun.

"I want you ready for me always," I warned, pausing to make sure he understood what I meant. "You can take care of that before you come over or you can do it here upon your arrival."

He nodded and whispered, "Yes, Sir."

"Sometimes I'll have a preference about it, sometimes I won't. But I'll always make sure you know what I want."

"Thank you, Sir."

"No orgasms unless I ask them of you," I said next. "Don't even touch yourself unless I've told you to."

"Yes, Sir."

"I want you to go get tested on your lunch break tomorrow."

He swallowed, chest going hollow with his breath.

"And I'll do the same. Once we're both in the clear, I'm going to take you bare. Is that a problem?"

"No, Sir."

"I might use condoms during role play. And if and when I decide to share you, anyone else who even looks at you will be wrapped."

Silas managed half a laugh on his next breath. "Thank you, Sir."

"You will eat three meals a day, and you will stay hydrated." I traced the backside of my teeth with my tongue. "If I find out you are not taking care of yourself, you will not like the punishment I come up with. Are we clear?"

"Crystal."

"Do you still like the blindfold?" I asked.

"Yes, Sir. Very much."

"Okay." I dropped the knot on my towel and pulled his body toward mine. "Then let's continue."

CHAPTER 23
SILAS

The bruises from my first night with Marshall were finally starting to fade and the intensity of their pain lessened. No matter how hard I shifted my weight in my office chair, I wasn't met with any more than the occasional bite of remembrance. It hadn't been long but felt like an eternity since our first scene at his house and a lifetime since our most important negotiation, but we were still working to find a routine that worked with both of our schedules. I'd gotten tested, as he required, and we were both now in receipt of my negative test results. We just hadn't had an opportunity to get together.

He saw his brothers often, but every Friday night was spoken for, which didn't bother me at all because that meant I could promise Friday dinners to Lincoln, which he loved. He was nervous about the development of my relationship with Marshall, mostly because of not wanting things to change between us. When I told him they didn't have to, the relief was palpable and he'd jumped onto my lap and kissed me on the mouth.

It was nice to still have that with Lincoln.

Nice for Marshall to understand the difference between romantic love and platonic love and to not be threatened by it.

I'd spent a Tuesday and Wednesday with Marshall but had finally caved and told him I didn't want to overdo it. I wanted to dive headfirst into things with him, but I also didn't want to appear too young or too eager. Like, I didn't ask to come over; I waited for him to invite me. Honestly, that was probably part self-preservation and part submission. There was meant to be a natural order about things between us and throttling my desire to be with him twenty-four hours a day seemed to align with the latter.

A knock on the conference room door had me looking up from the blank screen on my laptop and into my dad's tired eyes. He had on brown slacks and a white button-up, which I'd always thought was overkill considering he was so rarely client-facing, but it was practically his uniform. I remembered him wearing a tie when I was younger but hadn't seen one around his neck in years.

"Silas," he said, mouth pulled into a tight line.

"Hey, Dad. What's up?" I closed the lid on my laptop and leaned back in the old chair, hoping the creaks meant it was strong enough to hold my weight and not on its way to collapsing.

"I wanted to see when you'd have that updated bid for me."

I bit the inside of my cheek. "I haven't started it."

His eyes went wide, his expression morphing into a mask of horror. He tried to school his reaction, but it was such a big feeling he couldn't get it all under control.

"Why not? It's due this week."

"We both know you weren't going to use my draft." I rolled my eyes at him, annoyed that he'd given me busy work for no good reason like I was a ten-year-old trailing behind him into the office again on spring break or summer vacation.

"Do we?"

"You don't take me seriously," I reminded him. "You didn't even congratulate me after getting my article published."

"Of course I did."

"You threw it in the trash. Marshall is the one who congratulated me." My voice hitched at the use of Marshall's name, my throat not quite used to saying it at a normal cadence and not a moan anymore.

"I need your bid, Silas."

I shrugged. "I don't have it."

My dad worked his jaw back and forth and cursed under his breath. His entire body swayed, like he wasn't sure if he wanted to stay in the doorway, come in, or go out. The clock on the wall ticked closer to five, and I scratched the back of my neck, waiting for him to decide so I could pack my things up and leave.

"You don't understand what you've done," my dad muttered, shaking his head.

"If the answer is that I didn't waste my time on a fruitless endeavor, I know exactly what I did."

"I was going to use your bid, Silas."

He was so quiet, I barely heard him.

"Sorry, what?"

"I was going to submit yours for the final." He cracked his knuckles, shoved his hands into his pockets. "You were going to win us the job."

"You were going to submit mine?" I scoffed, pushing up out of my seat and grabbing my laptop. "You've done nothing but talk down to me about my design ideas since I graduated. You weren't going to use mine."

"Yours is the only design that will beat Covington." Marshall's last name rolled out of his mouth with a surprising bite of animosity. "We had to beat him."

"I can't decide if you're being real with me right now or not."

"Of course I'm *being real.*" It was almost a sneer, and I reeled back, putting more space between us.

"Be so fucking for real right now."

"Language."

"Language," I snapped back at him. "You refused to accept any of my ideas through the whole design process, and you submitted your work for the initial review period. Your design is the one that got us into the final round. Why would you change it to use mine at the last minute?"

"Because I wanted to win."

"You wanted to win." I sighed, tucking my laptop under my arm and trying to ignore the way my fingers trembled. "A month ago, I would have been so excited that you wanted to listen to my ideas finally, but now…now I just want to know what Marshall did to make you hate him so much that you'd even entertain the idea of listening to my ideas."

"It's not about him."

"Well, it's not about the project." I wanted to get out of the room, but my father was still in the doorway and the door was the only escape. "Or you would have collaborated with me in the first place. You would have read the article. You would have at least pretended to be proud of me instead of throwing my work into the literal garbage."

Marshall was proud of me. He'd offered me a job. And with the way this conversation was going with my dad, I might have to take him up on it after all.

"You really didn't put anything together?" he asked, scratching the side of his neck.

"I really didn't put anything together."

"You've just put us out of business."

A laugh gurgled up out of somewhere inside of me, terribly loud and horribly ill-timed. I tried to slap my free hand over my mouth to cover it but was half a second too late.

"You're laughing," he said.

"This is just the most ridiculous conve—"

"You're fired."

The laugh died in my throat, and I looked at my dad. Maybe I saw him for the first time…like really *saw* him.

"I'm fired?"

He nodded.

He shook his head.

"Okay," I conceded, gesturing toward the door he was blocking. "I'll go pack up my things."

He squared his shoulders, trying to fill the doorway. "That's it?"

"You're giving me whiplash, Dad. Do you want to fire me or not?"

"Do you even care that I'm firing you?" he shot back.

"If you took me seriously as an architectural designer, I might." I managed a tired shrug. "But you don't. And at the end of the day, you and I don't see eye to eye on design, so maybe it's better that we don't work together. Maybe it's… maybe it's time."

I left off the other part, that maybe it would be better if we didn't work together because whenever he found out I was involved with Marshall, things were going to get really hairy between us, and he would definitely fire me over that. He might even disown me.

He'd also ignored my question about why he hated Marshall so much. I knew they'd been in school at the same time, my dad being an adjunct professor when Marshall was a student, but I didn't understand the basis of the issues. A clash of personality seemed not enough to warrant the dislike my father carried. Whatever the problem, though, it wasn't for me, but it would sure help shed some light on why my dad had finally decided taking Marshall down was an adequate use of *my* talents.

"We can't lose this bid, Silas," he said.

I finally took a step around the side of the table, heading for the door while being terribly uncertain if my legs would get me there. I'd never stood up to my dad before, and I was scared out of my mind. Walking out of the door was the same as walking off a cliff, and I'd wanted to enjoy the start of my relationship with Marshall, not put it to the test.

"We didn't," I said sharply, pointing at his chest. "You did."

That seemed to catch him off-guard, and he wobbled on his feet just enough for me to slide past him. I went to my office and tucked my laptop into my bag, grabbed a framed photo of me and Lincoln off my desk, then checked my pockets for my wallet, phone, and keys, and walked toward the door. I stopped before getting it open, shifting everything around to get to my keys.

There wasn't much on the ring. A key to my apartment, my car key, the key to the office…I twisted the last one off of the ring and walked back into the office. My dad was still half in the conference room, facing the table like we were still in conversation. I set the key on top of his desk and stared at his back for a minute.

"I'm sorry, Dad."

He didn't look at me, and he didn't offer me an apology in return. Not like it would have done any good. I knew in my bones that it wouldn't be enough to keep me there with him, and it was too late for me to do the work he wanted anyway.

Walking to my car, I tried to convince myself it wasn't my fault if the business went under. My dad was the owner and the boss, the failure and the loss would be his, just like any wins had always also been his. It wasn't my fault if Marshall won the Cahuenga job. It wasn't my fault if my dad lost his entire livelihood because of me…

The words all felt like lies, though, and by the time I got to my car, I was a sniffling and inconsolable mess. Before, I would have called Lincoln. He would know what to do. He would know what to say. But now I went back and forth between him and Marshall. Not wanting to ruin my friendship with Lincoln the same way I'd ruined the relationship with my dad, but also feeling desperate to be grounded in a way that only Marshall could offer.

Snorting up as much tears and snot as I could manage, I swiped through my contacts until I got to Marshall, and then I hit the phone button. It rang through and went to voicemail. I hung up and called Lincoln instead. He answered on the second ring.

"Are you off work?" he said instead of hello. "Do you want to get a drink?"

I cried.

"More than one drink then," he said. "What's wrong, Si?"

"My dad fired me."

The only sound was the wetness of my crying until Lincoln cleared his throat. "I know that feels bad right now, but it's the best thing to ever happen to you."

"How can—" I got cut off by a beep and a flash on the screen. Marshall was calling me back. "I've got to go."

"You can't just hang up on me after dropping that bomb."

"Marshall is calling," I said through a fresh wave of tears.

Lincoln made a knowing sound that made me cry harder. "Kay. Text me later."

"I'm sorry."

The phone beeped again.

"It's fine, Silas. It's normal," he said. "I love you, and you'll be fine."

"I love you." Another beep, and I accepted the call, hiccupping a sob into the receiver. "Hello?"

"Sorry I miss—" He cut himself off, like he had it all

rehearsed but realized something was off. "Are you okay, Silas? What's wrong?"

"Yes, I think. No, maybe. A lot is wrong."

"Are you hurt?"

"No."

"Are you in danger?" he asked.

"No." I laughed and choked on my own snot. "My dad."

"Is he hurt?"

"No, he's…he's alive," I said, forcing a breath. "He fired me."

Marshall was as quiet as Lincoln had been, but then he asked me again, "Are you all right, Silas?"

"He's mad I didn't write the bid. He said it's my fault he's going to close." I choked on a sob. "It's a lot."

"Yeah, I imagine it is." His tone was as soft as his mouth when he'd almost kissed me for the very first time. "Where are you?"

"In my car at the office."

"I'll be home in twenty minutes. Meet me there."

I'd never been more thankful for an order in my life.

"Yes, Sir," I whimpered, wiping my nose with the back of my hand. It was embarrassing to be so upset over something I wanted, something I needed. My tears were creeping toward hysterical, and I didn't think Marshall would ever cry this hard about anything in his whole life. My reaction was unstoppable, but every time I choked on my own tears, my body curled in on itself. I felt like an overly emotional child, and for as much as I didn't want Marshall to see me like this, there was no place else I wanted to be.

CHAPTER 24
MARSHALL

made it home five minutes before Silas arrived. I'd barely had time to undo the cuffs of my shirt when he pulled into my driveway and cut the ignition. He sat in the driver's seat for a while, a fact I knew only because I stood in the open doorway and watched him. He could have as much time as he needed, so I left the door open and headed back into the house. On the phone, he'd sounded inconsolable, but it appeared he had cried a lot of that out on the drive from work to my house. I was certain he had more in him, though, and together we would wring him dry of it.

Eventually, I heard his footsteps shuffle up the porch, then he kicked out of his shoes and moved them into their place against the wall. I'd never asked him to take off his shoes. He'd just…done it and never stopped, and if that wasn't the best description of Silas as a person, I didn't know what was.

"You look like you need a hug." I greeted him from the kitchen, pouring myself a glass of wine. Alcohol was the last thing Silas needed, and I would make sure he didn't get any.

He glanced up at me, eyes ringed red and the tip of his nose wet from tears or snot, or most likely both, and he shrugged.

"Even if you want one, I'm not offering. At least, not right now."

"Alright," he grumbled.

I chewed on my lip, studying him to make sure what I said to him really had time to sink in. This was a test for us both, because even though I was Silas's boyfriend, I was still his Dom, and while it was easy for those two things to engage with each other most days, there were times when one or the other would have to take precedence. Whether we liked it or not. And Silas did need a hug. I wanted to hug him. I wanted to wrap my arms around him and let him cry and protect him from whatever had gone down with his father, but first...

But first.

"The rules are the rules, Silas. When you're happy to be here and when you're not." I paused. "Did you come straight from work?"

"Yes."

"You can use the guest bathroom to clean up then," I said.

Silas tucked his chin toward his chest and sighed heavily.

"The attachment is already in the shower for you."

He worked his jaw back and forth, then nodded briefly. "I'll be right back."

"I know."

He swallowed hard enough for me to see his Adam's apple bob, then he headed down the hallway like the weight of the world bore down on his shoulders. I waited until the door closed, then I went back to the kitchen to have at the wine I'd been pouring at his arrival. The red blend was fruity and dry, and I appreciated the way the flavor raced down my throat with every swallow.

In the bathroom, the shower turned on, and I groaned, pressing down against the base of my shaft to fight off my arousal. The effort was futile. Knowing Silas was in the shower naked, knowing he was in there preparing himself for me...

The erection was hot and heavy between my legs.

I finished the glass of wine and waited for the shower to turn off, except ten minutes later, it still ran. I washed my empty glass and Silas was still in the shower, so I made the executive decision to go check on him. Knocking on the door before twisting the knob, I gave him a heads-up about my arrival, which was met with a sniffling hiccup of a cough.

"Is everything all right in there, Silas?" I asked.

"Yes," he mumbled.

"Have you taken care of things?"

Another sniffle. "No."

"Have you been crying the whole time?"

The glass door of the shower was covered in steam, but I didn't need him to wipe it away to see how his shoulders trembled with confirmation. I should have taken my clothes off, but I didn't think it through. I pulled the door back and stepped under the spray, welcoming Silas into my arms. I held him briefly, kissed the top of his head, then reached around him for the nozzle attachment.

"Let me help you," I whispered against the shell of his ear. He frowned against my chest, and I fought with the shower behind him, slicking the nozzle, pressing it between his cheeks and easing the steel length inside of him. Silas cried and tensed against me, fingers barely resting on my hips when I got the nozzle fully inserted.

"You're dressed," he murmured.

"You just now realized?" I stroked my hand down the length of his spine and sighed into his hair. I could feel him fighting his muscles to settle, even though he vibrated with all of the tears he still needed to let out.

It was going to be a long night.

"Let's sort you out so we can sort you out." I wrapped my arm around his back and banded our chests together. I was soaked, hair in my face and clothes sticking to every crevice of my body, but I'd deal with it later. My comfort was secondary.

He nodded his consent, because while we'd agreed he would do this, we'd never truly discussed my involvement with the process. I think he understood, though, that it was my job to help when he needed it, and in that moment, he needed it.

I flipped the valve on the shower head, and Silas started, going tense again before baring his teeth against my shoulder and letting out a whimper that had no business turning me on as much as it did.

"There you go," I whispered to him, holding him tighter when he tried to fight away from me.

Together in the shower, we filled him, and when he grunted at me, I flipped the valve back to the overhead spray. Silas dug his fingers harder into my waist when I eased out the nozzle, and then he let everything go. Neither of us checked it, because the cleanliness was only half the point, at least as far as I was concerned. Silas was a twenty-five year old, virile man who bottomed exclusively. I didn't need to check to know he took care of himself that way.

He still cried against my chest, so I kept him in my arms after I turned off the water, only pulling away long enough to wrap him in a towel. I set him on the closed toilet, then stripped out of my soiled clothes. Leaving them in a pile on the floor of the shower, I wrapped the other towel around my waist and turned my attention back to Silas.

Tapping my first finger against my thumb, I studied Silas carefully, knowing whatever decision I made for him, it had to be the right one. There were a lot of ways for me to get Silas to the place he needed to be, but not all of them were ideal. Some would do more harm than good; some could shatter trust where others would fortify it. Finally deciding, I guided Silas into the bedroom.

"Get dressed, sweetheart," I said gently, getting him some

sweats and a clean t-shirt from my dresser. My clothes were huge on him, but I loved the way they hung loosely on his slender frame. "Let's go into the dining room."

He didn't agree, but he didn't protest. Silas toweled himself off and wore my clothes like they were his, and then he followed me into the dining room. I pulled out a chair for him, and he sat down with another wet inhale. Detouring into the kitchen, I poured myself another glass of wine and got a water bottle for Silas. I took both to the table and set them down.

"Drink," I said, and he begrudgingly twisted the cap off and took a sip. I narrowed my eyes, and he took a regular-sized swallow. "Wait here."

After a quick stop in my home office and then my living room, I was back. I dropped the newest issue of *LA Design Digest* on the table in front of him and a legal pad and pen on top of that.

"Transcribe the article."

"What?"

He looked up at me, eyes wide and confused. I sat down in the seat opposite him and took a drink of wine. We were both going to be there for a while.

"Transcribe it. Copy it. Write it down."

I could see the protest in him, but he swallowed it back and flipped open the magazine. It took over an hour for him to get through the whole thing, two bottles of water, and the rest of my glass of wine. Finally, he made an exhausted sound and dropped the pen on the table.

"There."

I pulled a red pen out of my pocket and slid it across the table and into his hand.

"Now annotate it."

"I'm sorry, what?"

I arched a brow. "Annotate it."

He probably didn't realize it, but he hadn't cried in almost twenty minutes, and if the set of his brow was any indicator, he'd gotten himself through the worst of it. Silas and I both knew he came over looking for pain. He wanted the emotional reset that came from being hit hard enough to catapult his brain right into subspace, but I saw immediately on his arrival that wasn't what he needed. Silas needed to recenter around himself and remember he was better than Stanley had made him feel, and he had to do that on his own, not by my hand.

Forty-five minutes later, Silas capped the pen and shoved the paper and magazine toward me.

"Annotated," he said.

I'd read the article enough times to know the ins and outs of it, but I was genuinely curious about the notes he'd make in the margins. Silas's notes quoted government-funded studies about energy and waste, and psychology journals and their opinions on the importance of introducing green spaces into urban areas. He made notes about a percentage he wished he had triple-checked before committing it to the final draft, and even a few lines about things he'd learned since the initial submission. In all, the annotation proved what I—and Stanley —had known all along.

Silas was ahead of his time.

The only difference was I'd recognized it as a benefit, and Stanley had seen it as a threat until it was too late for him to backtrack. He'd done the damage and, for whatever reason, blamed his own downfall on Silas's brilliance, then fired him to boot. There was no logic behind it, only the machinations of an old and desperate man. He'd acted that way once before, when he was much, much younger. It was such a blip in my memory, and I filed it away in favor of reading the final bits of Silas's notes, which ended just as intelligently as they'd started.

"Why did you decide to pursue architecture?" I asked.

He sucked his teeth at me then said, "My dad."

No new tears fell.

"Why did you continue with architecture?"

"Because I loved it."

"Past tense?"

Silas scrunched his nose. "I love it."

I stabbed my finger against the first page of his transcription. "You're too good at this to walk away from it."

"I never said I wanted to," he protested.

"But you thought about it. I could hear it in your voice when you called."

"How co—"

I cut him off. "Am I wrong? Are you telling me I'm wrong?"

He snapped his mouth closed and blinked hard a few times before looking down at his own handwriting. "No."

"You're too good to work for him forever," I said next. "This is a blessing."

"I've never even tried to look for a job. And I know you said I can work for you, but I—"

I raised a hand, silencing him again. "It would never work because I'm not foolish enough to hire someone who could put me out of business in less than three projects."

His cheeks burned, but he didn't argue.

"If you worked for me, I'd be obsolete before the end of the year."

"I doubt that."

"It's not your place to argue," I reminded him. "But what I was going to say was that I'm good friends with a consultant who recently moved to LA from New York. His name is Cory Callahan, and I'd like to get the two of you in touch. If you're agreeable."

Tears filled Silas's eyes, but they were so different from the ones he'd been crying earlier.

"Yes, please. Thank you." He cleared his throat. "Thank you, Sir."

"That's my job, sweetheart." I pushed my chair back from the table and came around to meet him in his seat, kissing the top of his head and tracing my fingers over his hair. "It's almost nine. Have you had dinner?"

"I came straight from work."

"But you've had lunch?" I asked.

"Lunch and breakfast," Silas answered, his stare on me as I carried my empty wine glass into the kitchen. "Just like you told me to."

"Good boy." For the first time since his arrival, a smile pulled at his lips. "Stay right there then. I'll get you something to eat, and then we can talk some more and finish our night."

CHAPTER 25
SILAS

woke up on my stomach, the smell of coffee in my nose and the press of Marshall's strong hands against the small of my back. He was a heavy weight on top of me, nose dragging up the back of my neck, trailed by his mouth leaving a blistering trail of kisses along my hairline. Beneath him I groaned, lifting myself off the bed to meet the hard length of his cock against my ass. He was naked and warm, his body substantial and his cock pressing against me like my favorite kind of invitation.

"You're awake?" he murmured, rubbing against me like a cat.

I spread my legs as much as his weight would allow to make room for him there.

"I'm awake. What time is it?"

"Too early for you to worry about what time it is," he said, nipping at my earlobe. Above me, Marshall shifted his hand between our bodies, pointing his cock—which was slick with lube—against my hole.

Taking him at his word, I closed my eyes and breathed in deep. I *was* awake, but my head ached from the embarrassing volume of crying I'd done the night before. After Marshall made me handwrite my article, he fed me veggies and fruit and made out with me until I was near tears again, desperate to get off. Instead, he tucked me into bed, and I fell asleep wrapped in the safe cocoon of his arms.

The slick, blunt tip of his dick brushed across my hole, but Marshall denied me. He entered me with two slippery fingers, thrusting with his whole body to get in. I buried my face in the pillow and groaned, trying to deepen the arch in my back to make access easier for him, but whenever I tried to shift or move, he stopped.

"If I want your help, I'll tell you," he warned, easing his fingers out of me.

I forced myself to stillness, and Marshall rewarded me with the thick stretch of his cock.

He cursed under his breath, sinking every inch of his dick into me with one agonizingly slow and slippery thrust. Staying still was work, every muscle in my body waking up hungry to respond. This was what I'd wanted the night before, and this was what he'd deprived me of.

"You feel…" Marshall trailed off, sucking a sloppy kiss against the sensitive spot behind my ear. He didn't finish the sentence, but he didn't have to. Feeling him bare was like heaven. The stretch, the friction, the veins of his cock…

Marshall grabbed my arms out from under me and pinned my wrists behind me, and my eyes rolled.

"God, I wanted to wake you up and slow fuck you, but when I get inside of you, I turn into an animal." He growled in my ear, pressing his weight down onto my wrists and slamming into me with enough force to knock the breath out of my lungs.

It was the best way to wake up.

My dick was hard as a rock, twisted in the sheets, and the tension only tightened with every pump of Marshall's hips. It was like being choked down there, the pressure an unexpected burst of pleasure. With a low grunt, he released my wrists and grabbed my hips, yanking me up so my chest pressed against the bed. The sheets unfurled from around my dick, and he thrust into me even harder than before. With my ass up in the air, he had a better angle and with the blood flow returning to my erection, I found myself lightheaded and gasping.

"Come," he told me, low and rough, and I didn't even have to try.

Within seconds, cum shot out of my cock. My body seized, muscles spasming, and above me, Marshall let out a low and rumbling roar. His cock thickened inside of me, his hot cum shooting deep into my body. There was no condom to keep us apart, and I struggled for air before throwing my face into the pillows to muffle the sounds of my pleasure.

"No," Marshall warned, a fist in my hair. He pulled me up forcefully, deepening the arch in my back and bringing my face up for air. "I want to hear every sound you make, Silas. They're mine."

I sputtered, another burst of cum leaking from my cock at his words. Behind me, Marshall had gone still, save for the heave of his chest as he breathed and the pulse of his cock as he continued to empty into me. I closed my eyes and went limp, letting him hold me upright by the hair, by the hip.

He eventually lowered me down to the bed, petting his hands over the slope of my back as I murmured content sounds into the space between us. He eased out of me with a groan, then rolled onto his back to my side. His arm lay outstretched in invitation, and I shuffled closer so I was half on his chest, half on the ruined sheets.

"How did you sleep?" he asked after his breathing had settled back to normal.

"All night."

He kissed the top of my head. "How are you feeling?"

"In what way?"

"Both."

"Physically, perfect." I reached down and gave a slow stroke of my cock, already going soft. My skin stuck to my palm, cum already cooling and drying. "When you were…when we…"

I trailed off, suddenly feeling unsure of how to explain to him what had happened with the sheets, with my body. It was one thing to admit I liked to be spanked, to be caned, to be deprived of my senses, another entirely to tread further.

"Tell me." His words were soft but had no room for argument.

"The sheets twisted around my dick while you were fucking me, and I liked it."

"Did it hurt you?"

I swallowed hard. "Yes. A little."

Marshall hummed and wrapped his arm around me, brushing hair back from my face. "And emotionally?"

"Good," I answered, which was true because, at that moment, I was. But I knew as soon as the adrenaline and arousal subsided, reality would come crashing back down around me. My dad had fired me, and that was worse than just losing my job. I wasn't sure what would become of our relationship after the conversation—the argument—we'd had the day before.

"Silas."

"I don't have another option," I said, closing my eyes and breathing in the comforting smell of Marshall's sweat mixed with the lingering undertones of his bath soap. "I'll find another job."

"Do you want me to get you in touch with my friend Cory?"

"It can't hurt."

"As soon as we're up, I'll call him," he said.

I pulled my lips together between my teeth and exhaled. "Thank you."

"Coffee is ready." Marshall stroked his fingers down my

shoulder, down my arm. He paused, almost as if deliberating before saying, "I need to shower and get ready for work, but you can make me breakfast. Everything you need is in the fridge."

A surge of complicated emotions exploded inside of me, somewhere between my chest and my stomach. I liked the command. I welcomed it, but for some reason I was beyond nervous about what it meant.

"Yes, Sir," I whispered, reluctantly untangling myself from Marshall's arms. My borrowed clothes were discarded on the floor, and I grabbed the sweats but not the shirt. Marshall watched me get half-dressed, and he stayed in bed long after I padded barefoot out to the kitchen.

The coffee pot was full, two empty mugs sitting beside it, and I poured one for myself. I'd fill his after he was ready for it so it didn't get cold. In the fridge, I found eggs and bacon. Bread in the pantry. In the other room, the shower turned on, and I flipped the gas on the front burner to medium-high.

The monotony of scrambling eggs and frying bacon was the perfect thing to follow the wake-up sex, and by the time Marshall appeared in the dining room, barefoot in a pair of navy slacks and a white button-up, with damp hair and a freshly shaven jawline, I wasn't terrified of what was going to come next.

He sat down at the table, same seat as the night before, and didn't say a word. He didn't have to. Warmth rolled through me as I poured him a hot cup of coffee then served it to him.

"Cream or sugar?" I murmured.

He answered with a small shake of his head. "No, Silas. Thank you."

I went back to the kitchen, mentally trying to fight back the arousal that had started to once again burn between my legs. I made up two plates of eggs, bacon, and toast, then brought it all back to the table and slid into the seat beside him. He didn't tell me to wait, but I found my hands folded neatly in my lap until he took the first bite of eggs. Only then did I pick up my fork and start to eat.

Marshall noticed, of course, raising an eyebrow at me without calling it out, and I blinked at him before looking down at my bacon. The strips were juicy and fatty, and I huffed out an exhale, thinking about Lincoln and his apology bacon.

"Is the bacon funny?" Marshall asked, taking a drink of his coffee.

"It just reminded me of Lincoln."

His mouth turned up into an amused smirk. "Tell me more."

"The morning after…the morning after you and I saw each other at Rapture that first time—"

He narrowed his eyes at me. "The morning after you were assaulted."

I sighed, nodding. "That morning, he made me apology bacon. We were eating it when you called. It's nothing. It just made me think of him."

Marshall picked up a slice of bacon and bit into it, chewing and swallowing before responding. "What does Lincoln do for work?"

The butter on my toast melted slowly, sinking into the grain of the bread the same way I wanted to sink into the floor. It wasn't that I worried Marshall would care about Lincoln's job, I just didn't want it to complicate things.

"He makes movies," I answered, biting into the crust of my toast. "Adult movies."

"He makes porn."

I shoved another bite of toast into my mouth. "Yeah."

"Have you ever?"

"I told you our relationship isn't like that," I said.

Marshall used his toast to slide the last bit of his eggs onto his fork. "I meant in general, not with him."

"No," I whispered, shaking my head. "I haven't."

"I wouldn't care if you had," he said. "Are you finished eating?"

The questions were so conversational, so far from what I expected.

There were two bites of egg left on my plate and half a strip of bacon. We both looked down at the leftover food, then I glanced up at him with my fork still in hand. "Am I?"

He licked his lips and smiled at me. "If you want to be."

I dropped my fork onto the plate. "Then, yes. Thank you."

He shook his head and stacked my plate on top of his, folding the last bit of my bacon into his mouth. "No, sweetheart. Thank you."

"I can take those," I protested, reaching for him as he stood to carry the plates into the kitchen. I hadn't cleaned up from preparing breakfast yet, and I didn't want him to see the mess I'd left.

"You're my submissive, not my servant," he said, turning on the water. I eyed him nervously, my coffee still in hand, while he rinsed the plates and the pans before arranging it all into the dishwasher and closing the door. "Do you want to stay here today, or do you want to go home?"

The question took the air out of my lungs because, for the briefest, most fleeting moment, I'd forgotten the two were not the same place. But before I could answer, Marshall spoke again, "You're more than welcome to stay here, but I'm not sure I want you to be alone. So if you do, I'd like Lincoln to come over until I'm off work."

Another rush of air out of my lungs, tangling in my throat at the impossibility of it all.

"I'd like to stay," I said.

Marshall scratched his cheek then checked his watch. "Is Lincoln up this early?"

"He'll answer if I call."

"Call him then. I'm going to finish getting ready for work."

"Yes, Sir," I mumbled, mostly to his back as he went toward the bedroom. My phone was somewhere in my bag, which I found by the front door where I'd left it. It had enough of a charge on it, and Lincoln answered on the fourth ring.

"M'hello?"

"Did I wake you up?"

"Of course." He yawned. "Are you okay?"

"Yes, but…I want to stay here today, and he has to go to work. Can you come over?"

Lincoln groaned, and I was so familiar with him, I knew it was the sound he made when he stretched first thing in the morning.

"Am I allowed?"

"He's the one who told me to call."

"Yeah," Lincoln answered. Another yawn. "Can I shower there? Is there coffee?"

"Yes and yes."

"Kay. Can I stay in pajamas?" he asked.

"You don't wear pajamas."

Lincoln chuckled. "Good point. I still have his address from your first date, so I'll see you soon."

He hung up, and I took my phone into the bedroom in search of Marshall's charge cord. I found it and him, standing in the en suite with his fingers in his hair. When it was damp, the gray around his temples was less pronounced, but he was no less sexy.

"Everything settled?" he asked.

I sat down on the edge of the bed. "He's on his way."

Lincoln arrived in record time, knocking on the door just as Marshall finished tying his shoes. We'd moved from the bedroom into the living room, and he pointed at the couch, indicating I should stay put while he stood up to let Lincoln in. I craned my neck to watch their interaction.

"You must be Lincoln," Marshall greeted when he opened the door.

I crawled up onto my knees but didn't have a clear view of the door.

"And you're Marshall," Lincoln said back, still sounding tired but somehow also sassy.

"Thank you for coming over."

There were footsteps in the entryway, the door closed, then both of them were in my sight line. Lincoln smirked at me, seated on the couch in a too-big pair of sweatpants and not much else. I didn't have to explain. I didn't have to say a word. Lincoln took one look at me and climbed onto the couch beside me, wrapping me up his arms and pressing a sloppy kiss against my temple.

"Where's the remote?" he asked Marshall. "I've got it from here."

Marshall huffed out a laugh, pulling open a hidden drawer in the side table and passing Lincoln the remote.

"After your phone is charged, keep it on you," Marshall said to me.

"Yes, Sir," I agreed.

"I'll let you know what Cory says."

"Thank you."

Lincoln turned on the TV and immediately started to scroll through channels, spinning his body around so his legs were over the back of the couch and his head was on my lap. I petted my fingers through his hair and smiled up at Marshall, tears threatening to spill again but not from sadness.

I didn't think I'd ever been so taken care of. So happy.

He must have seen it because he bent down and swiped at my lower lashes before anything was able to escape.

"I—" He closed his mouth and swallowed, steeling himself before going on. "I hope you have a good day, sweetheart."

"Sweetheart," Lincoln murmured, and I covered his face

with my hand. He licked my palm, and I smeared his saliva across his cheek.

"Thank you," I whispered, because I didn't know what else to say.

Marshall kept my face in his hold and pressed a very chaste kiss against my mouth. When he pulled back and stood, there was a look of worry on his face, and I chalked it up to his concern about my recent unemployment and being home alone with Lincoln. Before I could ask him what was wrong, he schooled his features back into his normal mask of casual dominance and adjusted the cuffs of his shirt.

"I'll be home by six," he said. "I expect dinner."

I grimaced, brow scrunching. Had he forgotten what day it was, or did he not care?

"Yes, Sir, but…"

"But?"

"It's Friday," I said, tucking his chin toward his chest. "You see your brothers on Fridays."

Marshall cursed under his breath.

"Do I get dinner?" Lincoln asked, the question muffled by my hand still covering half his face.

"You can stay if you want," Marshall told him, cracking his knuckles one at a time.

"I do like, but I can't. I just wanted to see what you'd say."

"Lincoln," I warned, throwing my head back and staring up at the ceiling. I hoped he wasn't going to antagonize Marshall forever because that would get so old, so fast.

"He's fine," Marshall assured me, brushing my hair backward and leaving one last kiss against my forehead. "Dinner for you and Lincoln, then. And I'll be home right after. Relax today, Silas. A new job will be waiting for you soon, I'm sure of it."

"I'll relax," I promised.

"He'll relax," Lincoln also promised.

Marshall gave us both one last look like he didn't want to leave, but not because of trust. Because of longing. Much like he'd cleared his last expression, he shook this one away as well, then grabbed his things and headed out the door.

"He loves you," Lincoln said, long after the sound of Marshall's car had faded into the distance.

I opened my mouth to argue, but the protest died in the back of my throat.

Lincoln rolled onto his side and handed me the remote, and neither of us said another word for hours.

CHAPTER 26
MARSHALL

Cory was, as I expected, more than agreeable about meeting with Silas. He'd also read the article so Silas's creativity was clearly only lost on his father. I texted Silas to let him know how to get in touch, then tried to focus on work. I went ahead and submitted the final draft of the bid on the Cahuenga Pass project because, with Silas out at Ayres, I had far less to worry about. It was a shame—from a business perspective—that Silas didn't want to come work for me, but I also appreciated how that was one too many relationship lines between us.

Knowing the bid was done and Silas was safe with Lincoln on my couch, my mind reluctantly traveled to other obligations that I'd been shirking since taking on both. The biggest of which being Hunter's revelation about a new brother. I'd looked him up a couple of times and didn't find much of him on social media.

Andrew Calavert.

There'd been a long-abandoned Facebook profile and a LinkedIn page that hadn't been updated since he'd graduated —from USC—with his J.D. a couple years after. If he had a job, I didn't know where it was. It wouldn't have taken more than a couple phone calls to find out, but I didn't want to make any assumptions. He was willing to meet with us at some point, and I could ask him then.

I glanced at my watch, knowing the end of the day was approaching faster than I would have liked. For the first time in my life, I was torn between two things that both deserved priority—Silas and my brothers. So I called Hunter, since he was the only one who knew about our unspoken agenda for the night.

"Hey," he said, already sounding weary. "Are you ready for tonight?"

"Not entirely." I paused. "Do you think we can table it?"

"The conversation?"

"Dinner," I said.

The quiet between us was thick. "Does this have anything to do with that boyfriend of yours?"

I'd never lie to any of my brothers, especially about something like this. And I'd already told Silas I'd be home after dinner, but if there was any way I could adjust that schedule to get back to him sooner, I wanted to try it. The revelation about our fifth brother was groundbreaking, but Andrew wasn't going anywhere. From what Hunter had said, although he'd agreed to meet us, he wasn't chomping at the bit to do so. We could put the reveal off another week…

"Yes," I told him, "But not in the way you're thinking."

"How am I thinking?" he asked.

"That I want to ditch out on you to get laid."

Hunter chuckled. "Don't you?"

I let my mouth tug into a smile, since my brother couldn't see it. "Of course, but he's going through something right now."

"Smith is about to be going through something too," Hunter interjected, "when he finds out there's another one of us."

Scrubbing a hand down my face, I leaned back in my chair and stared up at the ceiling like I could find the answer there. "You're right," I agreed. "Do you have any other information about him?"

"I have his phone number."

"Have you talked to him?"

"Just the first time. He knows about you and Smith and Finn. He knows we're telling them tonight, but nothing else."

"Okay," I said. "I'll see you at six then."

"Marshall, I know you like this kid, but being there for your family is the right choice."

"I can do both," I told him, hanging up the call and frowning down at my cell phone.

The rest of the day passed with the frown in place. So downturned, my jaw ached from it. The only reprieve from my day were the intermittent text messages from Silas about what he and Lincoln were doing and how they were feeling. He sent me a picture of the sandwiches the two of them had made for lunch, and he let me know he'd made plans to meet with Cory on Monday about a job. He assured me he felt a thousand times better than he had the night before, but I still didn't feel right about abandoning him to deal with the fact my father couldn't keep his cock in his pants.

This was fine.

It was as expected because I'd already told Silas I was going to be late, and Lincoln had already committed to staying there until I got home. The only thing that powered me through the rest of my day was knowing Silas had his best friend with him, otherwise the nagging nerves over Andrew would have eaten me alive.

By the time dinner rolled around, I was beyond ready to get out of the office and into our usual corner booth. My normal wine tasted like it had gone a bit sour, but I imagined that was more on account of my nerves than it was any fault with the restaurant itself. Hunter showed up next, which was out of character for him, and we exchanged a nervous glance.

"I'll tell them," he said, glancing past me, jaw tight.

Finn and Smith arrived within seconds of each other, taking their usual seats and getting their usual drinks. By all accounts, this should have been a standard Friday night dinner between brothers. I hated that I knew otherwise.

Hunter had the courtesy to wait until Smith and Finn had at least one swallow of their drinks before he flattened his hands against the edge of the booth and blurted, "There's something I need to talk to you about."

"You who?" Finn asked, head bobbling side to side like he'd made the most amusing joke of all time.

"All of you." Hunter's somber expression was enough to suck the amusement right out of Finn, which caused Smith to go tense to my left. I slid my leg over, knocking my shoe against his in a show of silent brotherly solidarity.

"That doesn't sound good," Finn muttered.

"No."

"Just spill it," I said.

Hunter pursed his lips, shooting me a glare before confessing to his vodka, "We have another brother."

Finn's eyes went wide, mouth gaping open, but he was quick to snap it closed. He looked from Hunter to me, then to Smith, and the way his face changed at the sight of our youngest brother had me swiveling to see him as well. Smith looked like he'd just watched a baby deer get shot, the expression on his face one of utter devastation tinged with horror.

"Hey," I said, squeezing his thigh in what I hoped was a reassuring way. "It's okay."

It was easy to forget I'd had this revelation three times before. Smith was the last to come to us. He'd never experienced the grief and confusion—and later, joy—that came from finding out there was another brother to bring into the fold.

"How did you find out?" Finn asked. He'd cleared his throat and downed his vodka, raising his empty glass over his head until the waiter saw him and headed to get a second.

Smith still hadn't moved, so I kept my hand on his leg, my foot against his.

"His mother died recently. The confession, as it were, was in her will."

"Must have been nice to not have a mom who was willing to sell you out," Smith muttered, and all three of us looked at him with varying degrees of concern.

The waiter brought Finn his second drink, which was gone in less than thirty seconds, but he refrained from ordering another. Smith's drink was untouched, save for his first sip of wine.

"Go on," I prompted.

"His name is Andrew," Hunter said, working through the short checklist of information we had about our mystery sibling. "He lives in San Diego. He's a lawyer."

"How old is he?" Finn asked, still eyeing Smith.

Our baby brother.

"Twenty-eight," Hunter said.

Finn groaned, dropping his head back against the booth. He sank into the leather and folded his arms in front of his chest.

"He knows about us," I said, taking over for my brother who was clearly running on fumes with the adrenaline of the confession wearing off already. "He's willing to meet with us."

"What if we don't want to meet him?" Smith muttered.

I knocked my knee against his. "Why wouldn't we want to meet him?"

"He's not…he wasn't…"

"He wasn't raised like us," Finn supplied, unfolding his arms in favor of violently stirring the ice around his empty drink with a cocktail straw.

"That doesn't change the fact we all share the same blood."

"The world doesn't need another Covington," Finn said.

"Calavert," Hunter corrected, scratching the side of his nose. "Andrew Neil Calavert."

Finn immediately pulled out his phone, and I knew my brother well enough to know he was searching for the newest addition to our family on all the social media platforms he had. He found nothing of note, same as me, then dropped his phone face down on the table with a sigh.

"At least he's not thirty-five," Hunter said, in a small glimpse of levity from the otherwise most serious one of us.

"Triplets would be a bit much," I agreed.

That earned a snort from Finn but also had Smith shaking himself away from me and climbing out of the booth. I let him go, until Hunter glanced from Smith's back to my face.

"You should go after him," he suggested.

"I think he wants to be alone."

"Yeah," Finn said. "So did I."

Remembering the destruction a very young Finn had brought into the house after Hunter's arrival was enough to have me out of the booth, chasing after my brother. We shared genetics, but Finn was the one who'd inherited father's temper. I always assumed it had skipped Smith, but after watching him leave, neither of the twins looked sure. I went after Smith, finding him in the parking lot of the restaurant with his ass propped against the hood of his car, hands jammed into his pockets.

"Hey, kid," I said, standing beside him and leaning against the car.

He stared out at the street, a very tense frown on his face. It was strange to see him so unhappy. Smith had always been guarded of his emotions, stoic, falling somewhere between Finn and Hunter on the emotional intelligence scale.

"Is this what it was like when I showed up?" He kicked his

foot out, scuffing some rocks before crossing his legs at the ankles.

"It was worse when Hunter and Finn showed up," I admitted. "I was a lot younger, full of hormones and feelings I didn't understand. I was older when you came around, but you were the one full of hormones and emotions then."

Smith made a disgruntled noise in the back of his throat.

"You know there's most certainly more than just the four of us, right?" I asked.

"Five."

"More than just the five of us," I said, letting him correct me. "Though, Andrew is hardly part of us, right? All we know is that we share half the same genetic make-up."

"That's all we used to share."

"We were all kids."

"You were almost thirty when you learned about me."

I sighed, scrubbing a hand down my face. "What answer do you want, Smith? Do you want me to tell you that nothing is going to change and everything is going to stay the same? Or do you want me to tell you that everything is going to be different now that there's another brother?"

"I don't know," he grumbled.

I knocked my shoulder into his, and the way he sagged against me confirmed my youngest brother needed a hug, not a tease. Slipping my arm around his shoulder, I pulled Smith into my arms and propped my chin on his shoulder.

"You're still my baby brother. You're still their favorite," I said, referencing Hunter and Finn.

"Aren't I *your* favorite?" he mumbled against my shoulder.

"Of course."

"What if the next brother is younger than me?" he asked.

"It won't change a single thing about who you are."

"Am I being childish about this?"

Smith tried to worm out of the hug, so I ruffled his hair

and set him free. "You're not being childish. You're being human."

He exhaled loudly and shifted back to rest against his car again.

"Do you want to go back inside?" I asked. "Finish your wine, get some dinner?"

"Not really."

"You don't look like the kind of man who should be alone."

"Probably not," he agreed.

My earlier war over which of my priorities needed to take the top spot raged back to life. Silas was home waiting for me, but Silas had Lincoln. In this moment, Smith didn't have anyone besides me.

"I'll invite you over," I said. "The guest room is always clean, but I need you to know that I have company."

Smith raised his brows, and I knew I'd accidentally given him the distraction he'd been hoping for.

"Who?"

"I'm seeing Silas Ayres," I admitted.

The corner of Smith's eye twitched, and I stared him down, waiting for him to say something.

Anything.

What he finally gave me was, "Alright."

"Alright?"

"Alright, I'll come over," he said, ignoring the confession that my boyfriend was closer to his age than mine.

"His best friend is also there, but he is going home after dinner. At least, I assume he is."

"You have more than one spare bed if not," Smith said.

"Yeah. Why don't you run back in and let the twins know you're coming home with me? We'll all take some time to regroup and then decide what we want to do about Andrew."

Smith grimaced, but nodded, then pushed off the car and trudged back into the restaurant. As soon as he was far enough away to be out of earshot, I reached into my pocket for my phone. I had to let Silas know I would be home earlier than I'd planned and that my brother would be with me. It wasn't quite how I'd imagined their first meeting going, but life was life, and this was the situation we'd all found ourselves in.

The real issue with the turn of events was that none of my brothers knew I was into BDSM, and I was minutes away from walking my distraught baby brother into a house with a man who was very likely going to call me *Sir*.

Quickly, before Smith returned, I called Silas, who answered on the first ring...like he'd been holding his phone and waiting for my call.

"Hello?"

"Silas."

I could hear the smile in his voice when he asked, "How's dinner? Is everything all right?"

"Dinner is..." I bit back the lie. Dinner was *not* okay, but I realized with the mistruth just how much about my life Silas didn't know. It wasn't anything I'd kept from him. Things were simply so new we hadn't had the time to have some of these discussions. He knew I had brothers, but there was so much more to our story. Just like there was so much more to mine that Hunter, Finn, and Smith weren't privy to.

"Sir?"

Groaning, I kept my stare trained on the door to the restaurant. "My youngest brother is coming home with me. He's your age. I actually think you know him from school."

I wanted to dig myself a hole in the asphalt and never come back up for air.

"Who?"

"His name is Smith. Smith Covington."

Silas laughed on the other end of the line. "I can't believe I never put two and two together."

"Did you know him well?"

"No," Silas answered.

I scratched the side of my nose, not ready to make the ask I needed. "My brother. He doesn't know how I am. The way I am with you."

"He doesn't know you're a Dom."

"Among other things," I said.

Silas paused. "Is this your way of asking me to not out you when he's here?"

"Yes," I said. The door to the restaurant opened and the recognizable silhouette of Smith's narrow shoulders filled the frame. "I'm sorry to ask you to compromise this part of yourself right now—"

He cut me off, an indiscretion I'd punish him for later.

"Not calling you Sir doesn't compromise anything," he said thoughtfully. In the background, Lincoln made wet, kissy noises. "My submission doesn't change whether I call you Marshall or Sir."

Lincoln made a dry heaving sound.

"I do love the way you sound when you say my name, sweetheart," I said. Smith was close, back in earshot, running a nervous hand through his hair. "Smith is ready to go now. We'll be home soon."

"I'll be waiting," Silas said softly, before adding, "Marshall."

CHAPTER 27
SILAS

It had been a really long time since I'd spent the entire day with Lincoln, and getting fired by my dad had sucked, but doing absolutely nothing with my best friend all day was exactly what I'd needed.

After getting off the phone with Marshall, I turned my attention back to the pasta I'd put to boil since I was still responsible for myself and for Lincoln, who sat at the counter with his chin perched in his hands.

"Everything good?" he asked.

"You can tell it wasn't." I arched a brow at him. "I don't know what's going on, but you have to play nice. You heard him. His brother…doesn't know."

Lincoln chortled. "Would kind of be weird if he did, right?"

"A bit, yeah," I agreed.

The pasta was tender, so I carried the pot to the sink and dumped the contents into a strainer. Lincoln was strictly a butter and cheese kind of guy, so there wasn't any sauce to bother with. I mixed the pasta with half a stick of butter and a few spoonfuls of the most expensive-looking parmesan flakes

I'd ever seen in my life and served us both up. There was enough left over to feed Marshall and his brother, though I doubted either of them would be hungry.

"I know his brother, actually," I said, climbing onto a stool to sit at Lincoln's side. "From college."

"Is he cool? Is that weird?"

"He was quiet then. A little moody. And why would it be weird?"

"Because you *know* his brother now."

"I didn't *know* Smith," I corrected, rolling my eyes. "He was cute, but it wasn't like that."

Smith Covington had been angry at the world but pretty enough to get away with it, and I was curious to see how he'd matured since freshman year. I didn't even know if he remembered me from school or if he just recognized my name from the work I'd done as an adult.

Either way.

"I just realized I'm still in pajamas," I groaned, shoveling a bite of pasta into my mouth before reluctantly peeling myself away from the counter.

"So?"

"So I don't want to meet Marshall's brother for the first time dressed in his gym clothes."

"You said you knew him from school."

"You know what I mean!" I called over my shoulder, already halfway to the bedroom. Lincoln's laughter—and his footsteps—followed behind me down the hall, and he made himself at home on the bed while I dug out clothes that looked somewhat more presentable.

Marshall and I were not yet to the shared drawers at each other's houses stage of the relationship, but I had at least one pair of jeans hiding out in his closet because I'd had them in my bag by accident Wednesday night. There wasn't much to do about a better t-shirt, so jeans and Marshall's old college rowing team shirt would have to do.

"Do I look passable?" I asked, plucking at the hem.

My nerves had stacked on themselves since I'd gotten off the phone, and I didn't know if I was more worried about meeting Marshall's brother or making sure I didn't slip up and call him Sir. It had been easy to not in the very first days of being with him, but now that I used it, now that he'd earned it…the feel of it in my mouth was as natural as breathing.

"If I found you attractive, you would be positively fuckable," Lincoln said.

Scoffing, I pulled him up from the bed and into a hug that had the sides of our noses brushing together. His lips shined with butter from the pasta, and I kissed him quickly against the corner of his mouth.

"Thank you for staying with me today," I said, threading our fingers together and walking backward toward the hallway.

"It was a hardship," he assured me. "Sitting on that comfortable couch, watching all the premium channels, eating that expensive food of his."

"We have all the premium channels."

"Our couch is garbage," he said. "I didn't realize it until today."

I laughed, making it back to the counter. "It is pretty nice. We'll have to get a new one."

Lincoln and I managed a few more bites of pasta before the garage door opened. At the sound of it, he turned to me with wide and playful eyes, then gave his shoulders a little wiggle.

"You ready?" he asked.

"No."

"Too bad."

He dumped another forkful of pasta into his mouth and

spun the barstool around so he had a line of sight toward the door into the house. I tried to eat some more pasta, not because I had the stomach for it, but because it was part of my deal with Marshall that I would keep myself fed and hydrated.

The door opened and he was there, tall and broad as always, with a slump in his shoulders that was so slight, if you weren't familiar with the way he normally carried himself you wouldn't have even noticed it. When he saw me in his shirt, he flashed a very brief—but hot—smile, then stepped out of the way to make room for his brother.

Smith was inches shorter than him and far slimmer, but even though they looked different, it was clear they shared a relation somewhere in the family tree. Smith also looked like someone had kicked him in the ribs, and the urge to protect him was strong. I understood why Marshall had made the decision to bring him home. He closed the door behind him and looked up, giving me the barest of glances but lingering seconds longer on Lincoln.

"Smith, this is Silas," Marshall said, closing the space between us and wrapping me up into a hug. He kissed the top of my head, and I managed a small wave to Smith, more of a gesture, just a raised hand in greeting.

"Nice to meet you."

Smith clearly came from money. He was all manners even as whatever emotions he worked through bore down on him.

"This is my best friend, Lincoln," I said, pointing at said friend.

"Nice to meet you," Smith said again, softer.

"Do you…want some pasta?" I asked with a shrug. "I know you and Marshall normally have dinner together, but it's early and I don't think you guys had time to eat?"

Smith exhaled, sullen, then sniffed the air. "No, I'm good."

"Butter and cheese," Marshall observed, sliding his hand

down my spine and letting it come to rest in the dip above my ass. "Have a bowl, Smith."

"I'll make it up," I offered.

Marshall gave me a knowing look, and I went to the kitchen to serve up some of the extra pasta. Lincoln had sat back down at the counter to finish eating, and Smith took the empty barstool beside him.

"Do you want any?" I asked Marshall.

He shook his head and tugged at the knot of his tie. "I want you to finish what you're doing and meet me in the bedroom."

"Yes…yeah." I cleared my throat and set a bowl of pasta in front of Smith.

Marshall cast a quick look down at the contents of my half-eaten bowl, then inclined his head toward the hallway. Lincoln waggled his eyebrows at me, and I gave him the finger.

"We're good," Lincoln said, seemingly to both of us, because Marshall didn't move until the words had left Lincoln's mouth.

I followed him into the bedroom and walked right into his waiting arms, burying my face against the front of his chest with a happy sigh.

"How are you?" he asked.

"I'm good. Honestly. Better now."

"Did you talk to Cory?"

"All set for Monday," I said.

Marshall hummed and slid his hands down my sides until they were bracketed around my waist and our bodies were notched together in the way that already felt so right.

"What happened tonight?" I asked, flattening my palms against the center of his chest. I dragged them up until I reached his tie, then fussed with the knot until it came loose. He answered me with an approving noise, so I pulled the tie off and set to work with his buttons.

"You know I have three brothers," he said.

I tugged the tails of his shirt free from his pants, then slid the sleeves down until he was only in slacks.

"Yes."

"Half-brothers," he said. "Different mothers who all sold us out in the name of a payoff."

"What now?"

"We all came to live with my father because after he found out about us, he bought us."

Marshall explained it like he was reading something as commonplace as a recipe, which seemed impossible. I undid his belt and pulled down his fly.

"I was the first, then Finn and Hunter. They were young. Smith…he came later."

"How much later?"

I helped Marshall out of his pants, then toyed with the waistband of his black boxer briefs.

"He was almost a teenager. He's always been the baby, but for years now it's just been the four of us."

"They're lucky to have you."

"We're lucky to have each other."

He still had my hands, so I left his briefs alone.

"Hunter was recently made aware we have another half-brother. He's down in San Diego, named Andrew. We just told Smith and Finn about him tonight."

The breath left my lungs like air leaving a sail. "Oh, shit."

He huffed out what might have passed for a laugh on a better day. "Smith is not taking the news well."

"How are *you* taking it?" I pulled Marshall toward the dresser so I wouldn't have to take my hands off of him, and he smirked at me but went along with it.

"It's old hat to me at this point."

"That can't be true."

Marshall buried his face into my hair and breathed me in

with a groan. His dick pressed against my hip, but he hadn't asked me to touch it, so I busied my hands by reaching behind me until I found the dresser drawer where he kept his lounge clothes. I slipped a folded up and clean pair of sweats between us, and he made a very unimpressed sound.

"It is true," he assured me, taking a step away. "What else is true is that you may put those on for me. I rather don't feel like doing it myself tonight."

This was new. It was a different kind of submission, but a welcome one as I sank to my knees in front of him. One foot, then another into the sweats and I was back on my feet again, settling the waistband around his hips and tracing the muscle where the soft material met his skin.

"I don't enjoy seeing any of my brothers upset," Marshall said slowly, like he'd picked the words out carefully to make sure they were the right ones. He definitely had that way about him. "As for how it makes me feel, we're all adults so it's not anything like it used to be before."

"Is your dad still alive?"

"So I'm told," he murmured. "Get me a shirt, and I have to be honest, Silas. I love the way you look in my clothes."

Heat flooded my cheeks, and I turned away to get a shirt from the drawer for him. Marshall held his arms up expectantly, and I dressed him in his shirt as well, smoothing my hands down the front of his stomach to set the thin fabric into place.

"I didn't want to meet your brother dressed in sweats, but I didn't have a clean shirt."

"You look perfect," he assured me. "Though maybe you should bring some clothes over."

"Are you asking?"

He chuckled. "When have I *asked* you anything?"

I shivered, thinking about the numerous times Marshall had, in fact, asked me things. All the careful and thorough ways he'd negotiated consent with me and the ways he continued to do so even as we settled into a routine.

"What would you like me to bring over, Sir?" I whispered, tilting my head back to look up at him.

He rubbed his lips together, licked the bottom one until it was so thoroughly wet with spit that my cock ached in my jeans just thinking about what it would feel like to slide into his mouth.

All the things we'd done together, and he'd never sucked my cock. I wondered if he ever would. Wondered if he would let me come in his mouth or not…

"Use your best judgment, Silas."

He pressed the side of his finger against the underside of my chin, then closed the space between us and brought our mouths together in an unfairly soft and chaste kiss.

"Yes, Sir," I murmured.

He groaned and licked his tongue across the seam of my lips, then stopped and stepped back.

"I need to go check on Smith," he said. "Or I'd stay in here with you all night."

"He's in good hands with Lincoln."

"Just like you were?" Marshall arched a brow.

"We watched TV all day," I explained. "I made us lunch, and I made us dinner, and I kissed him after I got dressed because I was so grateful to spend the day with him."

Even though Marshall had told me it was okay for Lincoln and me to still kiss, to still cuddle, to still be *ourselves*, there was definitely a part of me that had been worried about how it would play out in practice.

"You're allowed," he reminded me, raising my hand to his mouth and dusting a kiss across my knuckles.

I exhaled and nodded. "I know."

Marshall gave me a look so filled with longing I worried it

was going to knock me over. I reached out to steady myself against him, and he let out a gentle laugh.

"I don't want to keep you from your brother," I said.

"You couldn't if you tried," he promised, and I knew the truth of it in my bones. "Now kiss me again, Silas, then go finish your dinner."

CHAPTER 28
MARSHALL

Smith ate all the pasta Silas had dished up for him, and Lincoln sat beside him at the counter, expression wary.

"Sorry about that," I said, coming into the kitchen to pour my brother and me both a glass of wine. One thing that was nice about having a brother who idolized you was I never had to guess about his likes or dislikes. They very nearly copied my own. I poured a glass for each of us, and before I could return the bottle to its shelf, Lincoln cleared his throat and grinned at me. I poured a third, then a smaller pour for Silas who'd slid back onto his barstool doing everything he could to hide his erection.

"You're fine," Smith said with a sigh. "Now that I'm here, it's all feeling very dramatic."

"You're allowed to have feelings," Lincoln said.

I found myself curious what the two of them had discussed while Silas and I were in the bedroom, but I wasn't going to pry.

"More dinner?" I offered.

Smith clanked his fork against the side of the bowl but shook his head. "Wine is good."

"Wine is better with something in your stomach."

"I ate." As if to prove his point, he shoved the bowl toward me.

"Have some more," Lincoln suggested gently, and I was suddenly even more curious about their conversation than I'd been before.

"Tell me about your day, Lincoln," I said, picking the pot up from the stove and seeing Silas had made more than enough pasta to feed all four of us. Heat expanded in the middle of my chest at the forethought, and I dumped some noodles into Smith's bowl before shoving it back at him.

"I enjoyed the amenities," he said with a smile that definitely had the power to take lesser men down. I quickly understood why Silas loved him, and I found myself grateful he had such a kindhearted and reliable friend.

"Did you eat me out of house and home?"

"I'm a gracious guest, Mr. Covington. I would never."

To his left, Smith groaned.

Lincoln laughed. "Did I hit a nerve?"

"A time and a place for all things," I said, topping off all of our wine glasses in lieu of recorking the bottle. There wasn't much left anyway; there'd be no harm in it.

"I'll put a pin in that."

"No one calls me Mr. Covington in my own home, Lincoln."

"Okay." He made doe eyes at me, and I hoped he couldn't see through me, straight to the part that did enjoy being called Mr. Covington—in the bedroom. Lincoln turned toward Silas. "Did you put a pin in that?"

"Linc," he warned.

Thankfully, Lincoln received the message. "Is that one of those 'Mr. Covington is my father, please call me Marshall' kind of things?"

Scratching the back of my neck, I leaned against the far

counter so I had a clean line of sight on all three of my house-guests. "Something like that," I murmured.

Dejectedly, Smith finished his pasta, then made quick work of his wine and leaned back as much as the barstool would allow, which wasn't much.

"Do you want to sit on the couch? Get comfortable?" I asked my brother, again looking at Lincoln. "Are you spending the night?"

He perked up. "Is that an option?"

Sighing, I carried my wine into the living room, grateful I'd had the foresight to get a conversation-sized couch, not some-thing smaller. Not anything built for only one man.

"I have a guest room." I sat down in my usual spot on the couch, and Silas tucked in beside me, getting close without climbing on top of me the way we both clearly wanted.

"What about your brother?" he asked.

"I'm not staying," Smith answered for himself, but he was already in the kitchen opening another bottle of wine.

"Yes, you are."

"Fine," he grumbled, hints of the preteen version of himself bleeding out through his tired and frayed edges.

Smith brought his wine to the living room and set it down on the coffee table with an unhappy noise. "I'm going to change, then."

"You know your way around," I said. "You can take your usual room, and show Lincoln the other one, if you don't mind."

I watched over Silas's shoulder as the two of them trotted off together down the hall, and once they were out of earshot, I slid my hand between Silas's legs and squeezed.

"Please, don't," he whined, arching into my hold.

"Don't?"

"You're going to make me harder than I already am, and

these pants don't hide anything," he whispered. "If it was just Lincoln, I wouldn't care."

"But my brother."

He nodded, lashes fluttering as I made a loose fist around what I could reach of his shaft.

"I don't like you telling me no," I said, giving him a stroke.

Silas gasped, crawling half onto my lap and burying his face into the crook of my neck. "I never did. I never would."

"Never is a dangerous promise, sweetheart."

"You know what I mean," he murmured.

I looked quickly down the hall and realized Lincoln must be waiting for Smith to change because neither of them had reappeared. Taking advantage of the time with Silas, I held him against me, enjoying the warmth and flexibility of his body.

"If it wasn't my brother. If it was just Lincoln, or if it was just a stranger, would you like that?"

"Marshall," he groaned my name like a curse, and then there was nothing more to say because the conversation between Lincoln and Smith grew louder as they returned to the couch. Smith collapsed comfortably onto the sectional side, scooping his wine off the table with one fluid and practiced motion.

As the night dragged on, the question about putting Silas on display stayed in the forefront of my mind. I mindlessly played with Silas's hair while Smith alternated between watching whatever show Lincoln had put on and talking about how three brothers was plenty, but four was excessive. The whole time, debating if I was too possessive or not possessive enough to let another man put his eyes on what was mine.

There was something to be said for the trust required for a scenario that involved exhibitionism or free use, and I meant that from both ways. Silas would have to trust me to make good decisions on his behalf, to keep him safe in all ways. And on the other hand, I would have to trust not just him, but also myself. To put us both into a situation like that and let it send me into a spiral of doubt would be absolutely unforgivable.

We'd talked about free use during our initial negotiations, and it was something that sounded extremely enticing…in theory. In practice? I couldn't say. I'd never been in the kind of relationship where something like that was on the table. I didn't know if I ever would be again.

If I wanted to be.

Just shy of midnight, Smith stood up and grumbled something about being tired, then took his wine to bed with him. He was so much like me sometimes I worried for him. The way he preferred to process internally, the way he would be alone forever if someone didn't force him to share company. Smith was a monolith, while also still being my angry, petulant, and sometimes scared-beyond-words baby brother.

"Do you want to check on him?" Silas asked quietly, untangling himself from my lap and immediately looking over his shoulder to search out Lincoln who'd fallen asleep in the corner of the couch, tucked into himself like a hermit crab.

"Just real quick, yes."

We both stood, and we both ignored the way both of my knees cracked.

"I'll get Lincoln to bed," Silas said.

I brushed a kiss against the side of his head, then counted the steps from the living room to Smith's guest room. The light was still on, the door not yet closed. He sat on the edge of the bed, elbows braced on his knees and phone in his hand. I knocked on the door jamb and he looked up, his eyes bloodshot and tired.

"You got into a fight with that wine bottle and lost," I said, jerking my chin toward the almost empty glass he'd been holding all night like a security blanket. "You're not going to feel great about this in the morning."

"I know there's ibuprofen in the bathroom, and I'll be fine in the morning." He barely slurred, and I twisted my mouth into a sympathetic half-frown. "Do you want to talk about this sober?"

"I don't want to talk about this at all." Smith tossed his phone onto the nightstand and flung himself onto the bed.

"I haven't seen you this upset since you showed up on the porch the first day we met."

He grimaced, and I felt bad for hurting him with the barb, but I truly couldn't remember the last time I'd seen him act so childish about his emotions.

"I've never done this before," he said so quietly I almost didn't hear him. Smith scrubbed a wary hand down his face and then looked at me with desperate and imploring eyes. "What if he doesn't like me?"

"Shit."

I'd been looking at Smith's behavior all wrong. I'd incorrectly assumed his reactions had come from a place of jealousy. He'd never introduced a new brother to the fold before, he was worried about the dynamic changing, or so I'd thought. Pushing off the door frame, I went into the room and sat down on the bed, close enough to touch his leg and let him know I was close to him, not just emotionally but also physically.

"Is that what this is about?" I asked, squeezing his knee.

"What else would it be about?"

I huffed out a dying laugh. "I don't know, Smith. I didn't realize. But if he doesn't like you, he'll be the one missing out, not the other way around."

My brother eyed me doubtfully, then blinked at me so slowly I wondered if he was about to fall asleep mid-conversation. With a long exhale, I pulled the blankets up to his chest and tucked him in.

Something else I hadn't done in years.

"Do you remember?" he whispered, rolling onto his side and curling up in the fetal position.

I smoothed my hand over the knobs of his spine, steady up and down and up and down until he settled.

"Of course," I told him.

Of course I remembered the times he'd woken up from night terrors, sometimes screaming and sometimes crying. Sometimes terrified, but never alone. I didn't know if Finn or Hunter had paid Smith any mind at night when I wasn't at the house, but whenever I was, he never had to struggle through a sleepless night alone.

I sat with Smith until the cadence of his breathing changed, and I was certain he'd finally fallen asleep. Turning the light off on my way out, I pulled the door closed behind me and found my way to the primary bedroom where I knew Silas would be waiting.

I closed that door behind me too—and locked it.

"Is he okay?" Silas asked. He was on the foot of the bed, still dressed in jeans and my t-shirt, his feet bare.

"He'll be fine," I said. "Did you get Lincoln into bed?"

"I did." He sighed, then tilted his chin toward his chest and gazed up at me through the fan of his lashes. "Mr. Covington."

A sharp heat exploded low in my belly, and I shot him a warning glance. "It's Sir, and you know it."

"Sir," he practically purred it at me, and the heat sank lower, thickening my cock in a dangerous way.

"Strip."

I reached behind my head and tugged my shirt over and off while Silas scrambled out of his clothes. I loved the look of him there in front of me, limbs a few inches shy of being lanky, hair an inch or so too long to consider kept up. Silas was awkward and messy when he let himself come apart, and that was when I enjoyed him the most.

"You're a sight for sore eyes."

"Thank you, Sir."

His cock bobbed.

"I'm tired, Silas." I took a step toward him, then another and another. He backed up until his knees hit the bed, then he sat down because he had nowhere else to go. I crawled onto him, used my body to slide us both up until his head was on the pillows. He made the happiest sound, and my dick leaked against my sweats.

Reaching between our bodies, I pulled my erection out and tucked my dick between the tight slide of his thighs.

"Fuck, you're tight," I groaned, shifting my hips to fuck the sliver of space between his legs.

Silas whimpered and arched against me, murmuring my name when I curled my hand around his dick again and stroked. It was rough and disjointed, but I brought him off with my hand at the same time I used the tight grip of his thighs to get myself off. It was nowhere near the worst I'd done to him, but in the tired and vulnerable moments at the end of the night, there was a quiet kind of intimacy in the moment that took my breath away. With one last trembling groan, I sank my teeth into Silas's pouty lower lip and went still.

"Go to sleep," I whispered, kissing the place I'd just bitten.

Silas murmured something I couldn't hear, but when I rolled off of him and onto my back, he chased after me. Flinging a leg over my hip and arranging his head on my chest, Silas was asleep before I even finished getting myself settled beneath him. With cum on my cock and my hand, I kissed the tangle of his hair and let sleep take me too.

CHAPTER 29
SILAS

onday morning, Marshall let me stay in bed while he got ready for work. It was some kind of luxury, writhing around in his sheets while he dried off from his shower and got dressed. He told me to touch myself while he knotted his tie, and I made as much of a show of it as I could manage. Partially because I hoped he would come back to bed and get me off and partly because I was basically always horny now. Meeting Marshall had been like the flip of a switch, and *boom*. Suddenly everything was sexual.

He sat down on the edge of the bed with his shiny brown leather shoes between his socked feet, then he coaxed me onto his lap, and then onto my knees. I didn't need any additional instruction to know what he wanted from me. Carefully after loosening the waxed laces, I slipped his feet into the expensive Italian leather oxfords and tied neat bows. My fingertips danced across the pressed seams of the shoes, and it was Marshall's gentle but firm hand on the top of my head that guided me down until my chest was flat on the floor and my mouth hovered inches from the leather I'd just been admiring.

I kissed the top of each foot, but the pressure on my head didn't let up so I kissed his shoes better, using the wet inside of my mouth and my tongue until it was the same as kissing his mouth. My hips thrust forward searching for friction that didn't exist, and then Marshall moved his foot so the toe of his shoe rested against the underside of my chin.

"Good boy," he praised, and I rocked back onto my heels. "You call me after you meet with Cory and tell me how it went."

"Yes, Sir."

How could he talk about work at a time like this?

Marshall straightened to his full height, and I stayed on my knees because it felt so good to be there. His body swayed like he knew he had to go but didn't want to.

"How close are you to coming?" he asked.

We both looked down at my exposed cock, thick and hard, and pulsating like a lightning rod between my legs.

"Very," I admitted.

"You did such a good job with my shoes just now," he said, threading his fingers into my hair and tipping my head back so I was forced to stare up at him. "If you promise to clean them up after you finish, and you can do it in two minutes, you can come."

"You want me to come on your shoes." I curled a sweaty palm around my shaft and stroked. Two minutes would be more than enough time.

"I want to go to work with clean shoes," he corrected, brow raised. "And I'm leaving in two minutes."

His grip on my hair was punishing enough that I had nowhere to look besides his face. No other option than to catalog the fine lines that fanned out from the corners of his eyes while he watched me and the way one side of his mouth quirked up every time I whimpered. My orgasm crept closer, and Marshall nodded his approval, encouraging me along, and it was his visible consent and desire for me that sent me over the edge.

I did my best to angle my cock toward his shoes, but I was so hard I could have cut diamonds and the bend was painful. When I came, cock pulsing in my fist, the only sound that left my throat was a rasping gasp. My body still spasmed from my orgasm, but I knew time was ticking. He released my hair, and I kept a firm hold around the base of my shaft as I went back down to the position he'd had me in before.

I'd managed to shoot most of my load onto his shoes, and I groaned at the way the salt of my cum tasted with the sharp leather of his shoes. I licked and kissed and sucked him clean until he tapped me on the shoulder with his other foot.

"Impressive," he murmured, helping me to my feet this time. My dick was still hard, but he didn't shy away in pulling me close.

"I don't care," he said, the wool of his slacks dragging over my cum-sticky shaft. "Let everyone I meet with today wonder what I was doing before work."

My knees went weak.

Marshall kissed the corner of my mouth, using his tongue to lick a drop of cum from my lips.

"Call me after you meet with Cory," he said again.

"Yes, Sir."

"Will you be here when I get home?"

"I…don't know," I admitted.

Lincoln and Smith had both gone home early Saturday afternoon, and Marshall and I had spent the rest of the weekend together in varying stages of undress. I'd texted Lincoln to check in, much the same way he'd texted to check on all three of his brothers, but I hadn't seen my best friend since he'd left.

"Let me know when you decide," he said simply, dropping another kiss on the opposite corner of my mouth. "There is no right or wrong answer."

Heat burned my cheeks, and I had no idea how it was so

easy for him to read my mind. To guess what my worries or concerns were before I gave voice to them.

"I'll let you know," I promised.

One last kiss, and then he was gone.

Without my Dom to oversee me, I flung myself face-first onto the bed and screamed into the pillows. My entire body was alive with want, and I was desperate to know how I'd even lived before meeting him. I'd had plenty of partners, a fair amount of sex, a decent helping of kinky sex, but everything I experienced with Marshall Covington felt like it was happening to me for the first time. Like everything that had come before him was child's play or a poorly planned rehearsal for some main event I hadn't even known was coming.

I gave myself five minutes to roll around in his sheets, then I finally forced myself out of bed and into clothes. I really didn't have a lot to choose from at his house, so I definitely had to go home before meeting Cory for a lunch interview at twelve in Brentwood. Before leaving, I tidied up a bit, wiping down the places he'd smeared water across mirrors and counters in the bathroom, tossing his wet towel into the hamper on top of his dirty underwear. I debated starting a load of laundry, but I wasn't going to be there to move it to the dryer so decided to not. That was another piece of the relationship we hadn't discussed beyond making meals and cleaning dishes.

Domestic servitude.

I didn't love the idea of being a housekeeper, but I did get hard if I thought about cleaning up after Marshall. I'd have to talk to him about it next time I saw him.

With the house straightened up, I headed home, where I found Lincoln sprawled on the couch with one leg flung over the back and his tablet propped on his chest.

"That can't be comfortable," I said.

He dropped the tablet down to look at me. "I'm more flex-ible than you."

"I guess."

I set my bag down by the back of the couch, then climbed on top of him and situated myself between the wide spread of his legs. He only had on a pair of underwear, which was very usual, and the heat between his legs instantly made my hip start to sweat.

"How was the rest of your weekend?" I asked, swatting his pad out of the way.

With an amused noise, he set it on the table and threaded his fingers into my hair, handling me so differently from the ways Marshall did.

"I spent it all here," he said. "On the couch just like this."

"You haven't moved an inch."

"Not even to eat."

"No food?"

"Not even a crumb," he teased, chuckling under his breath. "How is Marshall's brother?"

"Fine as far as I can tell."

On Saturday morning, Smith had emerged from the guest room looking far more put together than he'd been upon his arrival. He'd accepted a mug of coffee, drank it, then been on his way. Marshall assured me it was very characteristic of his youngest brother to act that way, but the text message check-ins over the rest of the weekend had led me to believe otherwise.

"That's good," Lincoln said. "How was the rest of *your* weekend?"

"Very sexy," I said, moving to alleviate the building pressure in my dick at the thought of it.

"I'm sure." He patted the top of my head affectionately. "I like him. For you, I mean. I like him for you."

"I like him for me too."

"Has he admitted he's in love with you yet?" Lincoln asked, hand going still in my hair.

"No."

A gentle tug on the strands he'd wrapped around his fingers. "And you?"

"What about me?"

"Have you admitted you're in love with him?"

Groaning, I removed myself from Lincoln's lap, tucking into the spot on the couch between his legs and the arm. I pulled my knees to my chest and propped my chin on them, frowning across the small space at him. "I'm not."

He rolled his eyes.

"It's barely been a month. Not even," I protested.

"I loved you the second I laid eyes on you," he countered.

"That's different."

"Is it?"

"Isn't it?" I shot back.

Lincoln shrugged and picked his tablet back up, swiping the screen to whatever he'd been reading when I'd gotten home.

"Aren't you meeting with that friend of his today?"

"At twelve," I said.

"What are your plans until then?"

"Annoying you until it's time to shower, I'd imagine."

"Do either of those things involve you getting up and getting coffee and toast from the kitchen?" he asked. "I wasn't kidding when I said I hadn't moved all weekend."

Laughing, I shoved Lincoln away, leveraging myself off his knee to get up and head for the kitchen. Coffee did sound like a good idea, and so did a lazy morning on the couch with my best friend. It was nice to sit with him, to read with him, to be close to him. But the whole time his question echoed through my head.

Is it?

Being with Lincoln was so different from being with Marshall, on account of the fact the relationship was platonic and the other romantic, but love, at its core, was the same, wasn't it? I didn't know, and I also didn't want to think too hard about it and end up ruining one or both of my relationships.

Finally, just after ten, I dragged myself into the shower and into work clothes, which was weird, all things considered. I checked my phone and sent Marshall a text to let him know I was getting ready to head out, then I kissed Lincoln on the head, and made my way to Brentwood to meet Cory Callahan.

I had just pulled into a parking spot when my dad's name flashed across the screen in my car, and the ringtone blasted through my speakers. Frowning, I pushed the green phone button to accept the call.

"Hello?" My heart rate immediately spiked, not sure of why he was calling or what he wanted.

"Silas." My father cleared his throat, anger already evident in his tone. "It's almost lunch. I'm calling to see if you're planning on coming to work today or not."

A laugh bubbled out of me, unstoppable. "Why would I come to work?" I asked. "You fired me."

"I didn't fire you."

"You literally did," I reminded him. "Told me to clear out my office, which I did."

"Obviously that was just in the heat of the moment."

The minutes on my car clock ticked from 11:55 to 11:56.

"You fired me," I said again, wondering if saying it a second time would jog his memory. "And I have a job interview, so I've got to go."

"Silas—"

I hung up the call before I could hear whatever else he had to say, then I silenced my ringer before shoving my phone into my pocket. He would most certainly call me back, and I wasn't going to let him ruin the interview Marshall had set up for me.

Finding the restaurant was easy, finding Cory was somehow even easier.

At a table for two against a window that faced the street, he sat comfortably in a pair of gray slacks and a green button-up shirt, sleeves rolled up to his elbows. I worried I was over-dressed, with a tie, but it was a first impression and I'd learned at least *something* from my dad's antiquated ways.

"Mr. Callahan," I said, approaching the table with my hand extended. "I'm Silas Ayres."

Cory set his menu on the table and looked up at me, eyes blue as sapphires. He smiled and stood, sliding his hand into mine for a quick and solid handshake.

"Cory," he said. "Please. Mr. Callahan has a time and place and neither of them are here or now."

I thought back to the conversation with Marshall about Mr. Covington and wondered if the two of them had more in common than just career paths. Cory was short, but carried himself like he was taller than me, which was saying something.

"Please, sit," he said, gesturing to the seat across from him.

I slid into the open chair and spread my napkin out over my lap.

"Thank you for meeting with me." I folded my hands together on the edge of the table, hoping he hadn't noticed how sweaty my palms were when we shook.

"Anything for Marshall," he said, sitting back into his chair. He glanced at the menu, then across the table at me. "I'd ask you to tell me about yourself, but I've honestly read up so I know a fair amount about your background."

I fought hard to keep my head up, face forward.

"Marshall made sure I'd read the article you had published in *LA Design Digest*, but I'd of course read it before he even brought you to my attention." Cory smiled, and it was impos-sible to not be put at ease. "Your innovative ideas in our field are admirable."

"Thank you, Mr...Cory."

The corner of his mouth twitched, and he scratched the side of his nose.

"I don't actively design the way you and Marshall do. I'm a consultant these days, called in to review and elevate things others are already working on, and I have to be honest, I think that's something you'd excel at. You approach architecture differently than most people do, don't you, Silas?"

My breath hitched in my throat because he was right, and it was something no one else had bothered to notice before him, or if they had, they'd never articulated it. My dad had always thought I designed carelessly, but that wasn't it at all.

"I do," I admitted.

"Does that sound like something you might enjoy?"

I managed a rough nod.

Everything was happening so fast, and I didn't know how to make sense of it. Cory's role as an architectural consultant was very close to a dream for me, and two minutes after meeting him, he was basically offering me the opportunity on a golden platter?

"I do like designing myself, though," I made sure to add.

I didn't want to walk away from my roots entirely.

"So do I," he agreed. "How amazing to do both, right?"

"I…" Nodding, I cleared my throat. "I don't know, but I'm sure it is."

"You'll know soon, Silas. You'll know soon." Cory smiled at me, and it was infectious. He smiled, and I smiled. He sounded sure, and I felt it. Whatever Cory contained and bled, it was contagious in all of the best ways.

"Thank you," I whispered, blinking hard.

One of my biggest fears in life had always been drowning in the legacy of my father's designs, and for the first time, I had support in my life offering me a way out of that future. I dropped my hands into my lap and wiped them off on the napkin, hoping I didn't do something embarrassing like throw up all over both of us.

"Don't thank me," he said, leaning back and lifting his arm to flag down a server. "You're about to make my job infinitely easier, and you're going to make me look *really* good."

I laughed, the tension leaking out of me and melting into the floor.

I had Marshall to come home to, Lincoln in the wings, and a job offer in front of me that was about to change my entire life. Even though my phone was in my pocket, missed calls from my dad going ignored and undoubtedly only making things between us worse, I'd never felt better.

CHAPTER 30
MARSHALL

On Wednesday, Hunter showed up—unannounced—at lunch, looking like someone had kicked his puppy. I worried, in this instance, the puppy was our youngest brother.

"What?" I asked, closing the lid on my laptop and leaning back in my chair for a stretch. I'd been hunched over it for hours crunching numbers and waiting for either a confirmation or rejection about Cahuenga Pass so I'd be able to put Silas out of his misery over the whole thing.

I hadn't seen him since the weekend, which was…fine.

He'd been in touch, which was not only appreciated but required, and I knew at home with Lincoln he was in good hands. Figuratively, at least. If not literally, on occasion. But always platonically. I'd worried getting used to the tactile nature of their friendship would take me some time, but it had slotted into place in my brain just as quickly as Silas had found his way into my heart. I'd spent most of the morning toying with the idea of taking him out to Rapture over the weekend, but Hunter's arrival meant I'd need to save that conversation for later.

"Spoke with Andrew," he said.

Frowning, I gestured for him to come in and close the door behind him.

Hunter was dressed for court, a navy suit and burgundy tie. He dropped his bag on the floor and sank into one of the leather guest chairs opposite my desk. The material creaked beneath his weight, and he grimaced, rolling his eyes at me.

"This chair is absurd."

"It's design."

"It's uncomfortable," he said.

"You can stand."

"Can we go?" He did stand after that, leaving his bag on the floor. "Get lunch or something."

I glanced around my office, at the blueprints and the general state of the place, then stood. "Yeah. Lunch is good."

We walked down to the same cafe we always favored on his midday visits, ordered the same sandwiches and the same drinks. It wasn't until our orders were in that I leveled my brother with a look meant to push him into telling me more about his call with Andrew.

Hunter opened with, "He's requested to be written out of the inheritance."

"That's…"

"Surprising," he supplied, and I nodded my agreement. "He doesn't want anything to do with the Covington name."

I bit down hard on the tip of my tongue. "Or the Covington men?"

Hunter snorted a laugh that died in the back of his throat. "He maintains he will always be a Calavert."

"Fine with me."

"And Smith, I'm sure," Hunter said. "But he does want to meet us."

"Why?"

The waiter appeared with our lunch and refills on our water, which was appreciated since I was relatively confident we had ended up in the Sahara for how dry my throat was. I'd welcomed three brothers into my world over the course of my life. There was no reason for a fourth one to throw me off so dramatically. I'd done my best to hold it together for Smith's sake, but when I was alone…

"Curiosity, I imagine."

I sighed. "I've been meaning to check on Finn. How did he take the news after Smith and I left on Friday night?"

"In stride, as usual."

I believed that about Finn, who was so amenable in all things I couldn't remember a time I'd ever seen him upset about anything that well and truly mattered. It was as if he'd managed to get all of the nonchalance in the genes, leaving Hunter, Smith, and me to carry the burden of always worrying in one way or another.

"And Smith?" Hunter asked.

I had texted him and Finn over the weekend, and I'd checked in again with Smith after he'd left, but if my own feelings were any indication of the matter, all four of us would be feeling the aftermath of this revelation for quite some time.

"He says he's fine, but he took a glass of wine to bed with him on Friday," I said. I didn't tell Hunter how he'd asked me to sit with him until he was asleep. Those moments had been ours…always. "I'm going to search him out tomorrow to make sure."

"I talked to Smith yesterday, by the way," Hunter confessed. He'd eaten through half his sandwich already.

"And?" I arched a brow.

He shrugged, but it was obvious there was something else he wanted to say.

"How are *you* with all of this, Marshall?" he asked.

I glanced down at my lap and smoothed the white linen napkin over the top of my thighs. There were crumbs, a smear of mayonnaise, my trembling fingers.

"I'm fine," I said, whether it was the truth or a lie was uncertain.

"Fine because you're distracted by Stanley's son?"

The silence between us was deafening, and I leveled a sharp look across the table. "His name is Silas," I corrected.

Hunter flashed a brief smile. "Him and Smith graduated the same year, yes?"

They were the same age, yes, but I only knew the year Silas had graduated because it had been in the bio *LA Design Digest* had attached to his article, which I'd practically committed to memory.

"What's your point?" I asked, instead of confirming or denying.

"Just making an observation."

"Your honor, I object."

Hunter snorted. "On what grounds?"

"On the grounds you're being an annoying gnat." I ate the last bite of the first half of my sandwich with my brother's amused laugh in my ears.

We lapsed into another silence while we finished our meals, and Hunter didn't bring Andrew up again until our plates were cleared and the check was on the table.

"He does want to meet," he said again, as if I'd forgotten.

"When?"

"Up to us."

"Then we'll talk about it on Friday." I paused. "Do you want to meet him? This is all taking his wants into account, but not ours. Just because Andrew, who is too good for our name and our money, wants to meet us, doesn't mean we have to."

"Finn likened us to sideshow acts when I told him."

It was an astute observation, and I knew that was how the whole thing would land with Smith as well.

"We'll discuss it Friday," I said again.

Hunter nodded, then reached into his pocket and pulled

out enough cash to cover the whole bill. "Lunch is on me," he said.

"I won't argue."

We finished our drinks and walked together back to my office so Hunter could collect his bag and head back to court or work or wherever it was he disappeared to during business hours. Before he left, though, he stopped me with a gentle touch against my forearm and a very serious expression on his face that had him looking so much like our father I wanted to throw up a little bit.

"What?" I asked after he'd taken too long to say anything of note.

"Be careful with Silas," he said softly.

"Careful how?"

"He's young," Hunter said.

"Do you think his best friend is warning him about me?" I asked, already knowing enough about Lincoln to hear the question in his voice. "Be careful, Silas, that man is old?"

He rolled his eyes to indicate yes.

"I am being careful," I conceded, which felt like a lie on my tongue.

Silas, if anything, had me acting very recklessly. Going all in on a relationship I'd never thought possible just because I was scared of it slipping through my fingers if I didn't act quickly about it. But my feelings for him were true, and they were strong. I'd almost slipped on more than one occasion and told him I loved him. I wasn't even sure if the way I felt for him was love…or something more or something less.

"I am fond of him," I settled on as a confession to Hunter. "And I am careful."

"You've never had a relationship, Marshall."

"Not that you'd remember," I agreed. "Not anyone that mattered."

"And does Silas Ayres matter?" he asked.

"Very much," I whispered.

My voice cracked, and Hunter's nostrils flared, but he didn't call me out about it. I knew he'd heard it, also knew he'd cataloged every tic and twitch my face had made while I talked about Silas. It was the lawyer in him, always looking out for tells. For lies and truths that would either fit or go against whatever narrative he was being told.

"What are your thoughts about Andrew?" I asked, realizing we'd talked about Finn, about Smith, about myself, but not yet about him and how the appearance of a new brother—who wanted little to do with us—made him feel.

"I don't think about him one way or another," Hunter said with a shrug.

"How analytical of you."

He slid his bag up onto his arm and gave me an almost sorrowful smile. "How else am I meant to be?"

Before I could counter, he gave me a quick wave, then turned on his heel and headed for his car. I stayed there and watched him go, seeing the most practical of my brothers in a new light. Hunter was pragmatic on his best days, and if he'd accused me of being too emotional in my decision-making, I found him to be quite the opposite.

No real emotion at all.

Heading back into the office, I pulled my cell phone out of my pocket and dialed Finn.

He answered out of breath. "Hello?"

"Busy?"

"Wouldn't have picked up if I was. What's up?" he asked.

"Just wanted to see how you were handling the whole Andrew situation," I said, sitting down at my desk and getting my work back online.

"Better than Smith but probably worse than you," he said.

I laughed. "That's a big range."

"I don't like that he doesn't want the inheritance, but I'm also glad he doesn't," Finn said.

"You never shared well."

He made a thoughtful sound. "I don't see why he wants to meet us at all."

"Do you want to meet him?" I asked the same question I'd asked of Hunter. The same one I would also ask of Smith on Friday night at dinner.

"I haven't decided," Finn said softly.

"You don't have to."

"I know, Marshall."

"I told Hunter we'd discuss it on Friday."

"Then let's talk then," Finn said. "I've got to get going but didn't want to not answer when you called."

Something tightened in the middle of my chest at the casual way he let that confession settle between us.

"Right. Hey, Finn?"

"Yeah?"

I swallowed hard. "Love you."

"Oh, God." He groaned playfully. "That boyfriend of yours has made you soft."

"Fuck you."

He laughed in my ear until he was out of breath, then a quiet, "Love you back."

The call disconnected in my ear, and I dropped my phone onto the desk and went limp. With my legs splayed out and my arms hanging over the armrests, I stared up at the ceiling feeling out of my element for the first time in a very long time. It was okay, I reminded myself. I was allowed. There were so many things going on at home and at work, it was perfectly acceptable for me to feel a little burnt out and exhausted over the weight of it all.

There was a light to be found in all of it.

A relief.

And that lived in the small spaces between Silas and me. When he was on his knees or on his back, in the throes of submission, and I stood strong and sure in my dominance. Being with Silas wasn't work at all—it was a reward. It was salvation.

And, suddenly, the responsibilities of the day melted away into nothing I wanted anything to do with. I wanted to go home, find Silas on my couch, and go to my knees in front of him in thanks for the life he'd already started to build around me. Maybe that was too much, too soon, or maybe it was too little, too late. Maybe it was not enough or just the right amount, I wasn't certain.

I was invested.

I was in love.

I closed everything up for the day and made my way home, not knowing if he would be there or at his place with Lincoln. Pulling up and finding his car in my driveway was like Christmas morning, and it took all my restraint to not run through the house calling after him.

He was easy enough to find.

All I had to do was follow the sound of whatever early 2000's punk band he had playing from his phone. It was on my nightstand, and Silas was in my bed, legs crossed at the ankle and a book propped open on his lap. He also had his laptop beside him, wearing not much more than a pair of underwear, and the sight of him there stopped me dead in my tracks.

"Are you busy?" I asked.

He looked up, startled, and then pleased.

So fucking pleased.

"I was reading through some stuff before I start with Cory on Monday."

I undid the top button on my shirt and stalked toward him.

"Monday?" I asked.

"I was going to tell you when you got home."

I crawled onto the foot of the bed, closed the space between us. Silas moved his book and his computer out of the way to make room for me between his legs. He looked like a king there beneath me, or more like a spoiled prince, ready to be pampered.

"We need to celebrate," I said, dipping down and kissing his hip.

"You're the boss," he murmured.

I glanced up at him, tugging down the waistband of his briefs to kiss him lower, and lower still.

"Well, if that's the case," I said, burying my face between his legs and breathing him in. "Then I think you should call me Mr. Covington."

CHAPTER 31
SILAS

There was something intensely erotic about having Marshall between my legs. With his shirt on and undone, his belt out of the loops but nowhere close to being open enough to get his pants off…I shoved my laptop as far away as I could manage, and then he had my cock and balls out, the elastic waistband tucked beneath them. He made a bit of a show of rubbing his cheek up the length of my shaft, letting his lips drag across my hot skin as I got hard embarrassingly fast.

"Mr. Covington."

The words caught in my throat, and the look he gave me, glancing up from beneath the fan of his light brown lashes as he slid my briefs down my legs and off was almost enough to make me come on the spot.

"Yes, Silas?" he asked, running a line up the length of my cock with the tip of his nose.

"I…I don't know."

"What do you *want?*"

His breath puffed warm against my balls. It felt unreasonable for me to tell him what I wanted, but he'd asked and that was the point of this relationship. Wasn't it? It was only that I'd dreamed about this for weeks and how it was only seconds away from happening.

"I want you to suck my cock," I said.

Marshall curled his fingers around the base of my dick in a painfully loose grip. He slid from root to tip, a groan leaving his throat when his fingers expanded to the point of barely touching around the swollen thickness of the middle of my shaft. He'd asked me once if I topped, and never again, which I did appreciate. With my other partners there'd always been an expectation I'd give in eventually and change my mind, the implication that not being a top was a waste. Marshall had never given that impression.

"How do you like to have your cock sucked?" He cupped my balls with his free hand, and a shudder tore through my whole body.

"I...I like when it's wet," I admitted. "I like when it's loud."

"You like to hear your partners choking on it?"

Arousal tangled tight and low in my belly. "Yes, but also just...noisy."

"So you know they're enjoying it?" he asked.

"Yes, Sir," I whispered, clearing my throat and remembering his earlier ask. "Yes, Mr. Covington."

Marshall hummed, smiling up at me with a very dangerous heat. "You can come in my mouth, Silas. But I expect a warning."

"Yes, Mr. Coving—"

The rest of the words were lost because Marshall's mouth sealed around the tip of my dick and everything went white. He swirled his tongue around my flared crown, welling spit up in his mouth and letting it slide down my shaft like a waterfall. It pooled on my sac and slid down farther, slicking my crack. Marshall took advantage of that, using his fingers to tease my hole while he worked his way down my shaft.

His teeth grazed against the skin, and I bucked off the bed

with a desperate little whine that I almost didn't even recognize as my own. It was far from the first time I'd had my dick sucked, but watching Marshall do it was definitely a brand new experience for me. At my noises, he flicked a stare up at me, stretching to get more inches into his mouth.

There was no way he was going to make it past the middle of my shaft, and once he realized it, he set a wet and sloppy rhythm from there to the tip and back down again that immediately ticked every box of everything I liked in a blow job. Sliding one finger into my ass, Marshall hummed and moaned around my cock, and I had to fist the sheets to stop from grabbing his hair and lifting off the bed to fuck into his mouth.

Propping myself up on my elbows so I could watch every second was a mistake. The sight of Marshall between my legs, fully dressed and humping the bed while he choked himself with my cock was too much for me to handle.

"Mr. Covington," I forced out his name, resting a hand on the top of his head in case he didn't hear me. "Mr. Covington, you're going to make me come."

In response, he let more spit wet my shaft and he made another attempt to get closer to my base. The tight squeeze as he choked around me sent me freefalling over the edge. I arched off the bed, making sure to grab the bed instead of him, and with a rasping cry, I came. Hot jets of cum shot against the roof of his mouth, his tongue, and his answering sounds were that of a starving man who'd finally been fed.

Marshall drank down every drop of my cum, keeping his mouth sealed around my shaft until I went soft. And once the blood had fled to other parts of my body, Marshall managed to tuck my entire length into his mouth. Exhaling against the curly hairs that lined the base of my shaft, he hollowed his cheeks and sucked me *hard*, then lifted off entirely and rocked back onto his heels.

"Holy shit," I muttered, vision still white and glittering around the edges.

He swiped his mouth with the back of his hand, then we both looked down at the erection tenting the fly of his slacks, the dark wet spot bleeding through the fabric.

"You taste as good as I knew you would," he said.

"That was…thank you."

The tip of his tongue darted out, either worrying the corner of his mouth or licking the taste of me away, I wasn't certain.

"You never have to thank me for that." Marshall climbed off the bed and finished undressing, the sight of his hard cock almost enough to bring mine back to life on sight. "It might be my new favorite way to reward you."

"Oh," I whispered.

"As much as I would like to tie you spreadeagle to this bed now and fuck you until I can't even remember my own name, I did say your new job deserved a celebration."

"Consider myself celebrated." I scooted to an upright position, then onto my knees.

"I want to take you to dinner."

"Are you asking?"

Marshall made a very unimpressed sound in the back of his throat. "Not in the slightest. Come clean off with me and then get dressed."

My legs wobbled when I stood, but Marshall held out his hand to me and helped me to the shower. He washed us both with a surgical precision, paying no more attention than necessary to my half-hard cock. After rinsing, he toweled us both off and instructed me to get dressed in something nice.

I still didn't have many clothes at his house, but I'd gone home earlier in the day to get a few things because I was at Marshall's more often than not. Doing the best I could with a pair of black slacks and a white button-up, I sat down on the edge of the bed to deal with my socks and shoes.

After I was dressed, Marshall emerged from the closet in a pair of navy slacks and a pastel pink button-up. He was busy fussing with the cuffs, his feet bare and his hair still damp from the shower.

"Silas," he said, not looking up. "Get my socks and shoes from the closet."

He'd already set out a pair of dark blue socks and brown oxfords, and I brought both things into the bedroom. He sat on the edge of the bed in the place I'd earlier occupied, his legs spread and his hands resting comfortably on the tops of his thighs. He didn't even have to ask. He simply extended one of his feet toward me, and immediately I went to my knees.

"What are you thinking about?" he asked.

"Hmn?" I looked up at him, rucking up the sock to get it onto his foot easier. He had big feet with long toes, smooth knuckles with a dusting of dark hair on the first two.

"Your brow." He reached forward and stroked his finger up from my nose toward my forehead.

"Nothing." I relaxed my face and quickly shook my head to clear it. "I just…didn't know this was something I liked before you."

"Maybe you didn't like it before me. Maybe this is something special just for us."

There was a lot more to unpack with that comment than I think he realized, and as I put his other sock on and loosened the laces of his shoes, I thought hard about it. I knew people like that, who were only into things with their current—or former—partner. Feet weren't something I'd ever even thought of before Marshall, but as I slipped one foot into its respective shoe and then the other, I didn't imagine I'd think of them after him either.

I didn't want there to be an *after* Marshall.

"There you go again," he said softly, reaching for the knot between my eyebrows. "What are you thinking about now?"

"It's embarrassing," I said.

"I didn't ask how it made you feel." Marshall trailed his hand down my face until he had my chin in a grip barely on the gentle side of punishing. "I asked what you were thinking about, Silas."

I recognized an order when I heard one, and I recognized the flush in my cheeks when I felt it.

"I was thinking about how I didn't want there to be an after," I admitted.

He lifted one of his feet and brought it down between my legs, a gentle pressure against my cock, his fingers still warm and solid against my face.

"Who said anything about an after?" he asked.

I blinked hard, shaking my head. "It was just a thought."

"Are you not happy with me, Silas? Not fulfilled?"

"It's not like that, Sir," I whispered. "That's not how I meant it."

He hummed, pressing his foot down slightly on my cock, just until I gasped and leaned toward him…somehow asking for more and less at the same time.

"One of the things I admire about you is how you always look to the future." He stroked his thumb across the hollow of my cheek. "But with me, you don't have to."

Spit knotted into something hard to swallow in the back of my throat.

"Why not?" I managed to ask. "Why not, Sir? Mr. Covington?"

"You're here now," he answered. "I'm here now."

Squeezing my eyes closed, I blinked back an uninvited onslaught of burning hot tears. Was that all this was? A series of moments with no hope for anything beyond the present?

"Hey." Marshall tapped my cheek, took his foot off my cock. "Where are you right now?"

"Are you going to be here then?" I asked. "Am I? In the future?"

"Oh, Silas." Marshall slid off the bed, hauled me onto his lap and kissed the top of my head. "Now is every moment, in the moment. We're already in the future, and it's our now. The now is where we live and it's where I'll always find you."

"Please don't make me cry," I muttered into his shoulder.

Marshall chuckled, kissed the top of my head, and lifted me to my feet. He sat me down on the bed, brought my shoes between us, and slipped my feet into them, the same way I'd already done for him more than once. After tying up the laces, he prostrated himself and pressed soft kisses against the toes of my shoes, then rocked back onto his heels.

We were almost eye level, almost equal.

"I am in love with you, Silas," he said, words carefully chosen and strong in their delivery. Each one landed between us, stacking together to build a foundation I never understood I'd wanted until Marshall had offered it to me. "Before. Then. But most importantly now."

"You…"

"I love you," he said again. "It might be too soon. My brother would most certainly think so, but I know how I feel when I'm with you, when I'm *not* with you."

"I…" I looked up toward the ceiling to stop the earlier tears from falling.

"This doesn't need to be tit for tat. You don't have to feel the same way I feel."

"Sir."

With a groan, Marshall pushed up onto his feet and held his hand out for me. I let him help me up, then I stared down at our feet, at our fancy shoes that neither of us had managed to get into on our own.

"I love you," he said again, barely louder than a whisper. Brushing his fingers across my cheek, he tipped my head back and pressed our mouths together.

The kiss was gentle at first, unsure, and then he dragged his tongue across the seam of my lips in question, and I opened for him. Marshall groaned into me, a sound so deep it rattled my bones, and he cradled the back of my head with his hand so he had enough leverage to deepen the kiss. Weakly, with trembling fingers, I grabbed him by the hips to steady myself, and then I gave myself over to him entirely.

I knew he'd cut me off because he thought I didn't love him back, but such a thing couldn't have been further from the truth. I hardly knew Marshall, and I was violently in love with him. So much so, I didn't even have the words to tell him in a way that made sense. To make up for it, I tried to move my tongue around his in a way that made sense, a way that would let him know the feelings he'd shared with me were so much more than mutual. It must have worked because after he ended the kiss, he traced his fingertips across my kiss-swollen lips with stars in his eyes.

Marshall took my hand in his, kissed my knuckles.

"We have a celebration to get to."

"Sir."

He was one step toward the door, his body still turned toward me like he wasn't quite ready to put the required space between us to facilitate us getting to this celebration dinner he'd promised me.

"Silas."

I wanted to tell him I loved him back because it was the truth. He knew it, I could tell by his eyes, but there was something to the words of it and I wanted him to have that. But the words were still a tightly wound, wrongly shaped knot in the back of my throat.

He smiled at me then, and it didn't look sad.

"Dinner, Silas," he said, giving me a pull toward the door. "We need to go because I have plenty more planned for you, and I'd like to get to bed before tomorrow." The corner of his mouth tipped into a smirk. "Some of us have to get up for work. We don't all have the luxury of lazing around naked in bed."

CHAPTER 32
MARSHALL

My jaw ached from trying to get Silas's cock in my mouth, but the look of unfiltered pleasure as he came on my tongue was worth it ten times over. I chased the pain with a drink of wine and an eyeful of the man I'd just admitted I was in love with, and he hadn't said it back, but the way he looked at me from the other side of the dinner table was answer enough.

"What's good here?" he asked, looking at the menu without really reading it. His stare zoned in on the center of the page and never moved.

"I'll order for you," I assured him, reaching out and plucking the menu from his fingers. His cheeks darkened, and he folded his hands neatly into his lap.

"Thank you, Sir," he said quietly. "May I ask a question?"

"I always want you to speak freely."

He reached onto the table, pressing two fingers against the base of his wine glass and sliding it halfway toward him without picking it up.

"You said you had plans for me later, so why are we drinking?"

I chuckled, not sure if I was more amused with the question itself or the barely restrained disappointment that laced around Silas's words as he asked it.

"We've spent more time together than before, and I have a better understanding of how alcohol affects you," I explained. "No drinking, to a few sips, to a full glass. Some people disagree, but I find you still have your wits about you after six ounces of Merlot."

My answer acted as some kind of permission for him, and he raised the glass to take a drink, chasing a stray drop from his lips with the tip of his tongue. My eyes went straight to the movement, and he must have seen it because he smiled at me.

"I was worried it was some kind of test," he said. "Like if I drank it, you'd deny me later."

I raised a brow. "I might deny you still, but not on account of enjoying a celebratory glass of wine that I ordered for you."

Silas nodded and returned his glass to the table.

There was still something *almost* off about him that I couldn't quite put my finger on. I worried it had to do with me sucking his cock, with me getting on my knees to put on his shoes and kiss his feet. Just like there were people who thought the only way to play was to play sober, there were also dominants who would have considered it out of character or unreasonable for me to do either of those things. Obviously, I wasn't one of those men, but I now wondered if Silas would see it that way. If by indulging my own wants, I'd changed his perception of me.

"Now I have a question for you," I said.

He smiled shyly at me, scratching the side of his cheek before leaning back in his chair like he was finally getting comfortable. "Well, you most certainly don't need permission to ask me."

"Neither do you," I said, waiting for him to acknowledge the truth of it before I went on. "How did you feel about everything we did at home?"

Silas's eyes flashed wide, and he was no longer relaxed, leaning over the table with a hushed voice.

"Everything?" he repeated. "Should we talk about this here?"

I glanced around the restaurant, finding it busy but not overly so. There were tables in proximity, but no one was on top of us. If they wanted to eavesdrop, they would have to make an entire thing of it, which I sincerely doubted anyone would bother with.

"Yes."

"Well." His cheeks were darker than before, almost crimson. "I liked it a lot."

"Was it uncomfortable for you? To have me on my knees like that? For me to be between your legs that way?"

Silas's eyes darted around the restaurant. "It wasn't uncomfortable."

"You don't think me less capable of being dominant for it?"

He chewed the inside of his cheek, letting out a breath that sounded almost like a laugh. I hadn't realized how nervous the conversation made me until I tried to smile back and swallow, but my saliva caught in my throat. I cleared it, hoping to look somewhat dignified.

"I think it takes a real dominant to get on his knees, Marshall," he said softly, dipping his chin toward his chest and looking up at me before adding, "Sir."

"Good."

I looked away from Silas in search of a server to take our order, but what caught my eye on the other end of the restaurant was something else entirely. My brother Finn at a table, an empty chair beside him and a very well-dressed couple across from him. They looked very friendly, talking with animated expressions and raised glasses. I was about to excuse myself from Silas to go say hello when the man stood up from the table, leaving Finn and the woman alone.

My brother watched him walk away, then leaned in close and slanted his mouth against the woman's in a kiss that was almost too indecent for the public. She reached up to touch his face, a very obvious wedding set sparkling on her finger. Finn pulled away from her and sank back into his seat seconds before the man returned, and they went back to a group conversation like nothing had happened.

"Are you okay?" Silas asked, looking over his shoulder, trying to see what had caught my attention. He'd never met Finn before, only Smith, and there wasn't enough resemblance between us for anyone who didn't know we were related to pick us out of a crowd as siblings.

"Yes," I said, giving one last look to Finn before refocusing my attention on Silas. I didn't want to tell him I'd seen my brother because then I'd have to explain why I didn't want to interrupt his meal to introduce them. That thought process brought up an entirely different chain of ideas, ending with the fact that, sooner or later, I was going to have to introduce Silas to the rest of them. Friday night dinner felt like the best option, but those dates also felt off-limits until we sorted out the situation with Andrew.

"Are you sure?"

"Positive. Was just thinking about how I'd like you to meet the rest of my brothers soon."

It wasn't a lie. I'd explain the rest later.

"Oh. Are you sure?"

"Why wouldn't I be?"

Silas shrugged. "I just want them to like me."

"They'll love you," I promised, not caring if they did or not. It wouldn't have any bearing on me. "As soon as we sort out the mess with the new one, I'll invite you along one Friday."

Silas scrunched his nose and shook his head. "Friday is your time with them. I don't want to interrupt that."

"It's not an interruption—"

He grimaced. "It's also my time with Lincoln."

I opened my mouth and closed it again, nodding my understanding. "You're right," I said. "That was very selfish of me."

"Not at all," he whispered, and then the waiter was there to take our orders. Silas smiled—content—as I ordered for us both, and I watched him nurse his wine through the entire meal and the whole of dessert.

After we'd eaten and long after Finn and his mystery couple had left, Silas let out a long breath and folded his hands together on his stomach.

"That was quite a celebration, but I hope you don't have anything penetrative planned for me later."

I laughed, unable to keep the noise contained in my mouth. "I'm an adaptable man, if you haven't figured that out yet."

"Should I be worried?"

I dropped my napkin onto the table and stood, brushing some stray crumbs off my lap before walking around the table and extending my hand. Silas smiled up at me and let me help him to his feet. With our fingers twined together, I pulled our bodies close, like we were on the verge of a dance.

"Have I ever given you cause for concern?"

"No," he rasped.

"I'm not going to start now."

"I know, Sir."

"Good." I kissed him quickly on the mouth, then held his hand on the way out to the parking lot.

Public affection was a new thing for me, and I doubted it was new for Silas at all. He and Lincoln were so tactile with each other, I didn't even want to wager a guess at how many people had mistaken them for lovers or partners at some point and not just friends.

When we reached the car, I opened the passenger door

again and waited while Silas arranged himself in the seat and buckled in. As I was closing the door, he asked, "Would you tell me again?"

"Tell you what?"

"That you love me."

My tongue stuck to the roof of my mouth, and I closed the car door. I walked around the front of the car, climbed into the driver's side, and leaned over the console, taking his face into my hands and holding him right where I wanted him.

"I love you," I said for what must have been at least the fourth time that night. It didn't feel any less scary in my mouth, but Silas's reaction softened every time which meant I would shout it from the rooftops until we were both comfortable with the truth of my feelings.

I closed the small space between us and slanted our mouths together, kissing him hard and insistent. Silas moaned against me, going pliant as putty in the passenger seat. The sounds he made were enough to have me second-guessing my plan about nothing penetrative.

With great reluctance, I ended the kiss, but only so I could drive us home. As soon as we were back in the house, I was on him. My hands, my mouth, the press of my chest and my thighs against his. I backed Silas into the wall and buried my face into the crook of his neck like a famished man, licking sustenance from the curve of his throat.

He moaned, whispered a flurry of endearments that had my hands making quick work of our belts and flies. I pulled both of our cocks free and then shoved my fingers into his mouth, depressing his tongue.

"Suck them the way you like your cock sucked," I demanded, and he did, welling saliva up into his mouth and gagging around my fingertips. When his spit ran down my wrist, I pulled my hand free and reached down low. Taking his cock in hand, and then mine, I used the leverage of his back against the wall to make a tight channel for our shafts.

Stroking slowly, I nipped at Silas's throat. He trembled, entire body alert and on edge as I stroked our dicks together. Precum slicked and smeared around my fingers, and it was so far away from being enough. I wanted Silas sweaty and ravished and bleary from it all.

"Tell me when you're close," I whispered.

I hoped it was soon because I was on the edge.

"Sir," he rasped, hips thrusting against mine. "Close."

I unfurled my fingers enough to let his dick fall out of my grasp, and when he cried out in absolute agony, I shot my load all over his violently throbbing cock. Silas's entire body swayed, and he slapped his hands against the wall, on the verge of a tantrum that only made me come harder.

"Jesus fuck," I cursed under my breath, letting go of myself before the sensation turned overpowering.

Silas pulled his lips between his teeth, and he blinked up at me, a hard press of eyelids that looked like they were working overtime to hold back tears.

"Strip," I told him, taking a step back so I could watch the show.

His fingers fought him every step of the way, but he managed to get out of his clothes. Leaving them in a pile by the door, I next ordered him to his knees, and then lower, and then I told him to crawl. He followed behind me like an obedient—if not slutty—dog, ass in the air and cock jutting out between his legs. He crawled without protest all the way through my house and into the bedroom, and when I stopped, he stopped.

Together, we waited.

When I could hear my heartbeat back in my ears instead of feeling it in my cock, I went to the dresser to retrieve cuffs and a collar, some rope, an anal hook, and my favorite bamboo cane. I dropped all the items on the bed for Silas to see, then I pulled a bottle of lube from the nightstand and added it to the pile.

"Is any of this a no?"

We'd talked about caning before, and it wasn't a no, but it was also far from the enthusiastic yes I normally preferred.

"No, Sir," he said, voice slightly hoarse.

"Stand up. Maybe just a little penetration."

He climbed to his feet, standing tall as I fastened the thick leather collar around his neck. I loved the look of it, the way the supple leather contrasted against the smooth heat of his skin. I slipped rope through the O-ring on the collar and flipped the ends off his shoulders and let them tickle the small of his back. Next, the cuffs. Around his wrists with gentle kisses, and then I walked him into the closet.

It was a walk-in with a full-length mirror, and Silas had been in my closet plenty of times, but he'd never noticed the bolts—or the spreader bar—in the ceiling. Lifting his arms over his head, I hooked him up and stepped back. Admiring the way he was lifted onto his toes just enough to keep him off-balance but not enough to make him tired.

"Still good?" I asked.

"Yes, Sir."

Then, the hook. I lubed it, eased it into him and groaned at the way it made him sigh like a well-tended cat. I notched the curve of the hook against his ass and threaded the rope through the ring at the end, pulling it all taut and ensuring his head was held straight.

"Look down," I told him, and he tried, but the rope tugged the hook, the ball on the hook pushed against his prostate, and Silas was very close to crying about it. His cock was still hard, looking like it was about to burst. I pressed my finger against the underside of his chin and righted his face so he stared at our reflection, head on.

"Just like this, alright?" I asked. "Don't move from here. Keep your eyes open. Do you understand?"

"Yes, Sir."

He shifted his weight, and the cuffs clanked against the bar.

"I'm going to start gentle, but I won't stay gentle."

He managed a nod.

"My intent *is* to hurt you, Silas. I want to decorate your thighs with stripes so dark they'll last for weeks."

He whimpered, swaying on his toes.

"Ready?"

"Yes, Sir."

I situated myself behind him with the cane. The position was far from ideal, but with his cock hard enough to stay out of the way, I reached around and tested the bamboo against the front of his thighs. A few gentle taps at first to check the angle. I adjusted as necessary, shifting a little to the side so I could have better access, then I landed a few test strikes.

Silas's cock cried before his eyes did.

And I wanted to taste the mess from both sides of him.

"Sweetheart," I whispered, rubbing my cheek against his, watching him watch us in the reflection of the mirror. I wondered what he saw when he looked at himself, if he saw the gorgeous man that I saw or if he only saw his own shortcomings. I'd ask him sometime, but not tonight.

"Sir."

"I do love you," I told him.

The cane whooshed as it cut through the air, and then *thwap* as it landed hard against his skin. His knees buckled, and he jerked forward. All his angling shifted, the hook curled into him deeper, and I watched him alternate between trying to fight against the pain in his ass and the pain on his thighs. I waited while he settled himself, one thin bruise already blooming across his legs.

"How many years did you work for your father?" I asked.

"Eight, Sir."

"Eight, then. Eight years of wasted potential." I swung the cane again and again. Two times in rapid succession, very close to the first strike. He still jerked against the impact but brought himself back to center much faster.

Four.

Five.

Six.

I don't think Silas knew he'd started to cry, but after I licked the tears from his cheek, he understood. Lower, his cock streaked wet smears across his stomach, precum pulsing out of his slit with every breath.

"You like this," I murmured.

Tucking the cane under my arm, I slid my hand down the front of his thighs and pushed my fingertips into the bruises that marked his otherwise blemish-free thighs.

He was a goddamn work of art.

A masterpiece.

"Very much, Sir," he said softly.

"Two more," I warned. "But first."

Returning the cane to my hand, I tapped the tip of it against his balls, against his shaft. He dropped his head back before remembering himself and forcing his head straight, prying his own eyes open with nothing more than willpower and the need to serve.

"What do you see?" I asked, continuing to pepper taps against his most sensitive areas.

"The bruises you promised," he answered, groaning. "I see the man I love."

"Silas."

"I love you," he said, and I looked up until I caught his stare in the mirror.

He was flushed and tearstained, but earnest as ever.

"I love you," I said back to him for the first time, then

popped the fronts of his thighs two more times, harder than any of the other strikes had been. His skin bloomed and cracked, pinpricks of blood appearing beneath the cane. I let it fall to the floor, then I loosened the rope around his collar, slid the hook out, and dropped it beside the cane.

I stepped in front of him, blocking his view, and I slanted our mouths together and kissed him. Spearing my tongue into his mouth, chasing after the high his confession made me feel, I took his thicker than usual dick into my hand and stroked him until he screamed out my name and painted streaks of spend across my knuckles. Silas cried out, whimpered, babbled, and I was careful to undo his wrists from the spreader bar, to take his weight against my chest before he fell. Slowly, I eased us both down to the floor and cradled him in my lap, brushing damp hair back from his face and leaving kisses in the wake of my fingers.

"I love you," he mumbled against my chest, arms limp but halfway around me. "I dunno why I didn't say it earlier."

There were a lot of reasons, I was sure. But those were his, and rightfully so. It didn't matter he hadn't delivered the response immediately. The only thing that mattered was he felt the same. He'd let me love him on my own, and he'd let me remind him of his worth. He let me show him that as long as he was with me, his potential would never be wasted. And I needed to know that for myself just as much—if not more—as I needed him to know it.

CHAPTER 33
SILAS

Lincoln traced the bruised stripes across my thighs with the tip of his finger, his touch featherlight.

"These are really hot, Si," he said.

I huffed a laugh and pressed play on the next episode of the true crime documentary he'd decided we were going to watch over dinner. It was Friday, our newly appointed best friend night, and we were in the apartment, on the couch, my legs sprawled across his lap, his feet propped on the coffee table, and takeout containers within reach.

"I think so too."

"And this was a reward?"

Humming, I kicked out my left leg when his touch slid to a particularly sensitive bruise on the inside of my thigh. "We were celebrating."

Lincoln rolled his eyes at me and finished off the pad Thai left in the bottom of his white paper carryout box.

"Are you excited to start work on Monday?" he asked.

"I'm not *not* excited," I said. "But I'm nervous."

"Why?"

Marshall's words were as etched into me as the bruises were. Eight strikes for the eight years of wasted potential spent working with my father. If I thought about it in hind-sight, the accusation was biting, but it was closer to the truth than a lie. Working with my dad had been the easy road, and I'd walked down it happily with both eyes open. Thankfully, because of Marshall's own name and connections, I'd been able to turn down a different fork in that road, but it was a near thing.

"What if I'm not as good as everyone thinks I am?"

Lincoln rolled his eyes at me and made a point of pushing his fingers into a bruise until I cursed his name and smacked him on the side of his head.

"You're not," he said. "You're better."

"You don't know that."

"I don't know Marshall, but I doubt he'd risk his reputation on you if you weren't," Lincoln said.

"He's not risking anything," I muttered.

"Weird thing to say, but if you want to be wrong out loud, go off."

I flung the remote at him, then tried to pull my legs away. Lincoln managed to catch me around the knees, using his own body as leverage to stop me from extracting myself from his grip. He ended half on top of me, my legs tangled and his face pressed against my stomach. I pushed down against the top of his head, pretending to fight him off.

"I hate you," I said.

He made wet kissing noises against my stomach, and I kneed him in the ribs until he rolled off of me, wheezing and clutching his side.

"It's not that serious," I told him.

"I'm wounded."

I stood up from the couch and stretched, fingers threaded together above my head. Leaning back, I arched until my spine popped. The release of pressure felt so good, and then I bent forward, letting my arms hang low. My fingers grazed the floor, and Lincoln made a very playful sound in the back of his throat.

"You're hornier than normal," I said, straightening up and arching a brow at him. He gave me an annoyed look, rearranging himself on the couch while I collected the takeout boxes and carried them into the kitchen.

"Thank you for noticing." Lincoln collapsed onto the couch, stretching across the seat I'd just occupied. "Do you think we can go get me laid?"

It was almost ten.

"Are you serious? Isn't there an app for that?"

"The guys on apps are the worst," he said, clutching his hands together in prayer. "They're either vanilla or they want to piss on my face. There is no middle ground."

"I'm sure there's a middle ground."

"Please let's go out."

"It's getting late," I said.

"You're getting old in your domesticness or whatever the word is. Rapture is barely open."

"You want to go to Rapture?"

"Please." Lincoln batted his lashes at me. "Are you allowed?"

"Of course, I'm…" I stopped myself from finishing the thought because…. *was I allowed?* Marshall and I had talked about my relationship with Lincoln, but we'd never talked about going to clubs or anything like that without each other. It wasn't like I was going to play or anything. There was no way he'd have an issue with it.

"Check with Daddy," Lincoln said, jumping over the back of the couch and scampering down the hallway. "I'm going to get ready."

With a groan, I found my phone on the coffee table and sent Marshall a text.

Are you with your brothers still?

MARSHALL
Yeah. Everything okay with you?

Yes. Just Lincoln wants to go to Rapture.

Is anyone stopping him?

He wants me to go with him.

There was a pause, and the water turned on in the bathroom, shortly followed by the hum of Lincoln's electric toothbrush.

Be safe.

It's okay?

Why wouldn't it be?

Just keep your clothes on. Send me a picture of your outfit before you leave.

Better yet, just wear what I tell you.

A familiar heat pooled low in my stomach.
Lincoln spit toothpaste into the sink and started singing an old blink-182 song.

Thank you, Sir.

Do you have black jeans?

Yes, Sir.

A white t-shirt?

Yes, Sir.

That with sneakers. No underwear.

The denim was going to be hell on my cock, on my thighs.

Understood.

Do you have a harness?

"What did Daddy say?" Lincoln shouted from his bedroom.

I cleared my throat, lips parched. "We're talking about it."

No, Sir.

A shame.

And no collar?

My teeth chattered together as I closed my mouth, palms sweating against the phone.

No one has ever given me one.

Did you want one? Did you like wearing mine on Wednesday?

I don't know, Sir. And yes.

Wear what you're told, Silas. Have a good night with your best friend. Stay with him unless he finds someone to host, then come over to my house.

Yes, Sir.

Thank you.

I love you. Be good.

I love you.

I stared at the phone to see if any other messages were going to come through, but none did.

"We're good!" I called down to Lincoln.

He let out a whoop in reply and was waiting for me in the doorway of my bedroom when I made it down the hall. I dug out my black jeans and a white shirt just like Marshall had instructed, then stripped naked and got dressed again. My cock was plump from the conversation, thickening even more in response to the tightness of the denim. Lincoln didn't say anything about it, and neither did I, and then we were in my car and on the way to Rapture.

The club was in full swing by the time we got there, dozens of people already packed onto the dance floor. The new downstairs room had people inside as well, and for the first time since Lincoln proposed the idea, I wondered if coming to Rapture was a good idea after all. Marshall had been so insistent when we'd first gotten involved that what had happened to me was assault, and while I agreed with him, I also didn't. I hadn't been victimized, at least not in the way others had been. It felt wrong to call it that, and facing the door of the room where it had occurred, I struggled to make sense of it being both at the same time.

"Do you want a drink?" Lincoln asked, mouth warm against my ear.

He'd dressed to cruise in short black shorts, black leather boots, and a mesh tank top that basically exposed his entire chest, nipple and navel rings included.

"Wine," I answered.

"I'll come find you! Scope me out a winner!"

I nodded, stare still fixated on the private playroom. I didn't want to go in there, but my legs carried me there anyway. Inside, I found far more people than my last visit, what appeared to be a group of friends. They laughed and talked, having a good time. A man stood in the corner of the room, dressed in all black, and completely alone. He was either an asshole or a voyeur, I imagined. Maybe both. At some point, one of the men in the friend group pulled another to his feet and walked him over to the spanking bench I'd found myself over the last time at Rapture.

I watched them talk. Negotiate. And then I watched them start a scene.

"They're nice to look at, aren't they?" An almost familiar voice startled me from behind. I'd been expecting Lincoln with a glass of wine, but instead found a blond man closer to forty, soft-looking hair and broad shoulders. He wore a pair of dark denim jeans and a white t-shirt, a wedding band on his left hand and a leather cuff on his right wrist.

"Uhm. Yeah," I said.

"We've never met," the man said, extending a hand toward me. "But we talked on the phone. I'm Landon Miller."

"This is your club," I said dumbly, shaking his hand.

"I hope you don't mind, but security let me know when you arrived, and I just wanted to come find you. Thank you for coming back and taking another chance on us."

"Oh, it's really…I was happy to eat Thai on the couch all night, but my best friend wanted to come," I blurted. "Not that I've been avoiding the place. It's fine. You were great. It's great."

Landon gave me a shy—but somehow knowing—smile. "Message received. I only wanted to introduce myself in person and let you know if you need anything to come find me. If you can't, let any of the bartenders know, and they will."

"I appreciate that," I murmured. "Did Marshall put you up to this?"

Landon squinted, cocking his head to the side. "Who?"

"Nothing. My boyfriend."

"No one put me up to anything, Silas. I just want to make sure everyone here is comfortable and safe." He gestured toward the asshole voyeur in the corner with a quick jerk of his chin. The man responded with a sharp nod. "And like I said, we're observing more closely now to make sure we're living up to our promises as a risk-aware space."

So he was an employee, not a prick.

Though, he could have been both.

"I'm…I'm sorry, I just. This is all great. I'm really fine, though. I don't want to make a big deal."

Landon held up his hands and took a step back, cheeks almost pink, but it was hard to tell under the glow of the stained glass. "Again, message received, Silas. I hope you and your friend have a good night."

I nodded, watching Landon head toward the bar. He passed Lincoln, who made a show of shaking his hips extra as he sashayed his way through the crowd with a drink in each hand. Dancing bodies parted for him, their stares trailing up his backside as he closed the space between us. Then he was there, and the wine was in my hand, my best friend was at my side, and all was well in the world again.

"Find me anyone good?" he asked.

"Didn't have a chance to look. Just had a chat with the owner."

"The owner?" Lincoln's eyes went wide, and he lifted his whiskey to his mouth like it was tea. Pinky out and all that.

"He wanted to make sure I was sorted after what happened the last time."

My best friend groaned, and I wanted to match the feeling.

"We can go look now, though. Did you see anyone good on the dance floor?"

"Maybe, but it's hard to tell who is a couple and who isn't," he said.

"You know as well as I do that couples can be looking too."

Lincoln made a very pleased sound at that prospect,

nodding eagerly. "Such a valid point. Maybe we can check the upstairs first and then circle back down?"

"You don't want to stop at the bathrooms before we go?" I teased, elbowing him in the ribs. "See if anyone is waiting there for you."

"Oh, you mean Riot?"

I raised a brow. "Whatever happened with him?"

"He was okay at sucking dick behind closed doors but was not okay with my line of work."

Sighing, I looped my arm through Lincoln's and pulled him toward the dance floor. "Then he's not worth your time."

"I know." He took a decent swallow from his glass and smacked his lips together. Sliding his free hand around my waist, he pulled our bodies flush and started to dance. I lifted my wine over my head so nobody knocked into me and spilled it, tilting my head back and relaxing enough to let Lincoln lead.

We danced through songs that bled together with the same beat, and finally, out of breath, Lincoln buried his face against my throat with a laugh.

"I wish I wanted to fuck you," he said.

I laughed back at him, putting enough space between us to bring my wine down and finish it off.

"You really don't," I said.

"I know. I know." His stare lifted over my shoulder, and he tracked someone across the dance floor toward the back stairs that led to the original private loft.

"What is it, boy?" I teased. "What did you find?"

"You're an asshole," he murmured, taking my hand and pulling me toward the stairs.

When we reached the top floor, I immediately recognized the man he'd spotted on the dance floor. He was exactly Lincoln's type. A little too tall for his own good, kind of lanky like a baby deer who hadn't grown into their limbs yet. If

Lincoln had a type, it was pretty and awkward and this man checked both of those boxes.

"He looks lost," I said softly.

"Maybe I should find him then."

"I think you should." I gave Lincoln a little shove toward the bar.

He spent less than five minutes chatting up the stranger and putting him at ease. Ten minutes in, the man leaned in close enough that Lincoln could have kissed him if he wanted, and I knew my best friend well enough to know he did. Another few minutes, which felt like a record, and then Lincoln took the man's hand and walked him over to the place I'd set up camp against the wall.

"Who's hosting?" I asked, admiring how up close the man Lincoln had set his sights on didn't look like his bones were trying to jut out of his skin.

"He is," Lincoln said. "Safety first and all that."

"You text a friend anyway?" I asked.

"Yeah. Yes," the man said.

Ah, there were the nerves.

I looked at Lincoln, unable to not smile at the way his entire face was lit with interest, then I pulled my phone out of my pocket and swiped it open to an empty message.

Holding it out for the stranger, I said, "Text me your name and address."

He didn't balk at the reciprocal safety measures, which made me feel a little better about leaving Lincoln on his own. It was far from the first time either of us would have gone home with a stranger from a club—or anywhere else for that matter—but it was the first time either of us had done so after my…

Well.

After my last trip here.

He handed my phone back and I looked down at the screen, confirming there was a real address there and a name.

"Ethan," I said, arching a brow.

He nodded.

"Alright." I slid my phone back into my pocket and gave Lincoln a warning look. "Text me tonight."

"I will," he promised, wrapping me into a hug and smashing his mouth against my cheek. "Thank you for coming out with me. Are you mad I'm ditching you?"

I didn't want to tell him that while I valued our Friday nights together, I also valued every second I got to spend with Marshall.

"Not in the slightest," I promised.

"I think I needed the distraction."

I puckered my lips against the air and the top of his cheekbone. "Go be distracted then."

The two of them headed out, Lincoln in front and Ethan trailing behind. After they weaved through the dance floor, stopping once for a very passionate make-out session near the door, they were gone. I checked my pocket for my phone and my keys and headed out to the parking lot myself, ready to make my way across town to Marshall's.

CHAPTER 34
MARSHALL

"How is your boyfriend?" Smith asked, sliding into the spot beside me at our usual booth. His arrival before Finn's was unusual, though, and I threw a sideways glance at him as he settled in and reached for the wine I'd preemptively ordered for him.

"He's well. And how are you, Smith?"

My brother had spent most of the week avoiding me, which was on brand. His early arrival was not. Neither of us did well with emotions, but I'd had a whole lifetime of being prompt behind my belt, and he still struggled to manage his time.

"Great."

"Are you lying?"

He rolled his eyes at me, leaning back against the creaking leather booth and stretching his legs into what would eventually be Hunter's space. "Why would I be lying?"

I sighed, not wanting to press the issue when the twins were due any minute.

It was actually five minutes, and they showed up together, another unusual mark on the box for the night. If I was being honest, that didn't bode well for the conversation the four of us were due to have, but there was no way around it at that point.

"I see you're pre-lubed," Finn said instead of hello, raising his glass in my direction as he slid in to make room for Hunter.

"Jesus," Hunter muttered.

Finn laughed at him. "No, I imagine Silas Ayres is the pre-lubed one in that relationship, now that you mention it."

"He didn't mention anything," I said.

Hunter shrugged helplessly, and Smith took a larger than socially acceptable swallow of his wine.

"I guess we should just get down to it," I suggested.

I knew none of us would want to eat until we'd dealt with the Andrew Calavert-sized elephant in the room. While we all sipped at our drinks, I looked around the booth, appreciating the way the four of us fit together. The way we fit into each other's lives. It was a blessing, I wagered, that Andrew didn't want any part of that.

"I spoke with him earlier today." Hunter fidgeted with a gold signet ring he wore on his pinky finger, rubbing the top of the insignia with his thumb. "He's offered to come to LA since it's just him traveling, versus all four of us going to San Diego."

"I was looking forward to a road trip," Finn teased.

"I would rather shoot myself than be stuck in a car with you for two hours," Hunter said, now spinning the ring around his smallest finger. "I told him we get together every Friday, and he suggested next week."

"Eager beaver," Finn said.

"I'm sure he just wants to get it out of the way," Smith said, staring down into his wine. He was clearly still not in a good place about the new brother revelation, but I wasn't sure how to help him. He looked to me for reassurance, looked to me as a model, but was also so resistant to advice in the times it didn't suit him. I wasn't one to ponder the sorts of sex or relationships my brothers had—we'd never been that close—but Smith would do well with someone to drag him out of his head on nights like this.

"Either way. If that's the case, we'll have to change our reservation," I said.

"I'd rather we meet him somewhere else," Smith whispered.

I patted his thigh. "Adding him to the reservation once isn't going to make this restaurant any less ours, Smith."

"I hate to admit you're right," Finn agreed.

Hunter was still at it with his ring. I'd never seen him so nervous. He didn't respond to either of us.

And for the first time, part of me didn't want to meet Andrew. He had no interest in the Covington name, something my brothers and I were extremely proud to carry, issues with our father notwithstanding. And all he'd done since his arrival in our lives was cause nervousness and upset. It had always been my responsibility as the oldest to keep my three younger brothers safe, and Andrew's existence made it very hard to do that.

"You know…" I paused, swishing some wine around in my mouth to make sure the idea still tasted like a good one. "We don't *have* to meet him."

"What?" Finn's eyes went wide, alight with amusement.

Hunter's hand went still.

"We don't have to," I said. "It was different when we were younger…when *you* were younger. But we're all adults now, and we don't have to welcome anyone else into our fold."

Beside me, Smith went tense, his mouth tipping down into a very tight and miserable-looking frown. The twins were silent, and after a minute or two, Hunter began to tap away nervously at his ring again.

"I want to," he said softly.

"So do I," said Finn.

Smith shrugged one of his shoulders halfway toward his ear which felt like as much of a yes as I'd get in the moment.

"Okay," I conceded. "I just wanted to remind you that we don't have to if we don't want to. All of you are not yourselves right now, and I'm not a fan of it."

"And you are?" Hunter asked.

"Aren't I?"

Finn snorted. "He's just tangled up with that little boyfriend of his."

"Am I?" I gestured to the table, to the restaurant. "Is he here right now? Or am I here with my three degenerate brothers instead?"

"Have you told him that you love him yet?" Finn asked.

He clearly meant it as a tease, the way he'd shifted to press his back against the wall, one leg bent at the knee and pulled up onto the bench of the booth, his bourbon held lazily in hand.

My face must have betrayed my answer because his eyes went wide in shock. More than he'd shown two weeks earlier when Hunter had told us all about our new brother.

"We haven't even met him, Marshall," Finn chided. "What if we don't approve?"

"Smith has met him."

Finn turned his attention toward Smith, that playful amusement continuing to dance across his face. Smith was still uncomfortable, but I *felt* the way he was forcing himself to try and relax back into normalcy with us. Teasing me was something the three of them had always done, though in most instances they'd ribbed me about being single. My relationship with Silas gave them new material to work with, and I was happy to let myself be a distraction for them.

"What do you think about him?"

"He's fine. A little clingy."

Hunter was the one to laugh at that, looking at me curiously over the rim of his drink. "Is he now?"

"There's nothing wrong with enjoying physical affection," I said. "Sorry the three of you are absolutely touch-starved."

With the last few words, I turned my stare toward Finn. I'd been unable to get the vision of him kissing that clearly married woman out of my head. There'd been no opportunity between Wednesday and today to bring it up to him, and while he would have definitely called me out about it in front of everyone, I would never. I'd planned to take advantage of our first few minutes together at dinner to ask him about it, but Smith had arrived first and thrown that idea right out the window. Finn caught my stare and blinked at me slowly, his expression giving away nothing about whatever marital infidelity he was helping to facilitate.

"I do love him," I told my brothers. "And I would like you to spend some time with him, but I also don't think now is the best time."

"I can do two things at once, Marshall." Finn gestured vaguely with his hand, and I wondered just how true his statement would turn out to be in the end. "I can be angry Dad didn't keep it in his pants while Hunter and I were in first grade and eager to meet the man who's stolen my stoic older brother's heart."

"Exactly," Hunter added.

"Well, next Friday is out if Andrew will be here."

The three of them paused, then nodded in a slow kind of agreement.

"The week after that?"

"You know we can see each other on days that don't start with F, right?"

"He's starting a new job on Monday, and he needs time to settle in."

"He's not working with Stanley anymore?" Smith asked,

the earlier frown having finally leveled out into something that almost resembled a straight line across his face.

"His dad—" I paused, unsure if it was my story to tell or not. After a beat, I settled on the CliffsNotes version. "He's not working with his dad anymore."

Hunter and Finn gave me matching amused expressions across the table, arched brows and all. They really could have been twins in every sense of the word besides the one that counted the most.

"Where's his new job?" Finn asked.

"You can ask him in two weeks."

"You're no fun."

"So you say," I drawled, favoring a drink of wine over more conversation with Finn.

"I'll tell him yes then," Hunter blurted, and the tension was back.

"Yes," I said for the rest of us. "I'll make a reservation on Monday and send everyone the information. You can pass it along."

"Okay."

The waiter came by to check on our drinks and, as if on cue, my stomach growled loudly enough for everyone to hear.

"Are we ready to order?" the waiter asked, and beside me, Smith finally laughed.

———

We'd gone from dinner to a nightcap when Silas texted me about going to Rapture with Lincoln. I read and re-read the message on my phone, Finn's animated voice while he told Smith and Hunter a story about something that definitely didn't have to do with whatever he'd been doing at dinner last Wednesday, then gave Silas my answer.

A lesser man might have said no.

Hell, my first instinct had been to say no, but not because I was jealous or worried about Silas cheating on me. He was definitely attractive enough to do that if he wanted—which I doubted was the case—but I was more worried about his safety. He hadn't been to Rapture since the night we'd met there, since his assault, and I wasn't sure how returning to the scene of that almost-crime would sit with him. I took reassurance in knowing he had Lincoln with him, and even though Lincoln was femme and flighty, he loved Silas as much as I did—maybe more, while also differently.

If I wasn't threatened by their friendship, there was no need for me to be threatened by the two of them having a night out together. It was unreasonable to assume their Fridays would always consist of them being holed up in their apartment together watching movies and eating takeout. Especially while I was out myself.

Their apartment.

I rolled those words around in my head, not liking the sound of them. I liked Silas in my home and my space, but I wagered until I thought of it as ours, I had no right to ask him to give up the former. I was too buzzed on wine to have that conversation or those thoughts, so I shoved them into the back of my head.

During our text exchange, I'd given Silas instructions about what to wear and where to go at the end of his night, and I hadn't asked for proof or confirmation of either. There was already a trust between us that meant I didn't have to, and I hoped he'd noticed that during our text exchange. Even as I sat at the bar with my brothers, enjoying a fresh glass of wine, I had no idea if Silas was out at the club, at his apartment, or on his way back to my house. The uncertainty didn't bother me, and it was a new and unruly thing to have that sort of confidence in the devotion of another person whom I wasn't related to.

The four of us finished our drinks and said goodnight just before midnight.

When I got home from dinner, Silas was in the shower. My dick immediately pulsed against my thigh, knowing what he was doing in there…what he was getting ready for. Even if I had no plans of fucking him, Silas followed orders. He knew what was expected, and he always delivered.

It was one of the many things I loved about him.

Unfortunately for us both, I'd had too much wine to be of any use to him. I'd left my car in the parking lot and let Smith drive me home. When he saw Silas's car in my driveway, he made an amused sound but didn't tease or chide me the way Finn often did.

Deciding to let Silas finish up in the shower in peace, I padded into the bedroom and stripped out of my work clothes. After changing into a pair of plaid pajama pants, I sat down on the edge of the bed and prayed the room didn't start to spin while I waited for Silas. Thankfully, the floor and the walls remained at the correct angles, and then Silas was in front of me, dripping wet with a towel wrapped around his waist, held loosely in his hand.

"You're home," he said, a little breathless and a little surprised.

I hummed, beckoning him closer. He shuffled into the space between my spread legs, and I pulled the towel out of his hand, letting it fall to the floor. His cock was almost eye level, not hard but still impressively long and thick.

"God," I murmured, dragging my nose down his length. "I love your cock."

Silas made a desperate sound, swaying on his feet, and I pressed gentle kisses from root to tip, licking the taste of him straight from his slit.

"Sir."

"I think if I close my eyes long enough to make you come, the floor might come out from under me."

I tried anyway, letting my eyes fall closed as I licked the underside of his glans. It was too late, and I was too deep. Reluctantly, I let go of his cock and bracketed my hands over the slender swell of his hips. I leaned in and kissed the barely there V that dipped down below his waist.

Humming, I pulled away.

"Are you drunk?" Silas asked, laughing under his breath.

"Not drunk, but also not *not* drunk. And it doesn't help that I find you positively irresistible." I kissed his navel, and an inch lower, then took his hands in mine and kissed his knuckles. "Do you want to go to bed or watch a movie?"

Slowly, Silas lifted his hands and slid his fingers into my hair. And maybe it was the wine buzzing through my blood, but it felt a lot like magic.

"A movie is good if you can manage it," he murmured. "And a snuggle? Sir?"

I pressed my cheek against his stomach, wrapped my arms around his waist and breathed him in. My earlier thoughts about *my* house faded into oblivion as if he ever made the decision to leave me, I had no idea how I'd ever go back to existing without Silas in not just my space, but also my life.

"A snuggle sounds like a dream, sweetheart. A snuggle sounds like a dream."

CHAPTER 35
SILAS

On my knees at the edge of the bed, I tied the knots on Marshall's shoes, then rocked back onto my heels so he had enough room to stand. Me helping him get dressed had become part of our morning routine, and even though I was getting ready to start my new job with Cory this morning, I stuck to it. The only thing different from the mornings before was that instead of being in pajamas or naked, I was also dressed for work—casual, Cory had assured me—in navy blue chinos and a white, short-sleeved button-up. Marshall was in slacks as usual, which had always felt over the top for our line of work, but I'd never complain about how he filled them out in every possible way.

"Text me when you can, and let me know how it's going," Marshall said, helping me to my feet. It wasn't a question, but the command didn't need saying. He was the first person I wanted to tell everything, even first over Lincoln now in some instances.

"I will, Sir."

He reached into his pocket and pulled something out that was small enough to fit in his fist.

"Open," he instructed, and at first I thought he meant

my mouth, but then he moved his hand between our chests like whatever he was holding he meant to transfer into my hand.

I lifted my flat palm beneath his hand, not needing to look at the transfer to know he'd just dropped a key into my waiting hand.

"I am not asking you to move in," he said quickly, almost regrettably, "but I want you to be here as often as it suits you."

Somewhere in the back of my mind, I knew a permanent key had been coming. It made sense. It was logical. Marshall had a house all to himself, and I had a shared two-bedroom apartment. I would have offered him a key in return, but this exchange wasn't like the kind that happened between mid-twenty-somethings. Marshall giving me a key to a home he'd bought with his own money was so much different than a copied key to a month-to-month rental.

"I don't know what to say," I whispered.

"You don't have to say anything." He curled my fingers toward my wrist, capturing the key in the palm of my hand. I slid my hand into my pocket, letting the key drop past my fingers. "You don't have to call before you come over. You don't have to text. Treat my home as if it was also yours."

"Marshall."

"The only thing you have to do is remember the rule."

He slid his hands around my waist and pulled our bodies flush. Then both hands dipped lower, and he cupped my ass, fingers pressing gently at the seam of my pants.

How could I forget the rule?

"I remember, Sir," I rasped.

"If you're here more than one day in a row, you should just make a habit of it after you get home for the day. If that's inconvenient or if I have you otherwise entangled, we'll work something else out. Understand?"

"Yes, Sir."

Marshall smiled and tilted his head down, slanting our mouths together in a very chaste kiss—all things considered.

"I have to get to work." A peck against the corner of my mouth. "I'll talk with you soon. Do you want to celebrate tonight?"

"We celebrated last week."

Marshall took a step back, mouth twisted into a moderately disappointed frown. "Do you not deserve more than one?"

My cheeks burned hot at the call-out, and I wanted to shake my head and tell him no, I didn't deserve more than one. What had I done besides get fired from my job and take a handout from a man I barely knew but had somehow fallen in love with? Reducing the chain of the events of the past couple weeks felt unfair to everyone involved, but it was the truth of the matter.

"Whatever you want," I said instead, blinking up at him and hoping my face conveyed the submission I meant it to.

He studied me quietly, head cocked to the side in the way I imagined he looked when he was forty percent of the way through a design and struggling to tie the ideas together to reach the middle.

"Do you remember the night you came over crying, and I made you write a copy of your *Design Digest* article?" he asked.

I swallowed hard and nodded. "And annotate it," I muttered.

Marshall dragged his tongue across the front of his teeth and nodded back at me.

"Alright. Just wanted to make sure."

I groaned inwardly at the embarrassment of that night as a whole, which stretched far beyond the forced attention to my design ideas.

"I love you," I said, reaching for the key in my pocket. The sharp, freshly cut teeth bit into my palm, and the pain was grounding.

"I love you," he said back, kissing me once more. "Don't be late for your first day."

"I won't, Sir."

He left in a rush of cologne and soft touches that promised more later. Once the door locked, I sat down on the edge of the bed and put on my own shoes—sneakers, again at Cory's suggestion—then stared at the wall for a solid five minutes before heading for the kitchen.

I'd made Marshall coffee after getting out of the shower, and now with him gone, I prepared a mug for myself. He was still strict about the meals, which went without mention, so I grabbed a yogurt from the fridge and ate it while leaning against the kitchen counter.

When I'd come over the first time, Marshall hadn't had yogurt in the fridge. It had come up in conversation that it was what I normally ate, and after that, it appeared...and stayed stocked. Same, I realized, with the other snacks I tended to favor. Without request or fanfare, Marshall had stocked his house with the things I liked to eat, then he'd given me a key and asked me to make his home mine.

To make his home *ours*.

That level of commitment should have made me nervous, but instead, scooping the last bites of yogurt and fruit from the bottom of the container, I found myself comfortable with the idea of building a future with him. There were maybe a handful of reasons it was a bad idea, the age difference between us being one, my dad's never-ending hate for the man being another, but the pros definitely outweighed the cons.

Should it have been scary to think about packing up my bedroom and moving into his house? Probably. Where would my things go? What would happen to my bed? It all seemed trivial, which made Lincoln my biggest concern in the whole situation. There were some months where he could afford all the rent on his own, but not all of them, and I didn't want to leave him hanging.

I'd have to talk to him about it on Friday.

I finished the yogurt and tossed the empty container into the trash, then washed the spoon and my empty mug. I washed Marshall's mug too, then turned off all the lights in the house and locked the door behind me with my new key. On the porch, I leaned against the wall to dig out my key ring, sliding his right alongside my apartment key and car key. Shocked that the chain didn't somehow weigh a hundred more pounds from the addition, I gave the door one last check and headed to my first day of work.

The drive to Cory's from Marshall's took about as long as it took to get anywhere, but the typical traffic gave me more time to think. Not just about the invitation or about the changes it would bring, but also about the biggest change that I'd done a good job of ignoring up until that very moment.

For years, it had been me and my dad against the world. And even when that wasn't okay, it also *was* because it was all I had. I'd known since college working with him wasn't supposed to be a forever thing, but I'd always planned on him retiring sooner or later and handing me the reins. The Cahuenga Pass project made it clear he never truly planned on giving up unless it suited him, even if the cost of his stubbornness was my future. It was a shocking revelation to me, softened only by the very careful and kind way Marshall had helped me navigate through it.

Pulling into the parking garage at the address Cory had given me, I found a parking spot. I tossed my cell phone from hand to hand, knowing that sooner or later I was going to have to talk to my dad again. There was no way I could leave things the way they were: the firing, the tension, the things he'd said to me. It had to be addressed, right? Marshall always talked about what I deserved, and I deserved peace with all that mess, didn't I?

I sent him Marshall a quick message.

> When is Cahuenga Pass decided?

His response came quickly, like he'd been staring at the phone and waiting for me to message him.

MARSHALL

They're delayed, but before the end of the week I think.

Why?

> Just thinking about my dad.

Instead of another message, the phone rang. Marshall's face flashed across the screen, and I pressed the button to accept the call.

"I'm fine, I swear," I said instead of hello.

He huffed out a laugh into my ear. "I know you are, but I want you to know that even though it hasn't been announced yet, he knows he's lost it. He knows you were his only chance at it. That's why he reacted the way he did when you told him no."

Sighing, I rubbed the bridge of my nose. "Okay."

"Was that all?" he asked.

"For now."

"Are you where you need to be, Silas?"

I dropped my head against the headrest and stared at the concrete wall in front of my car. The elevator was at the end of the row and eight floors up my new boss waited for me. I had ten minutes until I was due to report for my first day. I was where I needed to be physically and mentally, Marshall's low voice and steady presence.

"Yes, Sir."

"Have a good day, sweetheart."

My heart twisted, tight and expansive at the same time in the middle of my chest. I loved when he called me that but didn't want to ask for more of it. The sparse use of the endearment made it that much more special when it did slip out. I tucked the sound of it away in my pocket—alongside my keys.

I sent a text to Lincoln for good luck, even though I knew he would be sound asleep, then forced my legs to carry me to the elevator. The ride to the eighth floor was nowhere near long enough for the first day jitters to subside, and seeing Cory leaning against the wall in the elevator lobby as the doors slid open didn't help much either. He smiled down at his phone, then up at me and held out his hand for a quick shake.

"Silas," he greeted, palm a thousand times less sweaty than mine. "It's good to see you again."

"Good to see you too, Mr. Callahan."

His cheeks flushed and he shook his head. "Please remember, Cory is fine."

"Cory," I repeated.

"Marshall has done nothing but speak highly of you since we met last." He gestured toward the office. "Want to follow me and we can get you caught up?"

"Yeah. Yes."

Following him through the maze of desks gave me a few moments to school my expression, to fight down the nervous bile that kept trying to force its way up and out of my stomach. Instead of taking me to an office, Cory walked me to a conference room, blueprints spread across the entirety of the table, his laptop open and a drafting program up on screen.

"I'd love your help with this." He tapped his finger against something on his laptop, and I sat down, pulling the computer in front of me. Immediately, I recognized the schematics, and I blinked up at him.

"What…what do you mean?"

He cocked his head to the side. "You don't have a non-compete with your father, do you?"

I shook my head and glanced back at what was definitely a design for the Cahuenga Pass project I was ninety-nine percent sure Marshall was expecting to be awarded before the end of the week.

"I was called in at the last minute to consult over it, which has turned into a more formal bid than I'd planned. I'm capable, but a little out of my element with some of it." Cory sat down beside me and tapped the tip of a pencil against the edge of the desk. "Was hoping you could help smooth out some details so I can get it submitted before Wednesday."

"That's two days," I croaked.

"End of day."

I forced a laugh. "Three. You know Marshall is—"

He cut me off. "It wouldn't be the first bid I stole out from under him, and it wouldn't be the first I lost to him either. We've known each other for years, Silas. Business has always been business."

I exhaled, the jitters from my first day of work turning into jitters about stealing a seven figure payday from the man I'd only recently admitted to being in love with.

"Are you uncomfortable with the idea of it?" he asked, mouth angled up into a smirk. "I was of the impression you were already bidding against him for it before you quit working with your father."

"That was different," I muttered.

"Was it?"

I swallowed hard, knowing in my bones that Marshall would be infinitely disappointed in me if I didn't put my all into what Cory was asking of me. He wouldn't want me to take his feelings into consideration when it came to work. From the last meeting at my dad's office to the night at his dining room table, Marshall had done everything he could to remind me of my talent and my worth in the design space.

"Three days," I repeated.

"You're young." Cory slid some paper around on the desk, erasing something before writing a different series of numbers on top of the shavings. "Younger than me, and you're full of the ideas this kind of project needs. I know I'm kind of throwing you in the deep end, but you're up for it, right?"

I thought about my dad.

Thought about Marshall.

And then for the first time in a very long time, I thought about myself.

"Yeah," I agreed, getting a feel for the mouse and the keyboard. "I'm definitely up for it."

CHAPTER 36
MARSHALL

Silas got home from work looking like someone had shit in his Cheerios. I'd called it an early day, eager to be home before him, but when he saw me on the couch with a glass of wine, his brow furrowed and he was quick to lock himself in the bathroom.

Alone.

Chasing my concern with a drink of wine, I headed down the hallway and propped myself against the hall across from the bathroom and waited for him to finish with his responsibilities. The water was on and off in less than ten minutes, and then Silas appeared in a puff of steam, towel held together below his navel with one hand, clothes gathered in the other.

"How was work?" I asked. "Thought we were celebrating tonight?"

"Work was fine," he muttered, looking down at his dripping wet feet. "It was good."

I gestured for him to move, and he padded into the bedroom. I followed behind him, sitting down on the edge of the bed while he toweled off and changed into a pair of basketball shorts and one of my old t-shirts. It hung baggy around his shoulders, and I loved the look of it on him. Standing before me, Silas shifted his weight, avoiding my stare.

"What's wrong?"

"Nothing, Sir," he lied.

"Do you want to tell me about your day?"

"Just getting familiar with how Cory does things." Silas shrugged his shoulders up toward his ears.

"You were much more excited about this earlier today," I reminded him. "Was it horrible? What happened to sour your mood between the last time we talked and now?"

"My mood isn't sour," he grumbled, fidgeting his hands together in front of him like a petulant child. Silas blinked up at me, tired but earnest. "It was just work."

I narrowed my eyes at him, but he gave me nothing else.

"Just work," I repeated, and he nodded. "Alright. We'll celebrate *just work* my way then."

He swallowed audibly, and I stood, taller than him… broader than him…stronger than him, and far more determined.

"May I please brush my teeth first?" he asked quietly.

I wanted to tell him no but letting him into the bathroom seemed better than keeping him in the bedroom. If he wanted to run, I would gladly chase him.

"Of course, Silas."

He gave me one more look before turning on his heel and heading into my en suite. After he'd walked away from me, I went into the closet, dug out a wooden paddle, and went after him. A spanking in the bathroom was not my first choice, and not even my second. It was less than ideal, and for the first time ever, I was envious of friends who had better-equipped play-rooms than I did. I could convert my office, but I liked the separation of work and home.

I'd spent enough time making my house work for me, with

the hooks in the ceilings and the bolts in the bed, but there was no real space dedicated for impact play beyond what I could come up with on the fly. That had always been fine, though. I'd never kept anyone around long enough for any part of my house to become boring or predictable for them. Maybe one day I would task Silas with the job of designing a dungeon. See if his skills were up for the challenge.

Dropping the paddle on the counter to his right, I caught his stare in the mirror. He looked at me and then the paddle; then he spit toothpaste into the sink and rinsed his mouth.

"Fresh and clean?" I asked

"Yes, Sir," he whispered.

"Good. Now drop your pants and grab the edge of the sink."

His exhale trembled, but he shoved his basketball shorts down to his ankles and hinged at the waist, sticking out his ass and bracing his hands like I'd told him to.

"Does this feel like a celebration to you?" I asked.

He shook his head.

"Good. Whenever you're ready to celebrate, you let me know and we'll start," I told him, picking up the paddle and testing the weight of it in my grip. "Until then, count them out and thank me.

Silas huffed, and I cracked the paddle down hard against both of his ass cheeks. He cried out, jerking away from the counter, and I collared my hand around his throat, pinning his face down toward the sink and delivering another strike against his ass.

"You're not counting *or* thanking me," I warned.

"One, thank you, Sir. Two..." He panted, shoulders heaving against my forearm. "Thank you, Sir."

He still had marks from my cane on the front of his thighs, and if he didn't pull his head out of his ass, he wasn't going to sit right for a week. Cory would be the last person to ever ask him for an explanation as to why, but it would certainly make settling into his new job more difficult than it needed to be. And maybe I was reacting poorly over his attempts to dodge the conversation, but our relationship was built on a trust that ran both ways, and I knew Silas had lied about work at worst or offered me disingenuous half-truths at best.

He caught up after that, forcing out his numbers and his thanks until my forearm started to ache from how hard I was hitting him. I gave him one more, an even ten, before dropping the paddle onto the floor and sucking in a much-needed lungful of air. Over the sink, Silas sobbed, gasping for breath, and I'd never felt smaller.

"I'm sorry," I murmured, folding myself over him and kissing the back of his neck. I pulled him upright and awkwardly reached around him to turn on the taps. The water ran cool over my fingers, and I lifted them to his face to wash away the tears that had become waterfalls over his lash line.

Instead of pulling away from me, he leaned in close, letting me wash his face before turning around and burying himself against my chest. I wrapped my arms around him and stroked circles across his shoulders and down his spine, my lips pressed softly against his temple.

"I'm sorry," I told him again.

"You were right for it," he muttered, sniffling hard and no doubt smearing snot all over my shirt. "I deserved the punishment."

"Why did you lie to me?" I asked, pulling him back enough that I could see his face, his splotchy cheeks and trembling lips.

"I...I didn't know how to tell you."

"Use words maybe."

"Cory is bidding on Cahuenga Pass," Silas blurted, covering his face with his hands. "He has me working on the proposal."

It was just like Cory to come in at the last minute and get his hands onto what had otherwise been a sure thing. But it made sense they were bringing in another option. The gap between what Stanley had offered against what I'd designed would have been insurmountable. I couldn't fault them for wanting to stack someone more competitive against me before making a decision. It also explained why the award had been delayed. They were giving Cory time to finalize what he wanted to present.

Rather, what he and *Silas* were going to present.

"And you didn't think you could tell me that?" I asked.

"We *just* talked about it." Silas angrily wiped fresh tears out of his eyes. "You've been expecting this job for weeks now."

"Silas." I smoothed his hair back from his face, held him gently in my hands. "This would not be the first job Cory stole from me, and I doubt it would be the last. Our careers have always run competitively, but with you on his side, I think that I may find myself at a loss more often than not."

Another wretched-sounding cry ripped out of Silas's mouth. He was a disaster, worse than the night he'd gotten fired. Putting enough space between us to bend down and pull up his shorts, I got him mostly reassembled before wrapping him back into my arms. He was soft against me like he always was, not arguing as I walked him out of the bathroom and bedroom, down the hallway and onto the couch. The cushions there were softer than my bed and far more forgiving than the dining room chairs or the barstools at the counter.

"Why do you hate that so much?" I asked.

"You asked me to work with you, and I said no. Then I just went and stole—"

"Bold of you to assume your win on this bid is already a sure thing," I teased, even though I knew it was.

He gave me a watery smile, shoulders heavy. "I didn't want you to be mad," he finally said. "I didn't know how to tell you."

"I would never be mad at your success, Silas."

He looked like he wanted to argue more, but I raised a hand to stop him. Reaching into my pocket, I pulled out my phone and swiped open to my bank app, then I dropped the device into his hand.

"Losing Cahuenga Pass isn't going to make or break me," I promised.

He stared down at my bank account totals, nostrils flaring. I tapped another tab that opened up my investment portfolio and I heard his breathing hitch.

"I also had a feeling something was up with this bid, but I wasn't certain."

Silas blinked hard at my phone and handed it back to me. "I didn't know," he whispered. "You didn't say anything."

"I didn't say anything about my financial security, but that doesn't mean it's not there. I didn't say anything about this bid because I wasn't sure what was going on." I slid my phone back into my pocket, regretting I'd left my wine in the bedroom. "There's plenty of things I know to be true that I don't say out loud."

"Like what?"

"For one, I knew I loved you long before I told you," I told him, and the flush on his cheeks turned far more solid than before. "Do you want another example?"

Silas looked like he wanted to crawl out of his skin as he answered with a choked off, "Yes, Sir."

"I want you to move in with me," I said.

He went still.

"I want you to move in with me. I want you to make my home into our home."

"I..." he trailed off.

"I also don't want you to answer that in any way right now."

"Yes, Sir," he whispered. "Yes, Marshall."

Something about the clarifier had been so needed. It was Silas's way of telling me he heard me not only as a dominant—as his Dom—but also as a partner. I worried sometimes that our age gap would create its own power imbalance, but with the simple use of my name, Silas once again rendered that fear moot.

"I want to celebrate your first day of work," I said again. "And later this week, when you snatch this award right out from under me, I want to celebrate that too."

He managed a weak laugh but nodded along with me.

"Friday, we're supposed to meet up with Andrew," I said. "But afterward, however Cahuenga Pass goes, I want to take you out."

"I don't des—"

"Silas, stop," I warned.

He groaned, throwing his head back and staring up at the ceiling. I leaned against the arm of the couch and studied him carefully, trying to make sure I didn't misread the situation.

"What is it?" I asked him slowly. "And don't lie."

He huffed, the callout clearly weighing heavier on him that he wanted to admit. I had no qualms about that. He could do with a reminder about who we were to each other and what I expected of him.

"I'm sorry," he said. First to the ceiling, then to me. He went to his knees, forced his way between my spread legs, and grabbed my thighs. "I'm sorry."

"Forgiven."

"Why?" he asked.

"Because I want to," I said, tracing my thumb across his lower lip. "Because forgiveness is my prerogative."

"I don't des—"

I cut him off again, "You're not in charge. What you deserve is not for you to decide."

"I want to make it up to you," he said next.

"There's nothing to make up, and if you don't stop, you'll find yourself over the sink again with ten more bruises to match the ones I just gave you."

I could see the argument in his face, and then I watched the fight go out of him.

"Is this settled?" I asked.

"Yes, Sir," he whispered.

"Can we celebrate now?"

Silas glanced up at me from beneath the fan of his dark lashes, expression half-coy and half-disbelieving.

"Did you still want…"

"I always want," I assured him. "And right now I want you to suck my cock until I get tired of your throat and want to move on to your ass."

"Sir."

His fingers slid up my legs, freeing my half-hard cock from my fly with relative ease. He sank down and took me into his mouth like getting me erect would be his penance, and I was content to let him chase his own forgiveness between my legs.

Silas went to work on me with a ferocious strength, spit pooling on my balls as he hollowed his cheeks and sucked me toward the edge. I slowly worked my fingers through his hair, lifting his head to slow him down enough that I didn't shoot my load into his mouth before I even had a chance to get him on my lap.

"Easy, sweetheart," I rasped, hips shifting off the couch in protest of my own actions.

Silas groaned, slowing down and easing up the suction. I closed my eyes and stretched my arms across the back of the couch, enjoying the way pleasure wrapped around my spine the longer he sucked me, content to enjoy the feel of him until he started to chase after friction with sharp pumps of his hips.

"Settle," I warned, tapping his head until he pulled off.

Rocking back onto his heels, it was the second time that

night Silas had gazed up at me with a wet face, though this time the tears were far more welcome than the first.

"Go get lube," I told him, and he was off in a flash, leaving his pants around his knees as he awkwardly raced down the hallway. He was back in seconds, the bottle still wet from the shower as he pressed it into my hand.

Flipping the lid, I squirted some into his waiting hand, then used my foot to kick him backward toward the coffee table.

"Get yourself ready for me," I said. "Spread yourself open so I can watch."

He cursed under his breath, bringing his heels onto the edge of the coffee table. He was bent like a W, his cock so hard he didn't even need to lift himself out of the way for me to watch him spear two slick fingers into his ass. I poured lube into my own hand and stroked my dick until it shined under the living room light, my stare alternating between the indecent-looking stretch of Silas's hole and the enraptured look on his face. He was bruised from back to front, cheeks wet with tears and spit, stomach smeared with precum. If I watched him carefully, I bet I could see him trembling from the want of it all.

"Silas, now."

I bracketed my hand around the base of my cock and held it tall. Silas climbed onto my lap and sank down slowly until my entire length filled him up, and once we were fully joined, he settled his hands on my shoulders and started to move. He rode me tentatively at first, not wanting to go too deep or too hard, but the need to have him quickly became too overwhelming for me to let him go slow any longer.

With a rumbling growl, I looped my arm around his waist and pushed into a standing position. Silas cried out in shock, then laughed, and I brought him down to the coffee table on his back. Angling one of his legs straight into the air, I pressed a sloppy kiss against the inside of his calf, then I fucked him the way we both knew he wanted to be fucked.

Silas shouted my name, coming almost immediately. Ribbons of white shot out of his cock, painting his chest, and I continued fucking into him with the same level of force until his balls were well and truly emptied, and then I fucked him even harder. Silas begged for more, whined for less, and I thrust into him harder and harder and harder each time. There was no way for me to get deep enough into him for my need to ever be sated, but I would surely die trying.

One final snap of my hips and the table gave way beneath our weight. Wood groaned and cracked, buckling under Silas's back. We both fell straight through to the floor, but I couldn't be bothered to care. My orgasm railed into me like a freight train, and I dug my nails into him with so much force he'd end up with ten more bruises whether that had been my intent or not.

Coming inside of Silas was like coming home, and I dropped my chin toward my chest to try and slow my breathing. Desperate breath after breath, my vision was still dark around the edges from the force of my orgasm. Silas's knee hooked over my shoulder, but I was pressed so tight against him with the table all around us, I managed to steal a kiss. The taste of his spit and his sweat were enough to bring me back into the present, and I moved out of him slowly so I didn't hurt either of us more than the fall already had. My knees were going to kill me.

Carefully, I pulled him out of the debris and onto my lap, trailing my fingers down his back to check him for splinters.

"Are you all right?" I asked. "Did that hurt?"

"I'm fine. I'm more than fine," he murmured against my mouth, the words trying their hardest to turn into a kiss. "That's my kind of celebration."

I laughed, burying my face into the crook of his neck and smiling against his sweaty skin.

"Me too, sweetheart, but I'm nowhere near finished with you."

Scooping Silas into my arms, I carried him down the hallway and tossed him on the bed. "In fact, I'm just getting started."

CHAPTER 37
SILAS

Tuesday, I couldn't sit down at work with Cory. Wednesday wasn't much better, but by Thursday, I could manage a couple hours at a time before having to get up and stretch my legs to ease the ache of the bruises on the backs of my thighs and my ass. Marshall had done a number on me Monday night, and the worst part was, I'd deserved it and more. I'd lied to him, for no reason at all. Marshall had never done anything short of putting me above him in almost all things, and for me to worry he'd be mad about my work on a competing bid—in hindsight—was ludicrous.

He'd been particularly sweet the rest of the week, whispering very affectionate praise every morning when I tied his shoes, and even better kisses when I brought him his coffee. I'd been at his house the whole week, but I was looking forward to getting back to my apartment and my things on Friday night.

At least, for a little while.

We'd agreed I'd have my usual date with Lincoln, and he would have dinner with his brothers, all four of them, and then we'd meet up at Rapture. Lincoln would come if he wanted, but at the end of the night, we would go our separate ways.

When I pulled into the parking garage at work, my nerves about Cahuenga Pass were beginning to get the better of me. I truly believed Marshall didn't care if he lost the bid or not, but *I* cared.

I cared.

And I found myself with no time to reconcile those feelings because when I walked into the office, Cory sat on the edge of a clean conference room table, bottle of champagne and two glasses to his right.

"Good morning," I said, pushing open the door and joining him in the space that had become a second, or rather third home to me over the last week.

He smiled brightly and raised the champagne.

"It is," he agreed.

The cork popped and champagne fizzed, and my heart somersaulted behind my sternum before sinking to the floor.

"Did you win it?" I rasped.

"I didn't," he said, pouring two flutes of champagne at eight-thirty in the morning. "You did."

"I hardly—"

He cut me off by jumping off the table and thrusting a champagne glass into my hand. "It was one hundred percent your thoughts and input that sealed this deal, Silas. If you want to have a lasting career in this industry, especially in this city, you've got to stop selling yourself short."

I thought about annotating my article for Marshall, and then I thought about the way my father had thrown my ideas into the trash.

"Force of habit," I murmured, clinking the rim of our glasses together and taking a sip. My mouth still tasted like coffee, but the bubbles helped me ease into a more celebratory mood.

My phone vibrated an incoming call in my pocket, and I realized I still had my messenger bag slung over my shoulder.

I hadn't even unpacked for the day before Cory had ambushed me with praise. Cocking a shoulder down, I dropped my bag into a chair and pulled my phone out of my pocket.

"It's Marshall," I said, flashing Cory the screen.

"I'm sure he's calling to congratulate you. I'll give you some privacy and then we'll regroup." Cory raised his glass again, then let himself out of the conference room.

I answered the call and sank down into one of the chairs. I didn't even feel the bruising on my ass. My entire body was numb from the shock.

"Hey," I answered.

"Are you at work?" he asked.

"Yeah. Yes. I…Marshall, I…"

"Congratulations, sweetheart." He sounded so fucking sincere, so proud. "No one deserved this more than you."

"You did."

"The email in my inbox says otherwise."

I let out a long breath. "I haven't seen the email. I just walked in, and Cory was here with champagne and then you called."

"Mr. Covington," he said, clearing his throat. "While your submission on Cahuenga Pass was remarkable in its composition, we regrettably find you outdone by Cory Callahan and Silas Ayres."

I blinked hard, swiveling the chair around and setting down my champagne flute before I dropped it on the floor.

"It says my name?"

"It says your name. Equal placement."

I closed my eyes and pressed my fingertips against my eyelids until I saw stars. How did the thing I'd wanted for so long—recognition—taste so bitter? It was unfair that Marshall losing the bid was the cost, cruel that my dad…

My dad.

"Do you think they emailed my dad the same thing?" I asked.

"I doubt they called him Mr. Covington, and it would be a stretch to call anything he's done remarkable, but…"

"Shit."

As if on cue, my phone buzzed with another incoming call. I didn't even need to look at my screen to know who it was.

"Is he calling?" Marshall asked.

"Yeah."

"You don't have to answer it, you know," he said gently. "You can talk to him on your own time and your own terms."

It was a weird thing, not being beholden to a man who didn't appreciate me. I stared at my dad's caller ID on the screen until my lack of movement sent him to voicemail.

"Are you there?" Marshall asked me.

"I'm here."

"You don't have to talk to him at all," he said.

"I can't just ignore him forever."

"Of course you can. That's what my mother did."

A silence fell and my phone gave a quick buzz in my hand to let me know there was a voicemail waiting for me.

"I'm sorry she did that," I told him.

"I'm not. It's what gave me my brothers, what led me to you."

I made a dismissive sound. "That feels a stretch."

"It's not for you to decide." Marshall hummed. "I just wanted to call and congratulate you on a well-deserved win, Silas. I'm looking forward to celebrating with you later tonight."

His voice dipped into a low rumble, and pleasure arced up the length of my spine.

"I'm looking forward to it too."

"I'll talk to you later. I love you."

I nodded, even though he couldn't see me. "I love you too."

The call disconnected, and I dropped my phone onto the table, knowing there was still a voicemail hanging over my head. My dad could be angry or resigned, and I wasn't sure which I preferred, so I left the message for another time, like Marshall had told me I could.

Sipping my champagne, I headed through the office until I found Cory behind his desk with his brow furrowed. He so rarely looked anything besides easygoing, it was an uncomfortable look to see on his face.

"Everything all right?" I asked.

He schooled his expression. "Everything is perfect. I just have an overbearing friend who needs to move across the country if he wants more control over my life is all."

Closing his laptop, Cory again raised his champagne in a toast. I mirrored the motion and let the bubbles chase away the anxious bile that had built up in my throat when I saw my dad's name come up on my phone.

"Is Marshall taking the loss in stride?" Cory asked.

"Seems like it."

"And…your dad?"

I shrugged. "He called, but I haven't listened to his message."

He gave me a tight smile. "Fair enough. We need to go through the project and get a little more specific with the time-line so I can send that over, and I think things are going to get rolling pretty quickly on this one."

I nodded, still dumbstruck.

"I have a couple others that landed on my desk this week I'd like you to look at as well. One in Orange County and another in New York."

"New York?"

"It's where I'm from originally," he said, standing up and tucking his laptop under one arm.

"What brought you to LA?"

"A man."

Of course it was a man. Wasn't it always a man?

Cory walked around from behind his desk, and I realized we were clearly heading back for another day of work in the conference room. He could have rented just the conference room and saved himself some money, but it was his business, not mine, and I wasn't about to tell him how to run it.

I could start my own business, I realized. Which had always felt like a possibility that was *just* out of reach for me. Even when I'd imagined inheriting the firm from my dad, small as it was, it had always felt like it was his. Something for me to take over, not something for me to build.

There was something in that idea, and I frowned at it, leading the way to the conference room. It didn't feel like an overstep to take the lead, and Cory and I worked well together, opening our laptops and sitting down at the table side by side. As peers and partners.

I spent the rest of the morning reviewing his other two projects while he began a draft of the timeline on Cahuenga Pass, and when we broke for lunch, I would have sworn the voicemail from my dad was burning a hole in my pocket. For lunch, I headed toward the beach to a little sandwich shop I only went to when I wanted to celebrate something. I'd have to share it with Marshall one day, but after the rush of the morning and the phone calls and the work on two new bids, I wanted some time to myself. Some quiet to think. But while I waited for my roast beef and cheddar, my finger hovered over the voicemail from my dad.

Instead of pressing it, I called Lincoln…and woke him up.

"Were you really asleep?" I asked when he yawned loudly into my ear.

"Really asleep. What time is it?"

"Noon, buddy. It's noon."

He made a very disbelieving sound in my ear that turned

into a stretch and a moan. "Aren't you supposed to be working?"

"I am, but it's lunchtime."

"Lunchtime," he repeated, yawning again.

"I'll let you get back to sleep"—I laughed—"but I wanted to let you know Cory and I got the job."

"You what?" Lincoln was wide awake now, and I had to cover my face with a cupped hand to hide my smile and my blush.

"We got the job."

"The one your dad fucked up?"

"Yeah," I said.

"The one your boyfriend thought he was going to win?"

My heart twisted, but not as badly as before. "That's the one."

"Fuck yes!"

I could picture Lincoln in bed, tangled in his sheets, fist pumping the air in celebration.

"Now I'm definitely coming out with you and Marshall later tonight. Celebration blow jobs for everyone!"

"You didn't even do anything," I teased.

"I'm hurt you would say such a thing. I supported you! Wholeheartedly."

I rolled my eyes, giving a pink-haired hipster a wave of thanks when they dropped my sandwich and a bag of chips in front of me.

"Yes, you did," I consoled. "I couldn't have done it without you."

"I know. I know. You're welcome, Silas."

Tearing open the wrapping on my sandwich with one hand, I couldn't help but feel *light* about the win for the first time since the morning. I did deserve this. I had worked hard. I always worked hard and would continue to do so. It wasn't my fault my dad didn't see it, and it definitely wasn't my fault he was too stuck in his ways to understand that architecture and design was a living, breathing industry that would have to change to stay relevant.

"I'm gonna eat," I told him. "I'll be home after work."

"I can't wait. Now I'm going back to bed."

Lincoln hung up on me, and I dug into my sandwich. I'd gotten partway through the first half when the chair across from me pulled out and my dad sank down into the seat. The bread and meat tangled into a ball and lodged in my throat. I choked on it, of course, slamming my hand against my chest to force it down into my stomach.

My dad didn't say anything while I fought through it, only silently sliding my drink closer after I'd managed to get it down.

"What are you doing here?" I asked.

"I knew you'd be here."

He sounded tired and looked it too. But of course he knew where to find me. I might not be under his thumb anymore, but I was still predictable.

"You ignored my call earlier?"

"I was busy."

"Celebrating?"

"Working," I said.

"With Cory Callahan."

I nodded.

"How did you get that job?" he asked.

"I interviewed for it," I said.

My dad sighed, tilting his head to the side like he was trying to decide if I was being deliberately obtuse or not. That was me, I wagered, his problem son.

"That's not what I meant."

"Marshall introduced us," I muttered.

"Covington?"

"Yeah."

"Why would he do that?" my dad asked, brow arched in accusation more than question.

I would have rather talked to him about the win, would have rather listened to him berate my ideas for being too ahead of their time, would have rather done anything than explain to my dad my relationship with his biggest business rival.

"What is your deal with him?" I asked instead, pushing my sandwich toward the middle of the table. I no longer wanted to take Marshall here. I wanted to find a new place to celebrate my wins.

"He's arrogant."

"Rightfully so," I shot back.

"He's always been entitled. Walking around like he's a gift to this industry. Even when he was in school, he was a prick about it."

"He was a prick about being talented?" I furrowed my brow at my dad. "That doesn't even make sense."

"He's never had to work hard."

I wiped my hands off on my napkin, then smoothed it back neatly over my lap. "I find that hard to believe. He's good at what he does and only part of that comes naturally."

"And what does he do, Silas?" The accusation was there, right on the tip of his tongue.

"I was talking about work. You know what I meant."

"You know what *I* meant," he said.

Sighing, I stared across the table at my dad, the lines around his eyes and the defeat in his posture.

"This is about more than work, isn't it?"

"My history with Marshall isn't your problem."

I laughed, shaking my head. "You've very much made it my problem."

"What is your relationship with that man, Silas?"

You don't have to talk to him at all.

Marshall's quiet reminder rang loud as a bell in my head, and I grabbed my phone and stood up in one swift motion.

"I'm not doing this with you," I told him. "Not now and not here."

"Silas."

"Not now and not here," I repeated. "I'm not a child anymore, and I don't appreciate you treating me like one. You raised me up to be just like you, but when it was time for me to stand on your shoulders, you shoved me down and kept me there. You tried to bury me with this grudge you're carrying, and I won't have it anymore. This win could have been yours, could have been ours, but now it's just mine."

It was a weird thing to realize that I'd outgrown my dad. To see the valley between us as something insurmountable instead of challenging. He would have been content to hold me back in all things and all ways as long as it suited him, then chide me for not being further along when it didn't. There was no winning with him. There wasn't even any playing the game. My dad, I realized, was still years in the past, back when I could barely hold a drafting pencil and my mom was still alive. It was sad, to know he'd turned into something stagnant so long ago, and his roots were too deep and gnarled to untangle.

The fact I'd cut myself free of him was a blessing because there was still time to extract my life from his before he pulled me down into the dirt with him. I wasn't sure if this was going to be the last time I talked to him, but…it might be, and that was okay.

It was okay.

I picked up the tray of my half-eaten sandwich and carried it to the trash and dumped it. My father didn't call after me, and he didn't chase after me. I supposed, in some way, that deserved a celebration too, even if my heart wasn't ready for that part quite yet.

CHAPTER 38
MARSHALL

As usual, I got to dinner first. Finn second. We weren't at our normal booth on account of needing more space to accommodate Andrew, but Finn still slid into the seat opposite me, a tight smile on his face. He'd done a stellar job of avoiding me over the past week and a half, which made it impossible to ask him about the couple I'd seen him with. So much time had passed since my initial sighting, the urgency had become less pressing, dying down to the point where I'd decided it wasn't my business at all if my younger brother was in the middle of tearing apart a marriage. I didn't want him to get hurt, but he was old enough to make his own decisions… and live with the consequences of them.

More than anything, I was hurt he hadn't told me. There'd been years where all three of them had treated me as a sort of confidant. I was older and more removed from their day-to-day lives, and all of them had taken turns confessing and crying on my shoulder at some point over the years. As the twins had gotten more settled in their own lives, that had died off, leaving me with Smith and his troubles. Eventually, he'd also outgrow the need for me, and I'd be left with none of them at all. Not in the way I'd grown accustomed to, at least.

"How are you?" I asked Finn, instead of anything else.

"Alive and thriving, Marsh." He rolled his eyes, some of the fight going out of him. "How are you?"

"Lost a job to Silas today," I answered.

Finn's eyes sparkled, and he fought his mouth back into a pensive line. "That so?"

"Mnhm."

"How do you feel about that?" he asked.

Smith was next to arrive, also taking his usual space to my left. The table they'd given us for the night was round, but I appreciated the way we tried to notch ourselves into our usual seats which would either leave Andrew between me and Finn or Hunter and Smith. I flashed a smile at my youngest brother, then turned back to answer Finn.

"Proud."

"Of who?" Smith asked.

"Silas," Finn answered before I could. "Taking money right out of our oldest brother's bank account."

"Oldest for now," Hunter said, taking his normal spot to Finn's right.

All three of us looked sharply at him, and he shrugged. "What? We don't know how many more of us there are running around. Just because we've only found Andrew doesn't mean there's not more."

The truth of that settled like a smothering weight over all of us, and it was only Andrew's arrival that snapped us back into the present. The implication of a new brother was a lot, the potential of more something unimaginable. The fact that Andrew walked up to the table like he'd known us on sight, the fact he was clearly a Covington...obvious by his build and the way his face was almost an identical match to Smith's, made the reality of the other options even more terrifying.

"Not sure which of you is Hunter," Andrew said, somewhat

awkwardly. But I watched him hold himself like Smith, watched him try to be brave.

"Want to guess?" Finn asked.

"Not really," Andrew answered, deadpan and dry...like Hunter.

"I'm Marshall," I said, standing and reaching across the table to shake his hand.

Andrew squared his shoulders and returned the gesture, putting everything else aside for the sake of maturity...like me.

"Andrew."

"This is Finn," I said, pointing at him. "Hunter. And this is Smith."

They all managed to get it together enough for handshakes, and then Andrew chose the seat between me and Finn, and we were all on our asses again.

"I'm glad you're older than me," he murmured at Finn.

"Why's that?"

"I think if you were younger, you'd be insufferable," he teased...just like Finn would have.

I glanced between the two of them, Finn battling his mouth into an angry line when I could tell he found the humor in the barb. Andrew's face a mask of indifference, like he'd unintentionally mastered Finn's humor and Hunter's delivery without even knowing better.

"Thanks for coming up to meet us," I said, flagging down our waiter. Andrew ordered a gin martini, and it was the first difference I'd noticed about him. "Though I'm not sure what your goal with this is."

"Do I need one? We're related. It makes sense to put faces to names. To shared DNA."

Beside me, Smith sucked his teeth. Like me.

"You don't need one," Hunter said.

And then silence fell over the table until our drinks were

served. Smith guzzled his wine, and I kicked my foot into his. He made an unhappy noise in the back of his throat but set his glass back down on the table. Thankfully, he'd gotten it all into his mouth and not all over the front of his shirt.

I scratched the back of my neck, tickling my finger up into my hairline while also waiting to see if any of my three—no, four—brothers were going to pick up the conversation again. When it became clear none of them were, I said, "So, Andrew. Hunter hasn't told us anything about you at all besides we have the same father and that you don't want to take his last name. Tell us something else. What do you do for work?"

"I also don't want his money," Andrew said quickly.

I glanced at his clothes, well-tailored but still off the rack. He didn't strike me as blue collar, but there was definitely no Covington money behind him.

"Good." I smiled. "How do you make yours, then?"

"Data entry," he said, biting the inside of his cheek. "What about the four of you?"

"I'm an architect," I told him. "You know Hunter is an attorney."

Andrew nodded.

"I'm in finance," Finn said, and I was grateful to see him engaged in the conversation, however minimally.

Everyone looked at Smith, who in turn looked like he wanted to crawl under the table and die. "I have a degree in design," he said. "I'm working with a historic preservation and restoration firm right now."

"Is that what you want to do?"

Smith swallowed. "Why wouldn't it be?"

"Just the way you said it." Andrew waved dismissively and reached for his martini. "Never mind. And you're the youngest?"

"For now," Smith muttered.

Andrew laughed awkwardly. "You'll have to forgive my next question, but…how did the four of you find each other?"

Finn and Hunter went tense, both of them lifting their glasses in sync like they really were twins. Smith was clearly lost in his head which left the answer to me.

Again.

"To be frank, it was a series of business transactions," I explained. "Our mothers all hit Willem up for child support of some kind and got buyouts instead. Which they all took. Yours clearly did not."

"Buyouts?"

"Cash for parental rights," I said, chasing the answer with some wine to erase how bitter it tasted on my tongue.

"That's horrible."

"It's just a thing that happened. It happened a long time ago, and now I have three brothers out of the deal," I said.

"Four," Hunter corrected.

"For now," Finn added on.

Andrew's brows stretched toward his hairline. "For now?"

"We thought it was just the four of us," Finn said. "But now here you are. There's no saying there's no other Covingtons running around."

"I'm not a Covington."

"No," Finn said warily. "You're not."

"Alright." I lifted my hand between the two of them, and Finn obediently stopped talking in favor of finishing his Manhattan. "And Andrew, Hunter says you're twenty-eight?"

"Yes." He licked his lips and looked around the table, curiosity finally getting the better of him. "What about all of you?"

"I'm twenty-five," Smith said. "They're thirty-five, and Marshall is almost forty."

"I'm thirty-nine," I grumbled.

"Almost forty," Finn insisted. On either side of him, both of my other brothers smirked at him, and I found myself even more outnumbered than before.

"Are any of you married?" Andrew asked next.

"No," Finn answered. "And we're all single, except for Marshall."

My mind wandered to Silas, and I smiled into my wine. I hoped he was having a good time with Lincoln, and I hoped he'd stopped beating himself up about winning the job. I was looking forward to celebrating with him at Rapture after dinner and celebrating properly with him in private after that. I'd have to come up with something good to get him out of his head long enough to appreciate how monumental his win truly was.

"What a smile," Andrew teased, and he looked so much like Finn, my breath caught. I managed to return the expression, grateful when our waiter returned with a second round of drinks and a welcome distraction.

The rest of the night passed well enough with only the occasional lapse into uncomfortable silence. It was clear by the end of the night that no matter how much Andrew had wanted to come into this meeting with nothing more than morbid curiosity, he was leaving with four brothers he'd not planned to keep. The same could be said for all of us, even if I could still feel the resistance pulsing out with Smith's too-tight smiles and sometimes too-loud laughs. We parted with hugs instead of handshakes and the promise that we'd make a best effort shot at getting together the following month.

I stood in the parking lot with Finn, Smith, and Hunter, and the three of us watched Andrew climb into his car and drive away with one last wave in his rearview mirror. As soon as the car turned the corner, Hunter slapped Finn hard on the back once, ruffled Smith's hair, and headed for his own car.

Finn and Smith and I repeated the routine, watching Hunter until he was out of sight, at which point I glanced at Smith.

"How was that for you?" I asked.

"He's a lot like Finn."

Finn snorted. "He's more like you and Hunter than me."

"A bit like Marshall," Smith suggested, which earned him an eye roll from me.

"Stoic in the face of emotion," I said, which wasn't even true for me anymore. Silas could take me to my knees with a single look; he just didn't know it.

"What's the rest of your night look like?" Finn asked.

"Celebrating with Silas," I said, "as long as the two of you don't need me."

"I don't need you," Finn said, stepping behind me to slide his arm around Smith's shoulder. "Do you, Smith?"

He looked like he wanted to, but he was more like me than he'd ever admit.

"I'm good," Smith said.

"We can go get a nightcap since we're not invited to Silas's celebration." Finn pretended to pout, pulling Smith toward their cars on the far edge of the parking lot.

"You don't even know him, and Smith has only met him once."

"I went to school with him."

"That was a lifetime ago," I said.

"For you maybe," Finn taunted.

"He's coming with me next Friday, so any celebration that happens after that, I'll make sure you get an invitation."

Finn linked his arm through Smith's and turned them both backward, throwing me a wink and saying, "Love is cute on you."

"Good night, boys." I waved them off, reaching for my keys. "Be safe."

"Yes, Dad!" Finn called.

Smith shook his head, and then I watched the two of them get into Finn's car and disappear in the same direction Hunter and Andrew had gone. Letting out a long breath that threatened to deflate me like a balloon, I gave myself a good five minutes of peace and quiet in the parking lot before pulling my phone out of my pocket.

It was later than dinner usually ran, quite close to ten, and I had one missed text message from Silas. It was a picture of him sprawled out on his couch, head resting on Lincoln's shoulder, both of them grinning at the camera.

> **SILAS**
> Ready when you are.

It appeared, at least on the surface, he'd recovered from the misery of his earlier success.

I texted him back.

> Do you want a ride?

> I'll get one with Lincoln so he can fuck off at the end of the night, but you'll have to bring me back on Sunday to get my car.

> What I'm hearing is it's a good opportunity to talk about your living situation.

> Maybe.

> That feels fast.

> But not.

> Stop thinking so hard.

> I'm leaving dinner. Going to run home and change. It's late but I should be there a little before 11:30.

Can't wait. We're going to leave now. Is that okay?

You don't have to ask me that.

I want to.

More than okay, sweetheart

Find me when you get there?

Always.

CHAPTER 39
SILAS

"I won't lie," Lincoln murmured softly against my neck. "I liked it better when I could take you home and spank you until you cried."

I snorted. "Sorry, you have to work for it now. Being dominant must be terribly exhausting."

"It is," he agreed, knocking his head against mine.

We were on the patio at Rapture, nestled together at a cocktail table with a clear view of the dance floor. We'd done a quick pass through the place after arriving, and Lincoln had prematurely declared the night hopeless before hauling me outside for a better view. I wasn't looking for the same thing he was, but I promised him the night was very young and he still had plenty of time to find someone.

"What happened to that man from the last time we were here?" I asked. "Ethan?"

Even in the dim light of the patio, I could see Lincoln's cheeks darken. I hadn't heard a peep about Ethan since the night we'd met him, and the text messages Lincoln had sent over the course of the night and into the next morning to let me know he was safe and alive.

"I haven't talked to him," he said.

"Why not?"

"I didn't get his number," Lincoln muttered. "An oversight."

"I have his phone number," I reminded him. "He put it in my phone the night you went home with him. Did you not remember that?"

Lincoln's eyes went wide, then shuttered. "I can't text him just because you have his number. That feels like some consent violation."

"Do you want me to text him?" I asked.

"That's the same," he said. "If I want to see him again, I'll just have to do it the old-fashioned way. By crossing my fingers and hoping for the best."

"That doesn't sound like you."

Lincoln gave me a forlorn look. "It doesn't matter, and I don't want to talk about it. He was fun, but it's complicated so it's better to just let it be. Less attachments."

"You sound very unattached," I agreed, face somber in my agreement.

"Hey." He snapped his fingers in front of my face, and I smacked his hand down to the table. "There's your man."

I looked into the club, and Lincoln was right. Marshall was there, easy to pick out for how tall he was, how elegant he looked, even in a sea of skin and leather. His hair still looked wet—he must have showered after dinner—and even though there was a whole dance floor between us, the scent of his soap filled my nose. He scanned the room looking for me, and I watched him the whole time until he found me. His approach after that was like a guided missile, cutting through the crowd with precision until he was right in front of me.

Up close, I gave a quick glance to his clothes, black jeans and a black t-shirt, mostly the same as what I had on but also a hundred times better put together. He gave me the same onceover, but I could tell by the heat in his eyes I was the only one who found myself to be lacking.

"I'll go get drinks," Lincoln said.

Marshall gave him a quick greeting and thanks, never taking his eyes off me.

"There's my brilliant project architect," he murmured, sliding an arm around my waist and hauling our bodies together. "Are you ready to admit how amazing you are?"

I huffed, cheeks burning. "To anyone except you," I admitted.

"We'll have to work on that."

Marshall leaned down and brushed his lips against mine. He tasted like toothpaste, fresh and clean. I smiled against his mouth and joined my hands together at the base of his neck.

"How was dinner?" I asked.

"He's far less horrible than any of us hoped. Very much like all of us in his own little ways."

"That's good, right?"

He nodded, pulling me into a proper hug. "It's good. How was the rest of your day?"

"I saw my dad," I blurted.

Marshall's arms tightened around me—an act of protection, I realized—and I let myself go weak and vulnerable against him.

"Are you all right?" he asked. "You should have told me earlier. You could have."

It was easier to be honest sometimes when I wasn't aware of Marshall's penetrating stare on me. In his arms, his heart beating inches above and across from mine was a safe place for my truths.

"I'm fine. It was…I don't know. He showed up while I was having lunch. He knew where to find me."

"And?"

"He wasn't angry, just defeated, I think. He implied there

was something going on with you and me, but I didn't tell him either way. I did tell him I didn't want to talk to him, and I left."

"Did he come after you?" Marshall asked.

I shook my head, and for the first time, I wanted to cry about the whole thing.

My dad had just let me walk away from him because he was angry at me on the day that I'd won the biggest bid of my career. My name was attached to the win. When I worked with my dad, they'd all been his name and his glory. Cory was the first person to give me credit that was due, the second person to see me as an equal. The first, of course, currently had his arms wrapped around my waist and his face buried in the crook of my neck.

"It's better this way," I said.

Lincoln was on his way back, his lithe figure slinking through the crowd and toward the patio.

"I'm ready to celebrate," I told Marshall, and I meant it honestly.

He pulled away and smiled down at me, leaving a kiss against the tip of my nose, then the corner of my mouth.

"He's here," Lincoln said out of nowhere, setting two glasses of wine on the table, his own drink still in hand.

"Who?"

"Ethan."

"Go get him, tiger," I teased, untangling myself from Marshall's arms so I could slap Lincoln on his ass.

"I don't want to look desperate."

"You'd look interested," I said.

"I'm going to wait," Lincoln said with a nod, his action decided. "He just got here, and he was with a few other guys. I don't know their deal."

"Are you sure your name isn't Thomas?" Marshall asked, handing me my drink before reaching for his own. He took the smallest sip imaginable, smiling at Lincoln the whole time.

"Why would it be Thomas?"

"You're a doubter." At Lincoln's blank stare, Marshall clarified. "You know, from the Bible?"

"Never read it."

"I thought it was something everyone just knew."

Lincoln offered him a lopsided smile. "The first time I ever stepped foot into a church was this one, Marshall. I don't know a thing about the Bible or Thomas."

"Lincoln?" A voice from a few tables away had all of us looking, but it wasn't Ethan who stood there.

"Riot."

"Can we talk?"

Lincoln looked like he wanted the earth to swallow him whole.

"You don't have to talk to him," I said softly, using Marshall's earlier reminder to me on my best friend.

"I know. It's good. If you guys wander off, I'll come find you." He leaned in close and dusted a kiss against the corner of my mouth. The opposite side from where Marshall had kissed me last, and instead of any sort of concern over how the affection would make Marshall feel, I only felt overwhelmed and washed in love.

"Does this mean we can begin the celebration?" Marshall whispered into my ear.

"What does the celebration entail?"

"Since when do you care?"

I chuckled, heat racing down my throat and spreading through my chest like wildfire. "We've never really…not in public."

He turned me so my back was to his front. So I could feel the heat of his erection against the back of my hip.

"Let's negotiate then," he murmured.

Fuck.

It had been so long since we'd discussed consent and action, not for lack of action but lack of need. We'd both established the ground rules and the limits and the expectations so there wasn't much left to say. I was always submissive to him. I'd even called him Sir in public before at times, but there were parts of what we did that hadn't left his house before. Those rules were set but only applied when we were in the privacy of his home. Taking those acts out of the bedroom was something new for us entirely.

"Do you have different rules in public?" he asked.

"I don't know. Before…before you, it was only scenes here and there. It didn't feel so intimate."

"Then maybe you were doing it wrong."

"Maybe," I agreed, resting my head against his chest.

"Is that your way of saying you don't want to do this here?"

Feeling bold, I took his hand and dragged it down my stomach and lower still until his fingers danced over the hard line of my cock.

"I do want it."

"Can I fuck you here?"

Arousal exploded between my legs and my dick jumped against his hand.

"That's delightful, sweetheart, but it's hardly consent."

"In a private room," I said, shivering. "With the door open."

"Not entirely in the open," he surmised, and I nodded my agreement. "Can I touch you over your clothes in the open?"

"Yes, please. Sir."

Marshall curled his fingers around my dick, through my pants, and I groaned, lashes fluttering. He stroked me with a rough hand before letting it trail up my body again and under my shirt. His fingers twisted and flicked my nipples, and it was very hard to not writhe and moan for him right there on the patio.

The public setting enhanced everything. The pleasure, the need, all of it amplified with the crowds and the bodies around us.

"What if I take you up to a playroom and strip you naked? Impale you with my cock while I torment the memory of those bruises on the insides of your thighs?" Marshall whispered, breath hot against my ear. "What if we *start* with that?"

I was nothing more than need. "Yes, Sir."

"That's enough wine then."

We left our glasses on the table, and I followed Marshall into the club. The music was louder, bass thumping in time with the rapid-fire beat of my heart. The only steady thing around me was Marshall's hand curled around mine. He led me to the downstairs playroom where we'd first made each other's acquaintance in this new way that had so quickly become familiar, then held out his arm.

I walked around to the front of him, almost on display like a woman at a ball, and Marshall eyed me with a dark and primal sort of intent. He sat down on the couch and pulled his cock out of his pants. He was hard. He was hard, and I wanted to get onto my knees and suck him.

"What, Silas?" he asked, stroking himself from root to tip.

Precum pearled against his slit and with a quick swipe of his fingers, it was gone.

"Just want you, Sir," I managed.

"Rightly so." He sucked his tongue across the front of his teeth. "Go find lube and a pair of nipple clamps. Get a pair of wrist cuffs while you're at it."

"Yes, Sir."

The downstairs playroom wasn't nearly as well-equipped as the upstairs space, and I quickly realized I'd have to leave him to get the things he'd demanded. He didn't seem bothered at the prospect, sprawled out on the couch with his dick in his hand like a king with his scepter.

I imagined he was that—to me.

I walked quickly upstairs, sliding into the first playroom. The door was cracked open, but there were people inside. Lincoln, I realized, with Riot there on his knees with a mouthful of cock again. Clearly Lincoln's work was only an issue when it suited him. Neither of them saw me, Lincoln lost to the pleasure of the other man's mouth, so I grabbed what I needed from the armoire against the wall and made my way back downstairs to Marshall.

He looked the same as I'd left him, and I went to my knees at his feet, all the things he'd asked for clutched in my sweaty hands.

"You're trembling," he said, taking everything and setting it down beside him.

"I always do."

"I know. I like it. Now take off your clothes."

I managed to strip naked while still on my knees, resting my hands on the tops of my thighs, palms up after I'd finished the task. Marshall surveyed me like I was chattel, and the casualness of his perusal had my cock pulsing like mad against my stomach.

"Definitely worth celebrating," Marshall said, almost under his breath.

He held open one of the cuffs and I set my wrist in it. Carefully—as always—he closed the clasp around my wrist and again kissed the delicate place where the leather met my skin. I shivered, arousal coursing through my fingers as he repeated the motion with my other wrist.

"Over your head," he said next, and I raised my arms, which gave him clear access to my chest.

Marshall leaned over, resting his elbows on his thighs so he could toy with my nipples until I moaned and gasped his name.

My nipples were hard, erect, and he attached the clamps to each one with a brutal efficiency. I managed another gasp when he tugged the connecting chain between them, and his smile was absolutely feral.

Hooking his finger under the chain, he lifted it up, tugging at my nipples to the point of discomfort. I realized too late what he wanted, and he grabbed my chin with this other hand, pulling my mouth open and easing the chain between my teeth. My chin quivered, every tremble like a thousand pounds of pressure on my chest.

"Perfect," Marshall mused, beckoning me to my feet, then onto his lap.

I turned so my back was to his chest again and straddled him…somewhat awkwardly not being able to see. His cock was slick with lube, poking against my backside, and then he reached up and bent my arms back, dragging my joined wrists together behind his head. I'd never felt so exposed, my muscles tense from the predicament bondage he'd managed to put me in without even a foot of rope in sight.

My lashes fluttered, and a slick finger eased into me, turning and pressing against my prostate. I tried to cry out, the sound muffled by the chain between my teeth. Marshall hummed, sounding pleased, then slowly fucked my hole with his finger until I writhed on his lap as much as the bondage would allow.

To my relief, he replaced his finger with his cock, and I sank down onto his lap, impaled as he'd always planned. Marshall eased me all the way down around him, curling his hands over the still dark bruising on the fronts of my thighs. He spread my legs a little bit wider, fingers pressing against the marks from earlier in the week.

"Ride me," he whispered into my ear, grasping the smallest sliver of flesh between his fingernails and pinching down on me.

Hard.

I jerked on his lap, pain lancing up my thigh, through my nipples. The muscles in my arms were taut, stretched behind him, and then he pinched another spot, then one on both sides, and I couldn't stop myself from shaking on his lap. The pain was fucking acute and all over at once. Marshall groaned low and deep in my ear, then slapped the inside of my thigh hard, the biting sting of the impact a warning.

"Silas," he warned. "I gave you an order."

I didn't remember how my legs worked. All I knew was to hold my arms up, keep my head steady so I didn't pull too hard on my nipples, but another quick slap against my thigh reminded me and I started to move. Beneath me, Marshall was all tension and restraint, and I did exactly as he'd asked. My hips were jerky, circles aborted because the pleasure inside of me was still too clouded from the pain outside me.

"Help," I pleaded, the word barely more than a garbled whisper. The chain caught on a tooth, and I sobbed.

"What's that?"

"Help me, please. Sir."

Marshall dragged his hands across my battered skin, sliding one up to my throat and the other to my hip. He was still dressed, the only bare part of him his cock which was fully inserted into my body. The denim of his jeans rubbed against the bruised backs of my thighs, and his hand collared my throat like a hug. My dick throbbed, hard and angry between my legs.

Ignored.

"I'm going to fill you up with so much cum it leaks down your thighs," he said into my ear, biting down on the lobe and taking over the movements required to get us there. "My fucking prize."

Marshall bracketed my hip with his other hand, pushing me down as he slammed up into me. The way he fucked me was measured yet barely controlled. The force of him enough to jostle one of the clamps free of my nipple. I shouted in agony as the blood rushed to the right side of my chest, and Marshall grunted, going still as I convulsed around him. He was close to coming. I could tell by the way he moved. I'd learned his body, become familiar with his sounds.

Eventually, his pace faltered, his breath caught, and Marshall raised his hands back behind him, tangling our fingers together. He used my neck to muffle the sounds of his pleasure, thrusting twice more beneath me before going utterly still. Cum pulsed from his cock, filling me just like he'd promised.

"Mine," he rasped.

Low.

Final.

I closed my eyes and went limp against his chest.

Sated and overflowing in more ways than one.

CHAPTER 40
MARSHALL

I spent the entire weekend making love with Silas.

Before dinner on Saturday, I hogtied him in the middle of my living room and fucked him until he couldn't breathe. After, I paid close attention to the rug burn on his knees and elbows in the shower, making sure to kiss every inch of skin I'd marked, bruised, or otherwise abraded. Sunday morning, I'd brought him coffee in bed, then I sucked his cock until my jaw couldn't take the girth of him anymore. He hadn't finished, so I let him jerk off on my feet while I had *my* coffee, then I kissed him long and hard after he licked my toes clean.

Silas was perfection in all ways. I told him often how much I loved him, how grateful I was to call him mine, but I didn't ask him to move in again.

Occasionally, I found myself aware of the power imbalance between us: the wealth gap, the age gap, the experience gap. It took conscious work to ensure I wasn't exploiting it. Hell, it was the deciding factor in why I shoved Silas at Cory instead of hiring him myself. The living situation needed to be treated with the same care. Silas knew where I stood. If he wanted to meet me there, I'd be happy for it.

Until then, I was content to keep him in my bed—often

tied and trussed—until he told me he needed to go home to check on Lincoln and get clean clothes. Apparently there was something wrong with my washer and dryer, even though it cleaned his cum off my sheets just fine.

Nevertheless, the week crawled toward Friday, and if Silas had any nerves over the impending meeting of the brothers, he wasn't showing them. He was focused on two things, work and me, and I had no complaints about either of them.

On Wednesday afternoon, he called me to get my opinion on something he was thinking about for a bid Cory had him drafting up for a job in New York, but our call was interrupted by an unexpected visitor stepping out of the elevators.

"Let me call you later, sweetheart," I said, waiting for him to answer back before hanging up the phone. I kept it in my hand, watching an older and far more miserable version of Silas make his way through my office.

"Do you have five minutes?" Stanley Ayres asked me, looking worse for wear from the last time I'd seen him.

"Depends."

"I want to talk about Silas," he said.

I stood up, frowning and shaking my head. "Then no. I don't."

"Covington," he protested.

I waved him off, coming around the front of my desk with the full intention of ushering him to the elevator and back to wherever he'd come from.

"I'm not going to talk about Silas with you," I said.

"Because you're fucking my son?"

I snorted, biting back the truth of the matter. I was doing far more than fucking him.

"I'm not going to talk about Silas with you," I repeated, stabbing the down button on the elevator.

"Does he talk about me with you?"

"Ask him," I suggested.

"He's not answering my calls."

The elevator doors slid open, and Stanley begrudgingly stepped inside, turning to face me with his arms limp at his sides. Silas hadn't even mentioned his father since the lunch interruption had come up. I wondered if he'd blocked his dad or chosen to willfully ignore the calls. Either way, it made me appreciate my father's concern for me and my brothers was in name and reputation only, not anything that actually mattered.

"I don't know what to tell you, Stanley."

Regret flashed across his face as the doors closed on him, and with a sigh, I turned and leaned against the wall. Pulling my phone out of my pocket, I sent a quick message to Silas.

> Your dad just showed up here asking about you.

SILAS
> Jesus. I'm sorry.

> Are you ignoring his calls?

> Yes.

> Did he seem upset?

> Defeated.

> Sorry he bothered you.

> Not a bother. Just wanted to let you know and make sure you're okay.

> Always.

It was an overstatement, but nothing worth arguing about.

The elevator doors slid open, and I was ready to rebuff Stanley again but instead found Smith, tie loose around his neck and exhaustion marring his features.

"Hey," I said, nose scrunched.

Smith stepped out of the elevator and headed for my office without an invitation. I went behind him, closing the door after he collapsed into one of the leather chairs opposite my desk.

"You good, baby brother?"

Instead of sitting behind my desk, I took the seat next to Smith, waiting for him to tell me what was on his mind.

"I want a new job," he blurted, frowning.

"Okay." I rubbed my hands together, immediately running through the rolodex of contacts in my mind who would be able to help Smith get out of his current firm and into something new. "Bored of the history or what's going on?"

"No. Yes. I mean…I want a new career."

Biting my tongue, I waited until it hurt so the pain would stop me from saying something regrettable to my still very impressionable youngest brother.

"What brought this on?" I finally asked.

"I'm bored."

"Of work specifically?"

"Yes," he said.

"Smith." I groaned, shifting my weight around and propping one ankle up on my knee. My slacks hiked up and I wrapped my hand around my ankle bone, tapping my fingers against my shin. "We argued about this after you graduated high school, and you were adamant it was what you wanted."

"Can't people change their minds?" he snapped.

"Of course they can," I said carefully. "But I want to understand why you're having this change of heart."

"I don't need to explain myself to you, Marshall."

"Then why are you here?"

"This was a mistake." Smith stood to go, and I grabbed his wrist to stop him. He let me, so I tugged him back down into the chair.

"What's really going on, Smith?" Leaning forward, I kept

my fingers curled around his wrist, both our hands resting on top of his leg.

Of all my brothers, Smith was the most like me, which meant I should know how to handle him and his moods like they were my own. The outburst sounded rash and unprovoked, though. I expected it was a knee-jerk response to finding out about the existence of Andrew, shaking Smith's foundation in more ways than one.

"What's the point of it?" he asked, frowning at a spot on the wall behind me.

"You preserve history, Smith. You repair and restore it for others to enjoy."

"I'm preserving someone's *idea* of history," he shot back. "How do I know I'm recreating an honest truth and not something made up?"

This was definitely about Andrew.

Exhaling a long breath, I squeezed his wrist before letting it go. He didn't jump up again, so I wagered he was no longer a flight risk.

"I think," I started slowly, needing to play into his comparison without being heavy-handed about it. "I think sometimes it's a bit of both. We have our own preconceptions—"

"Misconceptions."

"Both of those," I conceded. "But regardless of the meaning of the filigree or the conversation around the choices made when we weren't in the room, the core of it all remains unchanged. Don't you think?"

I was talking about us. The foundation and lives the four of us had built.

"And you know, Smith, sometimes when you dig deeper into the history of a thing, you find more support than you started with and that's only good news for everyone. Right? It doesn't change the shape of a thing, just the strength of it."

My brother narrowed his eyes at me, fully aware that I

wasn't talking about building preservation anymore. But then again, he never had been.

"It still feels like a lie," he muttered.

"Do you think we felt that way?" I asked, giving him a small half-smile. "When you showed up?"

"You should have."

I winked. "Finn, maybe a little, but not Hunter and never me."

In a decidedly *me* move, Smith dragged his tongue across the front of his teeth. His jaw was set like he'd been carved out of stone, and I wanted so badly to shake him out of whatever headspace he'd thrown himself into.

"By definition, additions are more not less," I explained. "I have to see that as a good thing until it's not."

"Design can be overdone."

"It can," I agreed. "But in this case, it's not."

Smith grumbled and groaned, but I could tell by the sag in his shoulders he knew I was right. Relief washed over me, and I straightened up, checking my watch and then clapping my hands together.

"Are you on your lunch?" I asked.

"I left early."

My first instinct was to chastise him for letting his emotions own him so completely, but I was also relatively lost when it came to my emotions about Silas, so I probably would have done the same thing. Smith glanced at me nervously like he knew exactly where my mind had gone at his confession.

"Let's get out of here then," I said, standing up and gesturing for him to join me.

"I didn't want to interrupt your whole day, Marsh."

"A welcome distraction. Let me pack up and we can go."

"Where are we going?" he asked.

"To get lunch, as a start." I walked around to the other side of my desk, powering down my laptop and gathering up my things. "And then we'll just see where the day takes us, alright?"

"When does Silas get home?"

"Silas doesn't live with me," I said. "But if he gets to my house, it's whenever he wants."

"He has a key?"

"Of course," I said. "But he still lives with Lincoln."

Smith stood, fidgeting with the knot on his tie. "Why?"

I swallowed back any argument I would have had about why Silas chose to keep his apartment instead of moving in with me because just like I didn't want to answer Stanley's questions about Silas, I wasn't keen to answer Smith's either.

"Because he wants to."

My brother followed me out of my office, close on my heels and flicking off lights as we went.

"Doesn't that bother you?" he asked.

"Not at all."

I pressed the button for the elevator, half expecting another one of my brothers to be there when it opened. It was blessedly empty, and Smith and I stepped inside and turned our backs to the wall.

"A little bit," I admitted, glancing at his reflection.

The corner of his mouth quirked up into a smile, and I exhaled a shaky laugh. "It's his choice though," I said. "Just like it's your choice if you want to walk away from restoration."

"I don't," he said.

"I know."

The doors slid open on the ground floor, and we stepped out together.

"Did you drive?" I asked.

"I walked."

"Of course you did." I jerked my head toward the parking garage entrance, and Smith again followed after me.

"I like the air," he said. "It helps me think."

"I wasn't arguing about it."

We reached my car and sank down into the seats. I tossed my bag into the back and pressed the ignition switch. The car roared to life, echoing loudly in the cavernous garage. Backing out of the spot, I braced my hand against the passenger headrest, giving Smith's hair a ruffle before putting the car into drive.

"What are you hungry for?" I asked.

"Whatever you want."

"Wrong."

"Sushi," he muttered, turning his attention to the corner of the windshield.

He was apparently not entirely done with being petulant about Andrew, and that was fine. I had patience, and I could wait him out.

"Nobu?"

"Too bougie." Smith swallowed hard, thumping his head against the headrest. "Maybe that place in the valley?"

I scrunched my nose, checking the rearview mirror before changing lanes so I could get on the 110.

"The one in Studio City?"

"Yeah."

"Anything you want, Smith."

I reached over and gave his leg a squeeze, shaking until he rolled his eyes and smiled. I wasn't sure how to talk him through whatever was going on in his head, but I definitely wasn't going to give up until I figured it out.

Everything else would have to wait.

CHAPTER 41
SILAS

"**D**o you want to come over to Marshall's?" I asked Lincoln, balancing the phone between my ear and my shoulder.

It was just before six. I'd come here right after work to find the house dark and quiet. I texted Marshall to see how late he planned to be, and he said he was out with Smith who needed some one-on-one brother time. I'd just gotten out of the shower, cleaning myself in the ways Marshall expected, and I didn't have any plans for the night since he wasn't going to be back until late. I could have gotten dressed and headed home, but whether I'd admit it to him or not, I had started to think of his house as my home.

"Of course, I want to come over to Marshall's," Lincoln said. "Do you want me to bring dinner?"

My stomach growled. "From where?"

"You tell me," he said.

"Will you get me a shawarma salad?" I asked.

"Perfect choice. Be there soon."

Lincoln hung up on me, and I tossed my cell phone onto my bed.

My bed.

The bed.

Our bed?

Fuck. I didn't know.

Sinking down onto the edge of the mattress, I dropped my head into my hands with a frustrated groan. I wanted to live here—with Marshall—but it was scary at the same time. We hadn't been together long and there was very much a part of me that worried once the newness or the novelty wore off, he wouldn't want to be with me anymore. Biting the corner of my thumbnail, I tried to convince myself my fears were unfounded, but there was only one person strong enough to remind me of that, and it definitely wasn't the one who'd just bit his nail so close to the quick it was bleeding.

Half an hour later, Lincoln was banging on the door, and I still hadn't managed to get a bandage around my thumb. I jumped up to let him in, then shuffled off to the bathroom while he busied himself with dishing up our dinner in the dining room. With my hangnail secure, I caught up with my best friend making himself at home at Marshall's table.

The dining room table.

Our dining room table?

Fucking fuck.

"I feel like I haven't seen you in forever," Lincoln said when I sat down beside him.

"I saw you Friday," I reminded him.

How could I think about moving out when three days felt like a lifetime? I scooted my chair closer to his so I could twine my foot around his ankle. Beside me, Lincoln let out a noise that was half-laugh and half-sigh.

"Do you want me to be home more?" I asked.

He groaned and shook his head. "I want you happy. I just have to get used to how that looks now."

I pulled the plastic wrapping off the fork and twisted it around my fingers until it was thin enough to tie in a knot. I wrapped the strip around Lincoln's wrist and tied it, hooking my finger beneath the plastic to make sure it wasn't too tight in his arm.

"What's this?" he murmured, turning his arm upside down to look at the whole piece.

"Like a collar," I teased gently, "but for best friends."

Lincoln snorted, knocking into me with his shoulder. "You could have just pissed on me to mark your territory."

"It's not like that." I bumped back into him. "Even if I'm here, I'm still your best friend. Nothing between us has changed except now we aren't up each other's asses all the time."

"It is a small apartment," he agreed, voice going soft. "But it's ours."

"It is."

"And now…Marshall's place is yours. His and yours."

I swallowed hard, dropping my fork. "He does want me to move in, but I haven't told him yes."

"Why not?" Lincoln shifted, knees pressing into mine. He took both of my hands into his and kissed the bandage on my thumb. "You love him. Why not? Please don't say it's because of me."

"Not only you, but I love that you think so highly of yourself."

He scrunched his nose at me, and I leaned forward and pressed our mouths together. Lincoln made a surprised sound, but then softened, letting his tongue slide out to search for mine. The kiss was quick and chaste—all history between us considered—but it was enough to ease the tension that had wrapped around us both.

"You're my best friend," I said, kissing the corner of Lincoln's mouth for good measure before pulling away. "That's never going to change."

"I think when you move in with him, I'll probably move too."

"What?"

Lincoln shrugged, untangling himself from me enough to get to his dinner and start eating. He managed a few bites before answering me.

"There's no point in having a two bedroom if you're not there," he said.

"You can get another roommate."

"I don't like the idea of someone in your space."

Lincoln shoved another bite of lamb into his mouth and made a show of chewing. Picking up the container my salad was in, I gave the whole thing a shake, then opened it up to find the chicken and the sauce mixed in with the lettuce. I took a bite for myself, giving him time to process the conversation.

"Would you get a studio?" I finally asked.

"That's probably safest. Less rent to worry about."

Another huge bite of lamb, and I matched him with a forkful of salad.

"Have you looked anywhere yet?"

"Yeah."

Something a lot like jealousy lanced through me, even though it had no place. Lincoln saw the writing on the wall, and he was trying to prepare and protect himself for what we both knew the eventual outcome would be. He didn't know about my hesitation because I hadn't told him. Not because I'd planned to keep it from him, but because everything still felt so fast and new when I thought about it.

"Do you think it's too soon for me to move in?" I asked.

"Do you love him?"

"Yes."

"Does he treat you well?"

I thought of the bruises all over my ass and my legs. The

hickey on my hip. The rules and the expectations. The correction and the reward.

"Of course."

Lincoln threw me a sideways glance. "And you treat him well?"

Laughing nervously, I moved some lettuce around the takeout container. "Don't I?"

Lincoln shrugged, unbothered. "It's not all about you. You have to give him the things he needs in return, right?"

"Of course," I said, scrubbing a hand down my face. "I'm supposed to meet his brothers on Friday."

"That sounds serious."

"What if they don't like me?"

"Then I imagine I won't need that studio apartment after all," he answered, taking the last bite of his lamb before sliding the container toward the middle of the table. My expression must have blanched because Lincoln was quick to smile and smooth back my still-damp hair. "I'm kidding. I'm kidding. Marshall doesn't seem like the type to let other people sway his decisions."

"He loves his brothers more than anything."

"More than you?"

"Different from me. Obviously."

"He's a good man, Silas. And so are you." Lincoln plucked a pickled turnip from my salad and chomped down on it. "Everything is going to work out the way it's meant to."

No matter how good the shawarma was, I wasn't very hungry anymore. I managed to get through half of the salad before giving up and stacking my Styrofoam package on top of Lincoln's.

"Do you have to get home?" I asked.

He stretched, his slender body taking up all the space the table allowed. "I don't have to do anything. When is Marshall home?"

"No idea. He's out with Smith."

Lincoln's eyes turned into hearts, and he crawled onto his knees, leaning toward me as I gathered up all our trash and leftovers from the table. I carried everything into the kitchen, rolling my eyes when Lincoln turned toward me, his entire expression one of mischief.

"Smith is cute. Is he gay?"

"I don't know what Smith is," I said.

"Shame."

I rolled my eyes. "What about Riot? What about Ethan?"

"What about them? Oh! I haven't even told you about Darian."

"Oh, my God."

Lincoln jumped up from the table. "Smith is cuter than both of them."

"Please don't put the moves on my boyfriend's brother."

"I'll think about it," he said with a laugh.

I cleaned up the table, then joined him on the couch. As soon as I sat down and got comfortable, Lincoln rolled onto his side and plopped his head in my lap. Folding his hands together behind his head, he lodged his elbow into my stomach until I angled him up and found a position that didn't make me want to cut his arm off.

"While I'm thinking," Lincoln blurted. "What if I'm not a Dom?"

I turned on the TV and promptly dropped the remote on his face.

"What?" Bending over him, I tried my best to dust a kiss across the quickly darkening red spot blooming on his cheek. It was hardly enough, so I swirled small circles over the mark until the furrow between his brows relaxed.

"What if I'm not?" he asked again, softly.

"Where is this coming from?"

He shrugged, shouldering into my gut again.

"Don't be that way," I coaxed, lifting my legs beneath him to jostle his weight around.

"It's nothing."

"Lincoln."

"I don't know. I just…I've been wondering. And, like, when I play…" he trailed off, frown deepening. He opened his mouth to say something else at the same time the front door opened. I looked that way, finding Marshall's frame filling the doorway, all shadow and darkness until he closed the door behind him and stepped into the light.

He still took my breath away.

"You're disgusting for him," Lincoln muttered.

I cleared my throat and pushed my fingers against his cheek.

"Hey," I called out to Marshall, who smiled when he saw me.

"Hey, sweetheart." He toed out of his shoes and dropped his bag, coming into the living room. He saw Lincoln on my lap, sprawled out across the couch. A moment of indecision flashed across his face, then he lifted Lincoln's legs and sat down beside me. My best friend readjusted himself over the top of us, and Marshall slid his hand around the back of my neck until I leaned in close enough for him to kiss me.

"Ewww," Lincoln groaned, covering his eyes.

"What did you have for dinner?" Marshall asked, kissing the corner of my mouth. "The house smells delicious."

"This hole in the wall Middle Eastern place we found after we moved into our apartment," I said.

"The," Lincoln corrected. "Mine."

"Fuck you." I smacked his face again and gave Marshall a smile. "I had a salad, and he had lamb."

"It smells great. You'll have to take me sometime."

I hummed happily and nodded.

"How was your day?" he asked, squinting. "I tried to call you a little while ago, but you didn't answer."

I patted my pockets, shoving Lincoln up with a knee to get to them. They were empty.

"Oh, shit." Heat burned my face. "I left it in the bedroom. I wasn't thinking. Or I was thinking too much. I…sorry, Sir."

Lincoln made a very contemplative sound, then rolled onto his side to face the TV, leaving Marshall and me both grunting for how bony he was.

"It's all right." Marshall stretched an arm across the back of the couch and pulled me to him so our legs touched beneath Lincoln's weight. "Did the two of you have a good night?"

"Yeah. Yes. What about you?"

"Smith is struggling with the new brother thing," he said, "but I think he's in a better place now."

"Good."

I handed Lincoln the remote since I didn't think he was at all interested in the news, and when he started to scroll through the channels, I rested my head on Marshall's shoulder. It was some kind of perfection in that moment, I thought, my boyfriend and my best friend in the same place. The peace, the steadfast comfort I stole from the both of them.

Half an hour later, Lincoln rolled onto his back and blinked up at me. His eyes were a little red in the corners, lashes dark and fanned across his cheeks.

"I'm gonna move," he said.

I bit the inside of my cheek and managed half of a nod. The set of his jaw and sheen in his eyes confirmed he'd been thinking hard about it since we'd talked, and he'd made up his mind.

"Thank God," Marshall said, reaching between their bodies and shoving his hand under Lincoln's hip. "You're ridiculously bony."

It wasn't what he'd meant, but Marshall didn't know that.

Lincoln gave me an uncertain smile, then moved off Marshall's lap and onto mine.

"Can I ask Silas to get me a drink?" he asked Marshall.

"You can ask, but he doesn't have to do it."

Marshall stretched, arms and legs out until something cracked. He was still dressed from work, and there was no way that was comfortable for him.

"Would you get me a drink?"

"What do you want?" I asked.

"Some wine," Marshall answered on his behalf.

Lincoln's nostrils flared.

"Did you want a glass too, Sir?" I asked, unwrapping Lincoln from my lap to stand.

"A small one."

"Can I help you change first?"

Lincoln made an unimpressed noise in the back of his throat, but he already knew the truth of me, and he'd known the truth of my relationship with Marshall long before I'd been willing to admit it to myself.

"Of course, Silas."

"Get your own wine," I said to Lincoln, shoving him toward the kitchen.

He grumbled but laughed, heading for the kitchen while I trailed Marshall into the bedroom. I could have made undressing him a whole thing, but I didn't want to keep Lincoln waiting too long, considering how tentative things were between us with both of our upcoming relocations.

Marshall watched me quietly as I undid all the buttons on his shirt and stripped him out of it, moving to his belt and pants next, and finally his underwear. On my knees in front of him, I pressed my cheek against his groin and inhaled deeply. The musky smell of him wasn't just arousing, it was also comforting. His fingers carding gently through my hair while I breathed him in only doubled all of those feelings.

"Is everything all right?" he asked quietly, letting me lean on him.

"Better than," I promised.

"With Lincoln?"

"It will be."

Marshall helped me to my feet and pulled me against his chest. His hands slid around my waist and down, cupping my ass as he pressed our mouths together. He kissed me urgently but quickly, then shoved me away with a low growl.

"I'll have my way with you later," he warned, giving a slow, overhanded stroke to his already thickening cock.

"Thank you, Sir."

"Get me some clothes."

I nodded and turned for the dresser, but no sooner had I got the drawer open than he was on me, hand reaching wildly into my pants and between my legs. Marshall grabbed my balls, kneading them almost too aggressively in his hand. I gasped, grabbing the dresser for support while he had his way with me, which apparently ended when I began to pant and beg him for more.

"I can't get enough of you," he whispered, nipping at my earlobe before reaching around and taking the clothes out of my hand. I was half-dazed with pleasure while he dressed himself behind me, looking smug and self-satisfied with the problem he'd created between my legs.

"I want you to take your phone into the bathroom, Silas, and I want you to record yourself jerking off," he said.

"Sorry. What?"

"Is recording a limit?"

I shook my head to clear it, the chain of events giving me whiplash. "No, Sir."

"Take your phone and record yourself jerking off," he repeated. "You can't take that erection and those basketball shorts back out to your best friend."

We both knew it wouldn't have been the first time Lincoln saw my erect cock, even if he had no interest in it, but getting myself off didn't sound like a horrible idea so I wasn't about to bring it up.

"Yes, Sir," I rasped.

Marshall gave me a slow and lingering look, then nodded his chin toward the bed. I scampered over there for my phone and took it into the bathroom.

The hardest part was finding a good angle, a comfortable position. In the end, I propped it up against the wall and sank down to my knees in front of it. Spitting in my palm, it didn't take more than five minutes for me to make myself come. The orgasm was lacking because I was alone, but it did enough to relieve the pressure in my balls that I'd be able to get through the rest of the night without poking Lincoln's back with it. I licked my hand clean and thanked Marshall before ending the video, then I washed my hands and left my phone on the bed before returning to the living room.

I found Marshall and Lincoln there, the former on the brand new coffee table and the latter on the couch. Marshall was leaned in, Lincoln's hands held in his as he said something that obviously wasn't meant for my ears. Lincoln nodded, sniffling, and behind them I cleared my throat. Lincoln startled, but Marshall—as always—held steady, keeping his body language the same but shooting a look in my direction.

"Are you sorted?" he asked.

I nodded.

He looked at Lincoln. "Are *you* sorted?"

Lincoln nodded.

"Alright then." He gave Lincoln's hands a squeeze, then angled his head toward the kitchen and asked, "Who wants some wine?"

CHAPTER 42
MARSHALL

By the time Friday rolled around, Silas was nothing except nerves and skin. He already knew Smith from school, and they'd met as adults, but the twins were a mystery to him. Even though I assured him they were harmless, he didn't believe me, and he'd wound himself up into a knot of anxiety by lunchtime. I told him to come home after work, that we would ride to dinner together, which we would. But I needed to step up and bring him back under control before then.

I got back to the house before him, stripping out of my work clothes and waiting for him in the guest bathroom.

"Hi," he said nervously, stripping out of his clothes and kicking them into the corner. "Did you want to watch or help?"

I exhaled a laugh, the corner of my lip twitching into a sly smile.

"I want to watch," I said. "Does that bother you?"

He shook his head and climbed into the shower, turning on the water before dipping his head beneath the spray. He slicked his hair away from his face and rubbed his hands across his chest, sliding one down toward his cock. He gave himself a quick stroke, then let go.

"It doesn't bother me."

"Do you normally touch yourself when you do it?" I asked.

I'd been in the shower with him through it one time, but I'd never thought to ask about his normal habits or tell him that I didn't want him jacking off if I wasn't around. As much as I liked the idea of controlling Silas's body that way, it gave me a thrill to know there were times we were apart when he needed to chase his own pleasure.

"Yeah," he admitted, chin tucked toward his chest. "I mean yes. Yes, Sir."

"Now I very much want to watch."

Silas nodded, slicking up the nozzle and bending awkwardly to ease it into his body. He flipped the water and raised onto his toes, grunting as the warm water began to flow. He waited, waited, tugging softly on his cock as the water filled him up. The urge to climb in with him and hold my hands flat against his stomach, to feel him swell from the pressure was almost insurmountable, but I decided to touch myself instead. He switched the water back to the overhead spray and let the nozzle slide out of him.

The tension in his muscles from holding the water in was evident. And when he gingerly stepped out of the shower, I slid my back against the wall so he could have a clear path to the toilet.

"Are you really going to watch?" he asked, sitting down.

"I'm really going to watch."

Silas stroked himself with more intent, a strong pull from root to tip. Slow, slow, and then faster. His hand was still wet with lube as he jerked himself off and emptied into the toilet at the same time. His body seized and shivered, and his hand slowed down again. He hadn't finished, but he was as hard as I'd ever seen him before.

I'd have to rethink my stance on letting him jerk off without me.

"Do you normally finish in the shower?" I asked.

He climbed back under the spray and washed between his ass cheeks, washed his balls, his cock, then turned off the water. "Sometimes, Sir."

I pulled the towel off the bar and held it open. He walked into it willingly, and I wrapped him up in the thick terry cloth, kissing the top of his head.

"Not anymore."

"Yes, Sir," he whispered.

"Are you nervous about dinner still?" I asked.

"Very."

"I think I've figured out how to help you."

Silas groaned but let me lead him to the bedroom just the same. Once in front of the bed, I tugged the towel away from him and shoved him forward onto his hands and knees. He went easily and willingly, rolling his damp forehead across the comforter.

"Sweetheart," I said, voice low. "You look good enough to eat."

So I did just that.

Climbing onto the bed behind him, I dug my nails into his ass cheeks and spread him wide. I speared my tongue into his asshole, licking and sucking and kissing him there until my spit ran down his sac.

"Touch yourself but don't come," I said, diving back in.

Silas was a writhing mess by the time he got close, barely managing to get out the warning.

"I'm close, Sir."

I pulled my mouth away and slapped my hand down hard against his ass.

"Not helping," he groaned, burying his face into the blankets and fisting the sheets with *both* hands.

I chuckled, flipping him onto his back and knocking his legs apart. His cock was thick and red, erect against his stomach and smeared with precum. I bowed my spine and licked a stripe from his balls to his slit, spreading his legs wide with my hands. He still had bruises all over his legs and ass from our earlier scenes, and I'd never seen anything more perfect every time I looked at him.

"I wasn't trying to." I took the tip of his swollen cock into my mouth and sucked hard, relishing the salty heat of his arousal against my tongue.

"Marshall." He gasped. "Sir."

Silas's fingers threaded through my hair, and his hips arched off the bed.

"It hurts," he whispered.

I gave him one last suck, then sat up and rocked back onto my heels. Gathering my own saliva into my mouth, mixing it with his precum, I spat into my palm and took my own shaft into my fist and stroked. Silas lay sprawled out like a starfish until I moaned and sighed, then he propped himself up on his elbows and watched me stroke myself off in front of him.

"Look how hard you make me," I told him. "Look how good you make me feel."

"I see it."

"Touch yourself," I said. "I want you close. I want you hungry to come so the only thing you think about the rest of the night is *me* and how badly you need *me*."

"Sir."

Silas wrapped his trembling hand around his cock, loose and gentle, and teased himself more than anything else. I let my stare drift from his cock to his face, the flush on his cheeks and the way it colored all the way down to his chest. He screwed his eyes closed and lifted off the bed, his entire body covered in sweat, his muscles quivering.

"Oh, fuck, Silas." I dragged my hand up the inside of his thigh and threw my head back with a groan that rattled me straight down to my bones. My orgasm rolled through me like a freight train, low and long and loud. I angled my cock downward and shot my load all over Silas's shaft and balls, clenching my jaw at the needy sounds that fell out of his mouth when my cum landed on his skin.

Pumping until I was sensitive and empty, I smeared my release all over his otherwise clean skin. Using my cum as lube, I made a rough first around his cock and stroked my spend into his skin.

"Marshall. Sir."

He fought himself.

He fought me.

"Silas," I said.

"I need…" he trailed off, and I slowly released my hold on his cock.

"What do you need, sweetheart?"

"You," he rasped.

"Perfect."

Spreading my body out over the top of his, I stole his mouth in a blistering kiss, deep enough to kick my cock back to life. The urge to get inside of him and rut him down into the mattress was real, but I'd already taken too much time, and if we were too late for dinner, my brothers would tease me until I never wanted to see any of them again.

"I love you so much," I whispered into his mouth, reluctantly putting enough space between us so we could both calm down.

Silas let his arms flop onto the mattress, his face twisted up in a mask of pleasure and pain.

"I love you, Sir."

"What do you need?" I asked.

He screwed his eyes closed and let out a long breath. "You."

"Who matters?"

"You," he choked out.

I hummed, grabbing his wrist and pulling him into a seated position. "Good. Now get dressed. We're going to be late."

My legs weren't much more than jelly, but I fought my way into something halfway presentable, and Silas did the same. Earlier, I would have expected him to moan and groan over the color and the cut of whatever he chose, but he moved quietly around the room with much more ease than before. My plan had worked, even if it was a little cruel to send him into the lion's den ready to burst.

He held my hand the whole way to dinner, and after we parked, I kissed his knuckles, his nose, the corner of his mouth.

"They will love you, but nowhere near as much as I do," I promised.

He hummed, giving me a weary smile.

"And as soon as we're back in the car, I'll make you come."

Silas's smile grew larger, and I couldn't stop myself from kissing him again.

"I could come like this," he murmured into my mouth, and I didn't hate the idea, but we did need to get into the restaurant before my brothers came looking for us.

For the first time ever, I was the last one to arrive.

We were back at the round table again, my seat open and the one beside it as well. Silas's grip on my hand tightened as we walked in, but I gave him a reassuring squeeze and pulled him up alongside me as we arrived at the table.

"Silas, these are my brothers. You've met Smith. This is Hunter and Finn." I pointed at each of the three of them in turn. "This is Silas."

"Oh, he is cute," Finn announced, standing up and extending his hand for a shake, which Silas returned. Hunter followed suit, and Smith offered him a wave. We all took our seats again, and beside me Silas vibrated so aggressively, I could feel it in my bones. I rested a hand on his thigh, maybe a little higher than was decent, but it was enough for his breath to catch in his throat and his body to settle.

"So," Hunter said, unusually talkative, "tell us about yourself."

"This isn't an interrogation," I warned.

"I asked a very standard getting-to-know-you question," he shot back.

"It's fine," Silas interrupted, clearing his throat. "It's fine. I'm twenty-five, I'm also an architect. I live…downtown. My best friend and I share an apartment."

I noticed the hiccup about where he lived, but I bit my tongue to stop from calling it out. I meant it when I'd promised myself I'd let Silas come around to the idea on his own. We needed that balance for things to work. Living situations weren't something I could dominate my way into, even if the thought of Silas and all his things being under the same roof as me and mine was enough to…

"That's sickening," Finn said.

I looked up in time to see him roll his eyes at me and raise his glass in a toast.

"What?"

"Your eyes," Hunter answered for him, gesturing vaguely at my face. "You're all…in love with him."

"Of course I am," I said.

Beside me, Silas exhaled.

"It doesn't matter what he does or what he likes," Finn decided. "Anyone who makes you look *that* lovesick has to earn a pass."

"He is also nice," Smith said from my other side. "From what I've seen at least."

"Thank you," Silas muttered, tucking his chin toward his chest.

It was smooth sailing after that, all of Silas's and my worry gone with Finn's nearly immediate and magnanimous blessing.

We made it through an enjoyable meal where Silas learned he and Finn liked the same kind of movies, he and Hunter shared an affinity for spreadsheets, and he and Smith, of course, did enjoy their chosen careers. They were agreeable in the ways that mattered, in the ways I knew would be sustainable.

After we said our goodbyes, Silas and I walked back to the car. He was quiet for the most part, almost at ease but still so very tense. As soon as the doors closed, he dropped his head against the headrest and grabbed the sides of his seat.

"Please help me," he moaned.

"I told you I would."

The parking lot was empty enough that I wasn't worried about getting caught. I undid Silas's pants and shoved my hand behind the waistband of his underwear. He wasn't hard, but his cock burned my palm when I wrapped my fingers around him. He made a gasping sound and lifted off the seat, hips thrusting toward my hand as I stroked him.

"Come, sweetheart. Come all over my hand and—"

I didn't even have time to finish the sentence before Silas bit out a sharp cry and came. Cum waterfalled over my fingers as he released, eyes screwed shut and fingers white against the leather seats. Part of me wanted to drag it out, to make it hurt more so it would feel better later, but he'd had the longest night.

We both had.

"Amazing," I praised, gently tucking him back into his pants.

He murmured something that wasn't coherent, going slack in his seat. With a laugh, I buckled him in, then held my hand up to his mouth. He licked and sucked me as best he could, and when I was satisfied with the work, I put both hands onto the steering wheel and drove us home.

I stripped Silas naked in the hallway, huffing out an amused breath when he collapsed face-first onto the bed. I followed behind him, scooping his body against mine and spooning around him. He made tired and happy sounds, and I kissed the back of his head and closed my eyes.

"I want to move in with you," he said, the words barely louder than a whisper and punctuated with a soft and final snore.

CHAPTER 43
SILAS

woke up with Marshall's fingers digging into my bruised thighs and his mouth around my cock. I had no idea how long he'd been at it for, but it took less than a minute of me being awake for him to suck my pleasure right out of me. I came with a tired and hoarse groan, my body clenching and aching at the sight of him enthusiastically swallowing my cum.

"This is mine," he murmured, kissing the tip of my dick before crawling up the length of my body and kissing me on the mouth.

He tasted like salt and sleep. He tasted like home.

Winding my legs around his waist, I pressed our bodies together. "I need you, Sir," I whispered.

The night before came rushing back to me—the edging, the torment, the eventual release. His brothers' approval and my midnight confession before falling into the deepest sleep I'd ever known.

"What do you need, Silas?"

Marshall was already reaching for the lube, slicking his fingers and smearing them between my legs. He pushed one finger into me, then another, and when I arched against him and moaned, he added a third. The stretch was monumental, but like all things with him, I welcomed it.

"This," I rasped.

He fucked me with his fingers and then replaced them with his cock. It was one slow glide as he entered me, seating himself fully and burying his face in my neck. Marshall cursed under his breath and then started to move. If I expected a slow and easy round of morning sex, I was wrong.

Marshall rutted me down into the mattress, fucking me with an unmatched intensity. He fucked me like he needed to come inside of me to get his next breath, and I would have been lying if I said I didn't love having that power over him. He curled his hand around the top of my head, leveraging our bodies so he could fuck deeper and harder. There was no real method to it, no pace, no consistency. He was already too close for that.

And I'd never been more in love with him.

Marshall came with a seize of his hips and a burst of cum that shot into the deepest parts of me. I tried to hold onto him, fingers scrabbling against his back, but he was covered in sweat and my hands shook with pleasure. I went limp beneath him, and Marshall thrust into me one more time before pulling out and rolling onto his back with a heavy grunt.

His chest heaved with every breath, and I wanted to crawl inside of his chest and live there.

"Sir," I whispered.

"Whatever you want, it's yours."

I climbed on top of him and slanted our mouths together, taking every pant and gasp that fell out of his mouth for my own. Marshall slid his arms around my waist and held us together, kissing me back deeper and with more tongue. It was kissing for the sake of kissing, even after my body heated for him again, and I humped myself against his leg. Marshall's hands stayed steady around my waist, and his mouth pressed firmly against mine.

He'd said whatever I wanted, so I came across his thigh with a whimper. His fingers dug into my hips as I rode out my orgasm on his leg, and he kissed me the entire time.

Eventually, the sun crept higher in the sky and my body slowed its desperate grind. The kiss turned languid and lazy until it wasn't anything more than shared breath and clacking teeth and smiles.

"When do you want to move?" he asked, pushing us both into a seated position before extracting himself from my arms.

Swallowing, I watched him find clean pants for both of us, not arguing when he got on his knees in front of me to help me into them. Marshall helped me to stand on shaking legs, then led me into the kitchen and up onto a stool at the counter.

"Same time as Lincoln," I said.

Marshall made us coffee, then cracked four eggs in a bowl and set to scrambling them. "When is that?"

"He's been looking, but I'm not sure."

"He doesn't want to stay where he is and get a new roommate?"

I shook my head. "He said it was our space."

"What a romantic." Marshall slid the finished eggs onto a plate, correcting himself, "Platonically romantic. If there is such a thing."

"I'm sure there is."

Next up was bread into the toaster, and then Marshall was on the stool beside me, breakfast in front of us both, coffee steaming and ready to drink.

"I can pay you rent," I finally said. "And bills."

"I don't want you to."

"What if *I* want to?"

Marshall finished chewing and set down his fork. After he swallowed, he dragged his tongue across the front of his teeth, the way he did when he was thinking about something. Slowly, I folded my hands into my lap and stared at my plate.

"Is this a limit, Silas?" he asked, looking at me from the corner of his eye. "Are you going to insist on this?"

I closed my eyes and thought long and hard about the answer I wanted to give. It should have been a limit. I'd never slacked off or tried to pass off my responsibilities onto anyone else, and I'd never intended to start with Marshall. But my relationship with him was very different than it was with Lincoln, than it would have been with any other boyfriend. Marshall was my partner, but he was also my dominant. That came with a different set of responsibilities and expectations, and we'd both known what they were when we signed up to be with each other.

Slowly, I shook my head. "No," I said. "No, Sir."

Marshall licked his lips, nodding before he said, "Are you sure?"

"I'm sure."

"Okay."

I picked up my fork and finished my breakfast, then I cleared our plates and caught up to Marshall in the bathroom. He stepped out of his shorts and held his hand out for me. The shower was already on, the water hot, and the steam filling the room. I walked into his arms and peppered his chest with kisses, feeling grateful and overwhelmed.

"Sir," I whispered, trailing a hand down his stomach. My fingers tangled into the hair around the base of his cock, and Marshall groaned at the touch.

"Yes, Silas," he answered, and I went to my knees.

I kissed the fronts of his thighs and the insides, lower down to the backs of his knees, his ankles, the tops of his feet. I dragged my cheek across his skin like a cat, blinking back a wave of unexpected emotion and tears that threatened to spill over my lashes. Touching and licking and kissing my way back up, I took his cock into my mouth and sucked, and sucked, and sucked him down my throat until his hands were in my hair and his groans in my ears, and how had I ever wanted to fight any of this?

This was heaven.

I couldn't have designed a better partner for myself if I'd tried, and to think I'd ended up with Marshall by accident. Call it cause and effect or whatever words you wanted, but I was so much more than lucky to be on my knees in front of his man. To have a place there for as long as it felt right.

"Don't swallow," he warned, and then hot cum splattered onto my tongue.

Marshall's hands tightened in my hair, and he restrained his thrusts as he came in my mouth. A burst of his cum shot against my cheek as he hauled me up to my feet, then he crashed our mouths together again and licked the taste of him off my tongue. He consumed me wholly, lifting me by the bruised backs of my thighs. I wrapped myself around him, opening my mouth so wide it hurt so he could kiss me deeper.

Marshall walked us into the shower, my back landing hard against the wall. The breath left my lungs and entered his, and the sound he made was enough to ground me right back into my body with so much force I never wanted to leave. Marshall was all-consuming, like when I'd given in and admitted how much I wanted my future to have him in it, he'd opened the floodgates.

It should have been too much, but I knew Marshall would never let me drown.

He managed to get us both washed and dried. Dressing took more time because he allowed my hands to roam over the dampness of his body a little longer than was necessary to get his clothes on. He dressed me in return, leaving reverent kisses on every faded bruise he'd ever given me. The passion finally quieted to a simmer, and Marshall sat beside me on the edge of the bed, our thighs pressed together and pinkies twined.

"Are you sure Lincoln is going to be okay with this?" he asked.

I still didn't know what the two of them had spoken about earlier in the week, but Marshall's concern enhanced my own.

"He says he will be, and I have to take him at his word."

"I know he's your best friend, and I want to make sure you know he will always have a place here. Us being together and living here doesn't mean your relationship with him needs to change."

Happiness swelled in the center of my chest, and I managed a nod in reply.

"Thank you."

"It's decency," he said. "Doesn't need praise."

"Thank you anyway," I told him.

A small silence fell, but I could tell he had something else he wanted to say.

"What?" I prompted, tightening the curl of my pinky finger around his.

"What about your dad?" he finally asked. "He suspects we're involved."

"It's not his business."

"Are you going to ignore him forever?"

"He doesn't like my designs. He fired me. He expected me to unfire myself to save him." I paused, fighting down the anger that threatened to bubble up at the thought of my dad. "He doesn't deserve to know the version of me that you've built."

"I've hardly—"

"Marshall. Sir," I cut him off. "Stop."

He laughed, brow raised. "Stop?"

"I'm not the same person I was the night we…well, we didn't meet, but you know."

"I remember."

"I'm not the same," I said again. "I'm who I am today, I have the things I have because of you. Arguing about this is a limit."

Another laugh, and Marshall raised his hands in surrender. "Alright, sweetheart."

"So, I don't want to talk about my dad right now. Maybe in the future, but not for a while."

"Understood." He cradled my cheek in his hand, angling my face toward his and gently pressing a kiss against my lower lip. "Whatever you want, Silas. Whatever you need…that's what you'll get from me."

The earlier wave of emotion was too strong to hold back any longer. Wetness beaded on my lashes before spilling down my cheeks. I covered his hand with mine and nodded, leaning in and bringing our faces close again.

"I know," I told him. "I know. I'm yours, Marshall. Sir, I'm so fucking yours."

Feeling bold, feeling strong, I kissed him. I climbed onto his lap and took his face into my hands, using my body and my mouth to make sure he understood just how much I meant it when I told him I loved him, I wanted him. I needed him.

Marshall hummed against my mouth, smiling against my teeth.

"I'm very glad to hear that, sweetheart," he murmured, trailing his hand lower and curling his fingers around my throat…the best kind of collar. The one I wanted to wear for the rest of my life. "Now why don't you get on your knees and prove it?"

EPILOGUE

SILAS

stepped out of the shower, cleaned and prepped, just like Marshall liked for me to be. It had only been two weeks since we moved in together, but I hoped the newness of sharing a space with him would never wear off.

"Silas," Marshall called out for me from what sounded like his office, and my heart leapt into my throat. Normally, if he got home and I was in the shower, he would join me. Sometimes all the way under the spray and sometimes only in the bathroom itself while I took care of business. I didn't mind either; I just liked being around him.

"Yes, Sir?" I called back to him, half out of the bathroom and half in. I used the towel to get as much water out of my hair as I could manage before wrapping it around my waist and heading toward the sound of his voice. "Where are you?"

"My office."

I padded barefoot and naked through the house and down the hallway, finally finding Marshall behind his desk. He had the blinds pulled, the only light in the small room coming from the glare of his computer screen. Normally he had the windows open, the lights on...I'd never seen the space so dark save for the end of the night when we were getting ready for bed.

Marshall's office was a comfortable space, a large oak desk, a drafting table, a white leather couch and a small side table that matched the desk. In lieu of bookshelves, he had books and magazines stacked haphazardly around the room. It was a mess he'd promised to go through as his home office had become a catchall space for the things of mine that didn't have a place yet.

"There you are," he said as I entered, standing up and stretching his arms over his head. He gestured toward the couch, and I sidestepped toward it as he came out from behind his desk.

"When did you get home?" I asked, accepting the kiss he dragged across my lips before sinking down onto the couch and pulling me onto his lap. The leather creaked beneath our combined weights, the smooth material cool against my still warm skin.

"Just a few minutes ago."

Marshall fingered loose the knot on my towel and tossed it onto the floor, and in the same motion smoothed his hand up my back to gently press between my shoulder blades. I went down onto his lap like he wanted, letting him manhandle me around until my cock was notched safely between his thighs. He was still dressed for work, expensive slacks that rubbed against my shaft with more texture than his hand but less than his leather gloves.

"I'm glad you're here," I whispered, pressing my forehead against a space on the couch beside his thigh.

"In this moment or…?"

"All of them," I answered.

Marshall hummed, pleased. "I'm glad you're here, Silas. I'm so very glad I get to come home from work to this."

He drew slow and lazy circles across my ass and the backs

of my thighs, fingers teasing my crack and my balls but never going through with the kind of touches I wanted the most from him. Groaning, my hips searched for some sort of friction, and above me, Marshall let out a low laugh.

"That's perfect, sweetheart. That's exactly what I want from you tonight."

"What do you want, Sir?"

"I want you to use my body to get yourself off while I spank you." He kneaded the sensitive spot where my ass met my thigh. "And I'm going to turn this ass purple while you do it."

"Yes, please." The consent left my mouth like a prayer. "Yes, please, Sir."

Marshall crossed his legs at the ankles, tightening the grip his legs had around my cock, and he cursed under his breath.

"You're already so fucking thick and hard, Silas. Are you going to make a mess of me?"

Before I could answer, he delivered the first strike against the back of my thigh.

It was reflex to push against the couch and try to get away, but his muscles held fast around my erection, and he made quick work of pinning both of my wrists together at the small of my back. Digging his elbow into my spine, Marshall spanked me a second time, a third, a fourth, and then the pain began to bloom into that perfect kind of pleasure that came from aching so acutely for another person.

I counted each impact in my head and at twenty, I groaned and gave in, thrusting my cock between his thighs. Marshall growled as I began to move, fingers gripping tighter around my wrist and muscles flexing to constrict my cock. He spanked me again, again, again, and my lashes fluttered. I moaned. I sighed. And all the while I thrust against his lap, the tip of my cock kissing the now hot leather beneath his legs.

Getting off like this was harder than I'd expected. It was

one thing to chase after something that felt good, another to see it through when the only thing I wanted to do was close my eyes and give myself over to Marshall's whims entirely.

"Don't stop now," he warned, landing a particularly hard strike against both my ass cheeks. The impact of his hand rattled down to my balls and I cried out, fucking into the crease of his thighs again.

The pain had turned into pleasure and my awareness of the instructions he'd given me had that pleasuring careening quickly back toward pain. Each time his hand connected with my ass, my body yearned to be free of his torture. The arousal coursing through my cock reminded me there was only one way out, so instead of focusing on the tingling agony every time he hit me, I redirected my attention to my cock.

It was hard to move, with Marshall holding me down so efficiently, but I managed to set a pace that catapulted me right toward the edge of an orgasm. Marshall hadn't let up, and I cursed the day his stamina ever began to falter. I loved the way he played with me, the way he fucked me like it was the first and last and only time we'd ever get to be together. Marshall did nothing in half-measures, and as a result, neither did I. The orgasm was close, but I wanted it to be bigger, I wanted the bruises on my ass to last longer. I wanted more and everything. As if he could somehow sense my delay —and I was certain he could—Marshall spanked me exceedingly hard on my thighs and down even lower toward my knees.

"I didn't tell you to play games," he bit out, and my whole body trembled. "I told you to come."

"Yes, Sir," I confirmed, thrusting three more times into the tight grip of his thighs before shooting jets of cum against the cushions of his couch and the soft weave of his slacks. I came with a gasping cry, my body jerking every which way his bondage would allow. Marshall landed one more slap against my ass, then went still while I rode out the waves of my orgasm on his lap.

Maybe I blacked out, but I came to in the fetal position, tucked against Marshall's chest with his arms wrapped around my shoulders. His fingers drew gentle lines down the outside of my arms, and I moaned happily against him.

"You made a mess of my pants," he murmured against the top of my head.

I smiled into his skin. "You're welcome, Sir."

Marshall kissed my hair. "Do you need another shower? What are you and Lincoln up to tonight?"

Sitting upright in his lap, I rubbed my eyes. "It is Friday, isn't it?"

"It is." Marshall helped me to my feet and then he walked us both into the bedroom. I followed him into the closet and turned my back toward his full-length mirror, eyes going wide at the sight of my backside.

"I hope whatever our plans are don't involve sitting."

Marshall had made a galaxy out of my ass and legs, a splattering of purple and blue and pink decorating me solidly from the middle of my thighs to the top of my ass cheeks. It was only going to get darker as the days went on, and I hated to think how uncomfortable it would be to go to work on Monday and sit down for eight straight hours.

"I hope they do," he said, unbuttoning his shirt and tossing it into the hamper. He changed into jeans and a black V-neck tee, lingering while I managed to ease my way into a pair of jeans and one of his old college t-shirts. Marshall always told me he liked the way I looked in them, and if my ass was going to be miserable, at least my top half was going to be comfortable.

I stuck my tongue out at him, and he took a quick swat against my backside. "I told you months ago I don't abide brats, Silas."

I yelped and jumped, landing right in his arms. He wrapped himself around me and slanted our mouths together, licking past my lips with a low, rumbling groan.

"Did you cry in my office?" he asked.

I reached up and pressed my fingertips against the tender skin just below my eyes. "Did I?"

"Tastes like it."

He licked my cheeks, rutting against me and pressing his own ignored hard-on against my hip.

"I think you did."

Tipping my head back, I gave him my mouth again, groaning as he returned to kiss me. He walked me backward out of the closet, stopping only inches away from the bed. He gave me a small shove to put space between us, eyes twinkling when I blinked him into focus.

"I'm going to be late if I don't get out of here," he said, checking his watch.

"Can't have that," I teased.

Marshall shot me a warning look, and I raised my hands in surrender.

"So, what's your plan?"

"I'm heading over to Lincoln's new apartment and nothing after that."

"Does he want to go to Rapture?"

"He always wants to go to Rapture," I said, rolling my eyes.

"If you head over there and want company later, text me and I'll come by after dinner. If you don't want company, that's also fine."

I smiled, heading after Marshall into the living room. I turned off the lights as we stepped into the hallway, and I stayed a few paces back to admire the broad swell of his shoulders as he walked ahead of me.

"I always enjoy your company," I told him.

"Same, but time with your best friend is important," he said, not for the first time.

"I promise I'll let you know."

We sat down together on the couch and put on shoes and socks, then gathered up our keys from the side table beside the front door. Marshall kissed me again, hard and thorough, before saying goodbye and heading to Cunningham's to meet his brothers for their weekly dinner.

I plugged Lincoln's new address into my GPS and drove to his side of town. He'd given me a spare key the day after we moved him in, so I buzzed in the lobby as a courtesy, then made my way up the stairs to his second-floor studio. The door was unlocked—very like him—when I arrived. He was half dressed, leather pants and unlaced leather boots, but as I opened the door, his back was to me. He had his cell phone in hand, arm limp at his side, and as I stepped into his apartment, Lincoln turned to face me with bloodshot eyes and tear-stained cheeks.

"Hey, Silas," he greeted me like everything was normal, like his tears were a figment of my imagination.

I opened my arms, and he walked right into them, pressing his snotty face against my shoulder and sniffling loudly into Marshall's shirt.

"Lincoln?" I asked, tentatively stroking my fingers through his freshly styled hair. "What on earth is going on?"

Silas and Marshall's story may end here, but this is far from the last you'll see of them. Lincoln's up next, ready for his HEA in an opposites attract romance called Burden of Proof. It features two versatile main characters who can't decide whether they're dominant, submissive, or a little bit of both.

Click here to get Burden of Proof.

ALSO BY KATE HAWTHORNE

———

Club Rapture: Risk Aware

Love by Design

Burden of Proof

Club Rapture: Giving Consent

Worth the Risk

Worth the Wait

Worth the Fight

Worth the Chance

Trophy Doms Social Club

Humbled

Edged

Praised

Bound

Shared

Trophy Doms New York

All In

Tied Down

Cried Out

Roughed Up

All in Good Time

Necessary Space

Necessary Time

Duality

Dual Destruction

Dual Surrender

Dual Defiance

Two Truths and a Lie

A Real Good Lie

A Cold Hard Truth

A Matter of Fact

Room for Love

Reckless

Heartless

Faultless

Fearless

Limitless

A Very Messy Motel Brothers Wedding

Relentless

Secrets in Edgewood

A Taste of Sin

The Cost of Desire

A Love Made Whole

Secrets in Edgewood: The Complete Series

The Lonely Hearts Stories

His Kind of Love

The Colors Between Us

Love Comes After

Until You Say Otherwise

STANDALONES

Rebound

One for the Road

Daybreak - Vino & Veritas

Unfettered

Dreams

A Thousand Lifetimes

COLLABORATIONS

With E.M. Denning

Irreplaceable

Future Fake Husband

Future Gay Boyfriend

Future Ex Enemy

With J.R. Gray

May the Best Man Win

ABOUT KATE HAWTHORNE

Kate Hawthorne is an author of character-driven LGBT romance, known for crafting emotionally intense stories with high heat and a kinky twist. Creating worlds where passion and angst collide, Kate's books bring you complex protagonists in fearless pursuit of self-exploration and happy—if not sometimes unconventional—endings for everyone.

Visit her website
http://www.katehawthornebooks.com

Sign up for Kate's newsletter
http://www.katehawthornebooks.com/extra

patreon.com/katehawthorne

instagram.com/kate.hawthorne

threads.com/@kate.hawthorne

facebook.com/authorkatehawthorne